The Trinity Prophecy

by Marissa Kinzel
with illustrations from Melissa McManus

ISBN: 978-0-578-68850-3 (Paperback)
ISBN: 978-0-578-68851-0 (Ebook)

Library of Congress Control Number: 2020908075

The characters in this book are entirely fictional. Any resemblance to actual persons living or dead is entirely coincidental.

Front Cover art by Melissa McManus

Printed by IngramSpark, in the United States of America

First printing edition 2020.

To Electra, my eternal cheerleader;
Mur, my backbone and lifelong support;
my mother, who I miss every day;
and you.

Chapter 1
The Snowy Mountain Prince

𝓝estled high at the peak of a snowy mountain there was a town of winter called Vetur. Within it lived its jovial citizens, the Veturians, who wrapped their fair blue skin in bundles of hand-woven clothes to keep the deepest bite of the cold at bay. They were overseen by a small castle court headed by King Vasilias Virvatuli and his Queen, Heilsa, both of whom were known for their kind demeanor and fair ruling. The Virvatuli royal family bore a special power—the power over the whims of the ice. They could conjure snow from nothing, build ice sculptures from the smallest drop of water. Every year, as a celebration of their history and hope for prosperity, the king and queen hosted a grand festival of the ice. Many commissioned special clothing, workers closed away their livestock stables, and all made haste to the central courtyard to view the spectacle. Led by the king, he cast out ice sculpture after ice sculpture, making them dance and sway, and the villagers danced with them. At the end of every festival, the king and queen would combine their abilities to create a snow flurry show, displayed like fireworks. Puffs of ice and snow exploded, scattering gently amongst the crowd. The queen would swirl the snow around, forming it into various shapes—sometimes, if she was feeling cheeky, she would create shapes like the villagers themselves.

One year, when the festival's snow flurries had calmed to a delicate sway, the king and queen gathered the crowd's attention.

"Everyone," Queen Heilsa announced. "King Vasilias and I have an announcement to make!"

"Our family will be growing by one member!" The king called out proudly, and the crowd erupted in cheers, taking piles of fallen snow and throwing them in the air. The royal family was beloved, and the promise of an heir was the promise of a bright future.

In the spring, a prince was born. He had lavender-white hair like his father, and wide, violet eyes like his mother. King Vasilias and Queen Heilsa raised him with care, training him to hone his gift of the ice from a young age while allowing him to explore Vetur and befriend the townspeople. The village and the castle were symbiotic, and the villagers raised the young prince like he was one of their own.

His name was Neros.

❄

Ten years later, the young prince bounded down the steps of the castle, sprinting through the courtyard past the castle guards and into the town.

"Your majesty! Care to help me tend to my sheep today?" A stablewoman asked as the youthful prince ran down the street.

"Not today, Veshna! Father is allowing me to explore outside Vetur today! I'm going to see lots of Endra!" He called, waving as he raced by.

Veshna chuckled. "Alright, alright. You be safe out there."

"I will!" He laughed, racing toward the edge of the mountain. Waving his hand, an ice board materialized at its edge. He leaped on it, sliding down the mountain with breakneck speed. There were other hills and valleys around Vetur, and the prince had practiced especially for this moment. He dodged the rocks and trees with ease, adrenaline pumping as he threw his hands in the air, cheering. Once he reached the bottom, he skidded into the grass and slowed to a stop. He stepped off the board, and with a flick of his wrist, it dissipated into snowflakes.

The landscape of the Endran plains was vast and full of color, an expanse of grass and greenery and flora and fauna as far as the eye could see. A blue-white haze protected a wonderland of waterfalls, and far off in the distance Neros could see a thick cloud of smoke circling over a great volcano. Directly to his left, there lay a dense forest that emanated an orange glow of autumn.

Behind one of the trees at the opening, Neros spotted a figure. She was small, like him, and she had long hair that looked like green leaves woven together. Her skin blended with the bark of the tree she hid behind, and if not for her decorated dress and bright yellow eyes, Neros would not have noticed her.

"You're blue," she said.

The prince smiled. "I'm not blue, I'm Neros!"

The girl frowned, concealing herself further behind the tree. "No, I mean your skin! It's blue! And—and you flew down from that mountaintop, all of a sudden. Where does it lead?"

Neros looked fondly back up the mountain, though his town was shrouded by a white haze of falling snow. "At the top of that mountain is my home, Vetur. My father is the king, and today, he said I'm old enough to explore Endra all on my own!" He smiled, placing his hands on his hips.

The girl didn't look so impressed. "Endra is peaceful. Your king was smart to let you explore now. But you're dumb for leaving home."

"What? Why?"

"Because you have no means of protection!" The girl came out from behind the three, gesturing to Neros with open palms. "What on your person would protect you if I attacked you?" As if to prove her point, the girl stretched out one arm, summoning long, limber vines from the trees' canopy. She sent them to wrap around Neros, constricting his body and pinning his arms to his sides as they slipped and circled his torso. The prince cried out in surprise as he was lifted off the ground and brought closer to the girl.

"See? You're defenseless!" She proclaimed, grinning in defiance. "How do you know that I won't kill you right here, right now?"

"Y-you won't!" Neros smiled, though strained.

"You don't know that!" She crossed her arms, glaring up at him. The vines tightened their grip, and Neros grunted at the feeling of thorns pressing into his back and sides. "I can!"

"But you won't!" Neros grunted, still smiling. "I can see it…in your eyes. You're a nice person!"

The girl squinted at him. Then, she threw her hands up in the air, and the vines receded, and Neros fell to the ground. He groaned, brushing himself off as he stood. Then, he smiled at the girl again and extended his hand. "Let's try again. I'm Prince Neros. What's your name?"

She gaped at him. "I just *attacked* you! Why are you offering me your hand like this?"

Neros' brows drew together, but his hand remained extended. "Because I want to be your friend, of course. Do people not greet each other like this where you come from?"

This time, the girl tossed her head back and whined. "Of course they do! Ugh! You're impossible!" She walked up to him and firmly shook his hand. Her skin felt like the bark it matched, but her grasp was still soft like his own skin. "I am Princess Anthea of Arboria. That's what this place is," She gestured behind her to the dense forest. "And I'm an Arborian. Skin of tree, hair of leaves. Neat, huh?"

Neros beamed. "That's amazing! There really are all kinds of people outside Vetur." The prince peered around her, attempting to see what laid beyond the thick outer layer of forest. Anthea blocked his view, even as he tried to dodge and look around her.

"Why are you so *nosy?"* She asked, sticking her face close to his and sneering.

"I-I wouldn't say nosy…maybe instead curious?" Neros suggested, offering a weak smile.

Anthea sighed. "Fine. Since you have no sense of danger, I'll show you where I live." She grabbed the prince by his wrist, and led him into the forest. It felt like a maze, and Neros hardly watched where he was going in favor of looking up at the canopy. It was breathtaking—a wide array of reds, oranges, and yellows splattered across every tree. The light reflected a dozen colors as it shone against the leaves, like a kaleidoscope of nature.

In time, the maze opened to reveal an expansive system of treehouses, all surrounding a larger tree with a trunk as thick as the base of the Vetur castle at home. Neros blinked, almost overwhelmed by it all. His jaw hung open, awe clear in his eyes.

"Wow," He breathed. "It's beautiful!"

"Welcome to Arboria, Prince Neros! The most scenic place in all of Endra." Anthea gestured grandly to the forest, and Neros took in its inhabitants. Arborians with skin of wood like the princess' and hair of varying colors walked and chatted idly amongst each other throughout the forest. Neros had never felt so close to the center of all nature in his life as he did in this moment. There were shorter trees, trees with willowing hair, red trees, and even a few that resembled the pines he was so familiar with at home.

"So, what makes you princess? Do you have a king or a queen as your parents?"

"Nope!" Anthea replied, slowly leading Neros to the central tree. "I was chosen to inherit my magic powers by the goddess Silva, who watches over this land!"

The prince's eyes widened. "You guys are that connected to the heavenly gods in Andolis?"

"Yeah, duh! Silva provides everything for us here!" The princess spun around, and Neros admired how her dress flowed freely as she turned. "But the Great Ancient Tree is the one that gives us Arborians the life force we need to survive!"

"That's amazing! So you live in a tree ecosystem, almost?"

"Pretty much! And no two Arborians are alike—everyone has small differences in their bark markups and hair type!" Anthea glowed with excitement, and it rubbed off on the prince. She tugged his hand. "Come on, I have to introduce you to my bestest friend of all time!"

As the princess tugged Neros around the Great Ancient Tree, he was able to observe more of the landscape. Behind the tree was a large spring, decorated with elaborated bushes of flowers and draping vines. Warm light filtered in through the trees, casting patterns in shadow across the water. On one side of the spring, there was a girl with rich brown skin, and short, pink petals blooming around her to frame her face in a bob. Her eyes were a soft pink, and they lit up immediately upon noticing Anthea's arrival.

"Anthy!"

"Rosea!" The princess waved, jumping across scattered stones to cross the spring and tackle her friend in a hug. "An outsider is here!" Anthea pointed to Neros. "He's blue!"

Rosea stared at him, instantly wary. "He certainly is."

"My name is Neros," He said, carefully making his way across the spring to extend a hand to the girl. "It's nice to meet you."

Rosea studied him for a moment, then offered a gentle smile, taking his hand and giving it a small shake. "I'm sure you heard Anthea say, but my name is Rosea. I'm a cherry blossom Arborian, so I look a bit different from the princess."

"You're very beautiful!" Neros complimented, smiling broadly. His earnest words brought a blush to her cheeks. Princess Anthea smiled in turn, whirling around behind Rosea and cupping her face between her hands.

"Rosea is the *most* beautiful! She's the only Arborian of her kind! She's a modern legend, you know? And we're the same age, so naturally, she's my best friend in the whole forest," Anthea beamed, proudness emanating from her being. Neros was captured by the princess' charm, and found himself listening to both girls' stories until nearly sundown. When he returned, his father sent him quickly to bed, but not before making him promise to tell him all about what he learned in the morning, over breakfast.

Over the next seven years, Prince Neros became engrossed with the history of Endra, pouring over the history of the land, trying to learn as much as he could about the world he lived in. He made frequent visits to Arboria, where he and Princess Anthea would share their knowledge and search endlessly for more information. Luckily, the history of Endra was recorded dutifully up until around the year 500, where darkness seemed to begin shrouding the land. Historical text dropped off after that, both in Vetur and in Arboria. Arborian texts resumed with a valiant retelling of a story of heroes who saved the world and rose to heaven. Vetur's history picked up far after, with the building of the castle and the honoring of the first king and queen, the first in recorded history with mystified ice power. These gaps intrigued Prince Neros, while Anthea believed that an important event was purposefully erased from history.

On a particularly cold winter day in Vetur, the pair sat on the floor of Neros' room, open books sprawled on every available surface. Neros wrote furiously in a notebook. Anthea scratched her head. Suddenly, she stood up, pointing at a large book open in front of her, with an oak cover and a strange, symbol-based text written within it.

"There!"

Neros jumped out of his skin, pencil line trailing off the page he was writing on. He sighed, beginning to erase the excess. "There's what, Anthy?"

She collapsed back to all fours, hands resting open-palmed on the book she'd been pouring over. "This book! This is written in ancient Arborian, and I'm rusty on the details, but there's something new in here we haven't discovered yet!"

"Really? Well, what is it?"

"This book talks about a *prophecy*."

At this, his brow furrowed. "A prophecy?" He scratched his head with the pencil, temporarily displacing the circlet that rested atop his head. He'd grown into it since he was a kid, when it hung low and pressed into his ears uncomfortably. He was grateful now that it rested above, though at times it was frustrating to re-center. Neros shook his mind of the thought, returning his attention to the princess.

"Yeah, a prophecy," She continued, turning the page in her book and turning it to display to Neros. There were images accompanied with the words on this spread, showing three figures with weapons, shooting magic up at a dark, clouded figure. "They say a dark power rose up from the underworld, Umbros. It is a vast sea of the dead that lies below us. In peaceful times, this darkness rose up suddenly, and...I guess some people had to come and save the world with magic." Anthea's brow furrowed. "I can't really translate the last half of it, but a prophecy means it was fated to happen, right?"

Neros nodded, peering closely at the book. The script was beautiful, no doubt, but wholly foreign to him. He frowned. "Yeah. In storybooks, aren't prophecies cyclical? There's no telling if something like this could happen again."

"I don't think it will," Anthea pointed out, turning the page to show three victorious figures, with a bright yellow light emanating from behind them. "This page says something about elimination of evil force. After that, it skips ahead to the creation of Arboria, the planting of the Great Tree and infusing it with its special power. Then we get the origin of the Arborians, which we've been over, where the Great Tree releases seeds that grow into saplings and eventually, us. Once every couple hundred years, a special sapling is sent out, imbued with magic chosen by Silva, and right now, that's me! There have been princes and princesses, but you know I'm the best there's been."

The prince laughed. "Without a shadow of a doubt, Anthy. I doubt your predecessors were half as witty and charming as you."

Anthea whacked Neros on the shoulder, rolling her eyes. "Neros, please, don't make me blush! We have a prophecy-mystery to crack!"

"I'm afraid that's where you'll have to stop for today, you two," A voice bellowed from the doorway. Neros and Anthea looked find the source, seeing King Vasilias standing strong. His presence was enormous, but he had a gentle smile and a soothing voice; he was the picture of the kind of man anyone could trust. An elaborate crown of ice glittered in the early evening light.

"King Vasilias!" Anthea jumped up, closing the book and tucking it under her arm. "Is it that time already?"

"Yes, it is. The sun will fall past the horizon soon, and your people need you, Anthea. I promise you two can continue studying soon."

"Alright, alright, if you insist." The princess bounded toward the door, ducking under the king's arm and whirling around to wave at Neros. "You can't keep me away forever, you know! I'll be back!"

The King's laugh bellowed, echoing throughout the hall. "I know, I know. Safe travels back to Arboria, young princess."

"You bet! See ya later, Neros! You, too, Your Majesty!"

Once the princess had long gone out of earshot, the king turned back to his son. "It's about time for our daily training, son. If you would, could you meet me in the training hall?"

Neros smiled, nodding. "Of course, father. Let me clean up here, first."

King Vasilias turned and walked out of the room, closing the door gently behind him. As Neros gathered up the books, his mind drifted back to what Anthea discovered regarding the gaps in history and the prophecy. Skipping around parts…Neros knew there was more to it than a mere mistranslation. For all Anthea claimed she was rusty, she had the power of the goddess Silva within her, so he trusted her summaries completely. Was there a specific reason parts of history seemed to be rewritten? He placed the books back on his shelf, pensive. He was grateful the castle court and his parents shared any resource they could in regard to his recent dive into the history of Endra. His father attributed his intense interest to his meeting with Anthea. *That princess got you invested in the lives of others, son, and for that, I am grateful, but tread carefully,"* he had said. *"You may not always like the answers you find."*

Neros made his way down to the training hall slowly, not entirely sure he was in the mood to train today. He had agreed, of course, as he had done every time previous—it was just as important for him to train his body as it was his mind. After his initial meeting with Anthea, future trips down into the world of Endra had not gone quite so pleasantly. His father warned him against such troubles, small monsters or the occasional bandit, and had taken to teaching him how to wield a weapon and fine-tune his ice magic. It was a careful balance of muscle and mental energy, as fighting with a spear and casting a spell felt entirely different, and took entirely different tolls on the boy's body.

The door to the training hall was tall and wide, a deep blue with silver studs and large handles. The doors were heavy—Neros always had to use both hands to push one open—and the hall within stretched for what felt like miles. Along the walls were various practice weapons, and enough training dummies to build up an entire army. Neros had always wondered if war was involved in Vetur's past, but Vasilias refused to say. If it was in the history books, it was written over or carefully removed.

The prince took a deep breath and heaved open the door.

Inside, the king stood with commanding posture, practice blade already in hand. Neros was glad he decided to wear loose clothes, as his summon to this room hadn't come with enough warning for him to change. He grabbed a spear off the far wall. His father, at times, had chastised his affinity for spears, saying he needed to broaden his horizons more if he were to become a prince worthy of inheritance to the throne. Neros understood, though he felt that in peaceful times such as these, he doubted he would need to learn more than his father was already graciously teaching him.

"Today," The king announced, dropping into a battle stance. "You will learn how to impart your magic energy into a weapon."

Neros' eyebrows shot up. "Really? Isn't that…Father, isn't that dangerous?"

"Of course it is. But without risk, there is no hope for reward." King Vasilias approached. He, unlike Neros, had managed to change into a loose tunic and pants (or Neros idly wondered if he was wearing that under all his kingly shirts and armor?) and pointed the tip of the practice blade at Neros. The point began to glow, ice magic pooling and gathering there. Then, the king cast his aim aside, shouting "Release!" And the magic shot from the tip of the blade, crashing into one of the training dummies and freezing it solid. "Do you see how it works?"

Neros had been too amazed by the spectacle to pay close attention. "Ah...perhaps, another demonstration?"

The king smiled. "It requires intense mental focus. You must imagine your magic energy coursing through your veins, ready to be released. The key is, instead of releasing it out of your fingertips directly, you connect with the wavelength of the weapon, to channel the energy into it instead. Here," The king reached out for the spear Neros gripped, and he handed it to his father. The king disappeared around a rack of spears, and returned with a long navy case, plopping it in front of his son. "There are weapons designed to make this process easier. Open this, Neros."

Neros obliged. He clicked the case open, revealing a long, shimmering spear with a diamond-shaped head. The shaft was pale blue in color, seeming translucent, as flecks of un-melting ice were embedded with the blue-gray wood used to build its shape. The diamond head was encased in winding, sharp tendrils, looking menacing without seeming malicious. Inside the head was a small orb of magic essence, floating aimlessly within its confines, emitting gentle blue light.

"This spear is called Vatnis, passed down through the royal family since Vetur's founding," Vasilias explained. "It was mine, but now, Neros, you are old enough to wield it yourself."

"It's beautiful. Thank you, father," The prince looked up, feeling doubtful. A royal weapon, in his own hands. It felt like a miracle and a mistake all at once. "But, I don't understand. You said this...makes it easier to channel magic?"

"Indeed," The king continued. "If you focus the energy into your hands, it will pass into the spear, and gather into this orb," He gestured along the shaft of the spear, pointing at the orb of magic dancing around the tip. "It will grow in strength until you cast a spell, where then it will all release at once."

The king stood, disappearing again behind a stack of practice weapons. Neros was left to attempt the technique for himself. He closed his eyes, focusing his energy into the weapon before him. Peeking an eye open to ensure it was working (it was, thank goodness), he strengthened the energy. The power of ice flowed through his veins, cold enough to chill any regular person, but to Neros it was comforting—like home. The orb grew larger and larger inside of its diamond casing, threatening to break out.

The prince thrust the spear forward, aiming for a row of training dummies. "Release!" The magic blasted out of his spear, recoil sending Neros stumbling backward and landing on his rear with a grunt.

"Very good!" King Vasilias encouraged, re-emerging from the stack of weapons with a fresh sword, one that looked more well equipped for the technique the young prince had just learned. "If you keep practicing, you will surely be able to master that with effortless ease. You'll even be able to build structures and sculptures with ice using this technique. In fact, at this upcoming festival, I'd like you to do the honor of showcasing the final sculpture."

Neros' eyebrows shot up. "Really?" To sculpt the ice statue at the end of the festival was an incredible honor typically reserved for the king alone. The performance contained most of the theatrics that the villagers looked forward to every year. The statue was crafted with ice, then secured with special magic to ensure it didn't melt for the rest of the year. Choosing what to sculpt, how to create it, where to throw in flashier moves—it was all an intricate process. If it fell to the prince, it would be quite a lot of pressure.

"Yes, my son. You are more than ready," Vasilias complimented, ruffling Neros' hair. Suddenly, he grew serious, squatting back into his battle stance. "Now, come at me! We need to hone your combat and magic skills if we're to start you on the right track to building with ice!"

Neros lunged forward, spear meeting his father's skill with the blade, and they parried for some time. The prince used his smaller size and speed as leverage over his father, but every time, his father's skill won out. Neros had a wild, passionate way of fighting, and Vasilias made no secret that it would turn into a weakness if he wasn't careful. The prince tried to take this to heart, but as Vasilias hurled ice wave after ice wave at him, it became harder and harder to remain calm and focused. One particularly harsh blow had Neros thrown backwards, spear fallen out of his hands, a vicious shiver coursing down his spine. He stood slowly, bracing his hands on his knees and breathing heavily.

"That's enough. You've learned a lot today, Neros. Leave your spear here: we will continue this later."

Neros only nodded his acknowledgement, and his father bid his farewell for the evening. Neros offered a weak smile and half-wave as he left.

God, Father is tough as usual in his training… The prince appreciated and respected everything his father did for him, but the process was arduous. Ice magic, though a comfort to cast, was unforgiving if it hit you, and Neros still found himself desperately trying to catch his breath, shaking off the bitter chill that wracked through his bones. He wiped the sweat from his brow. He knew he'd need a bath—to avoid one would mean certain sickness, especially with the hit he'd suffered.

But he would be fine. If he were to become a prince his father could be proud of, he would have to be.

The next festival of the ice came all too quickly for the young prince, and he felt he hardly had enough time to properly hone his skills. He slaved away during the smallest hours of night, until the sunlight began to peek over the top of the mountain and cast a soft yellow glow over the snow. His mother often came outside to join him, teaching him all her favorite show-stopping moves of years' past—a flourish of the arm here, a twirl there, a toss of his staff to the air, caught with whimsy and grace—their sessions were the opposite of that with Neros' father. Queen Heilsa often had tea brought out for them to enjoy in the quiet moments during sunrise, and though Neros felt exhausted, he was always happy and at peace (and, sometimes, his mother would allow him to slip away for an afternoon nap).

Neros stood in his bedroom, staring uneasily at himself in the mirror: he donned new garments today, made especially for the ceremony. A blue tailcoat on top of a respectable violet turtleneck, with sharp pants and shoes to complete the look. In this, he looked more princely than he ever had. The gentle, sheer details of his tailcoat paid a tribute to his power of the element, but also the roots he shared with the entire snowy town.

He fiddled with circlet, the bright purple gem in the middle glittering as he shifted it to be centered on his forehead. Nerves pricking at his insides, he fluffed his hair around it, unsure if he wanted to showcase his position so boldly today. His stomach twisted uncomfortably, and he took a few deep breaths to shove his anxieties away. *Today is going to be fine. You'll impress them. They already like you. The only person you can disappoint is yourself. And perhaps Father. But mostly yourself.*

Well, he didn't pride himself on pep talks.

"Neros!"

The prince started, whipping his head around to the door so quickly it displaced the crown he'd so carefully arranged. It was just his mother, who looked on with a gentle smile.

"Sorry, dear. I didn't mean to spook you," She chuckled behind her hand.

"It's alright, mother! Is it time already?"

"Indeed it is," She stepped into the room fully, walking up and re-adjusting his crown for him. "Are you ready?"

Neros shifted his weight nervously. "As ready as I will ever be, mother."

Queen Heilsa rested her hands on her son's shoulders, smiling. "You have worked so hard to prepare for today, Neros. You'll do a fantastic job, I know it."

His mother's faith offered him at least some solace, so he could at least bring himself to nod at her words. He silently followed her down to the courtyard, where the townspeople had all gathered in their traditional ice festival garb. This year, some villagers had opted to make small banners out of twill to wave in the air while festivities took place.

King Vasilias had a grandiose speech, as ever, and dispersed the townsfolk to partake in the usual activities: vendors were located around the middle of the courtyard, offering sweets and savory delectable treats to enjoy; there was a large rink for children to skate around, not far from a pond used for an ice fishing contest; gentle snow fell from the sky, punctuating the event with its silent grace.

When it was time to re-convene, King Vasilias' voice boomed out toward the crowd. Neros stood beside him at the makeshift ice podium.

"Ladies and gentlemen, citizens of our fine winter town of Vetur," He started. "It is time for a special surprise—our finale will be presented to you this year by none other than my son, Prince Neros!"

The crowd erupted in cheers and hollers, proud and excited faces lighting up among excited and curious ones. All of it made Neros' adrenaline spike with nervous energy. He resisted the urge to fidget. The king urged him to begin, giving him a pat on the shoulder. Neros nodded, steeling himself. *Alright. Let's do this.*

Spear in hand, he moved in front of the crowd. He focused energy into it, enough to last, but not too much—he couldn't have it explode in a burst of snowy fury, after all. The tip glowed, and children in the front cooed with interest. The prince waved his weapon experimentally, and flecks of ice sprinkle down from the tip. Neros smiled. *It's working!* He guided the spear skyward and shot off a flurry of ice and snow, watching as it burst outward in a firework-like fashion. It earned *oohs* and *ahs* from not only the children, but the adults, which only served to ease the prince's nerves even more.

Then, he began to dance.

Neros swirled around the circular courtyard, and the crowd parted to make room for him. The ice drifting out of the staff followed his movements, and he spun, moving his spear with him to make the flecks whirl around his entire body. He cast manual spells from his hands, multiple tiny snowballs forming and cascading in large arcs over the crowd. Neros continued moving his feet with grace and elegance known of the queen but keeping a power behind his magic reminiscent of the king. The crowd was enraptured, watching so intently that they even forgot to clap; their amazement ran deep as Neros continued his performance, methodically dancing around a particular section in the center of the courtyard—a section he had planned as the final resting place for the statue of the festival. As he danced, he added to it inconspicuously, and from the ground up, he built his finale piece: an ice sculpture that was a perfect rendition of his mother and father, locked in an embrace in perfect form for ballroom dancing. This went against tradition, wherein normally the structure served as an homage to the great Ice Goddess, Isolde: she who gave life and meaning to this region of Endra after The Fall of Umbros back hundreds of years ago.

To release the finale's fireworks, Neros pointed his staff at the statue, and fired off a powerful spell; it ricocheted off his parents' clasped hands and burst into a delicate shimmer of snow and ice, crackles of magic energy reflecting the light of the setting sun while the flakes drifted to the crowd below.

The Veturians surged in cheers, banners waving wildly and children jumping up and down, the picture of sheer excitement. In all their years hosting the honorable festival, King Vasilias and Queen Heilsa had never seen the villagers so thrilled about a finale performance. Neros' heart swelled as he looked out to a sea of admirers and proud supporters—his relief was practically tangible.

"Thus ends the festival of the ice! Thank you all for joining us, and we wish for your continued happiness and success!" The king bellowed. He turned to Neros. "Take a bow, son."

So Neros did, bowing to his audience, whose cheers still had not ceased. Eventually, the villagers began to amble away, needing to tend to their own shops and livestock and homes. Neros locked his spear safely into a harness on his back and went about helping the vendors take down and pack up their stalls. It would be tedious work without aid, and the prince was happy to oblige every year. The vendors respected his kindness, and usually sent him walking away with various trinkets and a few coins as thanks. This year was no different; pouch heavy and stress lifted, Neros bounded up the steps to the castle. The moon hung high and full in the sky, and it was late enough that the castle staff had been dismissed for the evening. The blue hue of the castle walls felt peaceful to the young prince, especially after a long day at the festival. He moved easily through the halls, finding himself following the sound of his parents' voices, but walked past the throne room and headed up the stairs to his own quarters.

Prince Neros dressed down for bed, nestled under the covers, and prepared himself for a long, fulfilling nights' sleep.

Just as he was about to drift off, a loud rumble roused him, coming from the direction of the throne room. His crown jittered on his bedside table. Neros shot up in bed—all the servants had gone home. What was happening? The castle rumbled again, and his gaze nervously flitted to the door. *Mom...Dad...* The prince was not the type to sit around: the very least he could do was see what happened. He grabbed his crown and set it atop his head as he stumbled out of bed to check on his parents. Before he could get out the door, the dim glow of his spear caught his eye.

He grabbed it, and ran.

Chapter 2
A Calamitous Jinx

*N*eros burst through the doors of the throne room, looking frantically around for the source of the rumbling—be it an intruder, livestock on the loose, or just Endra's magical plates vibrating with an overflow of magic essence. He locked eyes with his parents, who both appeared equally concerned.

"Mother, Father, what's happening?"

They shared a look. "What do you mean, Neros?" His mother asked.

The prince made his way to the center of the room. "There was a rumble, I felt it—"

Just then, the palace began to quake again, ice fixtures clinking as they knocked together from the movement. Neros whirled around, trying to locate the source, but it seemed all-encompassing; an uncontrollable shiver shot down his spine.

Low-life maggots of Vetur, the voice boomed. Do you understand the blasphemy you have done unto me?

"Who are you?" King Vasilias called, holding his wife closer to him.

Has it really been so long, King Vasilias, that you have forgotten my voice? How pitiful. You truly do deserve what is coming for you.

"What do you mean?" Neros stood firm, spear in hand, as though the disembodied voice was one he could spar with. He turned to his father, eyes wide. "Who is that?"

HMM…A NEW VERMIN AMONG YOUR FAMILY, IS THAT, KING VASILIAS? HAS THIS BOY TRULY LIVED SO LONG AND YOU HAVE NEGLECTED TO TELL HIM ABOUT ME? HAVE YOU LOST ALL YOUR FAITH? IS THIS HOW YOU CHOOSE TO CONTINUE MY LEGACY?

"Father, this voice…where is it coming from? What does it want?" Neros' wonder quickly approached fear, and he stepped closer to his parents to goad an answer from them.

The king stood firm, choosing not to answer and turning his head to the ceiling. "Why have you called to us? What seems to have frustrated you so?"

WOULDN'T YOU LIKE TO KNOW, KING VASILIAS THE VAPID? YOU DO NOT DE-SERVE A WORD OF EXPLANATION, YOU WRETCHED WORM. YOU DARE DEFILE MY LEGACY! NOW, YOU WILL PAY!

Heed my words carefully, vermin of Vetur: lest you learn to under-stand your mistake, this Curse will lay upon your family line for all of eterni-ty!

The throne room filled with a blisteringly cold chill, the walls emitting frost. A tendril of hazy mist soared down from the ceiling, spinning on its course and splitting in two, each strand knocking into the king and queen. They grunted, being pushed back into their throne seats, and right before the prince's eyes, their bodies began to be encased in ice.

"Mother, Father! No! You, whoever you are, what are you doing?" Neros called out to the chamber as he bolted for the thrones. Panic seared through his veins, and he had to stop whatever was happening, somehow.

FOOLISH BOY. YOU ENJOYED SEEING THEIR PERSONAGE SO MUCH OUT IN THE COURTYARD; I'M ONLY GIVING YOU A THAT WHICH YOU HOLD SO DEAR!

"You—you villain! Why do you refuse to explain yourself? Oh, Moth-er… Father…" Neros reached out to his parents, to stop the spread of the ice from consuming their bodies, but the cursed mist clearly had other plans. In an instant, a vein separated from the mist and bolted at Neros. The prince moved to block it with his right hand, but the cryptic energy wrapped around his appendage, squeezing it like a snake around its prey. It sank into his arm, an ice-cold sensation shooting up to his elbow before he tore his arm away, disengaging the mist. The prince grunted, searching the room for the offend-ing mage and cradling his arm close to his chest. "Fiend! What have…you done?"

IT IS A CURSE, DEAR PRINCELING. YOU REFUSED TO DO RIGHT WITH MY GIFT TO YOU, AND THIS IS YOUR PUNISHMENT, YOU WRETCHED MAGE. YOU ARE DOOMED NEVER TO CAST MAGIC DIRECTLY, LEST YOU WANT TO ENDURE INSUFFERABLE PAIN. YOU WILL FEEL MY WRATH IN YOUR BONES!

"No! W-wait, who are you? Why have you done this?" He cried, but it was too late. As quickly as Neros felt the presence arrive, it dissipated, leaving him in the near-empty throne room with his injured arm and ice-ified parents. The prince swore to himself, rising to his feet and stumbling over to his parents' side. He reached out to touch them, looking into their eyes as though they could start speaking words of encouragement to him. Through his iced hand, he could sense their pulses—a slowed, steady beating was the only sign the prince had that his parents were alive. He dared a look at their faces: they, too, had been solidified as stark images of fear and distress.

Neros sank to his knees, resting his head on his father's leg, where just moments ago so much warmth emanated from. A lump sat in his throat, heavy and swollen, and as he tried to swallow around it, he thought it would split in half. He choked back a cry, reaching up to grip at something, anything—but he could not feel anything, only hearing the soft scrape of his frozen hand against his father's leg. His heart hammered in his chest, adrenaline like a fire that could not be quenched; but, as much as he wanted to do something, he could sense the holy aura emanating from his parents' position. It was a power that far exceeded his own. *Damn it,* he thought miserably. *If only I had been able to properly communicate with that witch!* From his position on the floor, he glanced at the door—strange, that no one had knocked. Had no one else felt the castle rumble? Was it a trap designed only to affect the royal family…?

Perhaps, if someone else had heard, they could offer the prince some advice. Vigor renewed, Neros stood, scooping his spear off the floor and running for the door. He burst it open, met with the concerned, slightly out of breath faces of two castle guards.

"Is everything alright, your highness?" The taller of the two asked.

"I—um, did you hear anything in there?" Neros asked back, and the guard looked perplexed.

"Yes, milord. There was a rumble that seemed to be coming from here, so we gathered our weapons and came as soon as we were able. Are you sure everything is alright? You look as though you've seen a ghost, milord." He replied, taking a half-step closer to the prince, wanting to check for a fever but not wanting to be impolite.

"I–it's a long story, just…don't go in the throne room for now. I promise I'll explain when I get back. Okay?" Neros pleaded, his heart dropping to his stomach knowing that the strange voice he and his parents heard had been just between the three of them.

The guards exchanged a worried glance. "As you wish, sire."

Neros nodded to them both, taking off toward the southern annex of the castle, where his primary source of problem-solving was: the library. It was late at night, and very few of the guards were out, mostly stoically standing watch and offering the prince no more than a passing salute. Neros followed the torch-lit hallways as they curved and turned, until he arrived at the two wooden doors leading into the library. He pushed them open with great effort—they were always heavier than he remembered—and tumbled inside. The library was brimming with books, shelves spanning as far as the eye could see; rows and rows of shelves stuffed with books on all topics, recorded from as early as Vetur was founded. Thanks to the town's, well-documented history, so Neros knew there had to be something in here about curses.

The librarian gave him a tired look. "Prince Neros, shouldn't you be sleeping instead of studying?"

"I'm sorry, Runa, but this is urgent," Neros started, fiddling with his staff until it was strapped safely against his back.

Runa narrowed her ice-blue eyes, scanning Neros' figure up and down. Her gaze stopped, eyes widening. "Neros…your arm. What in the world has happened to you?"

Oh, no. Neros followed her gaze to see that he'd neglected to cover up his arm before making his way down here. "Um…" Somehow, the prince knew he wouldn't be able to talk himself out of this one. "I–it's my parents, Runa. They–there was a voice, and a great rumbling, I went to check it out, and—" he paused to collect himself.

"Is it some form of magic?" Runa asked, stepping out from around her desk and adjusting her glasses. She stepped closer to Neros, lifting his ice arm to examine it more closely. "Oh, my. It certainly is. What of your parents?"

"They—their forms are frozen. Please, Runa, I need to know where I can find answers here." The prince pleaded, eyebrows knit together in concern.

Runa narrowed her eyes. "Calm down, your highness. I have a few questions for you, first." She proceeded to rap her knuckles across Neros' iced arm, examining his face closely for a reaction. "Can you feel any of this?"

When Neros shook his head, she began to roll up his sleeve. "Now, then, just how far up does this go…?" She rolled his sleeve carefully, all the way up to his elbow. Runa sucked a breath of air through her teeth. "Your highness, this is quite bad. Are you aware of its effects yet?"

Neros shook his head again, and Runa huffed. "Very well. At least allow me to procure some coverage for you, so you don't draw the attention and concern of everyone in Vetur. They all care about you very much, you know," The librarian walked back behind her desk, gathering a few materials that Neros couldn't see. "Divination, curses, and spellcasting is in the western annex of the library, through a set of small doors. That way," She pointed behind her. "The most useful information will be found there. Good luck, Prince Neros."

"Thank you, Runa!" Neros smiled at her, breaking into a swift jog toward where Runa had directed him. It was useful to have someone with expansive knowledge of the castle library's organization; it had saved Neros countless hours of pointless searching in the past. Once he reached the doors, he pushed his way through to be met with a small room stuffed with well-worn books of all sizes and thickness, some stacked on the floor because there was no shelf room left. There was a single, small chair in the corner with blue cushions and a sturdy frame, as if someone had lugged it in from elsewhere in the castle to have a good space to read privately. Nodding to himself at the space, Neros set to work.

The prince pulled spellbook after spellbook off the shelves, filling his arms with books on magic knowledge and theory and plopped himself in the corner chair to set to reading. He skimmed the spellbooks he'd grabbed— ones focusing entirely on ice magic—but no curses came to light. Book after book, the most he could glean was more information on building sculptures and structures, not inflicting frozen-but-alive curses on enemies. Tossing the tomes aside, Neros dove into the theory books, absorbing theories on ice magic production, its effect on the spellcaster, and the long-lasting effects when cast upon others.

Though no conclusive evidence has been made on the subject, inflicting ice magic upon other mortals is widely ill-advised. Neros felt his stomach drop, though he kept reading. *Currently reported side effects have included brain cell damage, muscle atrophy, or prolonged dormancy post-thaw. Special circumstances do not apply (i.e. curses, altered magic, dark magic, etc.).* The prince sighed. This *was* different—it was a curse! He found himself growing increasingly frustrated at the lack of answers the books here provided him, and wondered what his father or mother would tell him to do if he went to them for advice. He closed his eyes, trying to imagine their gentle, smiling faces. All that surfaced were their frozen sculptures, eyes wide with fear, mouths open in unspoken protest. Neros' eyes snapped back open, and he forced himself to focus again on the theory books in front of him.

Many of them discussed the healing properties of water, but Neros knew that would be fruitless—pouring water over ice may melt it under *normal* circumstances, but most of the passages in this book were amended by saying curses were an entirely different story.

The prince searched for hours. He picked up dark tomes, light tomes, holy tomes, and tomes with strange, extra appendages. His endless scanning tired out his eyes, and the small room had no windows, so he was unable to perceive how much time had passed. All he knew was, for all the books in this room, there was inconclusive evidence for curses. Neros felt himself fading in and out of consciousness, and he sank lower in the chair, a tome about magic energy in mortals open over his chest.

"..ittl…Prince… Little Prince! Please wake up, milord!"

Neros blinked, eyelids still heavy from sleep. Panic overtook him in a moment, and he shot straight up, tome tumbling to the ground with a *thunk*. He scrambled to pick it up, close it, and brush it off, to feign composure. He looked up at who had awakened him—it was Runa, her lavender brows furrowed in concern.

The prince cleared his throat, matching her concerned gaze with one of his own. "H-how long was I asleep?"

"Not too long," She replied, plucking the book off his chest and examining its contents. "Magic Energy in Mortals, hm? Not a bad place to start."

Neros blinked blearily at her. "Start...? That was one of the last of the many books I'd scoured through, Runa. Just...just how much more research will I need to do before finding an answer?"

Runa looked over the top of her glasses, down at him. "You mean you've read nearly every relevant tome in here?" When Neros nodded, she looked at him with pity; it was no wonder he'd fallen asleep. "Very well. If that's how it is, perhaps...I need to see exactly what happened to your parents."

"But Runa—"

"No buts, Little Prince. I must see them. I'm one of few left who can sense magic energy in mortals around here. I might be able to tell you if they can be saved."

Neros' gut twisted uncomfortably. Whatever happened to his parents, the prince was firm that he should be the only one to bear the responsibility; after all, it sounded like the witch was punishing them for *his* actions. He didn't want to get the whole castle involved.

Before he could further protest, Runa had already turned on her heel to walk toward the throne room. Neros scrambled out of his chair, gripping his spear and jogging after her.

"Runa, you don't want to see them. I promise, I can handle this myself!"

"With all due respect, your highness, I will make that decision when I *see* them."

The prince worried at his bottom lip, fiddling with the spear in his hands. Small flecks of ice formed on his shoulders falling away and drifting to the floor behind him as he walked. It was an unconscious, nervous habit his mother had often scolded him for, warning him that one day he'd freeze himself to the wall or the floor. Neros always argued, but now he felt like she might have been right after all—a dull ache had made him aware that the ice was being produced. The prince willfully stopped the magic, turning the corner to follow Runa.

As the throne room came into view, so did two very guilty looking guards. Their eyes peered everywhere: to the floor, the ceiling, each other, before finally apologetically settling on Neros.

"We're so sorry, milord!"

"We—yeh looked so distraught, we wanted to see if there was anythin' we could do for yeh," The shorter guard supplied.

"And your arm, sire—it appeared dreadfully painful, we simply couldn't help it, we…we—"

"We peeked inside!"

The pair closed their eyes, awaiting punishment. Neros worried at his lip again, trying to hide his arm behind his back. *Oh, no, how am I going to cover this up now…?*

"Oh, that's right," Runa cut in, before Neros could punish the guards. "Your arm. I'd almost forgotten—here. Take this. It'll cover it up so you don't worry the townspeople." She dug around her pocket before procuring a deep purple leather glove, holding it out to Neros. He took it, sliding it over his arm. "It's one of my late husband's. He used to work in the gardens here, long ago. It might be a bit big, but it'll fit."

Neros looked over his arm, examining the fit of the glove; it was as Runa said. The glove itself was well-worn in places and a bit dirty, but as he extended his arm, he noted that it was long enough to cover where the cursed spot ended—just before his elbow.

"Won't the Veturians notice 'is other arm's not covered like the firs—*yow!*" The shorter of the two guards yelped as the taller one elbowed his side. "Whot? It's the truth!"

"I think the more pressing matter is Veturians *peeking in the throne room* when asked not to," Neros pointed out, to which the guard shrank inward. The prince sighed, moving past the two. "Well…you've seen it, now, haven't you? So there's not much I can do about that. Just…Agnar, you stand guard to make sure no one else enters. Brynjar, follow me and Runa."

The shorter guard, Agnar, nodded, saluting the prince and puffing out his chest. "It'll be m'sworn duty, prince!"

The remaining three re-entered the throne room, Neros the most nervous of them. On the throne remained the King and Queen. Runa let out a quiet gasp.

"What in the world happened, Neros?"

The prince avoided eye contact, staring straight ahead at his parents' figures. "They…I was in my room, preparing to sleep after the festival, when I felt a great rumble. I grabbed my spear, and ran right here. I…there was a voice, she called us vermin, said we deserved it, and then…well. You can see what happened next." His gaze sank to the floor. "She froze them, Runa. I did something to anger this witch, and she…she froze them."

Runa remained silent for a moment, walking slowly to the thrones themselves to examine the damage done. She inspected the King's body, then the Queen's, checking for any signs of life. Typically, in magical curses, she would be able to sense a life force still pulsing from within the ice. This would be a sign to Runa that the prince's parents could still be saved. If not…she feared how Neros would take the news.

"For what it's worth, I also felt a rumble. Agnar and I were conducting our nightly rounds, as usual, when the entire structure of the castle shook. We came running as quickly as possible, but our swiftness was met with no resolution. For the life of us, we couldn't find the source. Then the young prince came tumbling out of the throne room, telling us not to go in. And, well…" Brynjar trailed off, embarrassed.

The librarian hummed, inspecting the figures closely. Neros made his way toward her, while Brynjar retained a respectful distance, unable to bring himself to even look for more than a few moments.

"Brynjar," The guard jumped at the sound of his name, though Runa made no move to turn around. "Did you hear a voice? The voice Prince Neros speaks of?"

"Uh…unfortunately, no. Agnar and I only felt the quake, I'm afraid."

"Interesting." Runa placed her hands over Queen Heilsa's heart, closing her eyes. Neros peered at her, eyebrows knit together.

"Can they be saved, Runa?"

She was quiet for a long time. Neros feared the worst—his parents were going to be trapped, in a frigid comatose state, for the remainder of their life on Endra. He would need to rule Vetur by himself, keeping tabs on the state of the castle and the lives of the people. *The townspeople…they would riot, for sure. I'm too young to be king.* Stress tugged at his heart, and he looked desperately to Runa for an answer.

Runa sighed. "This is not pretty, Prince Neros, I will be honest about that. But…their spirits remain. I think, if you could find this witch, then maybe—"

"They can be saved?" He asked, hopeful.

"Maybe," She warned. "But you cannot trust that my word will be true. After all, you don't even know who the owner of this mysterious voice is. You are also the only one who heard it."

Neros frowned. "But I heard her, Runa! I *know* it was real!"

"Prince Neros," Runa leveled his gaze with a stern look of her own. "Perhaps the most logical course of action right now is for you to consider how we can best move forward."

"Move forward?" He gestured to where his parents' figures sat, immobile. "That witch cursed the royal family *for all time!* Do you expect me to abandon my parents, knowing they can be saved?!"

From his spot near the door, Brynjar cleared his throat. "If I may, sire, I suggest you consider the logistics of this situation. If you have no lead for the voice, how are you to begin researching this issue? You seem to have exhausted the library, have you not?"

"And without a lead, you have nowhere to go other than forward," Runa said. "You must understand that this problem goes beyond your own ability. This problem is greater than you are."

"I'll find a way!" Neros shouted, balling his hands into fists. "To toss them aside…how could I? Would you expect they do the same for me, Runa?" When the librarian remained silent, the prince's expression collapsed. He looked to the guard, who appeared equally apologetic. Frustrated tears pricked at the corners of Neros' eyes, and he turned sharply on his heel.

"Your highness—"

"*No!* Do not try to stop me! If you want to continue living as though my parents have died, so be it. The chain of command falls to the castle's court members, and you have my permission to lead them, Runa. But I am not going to sit idly by if there is even a shred of hope for me to cling to!" His frustrations growing, Neros stormed out of the throne room, re-strapping his spear to his back; Agnar peered at him curiously.

"Oi, yer majesty, are y'alright?"

Neros didn't look at him. "I'm going for a walk."

He continued down the hall, and if Agnar called out to him, he didn't hear. The only thoughts swimming in his mind were Runa's unbelievable suggestion, his parents' statuesque figures, and what he could do to save them. It all came back to the mysterious voice of that witch: who was she, and what mistake had Neros and his family made to anger her in such a way? *No one else could hear her…or at least, no one else did at the time.* The prince left the castle, swiftly descending the steps and embracing the frigid Veturian morning. The sun had just begun to peek over the mountaintop, signaling that many of the villagers would soon be waking up to tend to their livestock. Usually, Neros helped them; as the only child and prince of Vetur, he was more protected by the castle court than he was allowed to participate. This was fine, to Neros— he was plenty satisfied by the combat training his father provided and the opportunity it provided to be closer to the townsfolk. His mother would often solicit input from him as a result of his hands-on experience and knowledge of the troubles of the Veturians.

"Hoy, your majesty! You're out earlier than usual, aren't ya?" One of the livestock keepers, Veshna, snapped Neros out of his reverie with her call. "I was just about to let my sheep out for the day; care to help me tend to their pasture?"

Veshna was a stout, kindly woman with dark, loosely-braided hair and warm eyes. She wore simple, warm clothes: a homemade astrakhan hat, heavy cotton shirt and corduroy pants with a wool coat, all in earthy colors. Neros loved the way people dressed in town—his gift of ice magic also meant he was less sensitive to the cold, but he sometimes wished he could try their clothes on just to see if they felt as snug as they looked. Of all the townspeople, Veshna was by far the closest to Neros: she kept him safe from wandering merchants who passed through Vetur seeking young, naïve minds to scam, and in return Neros would help her with her chores. The prince thoroughly enjoyed his time with her, and she'd grown to feel much like family to him; she taught him just as many life lessons as his own father and mother.

Prince Neros smiled at her, relieved to have a momentary distraction. "Of course, Veshna. I'd be glad to help you."

Veshna welcomed him into her stables, and she opened the pen where her sheep had been sleeping, immediately putting Neros to work. He adjusted the amount of straw in their beds, tended to the vegetation in the pasture, and counted the current inventory of feed for her, taking notes as he went. Meanwhile, the sheep roamed their fenced-in pasture, grazing idly as Neros went about his work. Naturally, however, he couldn't prevent his mind from wandering. As he re-arranged the straw beds for the umpteenth time, he ruminated. *A mistake…tasting my own medicine? Was she talking to me, or was it bad business with my parents? I wonder if Vetur even has the answers I need, or if I should figure out an alternative.* Neros considered it, bogged down by the re-surfaced memories of his parents being frozen near-instantaneously. He moved back to the pasture, checking the fastenings on the fence to ensure their security, and ultimately ended up leaning against the fence, staring out into the snowy landscape. Vendors in the distance put up stalls to sell merchandise and trade, and other townspeople simply perused.

Without his notice, Veshna stood next to him. "Is there somethin' on your mind, dear?"

Neros jumped, turning to face her. "Oh! Um. N-not in particular."

"You don't need to hide it from me, your majesty. If you need to talk, you know I'm all ears. Always have been." Veshna smiled, eyes glinting in the sun.

The prince wrung his wrists, worrying at his lower lip. "I'm not sure how to phrase it."

"Then just talk. I'm sure you'll get to what you need to say eventually."

He nodded, taking a deep breath. He couldn't outright tell her about the curse—it was clear everyone in town had been completely oblivious to it. There was no way he would risk inciting a panic in his people when he himself had no idea what a solution looked like.

"What if…what if something strange happened to you one day? And you weren't sure…how to proceed. On one hand, there are people who care about the future, who want you to move on. And on the other hand, there is something mysterious, something…dark, that you feel will get worse if you leave it be? What would you do?"

Veshna brought a hand up to her chin, rubbing it thoughtfully and humming. "Sounds like you've got something big on your hands. You ask for help already?" Neros nodded. Veshna sighed. "And they were no help, I assume? Otherwise, you wouldn't be askin' me!"

The prince cast his gaze to his feet, cheeks coloring in shame. "It's a bit complicated."

"Everything's complicated, your majesty!" Veshna laughed. "But if I were in your shoes, I think I'd take a trip away from here."

Neros' heart nearly stopped. "Away from here? Why?"

"Well, the council won't miss ya, will they? An' sure, we will, but your parents'll hold down the fort as they so often have in the past. Right?"

At the mention of his parents, Neros felt the familiar lump rise in his throat. He swallowed around it, trying his best to smile honestly. "Right. Maybe I'll…go."

"That's the spirit!" Veshna clapped her hand on his back. "Now, go. You're no use 'round here if you're distracted. The sheep'll start grazin' your hair!"

Neros laughed, waving good-bye to her before hopping the fence and heading through the town square. He passed by the statue of his parents that he made the day before. He stared up at it, wishing he could go back to that moment, when he noticed something.

His parents' faces had changed.

The prince's brow furrowed, and he squinted, stepping closer, before seeing it was no illusion—the expression etched on his parents' faces in these statues was distinctly similar to how Neros knew they were in the throne room right now. Glancing back and forth to make sure no one was looking, he whispered a spell to cast ice magic to orient their faces to be smiling.

As the magic energy was pulled through his veins and out his gloved hand, he felt a sharp sting in his arm. He flinched, glancing down. *Was that… because of using my magic?* The deed was done, however, and his parents' faces were restored to their usual, warm smiles.

On his way to the edge of town, Neros stopped by a few stalls to pick up some materials: if he was going to take a day trip away from Vetur, he would need some food and water, and a shoulder-bag to keep it in. He was lucky to still have allowance left—and earnings from helping Veshna—so he could compensate the vendors for his purchases (even though a few still insisted he take their goods on account of him being royalty).

Bag sufficiently packed and tossed over his shoulder, the prince made his way to the edge of Vetur. He turned back for just a moment, contemplating all that he'd be leaving behind for a day or two. *I hope Runa can appease the courts. Will she have a good excuse for them, to keep them from bringing up my parents' absence? She doesn't know I'm leaving, either...* He frowned. *It's like Veshna said. They won't miss me.*

Neros turned back to the mountain's edge, renewed determination in his mind and a fire in his gut. "I will save you, mother and father. I have to. I'll find a way."

As he looked back down the mountainside, however, his attention was drawn to a hazy figure moving frantically in the distance, seeming to be coming closer with each passing second.

Chapter 3
The Way Forward

"*N*erooos!"

A girl ran in leaps and bounds up the snowy mountainside. Her hair, woven from vines and leaves, flowed effortlessly behind her. The expression on her face was urgent. Prince Neros recognized her immediately, though he remained curious, hands resting delicately on his hips.

Princess Anthea reached the top of the hill, bending forward to catch her breath. Neros' expression waxed concerned.

"Princess Anthea? Is everything okay?" He asked, reaching out to pat her back.

"I…no…it's not!" She stood bolt upright, fire renewed in her eyes. "It's Arboria. We've been attacked!"

Neros' eyes widened. *Attacked? Like what happened to my parents?* "What happened, exactly? Please, tell me everything."

"There's no *time* for that! Just follow me!"

Anthea gripped Neros' gloved wrist firmly, causing him to wince. He allowed Anthea to tug him along, and soon they were sliding down Mount Vetur. While this was far from what Neros had in mind when he went for this walk, he felt he had no choice but to follow. Their feet carved a path in the snow, white flakes flying behind them; Neros' heart pounded in his chest. *Calm down. She won't hurt you. She would never dare hurt you,* Neros assured himself. Still, he couldn't help feeling nervous, trailing behind Anthea at such

a high speed.

They skid to a stop at the bottom of the mountain, but Anthea simply launched them both into a full sprint. It had been a long time since Prince Neros had felt grass under his feet, but even longer since he had run with such urgency.

"Anthy!" Neros gasped between pants. "Can you at least tell me *some* of what is going on?"

"It's my homeland, Arboria! I told you! It's been attacked—by some force! The gods, I swear it! *Cursed!*"

"Cursed!? But how?"

"The Ancient Tree—it gives everyone life and magic energy—its roots have erupted from the ground, wrapping their wiry tendrils around all the Arborians! I only barely managed to escape, and I figured needed help—that was when I went to you. It's my people, Neros—the energy is leaving their bodies. None of them–they can't–they can't move."

Neros' eyes went wide. That was a far greater scale of curse than what was laid upon him. "Anthy, I-I'm so sorry."

Wait. Looking at the scenery around them, Neros felt at odds—they were running *away* from the woods, not towards them. He dug his heels into the ground, bringing the pair to a stop. Anthea yelped. "What's the big idea?! We're in a hurry, you know!"

"Anthy, we *passed* the entrance to Arboria. Where are we going? And why do you need me?"

"I told you, we don't have time for questions!" Anthea grabbed his wrist and *yanked,* earning another wince and quiet hiss from Neros as they started back into motion. "There's an oracle in a far-off land, and I can't brave the Endran terrain alone. Besides, you're my best friend! Is this *even* a question of whether or not I'd bring you?"

Neros thought of the people in Vetur. Their king and queen had fallen (even if not permanently), and their only prince had fled—for something now much longer than a simple day trip—leaving the ruling to the courts and Runa. What would *they* think? He knew Veshna wouldn't mind, but would the rest feel safe with the royal family gone? Neros ran off to help Anthea, a princess of a neighboring kingdom—but was it irresponsible?

"Uh, hello, Neros? Could I get some help here?"

Neros blinked, not realizing that they had stopped walking. Anthea was staring at him expectantly. Behind her was a wide river that looked twice as deep. Neros blinked again, processing what was being asked of him. *Oh. My magic.* He looked down at his now-gloved casting hand—the one that was crystalline ice underneath. *Is it going to be okay…?*

The harsh witch's words rang through his mind: *Cursed your bloodline… you wretched little mage… you will feel my wrath in your bones!*

Neros outstretched his hand, willing the magical energy to come forth from within. A swirl of icy white and blue manifested around his hand, and the ancient words of spellcasting rolled freely off his tongue. He aimed his magic at the river, and it shot from his fingertips, slowly freezing over the water's surface. The ice solidified and spread, thickening enough to be safe to walk across.

He could only manage to cover less than a quarter of the river's width before a searing pain tore through his arm and across his shoulders, rocketing down his spine. Neros cried out in pain, doubling over and immediately cutting off the magic flow, gripping his arm to his chest.

"Neros! What happened? Are you hurt?" Anthea rushed to his side, carefully taking his arm in her hands.

"I…I'm okay. I'm sorry, Anthea, I couldn't—"

"No, I should be the one apologizing to *you*, for dragging you along with me, and asking you to do stuff for me, without even noticing you're hurt! What is this glove?"

"Anthy, I'm fine."

"That's a bold-faced lie and you know it!" Her expression grew angry, then collapsed into sadness. "Don't you trust me? Can't you tell me…just what are you hiding under this glove?"

"I…of course trust you." Neros cast a nervous glance at his gloved hand. They were friends from a very early age, and practically grew up alongside each other—there was no reason for him to doubt her. Princess Anthea was just as beloved to the people of Vetur as the prince, King, and Queen. They experienced the joy of tending sheep in Vetur's village together; Anthea showed Neros all around Arboria, and they would play hide-and-seek together within castle walls.

He sighed. "Alright, I'll show you." Slowly, he removed the glove, sure

42

to avoid Anthea's gaze.

She gasped. "Neros… you can't possibly tell me you're okay after showing me *this*. Your arm…!"

Neros kept his gaze fixed on the arm in question, focusing on the glassy, cracked texture that it now bore. Cursed by a mysterious woman; Neros wondered who she was, or how strong her power was. His arm ached when not casting magic, but when he tried to use it, it felt as though his very life was force was being torn violently out of him. A few new cracks had appeared as well, from what Neros could see. His eyes widened—using his magic was more detrimental than he thought. He raised his eyes to meet Anthea's worried ones, then looked away.

"It's a curse. Last night, I was about to go to bed, and the castle shook violently. I followed it to the throne room, and a voice rang out in the halls. My parents, they…" Neros pursed his lips, swallowing thickly. "They've been solidified in ice. It…may or may not be permanent. And I…was cursed. Like this."

Anthea's fingers ran gently across Neros' arm, feeling the small divots and grooves left behind—the consequences of using magic while cursed. Unlike the prince's typically flawless ice blue skin, like fine porcelain, this arm looked like it had been transformed into thick ice, with cracks stretching like veins up to his elbow, unnatural fissures breaking off and curving toward the surface. If not for the tragedy associated with it, Neros may have found it beautiful. But the reality was that even as Anthea examined him, he couldn't feel anything aside from a faint ache—as though the princess was simply touching ice.

"This is serious, Neros. I'm right to assume you need to lay off the magic, right?" Anthea tugged the glove back over his hand. Neros only nodded. "That's all the more reason we should visit this oracle over in Paralia as fast as possible."

Neros lifted his head to level his gaze with Anthea's. "Right. I want to test the limits of this curse, as well. I haven't tried casting with my spear yet."

"Oh, yeah, your magic weapon! Well…save your energy, for now. It'll be slow, but I can handle the rest of this river."

Anthea positioned herself in front of the river, arms outstretched. She shouted in the ancient Arborian passed down to her from the spirits above, and light green magic essence swirled around her arms. Vines shot out from the beneath the grass, dislodging and plunging into the water's depths. They danced, latching onto the far wall of the river, growing—slowly, at first, then gaining speed. They grew thicker and larger in size, spawning smaller vines and leaves and even tree bark as they expanded across the river, toward them. Neros always loved watching the princess cast magic—he thought it held majesty and power in equal parts, a true blend of her fiery personality. After a few minutes, the might of her nature magic had crafted a sturdy bridge of thick, sprawling wood reinforced by vines and leaves.

Once the magic had faded from Anthea's arms, she set her hands proudly on her hips and smiled confidently at Neros.

"Not bad, huh?"

Neros chuckled. "You are amazing as always, Anthy."

Anthea grabbed his non-gloved hand, tugging him gently toward the bridge she created. The pair trekked across the makeshift structure, Neros being careful not to trip on the vines spiraling outward. It served to be a sturdy bridge, and they hopped off the other side, and Neros barely had a moment collect himself Anthea tugged on his hand again and continued their earlier pace. Ahead, there was a new region of Endra that Neros had never seen. It was marked by cascading waterfalls and copious grass-covered platforms, the bright, clear blue of the water nearly blending with the color of the sky. A small sign was stuck where the fields met the vast, deep lake. When they got close enough, Neros could make out what it read: Paralia.

The pair stopped at the water's edge, and they looked cautiously out at the scenery before them. Oddly, there was no sign of life—not that the pair could see, at least. Neros would be tempted to call it quiet, except that the rush of the waterfalls was the only sound Neros could place. He was admiring the lush grass and moss hanging off the rocks jutting out from the various cliffs when Anthea nudged him.

"So, Neros."

"Yeah?"

"Remember what I said a second ago, about, you know, saving your energy?"

"Yes, I do recall."

"Uh," Anthea giggled, rubbing the back of her neck. "I'm gonna have to take that back. We'll need to work together if we can hope to pass through this lake. It's way too far to swim."

"Too far?"

"We've gotta go way over there," Anthea explained, stepping next to Neros and pointing over his shoulder. His eyes were guided toward the very back of Paralia, past where the waterfalls converged. The land itself seemed to be pinched upward, as if forming some sort of opening for a cove. It was difficult to make out too many details from so far away, but it stood out from the rest of the landscape. "See that? They say that inside there is a labyrinth, one crafted specifically to hide away the most knowledgeable being of all: the oracle."

"I see. That is quite a long way," Neros mused, looking down at his hands. He curled them into fists. *You will never find answers if you don't try.* He felt resolute. He needed to see the Oracle: not just for Anthea, but for himself, too. "I want to try casting with my spear."

"Are you sure?"

"Yes. I've only just learned to do it, but I think it may be different enough to work." He steeled himself, pulling his spear free from the straps at his back. He walked to the water's edge, princess trailing close behind. He pointed the tip of his weapon at the water, taking a deep breath. *Focus. This will work. This has to work.* He willed the magic energy to gather into the tip of his spear—a crystalline diamond with a dim blue aura floating at its center. As the magic danced from his arms up the staff's length, the aura grew in size and brightness. It began to bounce around the inside of the diamond structure like a loose pinball.

"Vatnis of Vetur, honored spear of the noble King Vasilias, I command you: *build!*" Neros called, jutting the spear forward, pointing it skyward and aiming at a nearby grassy plateau. The water at his feet shifted and solidified, and crystal ice stairs formed, step by step, from the water's surface to the dense greenery above. The prince paused after its construction, and the light emitting from his weapon dimmed and faded.

Neros beamed.

"It worked!" Anthea shouted, tackling him into a bone-crushing hug. Immediately, she moved back, gripping his shoulders at arm's length. "Are you hurt?"

Neros glanced at his spear; the magic energy seemed to be stored in the weapon, instead of coming directly from his own body—so he felt far less pain. There was a dull, insistent ache where the cursed ice on his arm met his elbow, but he felt nothing abnormal otherwise. "I'm fine," He reassured, smiling in the hopes that she'd believe him this time.

When Anthea smiled back, Neros breathed a silent sigh of relief. "If you're sure," She commented, moving past him to check the sturdiness of the steps. Once she was satisfied, she cheered, taking them up two at a time.

"Anthy, be careful! They may be stable, but it's still ice, which is slipp—"

"I *know*, Neros! I'm not a sapling anymore, I'm not going to *slip*. Don't worry about me!"

The prince shook his head, knowing it would prove useless to protest. He followed her up, deciding to take the steps one at a time. From the vantage point of the plateau, Neros could see their destination far more easily. Where the cliffs had pinched together, the Endran crust itself opened up, giving way to a dark cavern below. Beside him, Anthea had begun to pull vines out of the grass of the plateau, using it as another bridge to connect to a nearby platform, also raised far above the water's surface. When her bridge made contact, both plateaus shook from the force. Across them, dark clouds of purple smoke pooled around the grass' surface, swirling higher and higher. The smoke transformed, becoming translucent fluid not unlike the water below them. Anthea was distracted, focusing her energy on securing the vine bridge.

"Uh, Anthy…?"

The water coagulated, forming a large, hulking figure. A face appeared where its head had settled, and its eyes glowed a bright, angry yellow. Neros gripped his spear a little tighter. He swallowed.

"Anthy! We've got trouble!"

The princess looked up from her kneeling position, and immediately frowned. "Oh, *great*, what is *this?*" She stood, crossing her arms as she walked across the bridge, heaving a sigh. Neros followed, staff at the ready.

"What do you want, you big oaf?" She hollered, frowning up at the beast.

It uttered broken, garbled words like it was trying to speak from underwater. "You intruders. No pass through sacred land."

"Sacred land? Out here? We're on important business, you know! We're here to see the oracle!"

The being frowned, hulking forward a few steps and staring directly down at Anthea. "You intruders. No allowed see Oracle! Is decreed by gods!"

"And what if we want to see the Oracle anyway?" Neros asked, squaring his shoulders and gripping his spear with confidence.

"NO! You not allowed!" The being growled. Neros started as its eyes shifted in color, now bright red. "No more disobey! Now, you die, intruders!"

"Die? Oh, no we won't!" Anthea's face grew serious, and she immediately began spellcasting, magic swirling around her as she conjured arrows made of leaves and branches. She moved her hand through her hair, willing it to become longer and molding it into the shape of a bow. She strung it with a spare vine from her head, pulled back, and fired. The arrow soared through the air, striking the space between the monster's eyes…and passing clean through. Water re-formed the shape of the head where her arrow had struck.

"Uh-oh," The princess said. "Neros, watch out!"

The monster swung a large, watery hand down, and the prince gasped, running across the bridge; he stole past the monster's side, diving out of the way. The monster's hand crashed down, separating like waves over the vine bridge Anthea created. The monster hurled its arm back into place—in the wake of his attack, the bridge snapped and collapsed.

So its body behaves like water, huh? Neros thought, eyes scanning for vulnerabilities. *Maybe…*

"Anthea! Shoot another arrow!"

"Why?"

"Just trust me!"

The princess shook her head and groaned. She pulled a spare arrow out of the quiver at her back, stringing it and taking aim.

"Where?"

"His arm!" Neros frowned in concentration. He aimed his spear, whispering chants under his breath. He glanced at Anthea—as she drew back her bowstring, he charged, leaping into the air. He jumped, swinging his spear, and when it connected with the monster's form, its arm froze.

This time, when Anthea's arrow made contact, the beast's arm shattered, a thick ice chunk stuck at the joint preventing a new arm from forming. It groaned, whirling around to face Neros as he retreated to another corner of the plateau.

"Insolent intruder! Your power cursed, me can feel it! Gods no want you to pass!" The beast roared, and Neros' heart stopped. *The gods don't want me to…?*

"The only cursed one here is *you,* you dolt!" Anthea cried out, drawing her bow back with a fresh arrow, grinning madly. "Freeze his leg, Neros!"

"Got it!" Ignoring the ache in his arm, he charged up his weapon and dove toward the guardian, swiping and freezing both of his legs. Anthea took her shot, shattering one and bringing the creature to one knee. The princess nimbly grabbed another arrow, firing it to shatter the remaining leg. The guardian cried out, shaking his fist at the two as they re-convened in front of him.

"You may defeat me, but you no survive other guardians and labyrinth!" The guardian proclaimed.

"We'll see about that! Let's go, Neros. We've got more water-butt to kick." Anthea puffed her chest out, defiant, as she walked across the plateau to begin making another bridge to cross. Paralia was a vast landscape, and Neros regretted not having more time to admire it. Bridge after bridge, the pair battled against guardians large and small, from shapes ranging from dozens of small spheres to ones larger than the guardian they fought first. The pair pressed onward, and Neros felt the ache in his arm swell as he battled, steadily worsening even in its resting state.

After hours of patterned fights, the pair reached the opening to the Paralia Coves. The drop was far, but the walls leading down to the floor were jagged and uneven, allowing for safer navigation. Neros moved carefully, their actions echoing off the cove's walls. Once safely on the ground, they set forth into the dark caverns ahead.

"I swear, we passed this stone before."

"What? Neros, no way," Anthea scoffed, looking disbelieving. "This is the first pink-gem-spattered rock that we've run into."

Neros groaned, running his hand through his hair and temporarily displacing his crown. "Anthy, you know I love you, but *this is a place we've passed.*"

He replaced his crown on his head, walking toward the rock and picking up a crystallized chunk of ice off the top. "I placed this here when we first passed by. I had a feeling we would get lost."

"I—come *on*, Neros! You didn't trust my instinct?"

The prince blinked at her, then laughed. "Not when the guiding nature of trees' roots aren't involved, no."

Anthea huffed, and Neros chuckled before turning back to the dark hallways of the coves. Soft blue light had filtered in from some of the cracks in the walls, but the deeper they travelled, the more the light faded. Torches replaced the cracks, but their light was not as comforting as Neros expected, their dim yellow glow more ominous than inviting. However, the prince thought it advantageous that the pink rock they passed happened to rest at a crossroads of two paths.

"We're lucky that the path we took curved back around to here. We're going to have to pay close attention from now on," Neros commented. "We went to the right before, which means the correct path lies to the left."

They continued down the corridor until it opened into a larger, square room with two doors; three stones sat in the center of the room, along with three holes placed around the room in a triangular fashion. There was a raised outer rim, and the spheres rested in the inner circle, where the holes were. A sign hung on the far wall. Neros approached it while Anthea examined the strangely colored spheres. The sign was written in a common tongue, though it seemed scrawled on hastily.

Neros read the script on the sign aloud: "You have been branded as intruders, but welcome to the Paralia Coves. The Oracle rests far beyond the depths of your intellect. You must solve every puzzle you come across in this labyrinth if you hope to see his forbidden place of resting."

"Forbidden? Why does no one want us to see the Oracle? Shouldn't that be written as his *sacred* resting place?"

"I don't know, Anthy. Maybe something happened." Neros searched the wall, pressing his palms against the rough surface. He passed over a stone jutting out from the wall, and he pushed it in. Neros jumped as the wall quaked, and a new message appeared in shining blue script. He peered at it, eyebrows furrowed. The message was written in ancient Veturian script—to Neros' surprise and confusion—and Neros found the handwriting to be beautiful. The glow of the text itself felt inviting, as opposed to the other warnings they'd come across.

Dear heroes who pass through this forsaken labyrinth: I will guide you through this trickery and mystery of element and intellect that lay ahead. Heed my advice, and your path will be have no turmoil. For this room, here are my words: All have weakness; all have strength. Endra is arranged in harmony, and so this room seeks to mimic it.

"Hey, Anthy," Neros started, not taking his eyes off the message. "What's on those orbs in the middle of the room?"

"They're beautiful stones! They have designs engraved into them. There's a leaf, a snowflake, and…a ball of flames. Why, what's that stuff on the wall say?"

Neros brought his hand to his chin, looking out into the room. "It says we need to heed its words to be guided through the labyrinth. It doesn't… seem like the glowing text here was meant to be seen by just anyone."

"Ooh, so you think we're special?"

Neros rolled his eyes, stifling a laugh. "Not what I meant, but we can go with that." He turned back to the wall, reading the script again. "It says all have weakness, and all have strength…and that this room seeks to mimic Endra's harmony."

Anthea hummed loudly, circling the stone orbs at the room's center. The prince stayed on the other half of the room, surveying the layout carefully. He and Anthea had poured over puzzles and riddles for a great duration of their childhood together; they would sometimes struggle for hours over a single riddle in the depths of a book, only to have to turn and ask the king for its answer instead. *But now Father isn't here to help us,* Neros thought to himself. *We're on our own.*

"Weakness and strength, huh?" Anthea mumbled, rolling the three stones so they laid side by side. "Do you think it means these weaknesses?"

"Like, elemental ones?" Neros hopped down from the outer rim, standing beside her to scrutinize the orbs. "So it looks like these would represent nature, ice, and fire, then, right?"

"And if we organize them by strengths and weaknesses, we'd say that fire is strong against nature, but weak to ice. Nature's weak to fire, but strong to ice…! It fits perfectly! Neros, Neros, let's move them!"

They set to work, rolling the orbs into holes where the pair thought they'd best fit. The stones were large, their tops sitting as tall as the princess' waist. It was a pair effort to move them into their appropriate spaces. The fire orb lay at the top of the triangle, with nature to its right and the snowflake to its left. Neros and Anthea braced themselves for movement, the unlocking of a door or a shift in environment of some kind.

But nothing happened.

Neros frowned, and Anthea groaned. "Great, it's not *literal*. Because these are totally arranged by elemental strengths and weakness! This *is* arranged correctly."

The prince hummed, sitting down on the ground to survey the orbs' placement. The room grew quiet as Anthea sat next to him, chin in her hands as she frowned at the stones herself. Neros thought about the riddle again. *Endra is arranged in harmony, and this room seeks to mimic it. But how?* It was from the ground that the prince noticed something odd: two of the stones were not glowing, but the Nature stone was. It was a faint, green light emanating from below.

"Why is that one glowing?" He asked, mostly to himself.

Anthea followed his gaze. "It's the nature orb, isn't it? Could it be because I'm here?"

"But that doesn't make any sense, Anthy. Otherwise, the ice orb over there would be glowing."

"Well, we could always switch the other two," Anthea commented, standing. "But I'd like to know how *that* makes any sense."

"Right? Because then, it becomes ice on top, fire to the left, and nature right beside…" Neros' eyes widened. "That's it!"

"What's it? Use your words!"

"The harmony! It's not their *elemental* relationships, it's the harmony of Endra itself!" The prince stood suddenly, moving to pull the fire orb out of its slot. "Vetur is in the north, and Arboria to the east. That's why it's glowing—it's the only one in the right spot! Anthy, quick, help me switch these!"

"What a weird riddle…" Anthea grumbled. Regardless, she helped Neros heave the stones into their proposed new arrangement—and as Neros predicted, both the ice and fire stones began to glow with faint blue and red light. The ground shifted, and the far wall gave way, crumbling into a pile of stones on the floor.

"Well then," Neros commented, climbing up to the now-destroyed wall and carefully maneuvering over the rocks to the alcove beyond. "I suppose this is our way forward."

Anthea followed swiftly behind.

The room they entered was a large circle, the blue rocky columns reaching from ceiling to floor, but not quite connecting to the ground. That being said, the ceiling stretched far beyond what Neros and Anthea expected, scaling twice their height and almost twice as high as the room prior. As soon as the pair entered, the ground shook, familiar purple smoke swirling at the room's center. The prince took a step closer to Anthea—and she to him— as he unlatched the spear from his back. Slowly, the smoke morphed into water, and a larger-than-life water guardian took shape before them. This one appeared to be wearing watery, yet sturdy armor, and held a large water-axe in both hands.

A calm, wise voice spoke out to them. BE CAREFUL, YOUNG HEROES. THIS MONSTER GUARDS MY RESTING PLACE. IT IS POWERFUL, BUT YOU CAN BEST IT.

"Intruders! How you make it so far?" The beast growled.

"We outsmarted all of your friends!" Anthea asserted, preparing her bow.

"You smart no more. Die!"

The beast swung its axe across the small room, knocking the prince and princess to the wall. It left a trail of water in its wake; Neros and Anthea pushed themselves off the ground and stumbled in opposite directions.

"We have to make a move, Neros! This guy means business!"

Neros could only shout back an approval, stumbling behind a chunk of stalagmite. He gripped his spear, heart beating fast against his chest. He turned around the corner and summoned the power of frost from within, channeling it through his spear and shooting it at the guardian. It landed, freezing the armored-looking water and slowly spreading, stopping just before the guardian's main body.

From the opposite side of the room, Anthea followed up quickly with an arrow, shooting the prince a thumbs-up. However, unlike the guardians outside, the beast's severed arm simply grew back. He swung his axe again, a wave of water crashing around both sides of the pillar Neros was using for cover and crashing into him, forcing him to the ground again with lungs full of water. He coughed, heaving liquid onto the ground. His eyes stung. Anthea called out to him, but he could barely hear her; he felt like he was drowning. *This is it? This is how it ends? Already, Anthea and I are faced with an enemy and I'm too…weak. Like the witch said. Mother, Father, I'm so sorry…* The prince choked up more of the viscous water, squeezing his eyes shut as his body jerked forward. His lungs *burned.*

He looked up at the monster through bleary eyes, firing another burst of ice from his spear and ignoring the insistent ache flaring in his arm. It crashed into the beast's arm, and Anthea shot him. The beast roared, turning its water axe to Anthea. She held her arms up to block the blast, absorbing what pure water she could. She grinned madly.

"Hit it again, Neros!"

The prince reached out to cast a spell, but the dull ache in his arm spiked.

"Anthea, I can't. My arm…!" He groaned.

"…Fine! I've got an idea," Anthea circled the room, forcing the guardian to turn alongside her. "If you're gonna just keep swinging that axe around, I'm going to make sure you break apart and *never recover!"*

The princess stomped, vines shooting from her legs and into the ground. They erupted beneath the water guardian and spun violently, sprawling out into nearly a tree-like pattern. The guardian's body splattered across the alcove, dissipating into purple smoke as it smacked against the walls. Then, the vines receded, and Anthea fell to her knees.

The princess heaved a deep breath, and Neros sighed in relief.

"Wow. I didn't know you could do that," He rasped.

"Neither did I," She replied between pants, a mad grin still on her face.

The remaining smoke cleared, and the room began to quake. Anthea stumbled to Neros' side; he hooked his arm around her shoulders so she could help him stand. The pair were prepared to run, yet no monster appeared: the ceiling opened up, and a heavenly light shimmered through the cracks. Neros and Anthea covered their eyes from the sudden shift in brightness. Glistening water droplets squeezed through, collecting at the room's center to take the shape of a small, old man whose beard and moustache trailed all the way to the floor. He floated, sitting cross-legged, and greeted the heroes with a warm smile.

"Thank you for releasing me from my prison, young prophetic heroes."

Neros and Anthea blinked at him, her eyebrow raised in a perfect arch.

"Whaaa…? Excuse me, did you just say *prophetic heroes?*" Anthea started.

"And, beyond that, who are you?" Neros added, standing fully to address the strange creature. He bore similarities to the guardians scattered across Paralia, but was—curiously—not malicious.

"Ah, of course. You have many questions. I am the Oracle: you may call me Pegaios. Sit, and I will tell you all I can." The oracle's voice sounded otherworldly, distant in a way that Neros could only describe by comparing it to someone speaking from behind a wall of water.

The pair exchanged a nervous glance, but did as they were told.

"You called us prophetic heroes," Anthea stated again, her eyes fiery and intense. "You *need* to tell us what that means. We've been studying Endra's history for the last *eight years* of our lives, and if you have answers, please…!"

"Wait, Anthy," Neros whispered to her. "That's not what you came here for."

"Yeah, but if he knows about that prophecy-mystery, I'm not gonna waste this chance!"

"Compose yourself, Princess Anthea of Arboria," Pegaios spoke, his words rolling and pattering as though they'd tumbled down a stream. "I have sensed the danger that befell your people—and I feel the curse you hide beneath that glove, Prince Neros of Vetur. I hoped—nay, expected—that you would come forth and seek my aid. I was the one who guided you through the labyrinth's puzzle, and it was my voice you both heard as you fought that final beast. As some may have told you, I was locked away here many years ago: but that is not the story you need to hear today. I am first obliged to tell you both of the first coming of the fated prophecy, from 500 years ago."

Pegaios outstretched his hand, summoning a long liquid staff from the pure water left over from their fight; then, he waved it above his head, fabricating a water-screen where colored, etched figures waving in an out of existence danced, before the projection was a large map of Endra.

"Long ago, Endra was a peaceful place. The species of all the lands lived in harmony, and the future of the world looked promising." The oracle waved his staff, and the map became overrun with purple splotches. "Until one day, a dark force began to rise from beneath the surface."

"From Umbros," Neros whispered.

"Precisely. Beyond the reaches of the sky, aloft amongst the cloudy heaven of Andolis, I rested, panicked that my visions of years prior had come to fruition." Another wave of his staff brought up the image of three orbs: one blue, one red, and one green. "I had seen visions of three heroes, coming together to stave off this evil, to banish and seal it away for all eternity. Using a great deal of my power, I called out to the world below, hoping to reach the minds of the heroes in my visions. I knew not what they looked like, only that they each needed to be masters of their elemental magic: one water, one flame, and one nature.

"Three brave, fortuitous heroes heeded my call, and searched for each other, coming together and learning to fight as one. They proved successful, destroying the darkness and sealing it back into Umbros, where it remained contained for many years." Pegaios swiped his staff, forcing the image of the happy, triumphant heroes away. "However, now I fear the prophecy may be repeating itself. Your lands have fallen under duress from curses of a dark, cruel nature, though I cannot tell its source. If nothing is done, Endra will surely succumb to the darkness and fall out of existence."

Neros paled. This was…far more intense than he expected. He stole a glance at Anthea, but she looked more determined than ever before.

"Tell us what we need to do," She said, hands curling into fists.

"You heroes make two, but my tale told of three: you must find the one whom you are missing."

"The one who can wield flames, right? But…where? Anthea and I have never been anywhere but Arboria and Vetur," Neros murmured, wringing his wrists in his hands.

"To the southwest, you will find the region you seek." The oracle tapped his staff on the ground; the sound of a water droplet amplified and echoed all around them, and a door appeared behind the oracle. "Take the door behind me to the springs. There is someone special there who can guide you along your journey far better than I. Meet him, and allow him to be eyes and ears in my stead. While you have freed me from ethereal imprisonment, I am afraid I cannot leave this place. Be careful."

"Can do!" Anthea smiled again, spring back in her step as she bounded to the door. "Thanks for the history lesson, great Oracle! You're amazing!"

Neros watched her back as she retreated to the springs. He turned, picking up his staff from the ground, holding it in his hands for a moment. *This...feels so wrong. Me? A hero?*

"You are hesitant, Prince Neros. What troubles you?"

Neros jumped, nearly dropping his staff as he whirled around to face Pegaios again. The prince's shoulders sank. "Your story...said there was a hero of water. My powers are of ice, Pegaios. What good can I do for Anthea? For my parents?"

The oracle grinned. Allowing himself to float to the ground, he walked up to Neros, resting the head of his staff on the prince's chest. Neros was surprised that it didn't feel wet. "You are a boy who has the mysteries of ice and snow tucked away in his mind, but something else sleeps within you. Do not allow your frosted curse to chill your warm heart. Believe in yourself, keep an open mind, and the rest will fall into place. Now, go. Best not to keep Princess Anthea waiting."

"R-right." Strapping his spear to his back, Neros bade the oracle farewell, pushing the door open and stepping into the springs beyond.

Chapter 4
Along the River

$\mathcal{T}$he expanse that lay beyond the door was beyond anything Neros could have imagined. If he thought Paralia's cascading waterfalls were magnificent in size and scope, the springs were limitless by comparison. Pool after pool of crystal-clear water shimmered in the late-afternoon sunlight, mossy vines hanging from where the cave's walls stretched overhead. The spring waters were alive with creatures, mostly small and appearing to be made of water like Pegaios was. Neros spotted Anthea having a rather animated conversation with one of them; he bounded over to see what it was all about, careful not to fall into the water rippling and swaying below his feet.

"So you're a water spirit, huh? Does that mean you can help us?"

"I'm afraid not, miss," The spirit replied, sheepish. "I'm just a spirit. Like Pegaios, we spirits are trapped here. If you're lookin' for a sprite, I think there's a lively one chatting over there under the trees. Thataway," It...gestured, Neros supposed, to a collection of trees and moss beyond the clearing.

"Perfect, thanks so much!" Anthea turned and bounded toward the trees. Neros sighed, following her so not to be left behind.

The back of Paralia was breathtaking, truly; Neros felt as though his entire spirit was calmed, his sore muscles healed, just from being among the water and spirits. As he caught up to Anthea, his gaze fell upon an excitable looking water sprite floating in front of her. It held a more distinct shape than the water spirits, with a bulbous head and tiny body, water-monocle covering one of its eyes, the chain made of equally viscous water and trailing around its body before dissipating into nothing. It was speaking—rather animatedly—to the princess, small arms flailing around as it was explaining… something.

"And so not all of us were destined to be guides, you see! We water spirits and sprites were here from the dawn of Endra, just like good ol' Pegaios. We're all here to protect Paralia. We bring life to the springs, and the spirits are the ones keepin' the water clean! So you've got them to thank for the unmatched beauty of this place."

"Wow, that's pretty amazing." Anthea spun in place, looking up at the bluish-green moss and leaves that swayed gently in the wind. The sun shimmered on the water, reflecting upward, almost making the water spirits and sprites glow. Anthea whirled back to the water sprite, hands on her hips. Neros walked up and stood at her side. "So, what's your name, then?"

"Pontius, miss! At least, that's what Pegaios named me eons ago, and it seems to have stuck since then! So, well, that's what you can call me. Oh! Listen to me prattle off, I've forgotten my manners completely. What can I call you? And you—" Pontius turned, moving his face a bit too close to Neros'. "Who are you? I didn't know the fine miss had a travel companion!"

"This is Prince Neros!" Anthea supplied, tossing her arm around him. "And I'm Princess Anthea. He's from Vetur, all the way up at the top of the mountain, and I'm from Arboria, deep in the woods!"

"Royalty!? Oh, my gods and goddesses, how could I have been so blind? It is my distinct honor to meet you, prince and princess!" Pontius bowed, deeply, and individually grabbed and kissed each of their hands. Neros was surprised to find that this, just like Pegaios' staff, wasn't wet. "What brings you all the way to Paralia?"

Neros bit his lip. "We, um…we seem to have fallen into troublesome times, I suppose you could say."

"We're looking for someone!" Anthea cut in, glancing at Neros. He nodded. "They're supposed to be off to the southwest. The Oracle said someone out here would be able to help us. Think you've got what it takes? It's gonna be a long, tough journey! I think. The Oracle never said how far away the place in the southwest is, but whoever it is, they're a legendary hero! Probably some fire-type, if we're going according to prophecy."

"Legendary—!" Pontius' eyes widened. "First you don't tell me you're royalty, then you neglect to mention that Pegaios has dubbed you to be two of *the* legendary heroes? Those come to save Endra from its fate as foretold? Oh, I would be *honored* to travel alongside you, heroes!" Pontius flew around the pair, shaking their hands—their fingers, really—viciously before returning in front of them. Neros shared a nervous smile with Anthea. "I may not seem like it, but I know quite a lot about Endra! Old Pegaios has been training me for a century now, and I can't believe it's finally my time to shine! Oh, quick, quick, we can't waste any time! Let's get out of here so we can start our adventure!"

Neros glanced at Anthea, apprehensive. Her earlier nerves seemed to have dissipated, however, and she was smiling. He found himself infected by her mood, and turned back to see Pontius holding what appeared to be two small spheres of water out toward them.

"What are these?" Neros asked.

"These are small parts of my body—" The prince's smile gave way to dread. *Is he serious?* "Don't look so alarmed, Prince Neros! You need these to allow my transportation power to transfer to you. I'm going to take us right back out to the waterfalls of Paralia. It's one of my special abilities bestowed onto me by Pegaios!"

Before Neros could respond, Pontius began flying around them, encasing them in a large, liquid bubble. The prince was unsure whether or not he should hold his breath, but he had no time to decide: there was a bright light, a weird pressure surrounding his body, and the feeling of being rocketed upward. Neros felt his stomach drop, and just as soon as it began, it was over, and the pair landed with an unceremonious *splat* in the grass.

The prince stood, and immediately lost his footing, tumbling forward in a fit of dizziness. He heard Anthea groan beside him.

"Oooh, that was…disorienting. Ugh, Pontius, is high-speed transport always this jarring?"

Pontius laughed, hovering over to her and scooping the water orb he'd handed her, shrinking it back down and replacing it on the chain of his monocle. "It's an acquired sense, your highness!" He floated over to Neros, who handed him the water orb before leaning back down on his knees. Nausea swept in and overtook the dizziness, and Neros had to focus all his effort into keeping his intestines *inside* his body. *An acquired sense? How does one exactly get used to this?*

The water sprite looked over the pair, and his cheer drooped into concern. "Oh, oh my. You two...you've never done that before, have you?"

Neros and Anthea nodded, and the prince's entire body protested the movement. He took a few slow, deep breaths to steel himself.

"Gosh, well, now I feel horribly rude for putting you through that without describing the procedure. You see, how it works is when you take the small orbs from me, they expand to the size of your body! Sometimes, if I don't have enough energy, this doesn't work, and I can't transport you anywhere. But as long as I've seen a place, I can transport you!" He paused, chuckling. "Well, that isn't *many* places right now, just Paralia, but the longer we're travel companions, the more places I can take you! Anyway, once the water expands, I use my magic energy to shrink you down real small and grab you, fly really high into the air, and that's when stuff gets crazy!"

Neros' jaw went slack. "It gets crazy *after* that?"

"You bet! Up until that point is standard fare for water magic." Neros blinked incredulously, but Pontius continued. "I'm able to vibrate incredibly quickly to travel at high speeds while carrying objects that are high volume, like you two! So I basically move really fast and SPLOOSH! We crash into our destination and the transit is complete. I returned you to normal size and as I did, the water orbs shrank. I need them back every time I do it, or else I lose them forever, and in this case, that's two less times I can transport someone somewhere! They're all connected to my little monocle chain right here," The sprite wiggled and twirled in place, his lengthy monocle chain spinning with him. "So that's what happened! It can be fairly disorienting if you've never traveled at high speeds like that before, so I do apologize for the apparent discomfort it gave you both. Are you feeling better, or shall I heal you?"

Anthea's eyebrows raised at that. "You can heal us?"

"Yes! Just another one of water's greatest properties, the property of healing! I can heal many wounds, and even regenerate a little, situation depending. Well, Prince and Princess? Are you still feeling queasy or disoriented? Prince Neros, if you don' mind me saying, you do appear to be a little green."

"No, I'm—" The prince moved to reassure Pontius of his wellness, but nearly stumbled to the ground instead. "A-actually, perhaps it would… behoove me to accept."

"Oh, boy! This is quite exciting—I haven't been able to use these abilities in eons! You've made the right choice, Prince Neros! Here, allow me."

Pontius floated closer to Neros, outstretching both of his small arms and focusing. He began to emit a dim, yellow-white light, and Neros could see small dust-like particles flashing and coursing through his arms, gathering into a large orb beyond where his hands extended.

"Quell the raging storm of these seas; *esi vesels!*"

As the sprite spoke, the glowing orb transferred from his hands to Neros' body, and he felt a warmth spread throughout; it was soothing, and (more importantly) immediately effective. As the warmth faded, so did his lightheaded queasiness. He bounced on the balls of his feet with renewed vigor.

"Wow, that was incredible. Thank you, Pontius."

"The pleasure is mine, your highness! And you, Princess Anthea of Arboria?"

The princess shrugged, smiling. "Why not? And, by the way, little guy, you can just call me Anthea."

"I could never dream of disrespecting royalty in such a manner! Princess Anthea, I insist." Pontius urged, floating over to her and performing the same spell.

Anthea giggled from the sensation, reaching her arms skyward to stretch afterwards. "Hoo, wow! That was amazing, Pontius. I didn't know there were other types of healing magic in the world. Now, then, we should really keep searching for that third prophetic hero of legend. The clock is ticking, and it's surely a long ways away. I mean, a fire elementalist? Where would we even find someone like that? The Oracle said southwest, but how far?"

Pontius brought a hand to his chin, humming. "Well, Pegaios could have been speaking of the Eldur Ignis Volcano. Situated at the edge of the vast Erimos desert, it's gotta be the hottest place I can think of. Well, other than the desert itself, but you know, that's more of a dry heat. Besides, the volcano is…a volcano! If you need a fire elementalist, that's your place."

Neros nodded. "I see. Pontius, do you know the way?"

"I know it is to the southwest, your highness!"

"And…do you know which way that is from here?"

"Of course!" He pulled another water orb out of his back pocket and enlarged it, turning it into something of a compass shape. "Part of the perk of being a navigator is knowing just what tools to conjure. Ah, yes, yes…it's this way!"

When the water sprite began floating away, Neros and Anthea had no choice but to follow. With a new companion at their side, Neros felt at ease—he felt he could trust Pontius not to lead them astray from their goal. *With him around, certainly we'll be able to find a way to unfreeze my parents.*

❄

The group walked for a while—straight west, and then south once they reached the river. Anthea tried to find their original crossing point, but her search proved fruitless. The farther they walked from Paralia, the less vibrant the foliage became, but Neros thought it was no less beautiful. The plains were an open expanse, and he could see a few towns scattered in the far-off distance. He wondered what sorts of people made towns here—were they Arborians? Veturians? He hadn't known many of his own people to leave the town, though Arborians lived in many places. *I wonder if a few of them would know anything about the volcano we're supposed to be looking for. They seem a bit…out of the way.* The towns in the distance looked off-course compared to the trajectory of the distant, brownish-red mountain that Neros could only assume was their destination. *Well, if that's the case, that's no mountain…that's a volcano.*

Neros had never been outside of Vetur and Arboria. The climate in both regions was, in his eyes, temperate: Vetur was cold, sure, but the citizens were happy. Arboria was never too hot or too cold, and even as the seasons passed the weather was manageable—Neros had even brought some Veturians to Arboria to visit once, just to escape a particularly vicious winter. Travelling to the volcano meant new territory for both of them—he wondered if they would be okay.

"What's on your mind, your highness?" Pontius' words spurred Neros from his thoughts, and he glanced at his new companion. "You seem deep in thought! Are you enjoying Endra's vast, luscious scenery as I am?"

"I was thinking about where we're headed, actually," he replied. "I've never been somewhere so warm. Come to think of it, you're just a water sprite, aren't you, Pontius? Will you be okay?"

At this, he laughed. "No need to worry, your highness! I won't evaporate even in the most arid of deserts. Just like you magically-inclined folk, it's all part of the package when you're a magical creature!"

Neros nodded, feeling a bit relieved. He couldn't imagine what he'd say to Pegaios if Pontius were to evaporate partway through their journey. Would he be able to assign them a different water sprite? Neros doubted it; Pontius seemed truly special.

"What a relief," Anthea said. "I'd hate to have to leave you outside or something. I bet you'll be a big help once we're in there." The princess bounded forward, and Neros had to lightly jog to keep up. "So, what do you think our future hero-partner is gonna be like? Do you think they're gonna be a girl, or not? I hope they're excited about saving the world!"

"I hope they're not too nervous about it."

"Aw, why not? Because there's only enough room for *one* nervous nilly in our trio?"

Neros' cheeks flushed. "C-come on, Anthy, you know that's not what I meant."

"Don't be nervous, either of you! This will be a grand adventure, I'm sure of it!" Pontius chimed in, swirling around the pair. Anthea rolled her eyes, but said nothing.

As the group continued to walk, the sun moved slowly across the sky. Neros was grateful for the quickly put-together bag of food and supplies he'd packed before starting this journey. *There's no way the meager amount I packed will be enough, though. I'm sure Anthea and I will have to forage around after a day or so. Well, maybe me more than Anthy.* He looked over to Anthea's satchel, which she pulled the occasional seed out of and popped into her mouth. Neros had forgotten that Arborians got sustenance from seeds and small pellets, making travel a non-issue for the species. When he was younger, he visited Arboria on holidays and between training, and Anthea and Rosea would keep him up for hours talking about the different towns they visited over different weeks of the year. Neros, admittedly, was a bit envious: he suspected that the princess got most of her negotiation skills from her various trips around the plains.

Hours passed; Paralia had left Neros' view by now, and the volcano was starting to look fairly sizable. To his right, he could see the distant haze of Vetur, and beside it, Arboria. From this distance, it was so small it almost looked like a bush. Neros smiled at the thought—he knew the truth of its vast, labyrinth-like vine systems and root ecologies. That forest was like his second home.

"Hey, Bubbles, what are those?" Anthea asked, gesturing to a couple of lumbering figures in the distance.

"Bubbles…? Oh, do perchance mean me, Princess Anthea?" Pontius chirped.

"Yeah! You're a water sprite, and you're bubbly, so. Bubbles!"

Pontius laughed, though it died quickly as he peered forward. "Oh, no. I've never seen creatures like that before. That purple aura they're emitting… that can't be healthy. Perhaps we should try to avoid them, young heroes."

Neros and Anthea nodded, deviating from their course a bit to avoid the opposing group. As they neared, however, the creatures seemed to spot them. They looked…almost undead, like skeletal beings barely held together by their own auras. Their bones rattled and wobbled as they moved, but they seemed no less determined for it. Once they locked on to Anthea and Neros, they broke into a jog.

"Great, *more* trouble? This area of the plains is supposed to be peaceful!" Anthea groaned, pulling out her bow and nocking an arrow. She drew it back and fired, whispering an enchantment that gave the arrow a greenish glow.

Neros watched in awe as it struck; the arrowhead expanded and turned into a complex net of vines that served to capture the creature, rendering it immobile. Its two friends were undeterred by this action, however, and continued barreling for the pair.

The prince knew he had little choice. He broke toward them, holding out his spear and stabbing it forward. He struck through one creature's ribs, and it howled out in pain. The one Anthea had captured was starting to wriggle away, so Neros shot a burst of ice magic from it using his spear as a vessel, freezing it to the ground. He did the same for the one he'd just knocked back. *Hm. This time, no pain.*

Neros turned around to see Anthea tousling with the other skeleton, but whirled around again to see that Pontius was nowhere in sight.

"Pontius…? Pontius, where are you?"

"In here, your highness!" Came the muffled, chipper voice of their water guide. "I've taken it upon myself to hide out in your bag here while you fight! It's quite unsafe out there for a sprite like me! I've not got the combat skills you two probably have, but as I learn information about these creatures, I'll tell you all I can!"

"Thanks!" Neros called, running to help Anthea. The skeleton had backhanded her, sending her to the ground. She kicked at its legs with her feet, but it backflipped away from her, outstretching its arms. It began to rattle, and hazy, purple smoke rose from the ground and swirled upward, summoning two more skeletal monster figures from beneath the surface. One lifted Anthea by the hair, swinging her back down with a *thump* while another took over to kick her in the stomach.

"You get away from her, beasts!" Neros shouted, sliding in and knocking one's skull from behind with his spear. Then, he spun, whacking the other in the ribs and willing them to freeze. He continued the momentum to knock the frozen skeleton into his neighbor, effectively freezing them together. Neros stabbed them again, cracking the ribs and causing them to screech. Reflexively, Neros' hands flew to plug up his ears. As their shouts dissipated, they receded back into the dirt.

Neros looked to the princess. "Anthy, are you alright?"

She groaned. "They got me pretty good there, huh, Neros?" She coughed, spitting a few splinters into the grass.

From his bag, Neros felt Pontius rustling around. He emerged, fraught with worry. "Princess Anthea! Oh, my gods and goddesses, how I wish I didn't have to see you in such a state! Here, here, allow me to heal you." The water spirit outstretched his hands, murmuring. "In this time of draught, let rain bring new life unto thee."

Water droplets formed all around Pontius' arms, shooting out like droplets of rain and soaking into Anthea's wooden skin. She began to glow with a faint light, and she visibly relaxed. Pontius ceased, seeming pleased with his work.

"Wonderful. That's better, isn't it?"

"Yeah, actually. Thanks! How did you do that?"

"That? Oh, it's not an uncommon practice, for water sprites and water-elementalists like myself and his highness to be able to do healing magic like this!"

"Like Neros?"

Neros blinked. "But, I…"

Pontius' eyes became saucers. *"What?!* You mean to tell me you don't know healing magic? Prince Neros, ice magic is an echelon above the rest! Most magically-attuned Veturians for all time have known water magic, have they not?"

He bit his lip. "N-not that I've known, though I suppose I never asked…"

"That's what was written in Pegaios' notes! Perhaps I'm thinking a few hundred years ago, but the power is likely still there. Ice is just freezing water, is it not? Surely the power to manipulate water rests within you too!"

Neros frowned, looking at his hands. *Perhaps it's not so different from what I know, but…* "How would I learn to use magic like that?"

"Not a problem, your highness. I'll teach you everything I know! It'll take a lot of persistent learning, but you'll get there! Then you'll be a man to be feared across all of Endra!"

There was no use to him not trying, but Neros was still hesitant. Would it mean he'd lose the ability to use powerful ice spells in the future? With his arm cursed like it was, though, he didn't see much of a choice. He nodded to Pontius. "That…sounds good to me."

"Perfect!" Anthea cut in, wrapping her arm around him. "With that settled, let's keep walking! It's late, and I'd like to make shelter somewhere safe. There should be a town a few miles ahead that we can stop at, and it would be the perfect place to rest for the night."

Neros nodded, allowing himself to be pulled along, his mind wandering elsewhere.

❄

In a few hours' time, they reached a small town built in the middle of the Endran plains. The sign on the outskirts of it read: *Welcome to Barmwich. Please be kind.* The structures looked like the homes he would find in Vetur, but they were made entirely of Arborian roots and sediment. They had leaf-thatched roofs and large, hulking wooden doors, but all the structures were woven with precise and perfect aesthetic sense. Oddly enough, Neros felt right at home.

A tall Arborian with long, cascading orange- and yellow-leaf hair bounded up to them, outstretching both of her hands to clasp them around Anthea's. *She's definitely an oak.* Neros noted.

"Princess!" The woman cheered. "It has been *seasons* since we've seen you! Gods, how have you been, dear? And who are these two you're traveling with?"

Anthea smiled. "Hello, Geneviève. This is Prince Neros, royalty from Vetur. And this is Bubbl–uh, Pontius. He's a water sprite from Paralia who's accompanying us to our destination. To tell you the truth, we were just passing through and hoping we could stay the night. We've got a *long* walk to the volcano tomorrow, and we want to be well-rested for it!"

Worry crossed Geneviève's face. "Oh, my. Eldur Ignis Volcano? They have fallen on some hard times, I've heard, from some of the Arborians brave enough to go there. Gods know they can survive, but that doesn't mean *I* have to like the heat!" She laughed before turning and shaking Neros and Pontius' hands. "You two seem like good folk, and if you're with the princess, I know you've got good hearts. Follow me, I'll show you to the inn."

The inn was down a couple of winding streets, built taller and wider than most homes. It had to have about three or four rooms total inside, if Neros' approximations based on the other buildings were right. It was managed by a group of willow-type Arborians, and Neros found himself totally unsurprised: willows were known to be good healers among Arborians, and many took to furthering their hospitality endeavors by opening clinics, potion shops, or inns in towns like these. Once inside, Neros could admire the tightly-woven branches and thoughtful architecture even more; it was almost overwhelming to take in. There were stairs behind the counter that likely led to the rooms, and the entire bottom floor was dedicated to a mixed tavern and front lobby.

A boy who looked a few years (or was it hundred years? Neros never really understood how Arborians aged) older than Anthea was at the counter, and he smiled warmly when he saw the princess. "My, my, do my eyes deceive me? Princess Anthea! You're a sight for sore eyes. What can I do for you?"

"Yeesh, you all act like I *died* or something," Anthea joked, but Neros could see she was relieved to be speaking to living Arborians. "There's trouble back home, so I'm finding a way to fix it abroad. We need a place to sleep so we can go to the volcano tomorrow."

"Just one room, or two?"

The princess seemed to mull this over a moment. *She's always carefully picking her battles*, Neros admired. "Just one," she said firmly. "I don't think I've got the coin to spare."

"You're the *princess*, Anthea! It's on the house. Now go get something to eat, and I'll get your room ready."

Anthea smiled as though it was her intention for him to say that all along. He directed the group toward the tavern, and they sat at a long table alongside a pair of Arborians with long, braided palm fronds draping down their shoulders, nearly to the floor. One wore a long, blue dress with zinnia flowers woven into the straps, and the man across from her had on what looked to be simple workman clothes—shirt, vest, and pants.

"We couldn't help but overhear," One piped up, concern clear in his tone. "You're going to Eldur Ignis Volcano?"

Anthea nodded. "Yeah, Geneviève was saying they'd fallen on hard times." The princess exchanged a glance with Neros. "Do you happen to know anything about it?"

"We do, actually," The other said, twisting in her seat to face them. "I heard the lava's all dried up out there. We've got a few friends that frequent the upper layer for mineral and material trades, see. Helps keep this town on its toes. But lately, they've been coming back completely dry. No one seems to know why, or how, but they're just about on the brink of civil war over it. You two are better off staying away from there."

Neros shook his head. "I'm sorry, but we don't have much of a choice. Why would they be on the brink of civil war?"

"The lava fuels their whole life, I heard. I think they might be dying. All the Embers up in the volcano there have been real closed off, so they don't really got much in the way of allies to ask for help."

"I agree," The man chimed in. "That's what I've always liked about that big ol' ice mountain and Arboria. Everyone felt like a friend, like we could ask them water and ice folk for anything and they'd hand it to us. Gods know we'd do the same for them."

Anthea and Neros exchanged another look. *Dying? Like the Arborians?*

The princess smiled wearily at them. "Right. Thank you for letting us know. We'll keep it in mind as we travel there tomorrow."

The group ordered their meals—a wide array of seeds and light caplets for Anthea, a bit of meat and vegetables for Neros, and nothing for Pontius—and they ate in grateful silence once it arrived. The atmosphere here was far more tense than when they walked in, and after hearing about the turmoil that overcame Eldur Ignis Volcano, Neros wondered if their other prophetic hero would even want to leave their home to search for the cause of the chaos. His gut twisted. *To be honest, I shouldn't have left home either. But staying in Vetur would have meant accepting there was nothing for me to do about my parents. But that's wrong. There has to be.* They would find a way to get this mysterious hero away from home. Maybe they could help them find answers, too.

Once dinner was done, the boy from the front desk returned to take them to their room. He introduced himself to Neros and Pontius as Wilton, and told them to make sure they asked for *him* if they needed something. Neros had to wonder if the rest of the willow Arborians who worked here were untrustworthy, somehow.

Anthea flopped down on the bed immediately, tossing her satchel off to the side and stretching out her limbs. "Ooh, this feels great! It's just like home. I almost feel spoiled."

Neros sat down on the bed opposite her, and resisted the urge to do the same. "Just like home, huh…?" He paused, considering her situation. "Are you going to be alright?"

Her arms flopped at her sides, and she stared at the ceiling. "…I think so. It's a relief to see some Arborians lively and well, you know? But it doesn't change all the lives I left behind…gods, even Rosea. All of their lives rest on my shoulders, and that weight is starting to…feel sort of crushing." She tossed her arm over her eyes, sighing shakily.

Neros' eyebrows drew together, and he looked to Pontius. "Could you give us a minute?" Pontius, sensing the mood, obliged.

The prince rose from his bed, perching cross-legged on Anthea's bed instead. She peered at him from under her arm.

"Didja have to send him away?" She asked.

"Well, I figured this way you could speak your mind with me more freely. We just met him, after all. While he's proven a worthwhile companion…I thought you might want to talk about this without him around."

She huffed. "Fair enough."

Moments of silence passed after that, and Neros wondered if she even wanted to talk more about what's been bothering her, when finally, she spoke up again.

"I hate feeling like a failure to my people," She said. "I've always been strong for them, but when those roots came out of the ground out of no-where, I just ran. I ran away from my problems, and then I dragged you away from *your* problems to solve this whole mess. I think…I think we just got lucky that the terrible curses put on our lands were related. But that doesn't change that all of those people might die if I don't act fast enough."

"I know what you mean—"

She sat up, fire in her eyes. "Do you *really*, though? I know you're trying to be sympathetic, Neros, but Arboria's population is more than *twice* Vetur's. And the only people in any *real* danger there that we know of are your parents. It's easy to try and save two lives, but *two thousand?* It's a lot taller of an order than you think it is."

Neros recoiled. "I-I'm sorry, Anthea. You're right."

The princess rolled her eyes. "You're so *spineless*, Neros! You just go along with whatever you're told to do, don't you? It's been like this your whole life! Your parents have guided you through everything, and now, with-out them, they're all you can think about, aren't they?"

He swallowed. "I…It's not just—"

She scoffed, crossing her arms and looking away. "I just don't know if you'll ever understand."

"I'm *trying* to, Anthea! I've been dealing with more than just the curse placed on my parents—I worry about the people of Vetur every hour I'm away. I'm *guilty* of abandoning them without a leader. The whole place could fall into chaos at any moment, and I—"

"But *none* of that has happened yet!" Anthea shouted, rising to her feet. "You're worried about ridiculous hypotheticals, Neros. You wouldn't know catastrophic tragedy if it slapped you in the face. Don't try and pretend like you know what I'm going through just because you have to re-adjust your magic and figure out a way to unfreeze *two people.*"

Neros' pulse raced, thrumming loudly in his ears. "Anthea, I'm not–it's not so simple to readjust the way I do magic."

Anthea rolled her eyes. "You've got a bubbly, happy guide who is more than willing to give you everything he's got to help you out. Must be *nice* to have things made easy for you, even in this hardship."

"But Anthea, I'm *trying* to help *you!* Please, just listen to me—"

"Oh, save it! You get to live in blissful ignorance of Endra's problems because the curse on your land doesn't affect anyone but you and your parents. There is little to no danger for Vetur's future, and I know Veturians don't live as long as Arborians, so even if something *did* happen, it's *way* easier for you to rebuild!" She groaned, running her hands through her hair in frustration. She got back into the bed, then, and burrowed under the covers, curling up into a tight ball.

Neros' stomach sank. "Anthea…"

"Just get out of here, Neros. Get Pontius and go to bed. We have a long day tomorrow."

"I—Anthea, please…listen…?"

The prince was met with silence. He sighed.

"I'll never really know the weight that's crushing you right now, Anthea. I'll admit to that. But…I want to help you shoulder that burden. I wish you'd let me. You're so stubborn, and brave, and strong, but you've really got quite a tendency to decide that you're the only one who's willing to carry the weight of your problems. I know Rosea wishes you'd share more with us, too." He sighed. "We're both going through a lot right now, and there's a lot of uncertainty on the horizon. We just have to believe in our fire hero, and hope that we can find some answers. That's all. You're my best friend, and I…I just hope you know that. Good night."

Turning to the door, Neros crept out into the hallway, closing the door gently behind him. He heaved a shuddering sigh. *That was…rough. I had no idea she felt that way.* Neros had to wonder if he really was inflating the situation he'd been put in. *It's true that there's no comparison between her concerns and mine, but…is all that truly what she wanted to say?* Runa's words pressed at the back of his mind, too. *She asserted this problem was bigger than I was, but now, am I to be so sure?* He sighed, looking down the hallway and expecting to see Pontius floating there, but it was barren save for the soft flicker of the wall lanterns. Neros gingerly navigated the inn, checking the restaurant area and then the lobby before determining that Pontius must have gone outside. The inn wasn't that large, and the town was smaller than Vetur's castle courtyard, so he had no doubt he could find Pontius quickly.

Neros left the building, walking through the grassy lawn around the outskirts. The light from the inn bathed the surrounding area in a warm glow, contrasted by the cool light from Endra's twin moons. Around the back, the prince could make out Pontius' small, floating figure. Neros also heard voices, which gave him pause. He ducked behind the wall to eavesdrop.

"They have done well to make it so far in just a day. I fear all of this has weighed heavily on their young minds."

"Not to worry, sir, I'll be the picture-perfect mood lifter! They'll be focused and motivated with our combined guidance."

"I have faith you will succeed. Be careful in the Eldur Ignis Volcano. The times there are tumultuous, I can sense. Young Neros and Anthea may have more trouble to deal with in ways that are not fighting Melanthos' monsters."

"I'll be sure to warn them, sir."

"Thank you, Pontius. I am glad you could go with them in my stead. Was that all you needed to report?"

"Yes, sir. Have a pleasant evening."

"You, as well. Be well."

The voices faded—one was clearly Pegaios, who was not around, and Pontius seemed undisturbed by this fact. Actually, Pontius seemed to be glowing, but that was fading, as well.

"Pontius?"

"Ahh!" The water sprite gasped, whirling around and waving his hands around in a panic. "Y-your highness? How long have you been standing there?! How much did you overhear?"

He laughed, tension from earlier rolling off his shoulders. "Relax, Pontius, I've only been here a few moments. But...was that Pegaios you were talking to?"

"Wh-what?! Who?! No! Not at all! I was speaking with no one! Just myself! I was speaking with myself!"

Neros raised an eyebrow.

Pontius deflated. "Oh, alright, you've caught me. It's one of my many special abilities: I can telepathically converse with the great Oracle! Not many water sprites can develop the skill as I have, and Pegaios deemed me most worthy of adventuring alongside you once we discovered I could use it." He explained amicably, but steadily sank into himself further. "I was discussing those strange, skeletal monsters you fought off earlier. They're abnormal on Endra's surface, so I had to confirm my suspicions with Pegaios."

"You said something about…Melanthos' monsters? Is that what we've been fighting? And…who is Melanthos?"

Pontius shook his head. "It's best if I explain it to both you and the princess tomorrow. How is she, by the by? She seemed rather conflicted after our arrival here in town."

"She's…" Neros looked back to where their room was at the inn. "I think she would like a bit of privacy before we go back up."

The sprite nodded solemnly. "Then, would you like to learn a bit about water magic?"

Neros' eyebrows shot up. "Truly? As in, right now?" He looked around. "But we're not near a body of water…"

Pontius laughed. "You and I are practically bodies of water, your highness! You don't know it, but the power to manipulate water is already at your fingertips. You just have to access that power. After all, many eons ago, Veturians used to have the ability to harness the power of water, and the Goddess Isolde only chose to bestow that of *ice* to the royal family. Over time, though, Isolde's gift made the royal family line so powerful that the Veturians stopped practicing water magic. Now, I don't know if any of them know it at all."

Neros' eyebrows drew together. "None of the Veturians know any water magic, as far as I know. That's so sad…"

Pontius tapped his hand under Neros' chin. "Cheer up, Prince Neros! It's by no means your fault. I'm sure Goddess Isolde had no idea that would happen, either. Besides, we're not here for a history lesson! Let's get some magic flowing! I'm sure it'll be easier without this pesky glove of yours," Pontius noted, floating down and tugging at Neros' gloved hand.

"Pontius, wait—"

The sprite gasped as Neros' glove fell to the ground, revealing his solid, icy arm. Pontius rapped his tiny knuckles against it, surprised at its solidity;

he carefully spiraled around his arm, assessing the damage. "Your highness... what treachery was done onto you? This...this is a curse most foul."

"I...I heard the voice of a witch, at home, and...well. When she froze my parents, I tried to reach out to them, to save them. She punished me by sealing my ice magic away, I think. I can use it, but it hurts. I already have a few fractures..." It was hard for him to look at his own arm, thinking of the witch's voice ringing in his ears: *you wretched mage...*

"My, my," Pontius hummed. "This complicates things a bit." He held out his hands, focusing healing magic onto Neros' arm. "Could you try to cast some ice magic for me, and tell me if it hurts as I do this?"

Neros nodded, extending his hand outward and calling the magic energy from his core, feeling its frigidity course through his veins and surface at his fingertips. Small ice crystals formed, and he felt the sensation of pinpricks at his elbow. "A bit...but not much."

Pontius hummed, concentrating further. "Then we may still be doing damage, so listen closely. I want you to take the energy you're using in this hand to cast ice, and to...transfer it, if you will, to the hand opposite this one. Pass it through your veins again, and try to focus your energy on warmth. Fluidity. Think like me! Or like water you see in the river. Rain that topples from overhead! Reproduce your ice, but make it warmer, so it can flow freely!"

"That...that doesn't make any sense!"

"It will if you just try to feel it, trust me!"

The prince huffed, closing his eyes and focusing on Pontius' words. He repealed the ice from his hand, and the sensation of pinpricks faded alongside it. Neros had never tried to cast magic from his left hand before; the only ice mages he'd ever known always used their right hands to cast magic and fight. *But I'm not fighting right now, so maybe...maybe the water will serve another purpose. Pontius seems to use it to heal. Maybe that's what he meant by warmth...?* He focused his energy to his left hand, trying to think of ice, but fluid. The river, the rain, the waterfalls in Paralia, the water that flooded his lungs when that final guardian swung his axe...and in his palm, a small orb of viscous fluid began to form.

Pontius beamed, losing all focus and dropping his healing energy to swirl around Neros and giving him—well, more like giving his face—a hug.

Neros noted that without Pontius' healing energy, conjuring the water magic didn't hurt him at all. His lips curled into a small smile, and the orb dissipated into mist.

"Oh, your highness, I knew you were amazing!"

Neros flushed. "It was only a small orb of water, Pontius."

"Nonsense! It's miraculous simply because you've never done it before!"

The prince only smiled, choosing to accept the compliment for what it was. His limbs felt like lead, and his eyelids heavy. He yawned, dropping to his knees in the dirt.

Pontius dropped in front of him, fraught with concern. "Oh, my, your highness, are you unwell? Well, of course, naturally that would take a lot of energy out of you. But, gods, I didn't even notice until now, you look..., well you look awful. How long has it been since you've slept?"

Neros thought about it. He'd collapsed while searching for answers in the library, but he only got a couple of hours, then. He'd walked all the way to Paralia, fought those monsters, picked up Pontius, and came all the way to Barmwich without sleeping. "Um...perhaps...a day...?"

Pontius sputtered. "One–a whole–wha–oh my–*Prince Neros*, we need to get you to bed immediately!" The sprite grabbed Neros' hand and pulled him to his feet; a feat of strength Neros could not comprehend with his oncoming exhaustion.

Once he re-entered the shared room, he closed the door carefully so not to disturb Anthea's rest. His heart sank when he saw her. *I hope she allows me to help her soon. If we can't cooperate, I doubt we'll survive.* Neros collapsed into the bed, rolling around until the blankets laid over his body in some haphazard way. He was simply too drained to bother more.

In an instant, he was asleep. His dreams were plagued by purplish, skeletal monsters trapping him in a frozen landscape.

Chapter 5
The Eldur Ignis Volcano

*T*he following morning, Neros blearily awoke to an empty inn room. He groaned, turning to peek at the window, watching the sunlight pouring in. *Anthea probably woke up hours ago. I hope she's around somewhere nearby.* He felt like he hadn't slept at all, after all that had happened. He endured nightmare after nightmare, and whenever he managed to talk himself down from an adrenaline high, he'd fall back asleep and a nightmare would pick up right where it left off. Never had the prince felt so *exhausted.* He sat up, rubbing at his eyes with the backs of his palms. Unexpectedly, his fingers caught around his crown. *I forgot to take it off...? Well, I suppose that's no surprise.* Neros barely remembered how he made it back to their room the night before, only that he was practicing water magic with Pontius. *Right...I wonder, can I still...?* The prince extended his frozen hand, focusing energy on making small ice crystals—ignoring the pain, he dissipated them, focusing on turning them into water droplets in his other palm. As the drops formed, the pain was alleviated, and he was able to hold them for a few seconds before they spun into snowflakes and dissolved.

Rising from the bed, Neros noted Pontius was also not in the room. He sighed, pulling his tailcoat on and re-adjusting his glove. *We have a long journey ahead of us today. I need to find Pontius and Anthea so we can get going.* He thought of Anthea, and their argument the night before. *I should probably also see if she's okay.* He knew what Anthea said was...harsh, to say the least, but he did feel like there was some truth to her words. *I at least have some faith in Runa and the councilmen to take care of Vetur in my absence, but Anthea's the only royalty in Arboria, isn't she? Sure, there are elder Arborians, but Anthea's the only one who looks out for most of them.* The prince sighed, wandering to the front desk and dropping off the keys with Wilton.

"Hey, you alright there?"

Neros blinked, then smiled. "Yeah. I'm okay. Have you seen Princess Anthea?"

"'Fraid not. She was always an early riser, though, so I doubt she's around here."

The prince nodded, waving and heading out. The weather was bright and cloudless, which was a relief. Neros felt as though their adventure had a time limit, and if they lost a day of travel for any reason, they might be in some trouble. *I could be overthinking it,* he thought, walking down the road and peering at all the various shops and stalls that had set up for the morning. The atmosphere here was completely different than the calm, serene one they'd seen last night. The warm glow of lanterns was replaced by busy streets full of merchants, awake and energetic in the morning sun. This, too, reminded Neros of home; specifically, during the time of the festival of ice. His heart sank. If there was a way for him to restore peace to the world in time for the next festival, he would do it. Even if it took everything he had.

Pushing those thoughts from his mind, he opened his satchel to check on his supplies. The hastily-packed bag was no surprise, considering the mental state he was in when he tossed the various items into it, but he still sighed at his past self. What was he thinking? Inside the bag were two apples, a canteen of water, a Veturian record of Endra's history, a rolled-up set of spare clothes, and a small twine-bound notebook. What started as a day-trip away from Vetur had suddenly turned into a lot more, and Neros knew he'd need more (and better) supplies. He scanned the stalls again—Arborians were notoriously good at making herbal remedies and potions, and having a few on hand wouldn't hurt. He paced the street, until he spotted a towering Redwood-type Arborian standing behind an overgrown-looking stand bursting full of wrapped up plants and bottles, all labeled with scrawled handwriting. As Neros approached, the Redwood waved.

"Hello down there! What can I interest you in?" He smiled.

"Well, I was hoping to pick up a variety of things, actually. I'm traveling to the Eldur Ignis Volcano today. Do you have any burn remedies? Or heat repellents?" Neros wasn't shopping for himself, necessarily—he's never had much issue with heat, considering he could usually create his own cooling source. With his curse, though, Neros had a feeling he wouldn't be generating any ice blocks anytime soon.

The Redwood looked nervous. "Eldur Ignis Volcano, you say? Well, it may not be so hot there anymore, but this section has my collection of herbs and potions that'll help you there." He gestured to the far corner of his stand, where an array of bluish-hued potions and floral arrangements rested.

Neros peered at his options. One of the bottles looked like it had ice crystals forming on the inside of its neck, and it was labeled simply: *Fuarite. Hmm…this may work, but I'm sure there's something more accurate.* He sifted through a few bundles of flowers, settling on a group of snowdrops and irises, their petals a brilliant white. Twine wrapped around their stems, and the label read *Fuarite Dry: Burn Remedy*. He flipped the label over, revealing a brief set of instructions: *Crush petals. Mix with water. Apply.*

Keeping the flowers in hand, he continued browsing. There were bags of seeds along the font of the cart, and Neros picked up some frost seeds for Anthea. He also grabbed a few standard restorative potions—just because Pontius could heal them, didn't mean they could rely on him all the time.

Neros paid the Redwood and continued down the street. Anthea had to be around *somewhere*, with Pontius; there was no chance that she would leave town without him.

Finding no luck on the main street, he decided to dip into a small patch of trees to continue his search. When she was younger, Anthea often took to hiding amongst the trees when she was upset or needed to think. Her connection to nature was unmatched—Neros had always admired her respectful cooperation with the trees and flowers. He suspected it was because she was borrowing their power whenever she needed to defend herself, and meditating among the plants—using a fraction of her life energy to restore theirs—served them well enough as thanks.

Sure enough, in a clearing of the trees, he found Anthea and Pontius, both sitting with their legs crossed. Anthea's palms were flush to the ground, and she emanated a faint orange glow. Each breath she took looked calculated, and she was the picture of calm.

Her eyes opened as Neros approached. She smiled, though it lacked its usual mischief. "Were you going to surprise attack me?"

Neros laughed lightly. "No, no. Not today. I just woke up, and you were gone." He shuffled around in his bag, holding out the pouch of seeds. "These are for you."

She quirked a brow. "Is this...some kind of apology gift? I should be getting that for *you.*" She accepted the pouch, looking a bit sheepish. "I'm sorry for what I said yesterday. We should be working together. I should've known better than to blow up at you." She rubbed at her face, sighing.

Neros patted the top of her head. "It's okay, Anthy. You were stressed, and you needed to vent. I...I was over-reacting, too, anyway. I think Vetur is in good hands, with the councilmen and Runa looking after it."

"Sure, but that doesn't mean I can just...you know. Say those awful things to you."

"You didn't mean it that way, though."

"Right, I didn't, but..." She rubbed her face again, dragging her hands down her cheeks and looking pitifully up at Neros. "That doesn't make it okay. I'm sorry, I really am."

Neros kneeled in front of her, pulling her into a hug. "I forgive you. I'll always forgive you."

"That kind of attitude is dangerous, you know."

He smiled. "I know."

"...You can let go, Neros."

Laughing, he released her. "Alright, alright. So, how was your meditation?"

"Refreshing! You know, beforehand, Pontius told me everything about what you saw last night. It's pretty convenient that we have a direct thread to Pegaios if we need extra guidance."

Pontius piped up. "You won't! I'm a perfectly capable and knowledgeable guide, after all!"

Ignoring the water sprite's reassurance, Anthea stood and stretched, scooping her pouch off the ground to examine its contents. Her eyebrows shot up, then she smirked, latching the pouch onto her belt. She hooked an arm around Neros' shoulder, walking them both in the direction of the Eldur Ignis Volcano. They made no further stops through Barmwich, their supply bags full enough for the trip ahead. Pontius acted as their compass, and if they kept at a good pace, Neros was sure they would make it to the volcano within a day or two's time.

On the way, Pontius told them about the mysterious man named Melanthos, and the monsters speckled throughout Endra.

"Melanthos is god of Umbros, the underworld," He explained. "And a hundred years ago, he incurred his wrath upon Endra, as the prophecy foretold. You know, the darkness that consumes the land that must be stopped by the heroes three!"

"So he's directly involved with the prophecy…" Neros hummed, stroking his chin. "Interesting. Around the time of darkness, much of Vetur and Arboria's histories went dark, as well. We never truly knew what happened."

"Oh, I only know what Pegaios told me," Pontius admitted. "But apparently, his darkened rage pooled into a huge mass in the middle of the Endran fields, releasing droves and droves of those purple-glowing, smoke-spewing skeleton monsters much like the ones you've been fighting. The war was destructive, and much of Endra was destroyed.

Legend has it that the heroes three defeated the enraged Melanthos, subduing him and forcing him to rest. For their efforts, they were awarded heavenly ascension, where they set to work restoring Endra to how it is today. As for Melanthos, he lies dormant in Umbros, carefully taking care of the dead, helping them to cross the winding River Sprygz."

"Why did he go berserk in the first place?" Anthea asked.

Pontius sank. "I don't know. Pegaios never told me."

"That's alright," said Neros. "The important thing is now we know a bit more of the prophecy. Maybe we can stop Melanthos from going berserk again, somehow."

Anthea nodded, and the whole group felt resolute as they traveled across the plains.

❄

Steadily, the ground beneath their feet became less vivid. Patches of dirt became larger and larger, soon growing entirely overrun by soot-like terrain that kicked up as they walked, getting caught in their throats.

"This must be the Ashen Terrain," Pontius said. "Seeing it in person, it's no wonder very few people ever travel to the Eldur Ignis Volcano. It's so smoky and ashy out here, it drives any potential tourist running in the opposite direction."

Pontius wasn't kidding. The volcano was very close by now—it was most of Neros' field of vision, actually—but the terrain for the past half mile or so had been nothing but soot. His white boots were barely recognizable, and the barkskin around Anthea's ankles had begun to blacken. He wondered if they'd be able to bathe once they arrived. His gut twisted; aside from the rumors in Barmwich, he knew next to nothing about the Embers as a species. Veturian record was bare when it came to the volcano as a whole, and Arborian texts only spoke of a myth from hundreds of years ago, about an Ember of colossal size who blazed the Endran fields to dust, resulting in the creation of the Erimos desert.

Neros had reason to believe the story was entirely fabricated, but he never called it to attention. Regardless, if *that* story was their only basis, Neros wondered if the Embers were violent people. They were…flaming, to some degree, weren't they? So Neros could only assume they would be a bit hotheaded. He wondered if he and Anthea would be welcomed there, or would they be branded as intruders, like in Paralia? He sighed; he really hoped they wouldn't have to endure the same run-around of battles as they did in the water world. Even despite the arid atmosphere, Neros could still vividly imagine the feeling of nearly drowning.

"The ground is starting to feel more stable," Anthea remarked. "We've gotta be hitting the side of the volcano soon."

Neros nodded. "I can feel it, too. Will we have to…climb it?"

"I don't think we have a choice."

He looked up—and up, and up—and he couldn't see the very top of the volcano. Anthea groaned beside him.

"I can't even make roots in the ground to make this go faster. We have to do this the long way."

Neros put his best foot forward; thankfully, it wasn't quite as steep as the mountain leading up to Vetur. It was also remarkably less hot that he anticipated. It was warmer than the grass they were used to, but not too much warmer than the ash they'd been walking on.

He hummed. "Do you think we'd be able to see the lava from out here?"

"Maybe," Anthea replied. "But those two at the inn said the lava dried up, remember? So I doubt we'll see anything now."

A bad feeling washed over the prince as they continued their ascent. First, an instance at the castle with his parents; then, the tragedy in Arboria rendering every Arborian immobile; and now, the lava dries up in an entire volcano? He feared to figure out the culprit behind all of this.

"This is *so* not as hot as I was expecting," Anthea's voice cut through his thoughts. "I think Geneviève just doesn't know how to keep herself cool."

Neros smirked. "Aren't you sucking on a frost seed right now?"

The princess smiled wide, showing off the seed between her teeth. "Yup!" She laughed. "You really know all my secrets, Neros."

Eventually, their walk became a climb. The volcano's rough outer edges had a few good footholds here and there, but navigating the cliff still proved to be tricky. The soot caked on his boots wasn't helping, either; one misstep and he would fall and tumble back to the base. Anthea was a ways above him, but she was much more of a natural climber than he was. *Breathe, Neros,* he told himself. *Just take it one limb at a time. Hand, then foot. Then hand, then—*

As he moved to secure his boot in place, the foothold broke off the volcano and tumbled down. Neros yelped, gripping his hands in place so not to fall as his leg swooped back to the cliffside.

"Are you okay?" Anthea called.

"F-fine!" Neros felt his voice quiver, so he placed his head against the side of the volcano to breathe. His pulse thrummed in his ears. *It's okay. It's okay. I didn't fall.* The spots beneath his palms and other foot began to quake, and his heart jumped in his throat as immediately as he threw himself to the next few footholds.

Once the quiver died down, he called out to Anthea. "Did you feel that, too?"

"I did. I thought this volcano was supposed to be inactive!"

Pontius hummed. "With a quake, normally some lava overflow would follow, but it seems like those Arborians in Barmwich were right. Come on, we're almost to the top! You can make it!"

Although they encountered no further quakes or missteps for remainder of their ascent, Neros still breathed a sigh of relief when they reached the lip of the volcano. The upper edge curved downward in a spiral shape, leading to what looked to be the most intricately laid out city Neros had ever seen. There were pulley systems, mine carts, platforms that operated mechanically to lift Embers to higher or lower platforms, and *shops*. The amount of shops scattered throughout the first layer inside the volcano was staggering. Some were tucked away in alcoves in the walls, and others were made to be like stands and stalls, similar to shop setup in Vetur and Barmwich. Bridges crossed over the outer rim to make simple traveling paths, and if Neros peered downward, he noticed that the colors seemed to change the farther down the volcano went. He could see hints of a blue aura emanating from below, though this upper portion seemed to be dominated by the color red. There were streaks along the volcano's walls that appeared to be recently-dried lava—the coloration was more vibrant than the surrounding muddy brown.

Most interesting to Neros were the Embers themselves, though. Most that he could see had red, or orange flames flowing off their heads—some had yellow—and their skin was a dark, dark brown. They looked like rock themselves, with rough skin. Many, if not all, had cracks; some had cracks spiraling down their arms, where others had simple scar-like shapes on their cheeks. Neros wondered how they got there, or if every Ember looked this way. As he followed Anthea down the spiral, many of them started to look their way, and began to whisper to each other. It was at this point Neros realized: they were the only non-Embers to be seen. *Anyone else who comes must only visit for a day, maybe a few hours.* It made sense to him, after all: the volcano was difficult to climb, and the Ashen Terrain was enough of a warning to stay away. Nobody seemed to be pulling out weapons to fight them with, which was a relief. Neros' spear could stay securely strapped on his back. Still, the prince did jump a bit when he heard the metallic *clang* of a nearby Ember smacking a mallet against some heated metal.

Anthea, however, was not perturbed in the slightest. She waltzed right up to him, offering her best smile. "Hello there, sir!"

The Ember had no flames on the sides of his head, just the top, which was curled into a neat-looking bun. He looked up from his work, and Neros was struck by how sharp his eyes looked—his sclera were yellow instead of white, and his irises a brilliant ruby. He rolled his shoulders back before speaking.

"Hello." His voice was remarkably—though unsurprisingly—deep. "And just who might you be?"

The princess brazenly stuck out her hand. "I am Princess Anthea of the forest kingdom Arboria. Nice to meet you! What's your name?"

"…Keahi." His gaze moved to Neros. "And who's your little friend?"

"I-I'm Prince Neros, sir. Of Vetur."

Keahi's stare turned stern, scrutinizing. "Why are you here?"

Neros fiddled with his wrists. "We're on a quest—"

"A legendary one!" Pontius piped up. "Prince Neros and Princess Anthea are in search of the final hero of prophecy! We were guided here by the great oracle Pegaios in the east."

Keahi frowned at Pontius, narrowing his eyes. "Prophecy? That stuff's all about magic, isn't it? I've got nothing to do with that. Go ask someone else."

He returned to his work, banging at his project. Anthea squinted, as though she wanted to say something, but she knew better of it. She turned on her heel and walked away. Neros trailed after her.

"How frustrating," She grumbled.

"Well, I don't think we can expect everyone to be nice to us."

"Neros is right! Let's keep moving, surely someone will be able to offer us some information!"

Most of the Embers were unwilling to talk to the trio. All of them had heard of the prophecy, but had no interest in talking about it further. After a few Embers were largely unhelpful, Anthea decided it was time to change her tactics. They walked across one of the long bridges, approaching the opposite end of what Neros now gathered to be the first layer of the volcano. As he looked below, he noticed the layer beneath this one had mostly orange-flame-haired Embers; the one below it, yellow-flame-haired. Then, there was a foggy mist of sorts, so Neros could only see a blue hue. *How curious…*

Anthea walked up to a shopkeeper, who had a wide array of swords, daggers, and shields displayed on a table. The shopkeeper grinned at them as they approached, but Neros felt like her posture was uneasy.

"Hello, travelers. How may I help you today?"

"Hey there," Anthea started, easing into an open stance. One hand on her hip, the other dangling at her side. Neros stood beside her, mindful not to cross his arms. "We've never been here before, and everyone seems a bit restless. I was hoping you could give us a bit of information?"

The Ember worried at her lip, but nodded. "Sure, I can answer a few questions. I'm not sure I'll be able to answer everything, though."

"It's no trouble at all, really, we're sorry to be asking so much of you." Anthea replied. *Her charm is turned up to the max,* Neros noted. She was typically a bit more brash and straightforward, but Neros remembered he *was* dealing with a master negotiator. Even Pontius looked impressed. Anthea shifted her weight, and continued. "A lot of the Embers we've spoken to so far have seemed kind of turned off whenever we mention the ancient prophecy…do you know why?"

Visible distaste crossed the woman's expression. "Well, you wouldn't know just from walking in, but we Embers are quite strictly separated. Down there," She gestured to the misty expanse behind her, far below where they stood. "That is where the Blue and White Embers live. If you two need anything to do with that dangerous practice, I suggest you take your questions there."

Anthea nodded, her expression unreadable. "Thank you for being so honest with us. I have one other question—this is a volcano, right? What happened to all the lava?"

The Ember's face fell. "Just a few days ago, it all dried up! Since it's stopped flowing, everyone's been in a bit of a panic. I'm sure that's why some folk haven't been all that sweet to you. You see, most of us in the upper layers rely on that lava to make all these beautiful blades and shields, and many of us use it for other crafting, as well. It truly sustains all life here."

The princess looked struck with pity—and Neros felt it, too. "What does that mean for you all now?" He asked.

"We Embers are at odds with each other," She explained. "We have been as long as I can remember. I don't know what this means for us now, but I have a feeling it's nothing good." She looked down, trying to hide her face behind her flames. "That's all I can tell you."

"You'll be okay," Anthea reassured her. "Thank you for speaking with us. I promise you, we'll find a way to help."

"It is none of your concern. But…I suppose I should thank you."

Neros tugged at his glove. "We should take our leave. Thank you again, and have a nice day."

The three of them turned and walked away, a somber mood settling over them. So far, the Embers struck Neros as a serious, almost segregated species. He wondered how their whole feud started, or if a group like this—especially in their current situation—could ever make amends.

"Turn those frowns upside down, you two! We're not here to save the Embers right now, we're here to find one! Understanding the social structure of this place will come naturally with time. We should see if we can't find an Ember willing to talk about magic with us."

Anthea huffed, crossing her arms. "But *how* are we going to find some-one when all of these Embers are so anti-magic up here? It's not like someone is just going to *look* like a mage in hiding, or something."

The prince brought his hand to his chin. "I guess that's true, but there must be something telling about the people around here. Let's just watch for a while, maybe travel to the layer below this one."

The princess agreed, and they set to searching. Navigating the volcano seemed intimidating, at first—there were many different motorized systems that were used for transit, and neither Neros or Anthea had much experience with such technology. However, they found the operation of the elevators to be surprisingly intuitive. Once they were both in, they closed the gate, pulled a lever, and selected a color off of a panel. In a second's time, the machine whirred to life and began moving at a leisurely pace.

"You know, perhaps I can't blame them for being anti-magic. The Embers seem to have accomplished great things with mechanical innovation alone," Neros mused. "It's incredible."

"Get that love-struck look out of your eyes, it's just a *moving platform*," Anthea sighed. "I swear, you're too easily impressed."

The elevator came to a halt, and the gate unlatched, pulling open by a unique cog-and-pulley system that must have been attached to some part of the elevator's moving structure, to signal when the occupants had reached the desired level. The group piled out, noting that the second level of the volcano was much like the first, except for one thing: most of the Embers had orange flames flickering around their skulls, with cracks in their skin that glowed to match. There were a few red Embers, and a few yellow ones, but it was dominated by the orange hue. Neros wondered if they lived like this intentionally.

On this layer, Neros and Anthea earned plenty more wary stares from the Embers themselves, and Neros was beginning to wonder if any Ember was friendly at all. *I can't blame them, though. I think I would be wary, too, if outsiders came right after a tragedy like this happened.*

Distracted by his own thoughts, Neros bumped into a red Ember, sending the young boy right to the ground.

"Oh, no! I am so sorry, here, let me help you up."

"No need." The Ember stood, brushing himself off. Neros took a good look at him; his hair was longer than most other Embers they'd seen, with red bangs that flared around his eyes while the rest of his hair remained in an almost impressively stable bowl shape. He had one large crack running down his right arm, and it reminded Neros of lightning; it revealed a moving, red substance that looked a bit like lava. His eyes matched his hair, a bright red emphasized by the same yellow sclera Neros had yet to get used to. Looking for someyhinf unique on his clothes, Neros found what he wore seemed standard fare: a plain tunic and pants with a sash around the middle. His eyes widened when he got a good look at Neros. "You're blue."

The prince blinked. "I—yes, I am."

The Ember narrowed his eyes, looking between him and Anthea. "You look lost. You don't belong here, but you seem as though you could use some assistance. Who are you?"

"I'm, um, Prince Neros of Vetur—that's a wintry mountain—"

"I know what Vetur is. And this girl?"

"Princess Anthea," She extended her hand, voice smooth and kind. "And you are?"

"Heath," He replied. "Though I don't think I am the one you seek, you ridiculous magicians."

Anthea's sweetness melted away in seconds. She groaned, "Ugh, do *any* of you Embers actually *like* magic, or believe in the prophecy?"

"Oh, I believe in the prophecy," Heath leveled her with an even stare, crossing his arms. "But you see, I have this *brother* who went below the gap to where the blue and white Embers live. To study *magic*. The fool."

Neros had a feeling that brother might be who they were looking for. "Forgive me, but why are you all so…against magic? We haven't gotten much of an explanation of it. We're here seeking out the third prophetic hero, but nobody seems to believe in it."

Heath sighed. "Follow me. I ought to give you the grand tour."

They started walking, and Heath gestured upward. "You used an elevator to get from up there to down here, correct?" When they nodded, he continued. "So, you've traveled between layers. The Eldur Ignis Volcano is made up of five of them: each layer is inhabited by primarily one color of Ember. You can tell what color an Ember is based on the color of their *magmatic core,* such as mine, which is red. The core is revealed through our cracks. Every Ember has cracks; some are just better at hiding them than others." He held up his arm as an example. "Now then, the top three layers of the volcano house red, orange, and yellow Embers, respectively. These Embers have lived their lives on innovation, thriving to create mechanical objects without the use of foolish *magic* to aid them. We create swords, daggers, lances, axes, armor, shields, bags, some jewelry, clocks, and other trinkets and knickknacks, all without the aid of magic spells. We think it's destructive. Do you understand so far?"

Neros wished he had pen and paper to take notes. "Yes, I understand. Please, continue."

Heath smirked, taking them into an elevator and shifting some of the knobs around, clicking the yellow key so it lit up. "Gladly. Normally, you would be able to peer over any ledge of the volcano and see our gorgeous, flowing lava, but now it has all dried up. We upper level Embers—remember, that's the red, orange, and yellow ones—believe it is magical trickery from the fools down below. I'm sure they believe the opposite, but you would have to ask my brother about that. Not that you should believe him," He added.

Anthea frowned. "Does your brother live down below? Why would he go there if everyone up here hates magic?"

Heath sighed. "If you go down below, I'm sure you'll meet him. You'll see why when you do." He led them out of the elevator, and Neros was beginning to wonder if each subsequent layer was supposed to feel warmer or not. He wasn't feeling any different, but there could have been a number of reasons for that. Magically inclined as he was made him less susceptible to some of the elements; however, a volcano full of lava would have been a natural exception, wouldn't it? There was no way for him to know now, of course, but perhaps after all of this had been sorted out, he and Anthea would have to make a trip back here. Heath had been a resource beyond imagination, as not much was written of these people in Veturian or Arborian history texts.

Pontius chirped from beside Neros' head. He leaned in close, whispering. "Prince Neros, I think I can sense someone special on this level! As helpful as this guy is, we should probably take a look around on our own."

Neros nodded. "Thank you for all your help, Heath. Is there anything else we should know before we continue to look for the other hero of prophecy?"

"I'd suggest taking to the blue or white levels of the volcano. The Embers you find down there will surely fit the magical implications of the prophecy. But whatever you do, do not believe anything my brother tells you. He speaks nothing but *lies*."

The prince glanced between Anthea and Pontius before nodding slowly. "O-okay. We'll keep that in mind. Thank you for your time."

Heath turned on his heel and left, waving a hand as he did. Anthea turned to Neros. "You didn't want to pick his brain more?"

Neros pouted. "I did, truly, but Pontius said he sensed a special aura on this level. Our third prophetic hero may be here."

Chapter 6
Apprenticeship

*A*nthea did not seem wholly convinced that Pontius could sense the prophetic hero of fire's *aura* so easily—as soon as they arrived on the level, he seemed to be twittering nonstop on the subject.

"It's the truth! I feel it coming from…this direction!" He urged, pointing across from where Anthea and Neros were standing. A few shops lay across the bridge, though they all seemed like the same types of shops as were on every other level. There was a clock-maker with two bright flaming buns atop her head, wrapped up in her work; a lean blacksmith with his hair tied back in a ponytail, concentrating on a rapier in front of him; and an older man, with no hair on his head at all but a plethora of elaborate-looking cracks, selling books.

"Well, there are three of them, and three of us. Let's split up!" Anthea suggested.

Pontius shrank into himself. "As much as I appreciate your…enthusiasm, Princess Anthea, I *really* would *much* prefer, *truly*, to stick to the sidelines, you see. I'm not much of a talker, or negotiator, or…conversational adversary of any kind! I can give you tips and tricks and information galore, but…I cannot gather it innately. I'm no good at it."

Anthea snickered behind the palm of her hand. "Okay, okay, I get it. Just stick inside Neros' spear and let us know if one of those people there seems extra special." Pontius nodded, tucking himself away in the head of Neros' spear. She walked shoulder-to-shoulder with Neros as they crossed the bridge, formulating her plan. "You should talk to the girl. She's cute, and she looks like she's making clocks. Super useful skill, could be hidden magical potential in there! The boy is just another blacksmith, I doubt he'll even take ten minutes of my time. We can talk to them for a little while, then switch, and *then* we've gotta buy some of the old man's books and re-convene to discuss our results. Got it?"

Neros' grin was wide. "Your tactics are solid, Anthy, I can't find I disagree."

"Perfect! Let's get talkin'!"

Speaking to the clock-making yellow Ember proved to be harder than Neros had hoped. She didn't seem like she'd noticed him at all upon walking up to her. She had glasses perched on the edge of her nose, and she gave off the impression that she would much rather be in a workshop than at a storefront. Her eyes were a radiant green, and as she screwed and snapped and locked pieces into place, Neros noticed her hair flickered and waved more than others. *I should have asked Heath if the flames atop each Ember's head is something they control.*

Shaking his head free of the thought, he stepped closer to her booth. "G-good day, miss."

She peered up at him from over her glasses, eyes going wide. "The outsider! You really are blue!"

Neros laughed, more out of nerves than anything. "My name is Prince Neros. What is yours?"

"Makana. Gods above, where are you *from?* I've never seen skin so pale and blue in my life!"

"I'm from Vetur, a mountain town—"

"I thought that place was fake!" She shouted, rising up from her work suddenly and crossing over the side of her stall to examine him. "So can you make ice? Can you? That's what I read in a book once, but I was sure it was fake. Magic is *ludicrous,* after all, super dangerous, but I just gotta know if you can do it."

"Um–well–" He stammered. "I-I can, but won't that get you in a bit of trouble…? You said it yourself, magic is dangerous."

"Nonsense! This is a rare occurrence! When do I ever get to meet a prince who looks like he stepped out of one of my mythology textbooks?

Come on, please? One icicle? Can you do that? Is that too much? Is a bead better? Will it melt right away? Oh! Can I use it in this clock I'm building?"

Her barrage of questions overwhelmed him. "It won't melt, I…" He sighed. "Fine, here." He moved his right hand around a bit, ignoring the sting that came from calling upon his magic. He procured three beads of ice: two small ones, and one medium sized. They floated for a moment before dropping into his palm, glimmering as they reflected the light off of her hair. Makana moved close, gripping Neros' wrist (and he tried not to flinch) and pulling his hand to her eye level before snatching up the ice beads and inspecting them from behind her glasses. Then, she moved back to her table and pulled out a magnifying glass, peering at them through that. A huge smile broke out on her face.

"That's asinine, what you've done there! I can't believe it's real. Can everyone from Vetur do this, or just you? Are you special?"

Neros' cheeks colored. "I don't know that I would say special."

"Sure he is!" Anthea's voice chimed in, and he felt the familiar weight of her arm around his shoulders. He almost sighed in relief, but she leaned in close to his ear and murmured, "That other guy was a total hack. Had nothing to say to me, just like Keahi up in the red level. What a waste."

Makana's jaw had dropped, and she gaped at Anthea. "Are-are-are you the *goddess Silva,* as shown in many legendary mythology books?!"

Now it was the princess' turn to look sheepish. "Wh-*what?!*" A loud laugh bubbled from her lips. "That's insane! No, no, I'm the princess chosen by Silva. My name is Anthea, but you can call me Anthy."

"A princess and a prince! Incredible. We Embers abandoned that royalty structure a long time ago, because it was too easy for one level to become tyrannical over the rest of us. Anyway, are you magic too? Can you make flowers? Or leaves? Or vines? Does it hurt to be here?"

"Whoa, whoa, girl! Slow down, let me answer you! I can make flowers, leaves, and vines, but I need some form of soil to do so. It doesn't hurt me to be here because my good buddy Neros bought me frost seeds!" She shuffled around her bag for one before showing it off, popping it into her mouth.

As the princess entertained more of Makana's curiosities, Pontius emerged and pulled Neros away from the conversation. "Your highness, you are very charming and excellent at making new friends, but—and I hate to tell you this—that's not our gal."

"It's not?"

"Truly. In fact, our 'gal' is no gal at all: it's that stubborn, quote-un-quote waste that Anthea mentioned earlier. Do you see him over there?" Pontius pointed with a tiny, watery finger. Neros glanced, trying not to blatantly stare—though he caught the Ember's eyes anyway. The Ember had been glaring, probably at the commotion he had caused (and Anthea had continued) with Makana next door to him. Neros tried to look apologetic, but the Ember merely rolled his eyes and went back to work. The prince sighed.

"Your highness, this may be harder than any of us anticipated."

"Truly," Neros echoed. He walked back to Anthea, tapping her on the shoulder.

"And so all Arborians are pretty spiritual—wha…? Hm? What is it, Neros?" She raised a brow.

"I'm going to try and talk to that Ember over there."

The princess gave him a flat stare. "You know, I told you he's not worth our time."

"But Pontius said he's the one we need."

She shifted her gaze to the water spirit, crossing her arms. "You're kidding."

Pontius shrank behind Neros' shoulder. "Unfortunately not, princess."

Anthea heaved a sigh, placing both hands on her hips. "If that's how it is. I'll change my game plan up a little bit here. You go talk to that *impossible* guy."

Neros sighed, slowly making his way over to the mysterious Ember's shop. The closer he got, Pontius chimed in his ear, "That's definitely him! I sense a magic aura unlike any other in this volcano! I know you may be tempted to tell me it's too soon to say, but when I get a hunch, I'm always right, Prince Neros."

The prince chuckled, adjusting his bag on his shoulder. "I'm not Anthy, Pontius. You don't need to go the extra mile to convince me."

Nevertheless, as he approached, he couldn't help but feel nervous. The Ember was intently focused, and even though he smiled and offered a small wave, he thought he'd missed catching his attention entirely.

"H-hello."

The Ember didn't look up from his work. "Can I *help* you?"

"Um, yes, actually. My name is Prince Neros, and I've traveled from Vetur in search of…a hero."

Still, his eyes remained trained on the rapier, though his motions slowed. "I'm aware of who you are. You're all anyone has been talking about today. You, and your friend over there."

"Ah, her? She's—"

"Princess Anthea of Arboria," He supplied, nimble hands carving intricate features into the hilt of the blade he was working on. "She informed me as such."

Neros deflated. "Right." He stood for a few moments, feeling a bit awkward as he shifted his weight back and forth.

The Ember sighed. "*Can I help you,* or are you just going to stand there?"

Neros' stomach flipped. *What kind of information do I need from him?* He fiddled with the hem of his tailcoat. "Do you believe in the prophecy?"

This time, the Ember looked up, his orange eyes piercing. They were sharp and narrow, made all the more intimidating by the glowing yellow crack crawling up his cheek from his neck, and down from his temple on the opposite side of his face. "The prophecy?"

"Um, yes! Endra's prophecy, you know, about the three heroes fighting back darkness? One of water, one of nature, and one of fire? It's, ah, it's the story of how the gods came to be!"

"I know of it."

"Do you believe in it?"

The Ember blinked a few times before returning to his work. His expression was impossible to read. "I don't have time to think about that sort of thing. I'm just a blacksmith."

"I understand. May I ask one more question?"

He leaned in to his work on the hilt, carving slowly and carefully. "What is it?"

"What is your name?"

"You don't need to know."

"Wha-wait! Why not?"

"You said you had one more question, and that was your question.

Now, if you're not going to buy anything, I'm going to have to ask you to leave."

Neros' shoulders sagged as he slumped back to Anthea, who had since moved away from Makana's booth and was perched against the railing overlooking the bottom of the volcano, appearing pleased with herself.

The prince quirked a brow at her. "What are you so happy about?"

"I had a feeling you'd have no luck, so I asked our little gal pal over here if she'd heard any rumors about people who could do magic. Special people. You know, like how Pontius thinks our little closed-off jerk is over there." She unfolded her arms and gripped Neros' shoulders. "And guess what she told me?!"

"That someone does magic?"

"That *that blacksmith* does magic! She said she heard a rumor that he practices in private, because upper layer Embers aren't supposed to know how to use magic at all. They forbid it! But that guy is a total rebel! No wonder he didn't want to talk to us, he thought we'd rat him out to the Ember authorities!"

Neros didn't feel so convinced. "But, Anthy, a rumor is just that. Hearsay. We can't prove that blacksmith does magic. For all we know, he's telling us the truth."

"Yeah, okay, but if you lived in a society like this and *you* wanted to do magic, would *you* tell two random strangers all about your abilities?"

He hummed. "I suppose not. But, still, how in the world are we going to prove whether or not he has magical prowess? Pontius' hunch and your newly acquired rumor aren't necessarily enough. We don't even know his *name.*"

"I think it'll take some extra sleuthing to figure that out. But we should probably stick to this layer. Any farther up and we'll get more stubborn boneheads who don't want to tell us anything about this *taboo rebel.*"

"Anthy, I *really* don't think you should call him that."

"Oh, so what? It's the truth!"

With Anthea taking the lead, they spoke to every Ember they could in the yellow layer. They had debated, for some time, whether going to the blue or white levels would prove to be useful. On one hand, if the blacksmith were sneaking off to take magic lessons, they could learn a lot. On the other, if the *gap* was as great as Heath implied, it could be safely assumed that the blue and white Embers wanted nothing to do with any of the upper level Embers. As much as the two wanted to learn as much as they could about their mysterious, potential new ally, they had to be careful what risks they took.

As they spoke to Ember after Ember, it became clear to Neros that everyone had *seen* the blacksmith at some point in time, but nobody really knew anything about him. He only came out to man the shop once or twice a week, and spent much of his time hidden from sight. He only started appearing down on this level around seven years ago, according to a few perceptive watch-makers they'd met. Before that, nobody seemed to know anything at all.

Magic was rarely a part of the conversation, much to Neros and Anthea's dismay. The princess was convinced that if he were practicing magic in secret that *someone* would know about it, or that his reputation would be in the pits as a result of it. However, they learned quite the opposite: that the master smith the boy was studying under, Aldebrande, now owned one of the finest weapon shops in all the volcano. Most people even said they'd seen red and orange Embers make day trips down to their shop just to get some of the exclusive goods the boy put out.

Positive reputation aside, Neros quickly learned two things: that no one knew for sure whether he could use magic, and no one knew his name. He sat next to Anthea at a table outside an eatery, both of them snacking on a curious Ember treat: various roasted meats stacked on a stick. It tasted smoky, though Neros wasn't sure what else he expected.

He slumped in his seat. "I suppose we shouldn't have expected this to be so easy, but it's still frustrating. I feel as though we've hit a wall."

Anthea sighed. "It may feel that way, Neros, but…maybe there's still something we can do."

"Such as?"

"So far, we've only snooped the clean way. You know, asking other people for information. But the Embers, intelligent and inventive as they are, seem to also be so gods-damned secretive that it seems the only way for us to do anything is to dig up the information ourselves."

"And how do you propose we do that?"

"Well, we haven't talked to that book-selling guy, right?" Anthea sat up, tossing her empty stick to the middle of the table. "Books hold a lot of the secrets that most are too afraid to speak aloud, right? We've always relied on books to teach us anything we wanted to know. It's how we got to know the prophecy we're entangled in so intimately; why wouldn't books teach us about this mystery blacksmith kid?"

Neros nodded. "I suppose that's a good point. Pontius?"

"I agree wholeheartedly! So well-spoken, Princess Anthea, it's no wonder you've been entrusted with the safety of all Arborians by the goddess Silva! What a level head in times of frustration!"

She waved her hand. "Stop with the shameless flattery. Let's go!"

Back at the shops, Neros noticed that the mystery blacksmith had disappeared. The book seller was still there, and Makana's station had a sign with foreign lettering scrawled across it, and a few numbers. Neros assumed it was a sort of "be back soon" message.

They turned to the book seller, Pontius resting on the prince's shoulder.

"I was wondering when you two outsiders would come talk to me," The old man said.

Anthea laughed. "Sorry, sir! We didn't mean to make it seem like we skipped over you."

"In fact, we're actually more interested in what you're selling," Neros supplied. "Do you happen to have any books on the legendary prophecy of old?"

"Ah, I heard you would be interested in the prophecy," He mused, bending over to rummage through his books, before pulling out a thick tome with a leather cover, intricately embossed with various insignia and more of that odd lettering he saw on Makana's shop sign. "This is all I have that has any mention of the prophecy, but it should be of great help to you. It's a history of the Eldur Ignis Volcano. I have many copies of this text, so it's no trouble for me to sell this one to you."

"How much?" Pontius piped up, reaching into his…pockets, Neros supposed, and pulling out a coin bag the prince didn't remember him having. He exchanged twelve copper-looking coins and in return, handed Neros the book for safekeeping. "This was a fantastic deal, your highness. You don't get texts like these from just anyone on any day."

"Thank you, sir, but I've actually got another question for you," Anthea piped up. "It's about the boy who works at the stall next to you."

"Oh, that boy? He's my apprentice."

Neros and Anthea blinked at each other. At once, they yelled: "*Your* apprentice*?*"

"No need to get all in a tizzy about it. I live over there; tonight, once you've had your fill of this book, come stay with me and we can talk about him a bit more." He extended his hand. "My name is Aldebrande. It's a pleasure."

All three of them shook his hand, thanking him for his time before finding a place along the wall to sit and pour over their new text. Neros brought out his Veturian-Endran history text, just for reference, and they dove in. It brought back memories of old times for Neros: the two of them would sit on his floor in the castle for hours and hours, switching from book to book and making diagrams and timelines to connect the dots of history together, from both of their kingdom's perspectives. Now, they had a third.

He watched curiously as Anthea pulled out a small scroll, unrolling it between them. His eyes lit up, recognizing it almost instantly as the very timeline they created when they were small.

"Anthy, I didn't know you'd kept this!"

"You never know when you'll need a little reminder of history!" She laughed. "I actually only have it with me by total chance. I nabbed it from my bookshelf before running out of Arboria. Everything was a blur then, but I just grabbed anything I could that may have held some significance."

Pontius peered over the document with a grin. "Well, this may be more important than you thought, Princess Anthea! Your documentation of Endra's history is startlingly accurate, despite a few gaps here and there. Though, what happened in those years has been kept from me, as well…perhaps this text from the Embers can reveal something new to us!"

Neros frowned, squinting at the book. "Hmm. Much of it seems to be written in their native language…I can spot a few bits scrawled in common on the side of the page, but they're purely annotations. Hm. Well, no matter! It isn't like we haven't cracked harder puzzles before."

Within a few hours, Neros and Anthea had decoded some key pieces of how the Embers recorded history. Perhaps most notable was the mention of a totally different god—Pyrrhus, the god of flame. The scrawled images of him made him out to be stockier and robust, as opposed to Isolde's and Silva's continually mentioned divine grace and elegance. He appeared to be a wrathful god, and the Embers separated from following his words barely a hundred years after the darkness was quelled. Curiously, there was a gap in recorded history from when the darkness began taking over and when it ended, just as their handwritten timeline dictated.

"Looks like no history was recorded for these hundred years or so," Anthea noted. "It's...sad. Do you think anyone was alive?"

"I–it's hard to say."

When the Embers stopped trusting in the word of Pyrrhus was when their advancements began to unfold at lightning pace. There was intense, detailed record of the first moving platform—an elevator—and the first stable bridges to cross the gaps of each layer of the volcano. Embers devised contraption after contraption; however, the details ceased whenever magic was involved. Anthea frowned.

"Well, this was obviously written by the red, orange, and yellow Embers. Ugh. I wish we could get some sort of recorded history from down below. You think Aldebrande has a connection?" She scrawled some notes on her timeline, drew a few lines, and began rolling it up.

"I can't say for sure, Anthy."

"But it's worth a shot to ask!" Pontius quipped, offering his most enthusiastic thumbs-up.

Anthea rose to begin walking to the place Aldebrande pointed them to—presumably, his home—but Neros was more interested in reading the rest of the volcano's history. He scooped up the book, picking up where Anthea had left off and continuing to read as they walked. Sequestered in pages deep in the book were folded slips of paper detailing large, intricately crafted reactionary machines that seemed to perform simple tasks, if Neros was reading the diagrams right. He absently wondered what they could be for. *Perhaps the Embers like this sort of intricacy in their daily lives...I suppose I can't blame them. It is a bit flashy, but it showcases a certain level of mental prowess in and of itself.* It seemed Makana wasn't lying earlier when she mentioned the discarding of a royal counsel—this text depicted a war from the years 800-850, where the royal King and Queen at the time had raised a prince who became corrupt with power. Images on the pages displayed a young looking blue Ember, with eyes orange and red like flames, angrily casting spells on people who ran from him in fear.

Neros closed the book, feeling a strange twist in his gut. *Perhaps…that's why these people hate magic. But I wonder, is there another side to this?*

He was pulled from his thoughts from Anthea's harsh rapping on Aldebrande's door. A lamp glowed dimly in the darkness, and it hit Neros how late it had become. He looked upward, and noted he *could* see the sky from down here, and it was rather beautiful. The stars glimmered, and the dark blue sky provided contrast against the persistent glow of the volcano's inside. Dried up or not, the whole layer seemed to emanate a yellow glow.

The door creaked open, and standing in the doorway was a slightly disheveled, but overall miffed-looking boy, with yellow-orange flaming hair tied back in a ponytail. A small set of glasses hung from his shirt collar, and he peered at them curiously before angry recognition flashed across his face.

It was the blacksmith from earlier.

Chapter 7
Hero of Flames

*N*eros blinked. Anthea spoke first.

"You! You're Aldebrande's apprentice! You *live* with him?!" Anthea said, running her hands through her hair and laughing. "Amazing! This is the *best* possible outcome."

"What are *you* doing here?" The boy frowned.

"Leof! Please, let my guests inside."

The blacksmith boy—Leof—pursed his lips, before stepping out of the doorway. "Master Aldebrande is in the main book room. Straight ahead."

Neros offered a smile as he passed, but Leof kept his gaze trained on the floor. Once Anthea and Neros were inside, the Ember closed the door and walked down the hall, turning the corner into what Neros could only assume were his own private quarters.

Aldebrande's home was small. Had Leof not answered the door, Neros would be surprised to know that the old man could afford to have *and* house an apprentice. Swords and daggers of all kinds lined the walls—rapiers, standard one-handed and two-handed blades, all with delicately carved hilts and special markings on each. There were shields, too, and gauntlets—Neros looked at his own glove. *I wonder if a gauntlet would better suit me for battle...* He shook his head. That wasn't why they were here.

The main book room was circular, and the walls were lined with books of all shapes, sizes, and colors—Neros couldn't break his eyes away from it. To him, it was a treasure trove of knowledge yet to be learned. The prince knew he could spend days, or even weeks, exploring and absorbing everything he could. Many of the book titles weren't in the common tongue, but the few that were boasted topics of great interest to Neros, like functions of kinetic contraptions, blacksmithing, and fine crafting techniques. Aldebrande sat in an old stone chair with cracked armrests. He smiled as soon as he saw Neros and Anthea.

"I'm glad you've come. Did you enjoy reading up on the Eldur Ignis Volcano's history as the upper-layer Embers recall it?"

"It was interesting, to say the least," Neros began, fiddling absently with his glove. "Though, it doesn't seem to be the full story."

"There are other books, but sadly, they are below my reach." Aldebrande shook his head. "Most of us upper Embers don't trifle with the mages who live deeper in the depths. A pity we can't seem to reach a compromise."

"Wow, there are Embers up here who *want* to work with the magic wielders?" Anthea chimed in. "That's news to me."

"There are few who are tolerant," Aldebrande explained. "I happen to be one. But let's put that conversation aside, for a moment; you came because you are curious about him, aren't you?" He gestured to the hall that Leof had disappeared down.

"Yes," Neros answered. "Anthea, Pontius and I are on a quest of sorts. We…have reason to believe the legendary prophecy from hundreds of years ago…that it is repeating, somehow. There have been strange curses inflicting other parts of Endra—both Anthea's home and my own have been struck by…unspeakable circumstances, not unlike the struggle that has fallen upon the Embers here."

"Ah, and the prophecy speaks of three heroes, does it not?"

"It does. Pontius, our guide, he said he felt a…special energy emanating from Leof, your apprentice. But…I don't think he believes us."

"Well, he has very little reason to, your highness," Aldebrande folded his hands together. "He has had some struggle growing up."

Neros' brows drew together. "Some struggle…? The look on your face…how long has Leof been under your wing?"

Aldebrande chuckled. "You can sense that much, can you? You're a perceptive boy. Leof has been my *apprentice* for three years, but he's lived with me for ten overall. Since he was around six, perhaps seven."

Their silence urged the mentor to continue. He sighed. "Leof is a unique boy. His parents…I believe they may have been orange Embers, living one layer above this. I don't know much about them, but I do know they adopted the same mentality as many of those who live up here: a harbored hatred of magic.

You see, many years ago, there were scuffles among the upper echelons—mind you, this was back when we still had a royal house and counsel—of whether or not magic was more dangerous than the smithing of weapons and armor that we had taken to like so much. Some thought magic was more pure, more akin to what the great god Pyrrhus wanted; others believed that separation was the only way to continue to innovate. You've read this in the history text, I'm sure.

The war depicted in the text was grueling, though short compared to our life spans. I was around 50 years old at the start of it—back in the year 800 or so—and it started with a prince who looked not unlike yourself, your highness. Unnaturally tall, for an Ember, and skilled in the art of magic. He was an anomaly, as we call them—a red Ember born from the blue King and his white Queen. He urged the people to be more agreeable to the intricate flame magic he would use, and tried to boast its benefits to us. No one took to his words, and he and his parents became angry. The rest of the details are…murky, at best, but under such duress, the prince became inflamed with power and frustration. He began using his magic to terrorize instead of aid, and many Embers cowered in fear while those who could forge, forged and fought back."

"Thats…awful. What happened next?" Neros asked.

"Eventually, he was subdued. It took many years to develop a new system of leadership, but what we have now—a board of five Embers, one from each layer—seems to be effective.

Since that war settled, blue and white Embers had taken to living in the bottom of the volcano, where the lava burns hottest. We don't interact much anymore, but there is still much tension between us."

"That's terrible that such a war happened, right under the noses of the rest of the world."

"That is true, Princess Anthea, but the threat of civil war is not eradicated. We are functioning, but we are all barely tolerant of each other.

Time has allowed for each side of this scuffle to breed extremists, those who squirrel away and prepare for when the gauntlet must be thrown again. But this is only the backstory; now, then, I'm sure you're curious about how dear Leof folds into all of this."

Neros and Anthea nodded. Aldebrande's expression grew sad.

"As I said, I met Leof around ten years ago, though 'met' is a difficult word to use. More accurately, you could say that I...found him. I was travelling up to the orange layer for some supplies: at the time, I ran a small business in making daggers and blades. I was known to do good work, but there was not a high demand for it, as the only ones who would buy my merchandise were wandering travelers, or merchants on the upper layers who serviced the occasional Arborian or others.

I digress. On my way to the store where I normally bought my tools, I came across an alleyway and a flicker of light; a young boy, facing away from me, snapping to produce the smallest sparks of magic as practice. I could tell he didn't want to draw attention to himself, but he was alone. His clothes were torn and tattered, and he looked to be about six or seven."

Neros felt a lump rise in his throat. "And his parents...?"

"Not in sight. When I spoke to the boy, he curled away from me, as though to defend himself. After some careful coaxing, he told me his name was Leof, and that his parents had thrown him out, though he wouldn't tell me how long it had been. Leof told me they called him an abomination for using magic, wanting to hone his skills. I will never forget the earnest look on his face when he told me he didn't understand why his parents were so mad.

I never met them, and I do not wish to. I took him down here, gave him a home, clean clothes, and a safe haven to practice whatever he desired. If he's continued to use magic, he keeps it secret from me. As he grew older, he learned very quickly of the tension."

"When you said he experienced some struggle, you really weren't kidding," Anthea mused, absentmindedly re-braiding her hair. She looked plainly guilty.

"For a long time, he would hardly interact with me. It was only about four years ago when he began asking me to teach him all that I knew. Of course, it took some deliberation, but I did begin teaching him. Everything that hangs on these walls was made by his hands alone. He seemed to like the work, so I continued to teach him, and in three years, he has grown to be a fine blacksmith."

Neros was amazed. There had to have been *dozens* of blades and armor hanging proudly on the walls, and Leof had made all of them, in only three years' time? It made Neros question nearly all of his royal training. Suddenly, he wished he had been taught a few more practical hands-on skills like this, instead of combat and diplomacy.

A deep, annoyed voice came sharp from the doorway. "Are you *through* telling these strangers my entire life story, master Aldebrande?"

"Leof, dear boy—"

"Don't. You've told them more than they could have ever wanted to know." He glared at Neros and Anthea, arms crossed tightly over his chest. "What do you two *seek?* I thought you were master Aldebrande's guests, perhaps to simply stay the night before continuing on your *adventure,* but instead it seems you've come to pry in affairs that you've got no business learning about."

"Leof, these two have traveled a long way in search of a hero of prophecy."

"And I am no hero," He said. Now that his face was in full view to Neros, he noticed that Leof had a small, sharp nose and strikingly angular eyes. The flames of his hair whipped and cracked, though no wind was around to blow it. If he looked closely enough, he could see the inside of Leof's cracks slowly moving, as though there was lava flowing beneath his skin. "As I have told them before. There is no prophetic hero on this layer of the volcano. They'll have to search deeper."

"But you're special!" Anthea stood suddenly, palms splayed open to him. He looked perturbed by her point. "You can do magic, can't you?"

Fear flashed across Leof's face—so brief Neros would have missed it if he blinked—before settling into a frown. He shook his head. "I don't know what you're talking about."

Aldebrande said you made sparks when you were little!"

"It was merely an illusion," He shot back, unfolding his arms to run a hand through his hair. "Listen. I am not *special.* I am not a *hero.* To you, I am barely more than a stranger. If master Aldebrande has welcomed you here to rest, then rest. I want no part of your adventure. Just leave me alone." He turned to leave, then turned back to Aldebrande. "Please do not tell them anything more about me, master. They've come too far to be misguided."

He turned on his heel and walked down the hall. The house had no doors, but if it did, Neros would sure he would hear it slam. Aldebrande stood and walked to the two, placing hands on either of their shoulders—well, their mid-backs, really, since he was too short to comfortably reach much further.

"That boy is a prodigy beyond my wildest dreams," He whispered. "I believe your plight, and your friend Pontius. Leof is one of a kind, and I always had a feeling that something great was in store for him. I will do my best to coax him into joining you. For now, I am sure you two have had a long day. Allow me to show you to the guest room."

❄

"That is a *terrible* idea!" Neros whispered harshly.

"You're just afraid, Neros. You've always been too afraid, but now, you have to swallow that fear and act!" Anthea shot back, pointing to the small makeshift map she'd drawn on parchment paper. "Aldebrande said if he practiced magic, he'd keep it secret, right? So we just have to expose him, and then he won't be able to turn us down."

"It doesn't seem to me like he's going to enjoy being exposed."

"Well, he doesn't take to typical methods of persuasion, does he? So this is all we've got." She rolled up the parchment and stuck it in her bag, rising to her feet and extending a hand to Neros. "Let's go."

He hesitated, then stood, politely refusing her hand. "I can't. I don't want to invade his privacy."

Anthea rolled her eyes, heading for the door. "Yeah, yeah, I know you're too proud to admit you're really curious, too."

She grabbed his hand, and together, they ventured down the hall—it was a small house, so the walk was short, but both the prince and princess tried to remain light on their feet. As they neared the door to Leof's room, Neros felt increasingly nervous. He had a terrible feeling about this. If he really *was* a mage, who could tell how powerful he was? What if he flew into a rage like the prince from two hundred years ago? Neros had left Vatnis—and Pontius sleeping soundly inside it—in the other room, and Anthea was not in an advantageous position herself. Could they go hand-to-hand against some-

one that powerful? Sure, it would be two against one, but Neros had plenty of doubts.

Anthea stopped at the doorway, crouching down and peeking around the corner; Neros tiptoed behind her. "Anthy, we *really* shouldn't be here—"

"Shh!" She hissed, peering into the room with who they assumed was their last prophetic hero.

Neros rolled his eyes, leaning over her to get a better look.

It was cluttered, but organized. Various in-progress projects were lined up on a long desk next to what looked like instructions. Along the walls hung finished swords and blades, but also tools that Neros assumed were used to make the blades: hammers, anvils, and a few carving tools. He had a bookshelf, and it was packed full to the point that some books were shoved sideways on top of the others. There was a shelf above the workbench that held mason jars of colorful salts, and a wooden box of coal. *At least it looks like he got used to living here,* Neros noted. If he hadn't, the prince imagined his room would be more barren.

Leof himself stood in the corner of the room at one of the workbenches, facing away from the door. He took a few deep breaths, as if to focus himself. He stole glances left and right, and Neros hid behind the wall to conceal himself, pulling Anthea as well. They couldn't risk being seen, but Neros' heart still hammered in his chest as he watched Leof's eyes linger in the doorway for an extra second. Then, he turned his attention back to the sword in his hand.

"Verschinge in Flammen," Leof whispered, waving his hand across the blade of the sword, stopping at the hilt. It glowed a bright orange, and flame transferred itself from Leof's palm to the hilt, spreading to the blade's tip. The magic energy fused with the metal of the blade, and the carvings began to emit a bright orange light. The Ember smiled, a barely noticeable change in his features—

"So you *can* use magic!" Anthea shouted, rising to her feet and tumbling into the room. Neros reached after her, but he was too late.

Leof gasped, whirling around and pointing the blade toward the princess. He frowned. "You?! I thought I told you to leave me alone!"

Anthea waved her hand. "But, you see, dear Leof—"

"Do *not* call me that," He growled, inching closer with the sword.

Neros stood and brushed himself off. "We-we're unarmed, Leof, please! We just want to speak with you for a minute."

Now the blade was pointed at him. "I told you I want nothing to do with you!"

The prince outstretched his arms in surrender. "Please, listen. All I ask is for one minute, just *one* minute of your time to hear us out. Then you can shove us away, and tell us to go to the bottom layers of the volcano to continue searching, and we'll listen. I promise, if you refuse us again, we will find someone else and leave you alone for the rest of your life. You'll never have to see us again. But all I ask is that you give us one minute to talk."

He spared a glance at Anthea, who gave him an impressed nod in return, as if to say *I can't get through to this guy, so I'm okay if you take the wheel.* Neros looked to Leof, hopeful.

The Ember squinted, looking between them. Then, he lowered his sword, and Neros sighed in relief. Leof turned away to place it back on his workbench. "Fine. One minute."

"Thank you," Neros said. *Now, where to begin…?* "You believe in the prophecy, don't you?"

Leof turned back to face him, arms crossed. He nodded.

"Good, that saves a bit of explaining. We believe that the prophecy has begun its second cycle—that it has been put into motion again. My family at home—Vetur, up on the mountain in the northeast—they've been struck with a terrible curse that has turned them into ice sculptures. I—" He swallowed thickly around a lump in his throat. "I've been afflicted as well. I had been gifted in my youth with the power to wield ice magic, but now, it hurts just to create small crystals.

And Anthea—she has been my best friend since we were small—she hails from Arboria, just east of Vetur. There, a curse has been cast upon all the Arborians. The great, ancient tree they all live in and worship has turned against them, its roots spiraling out of the ground and rendering the entire population immobile. Even here—the lava has run dry. On our way over, we ran into purple-smoking skeletal figures the likes of which we've never seen. Endra is in danger. We sought the Oracle in Paralia, fought monsters to see him, and he told us we needed another hero. Our guide, Pontius—who trained under the Oracle—told us that was *you.* You know how to forge weapons, you can wield them, and you know how to use magic. You're not like the other blacksmiths, and you're not like the other mages. Isn't that right?"

Leof sighed, but his expression softened a bit. "Suppose it is. Where would you have me go?"

"With us. We're searching for a way to break the curses inflicting us and our people, and to do it, we need a full trio to emulate the prophecy's first coming."

The Ember didn't look convinced, and Neros felt his heart sink. Leof sat down, and gestured for Neros and Anthea to do the same. They each sat on his bed.

"You're trusting in a guide sent to you from the Oracle that *I'm* the one you're looking for? What if his instinct is faulty? Or if the Oracle is falsifying information to ensure you fail?"

Neros tugged his glove back over his arm. "We trust them."

"The Oracle was locked away in Paralia Coves many years ago," Anthea cut in. "He has no reason to lie to us. Neros and I are good at reading people, and we can tell if someone has something tricky up their sleeve for us. We didn't make this trip completely unaware of the world around us— we've been studying it for our whole lives."

"Forgive me for being hesitant to believe I'm some special instrument of prophecy," he quipped.

"I didn't believe I was a hero, either," Neros said. "Up until a few short days ago, I thought I was a prince who could help his people with tending to their shops and sheep, who happened to be gifted with ice magic that, for the most part, I only used for fanciful festival displays."

Leof closed his eyes and breathed a long sigh. "You have had far more than a minute's time."

"And I am truly sorry for taking up so much more than asked. Can you give us an answer? Will you join us on our adventure?"

Moments passed, and to Neros, it felt like hours. He studied Leof's face carefully, looking for a sign that might mean success. If the prince didn't know any better, though, he would say that the Ember looked unbelievably nervous.

"May I sleep on it?"

That's not a no. "Sure. We'll prepare to head out in the morning, regardless."

"Thank you. Now, if you could, please leave me alone for the night."

"Not a problem. Thank you for listening to us."

Leof waved them away, and Neros and Anthea retreated to their guest quarters.

The princess stifled a yawn. "Good job, Neros. I think you really got through to him."

"I can't know for sure until tomorrow. I just hope he's sympathetic to our plight."

"After showing off your arm? I'd have to say he has a hole where his heart should be if he doesn't agree to come along after seeing *that*."

Neros' eyebrows drew together. "I–I didn't mean it as a manipulative maneuver, Anthea!"

The princess threw her head back and laughed. "Of course you didn't. You're too honest for your own good, you know that? Get some sleep."

"Yeah, you...you, too."

Predictably, Neros did not sleep well that night. The morning light did not awaken him, because it never showed—being many feet deep in a volcano would do that, Neros supposed, but he also could not be entirely sure that it was even daytime. He assumed it was, because Anthea was awake, and her sense of time and day versus night was far more keen than his.

Neros rubbed at his eyes, trying to push the tiredness away. He was less plagued by nightmares as much as he was uncomfortable—nothing against the Embers, but their idea of bedding wasn't exactly cushy. He'd removed his tailcoat to use as a makeshift blanket, and it now rested in a rumple on the floor.

"Good morning," Anthea said. She was in the middle of braiding her hair top-to-bottom, something Neros hadn't seen her do in quite some time. It was impressive how she managed to expertly twist the wiry vines and leaves into one large, neat-looking braid. "What a bed, right?"

He chuckled. "You could call it that," He rose, gathering his tailcoat and re-dressing. "Do you think Leof will have an answer for us today?"

"I hope so. We can't really afford to dilly-dally any longer."

From inside Neros' staff, Pontius stirred. The staff glowed bright blue, and then he emerged from it. He had a nightcap and gown on, which he replaced with his normal attire by twirling in place, water evaporating and re-forming over his body. "That's true, Princess Anthea! And I have a bad feeling about what may be in store for us if he refuses you."

Neros quirked a brow. "There would be...consequences?"

"Terribly adverse consequences! Horrible consequences! *Life-threatening* consequences, Prince Neros! If you are unable to emulate the prophecy's first coming by securing the Prophetic Hero of Fire, you will be unable to combine your powers and defeat the growing darkness plaguing Endra!"

Anthea frowned. "Can't we just...pick someone else?"

"Of course not!" Pontius wailed. "Pegaios is the one who selects the chosen heroes, and if he chose Leof, then Leof is the one you need!"

The more the prince heard about the prophecy, the more serious it became. On one hand, he was counting on Leof saying yes regardless; otherwise, Neros was fully prepared to beg. On the other, he would have at least liked to be secured by a contingency plan if Leof happened to refuse.

His gut twisted. He really, *really* hoped Leof said yes.

When they were both ready, they made their way down the hall to find Aldebrande and Leof. Neros stole a glance inside Leof's room as they passed—not to feel too hopeful, but it looked emptier than before. As they neared the doorway to the main room, Anthea stopped, holding her arm out to stop Neros from continuing.

"Anthy? What are—"

"Shh. They're talking."

Aldebrande's voice carried softly down the hall. "Are you certain about your decision?"

"I am." Leof's voice seemed to betray him.

"Leof, what has you so hesitant?"

"Plenty." Neros hoped he would elaborate, but it was almost as though he knew they were listening.

"Such as?" Aldebrande urged.

"It doesn't matter. I don't think they're going to give me much of a choice, regardless."

A soft chuckle. Then, before Aldebrande could speak again, Anthea shot down the hall. "You're coming with us?!"

Both Embers jumped, Aldebrande settling into a smile, and Leof, annoyance. "If you keep *spying on me* and *eavesdropping*, perhaps I'll refrain."

"You don't mean that at all. You've made up your mind, and now you're coming with us! Neros, he's coming with us! Hooray!" Neros emerged from the doorway with a weak smile as Anthea tackled Leof in a hug. The young Ember groaned, immediately trying to wiggle out of her grip.

"Unhand me *at once!*"

"Never! Now that I know you're coming with us, I won't let you go!"

Try as he might, the prince couldn't help smiling. "Doesn't he need to gather his belongings, Anthy?"

Bubble burst, she released him, allowing the Ember to propel himself three feet away from her. He brushed himself off before going down the hall, emerging seconds later with a well-packed backpack and a dark brown hooded cloak over his shoulders. It looked frayed at the edges, and Neros wondered if it was Leof's, or a gift from Aldebrande.

Leof looked between the prince and princess. "After careful consideration, I've decided I have nothing to lose by joining you. Master Aldebrande will be fine on his own." He paused. "Your highnesses, I will join you on your journey to save the citizens of Endra."

Neros smiled, the warmth of relief spreading through his chest. "We're happy to have you, Leof."

Back in the main body of the volcano, farther away from Aldebrande's house, Pontius rose from Neros' side. He looked different than normal: his eyes glowed a faint, bright yellow. When he spoke, his voice was deep and wise. "Heroes of the prophecy. I am glad to see you all together."

"Pontius…?" Neros queried, glancing nervously at Anthea and Leof.

"While I may appear as Pontius, it is I, Pegaios. I am merely utilizing Pontius' body as a vessel to portray this message to you. For the first time in many years, I have received visions of your path. However, my time is short, and so I will be brief. The hero of fire has agreed to join you, and this is a prospect of great fortune. Before you continue your journey, you must venture to the bottom of this volcano. There exists a trial the young Leof must pass, to gain access to a power required to battle against the turmoil ahead.

Proceed carefully. Take this time to build your trust."

After Pegaios finished, Pontius closed his eyes, quivered a little, and re-opened them. They were his typical, watery blue; he had returned to normal. "Wow, what a message! A secret power to be gained?! Right away, you're causing such excitement, Leof! This is incredible! Let's get down there immediately!"

Leof frowned. "I can't go down there so easily. What does this Oracle hope for me to gain from this, aside from unwanted harassment?"

"We'll be right here with you," Anthea said, wrapping an arm around him; again, he tried to tug himself free, but she was stronger. "So no worries! We'll kick some mage-Ember ass if they even dare to mess with you."

"I think the power Pegaios mentioned may not just be for you, but for all of us," Neros added. "Though he was rather cryptic in his delivery. Regardless, don't you think this is a good opportunity to enhance your abilities? You're a self-taught mage, are you not?"

Leof looked uncomfortable. "And if I am?"

"Th-there's nothing wrong with that!" Neros backpedaled. "Many mages are self-taught in some regard. But if the blue and white Embers know something special, I think you should try to learn from them."

The Ember hesitated, then sighed. Neros found his expressions difficult to read—he could only guess what Leof was thinking about any of this. Then, the boy tugged the hood out and over his head, so his hair was concealed. His face was also partly obscured.

"That's an argument I cannot disagree with. I'll show you the way down."

Chapter 8
The Trial of Mages

$\mathcal{L}$eof's hands ran over the keys of the elevator expertly; he flipped the color-coded palette over to reveal blue and white buttons; he pressed the blue one, knocked the lever back, wound up some cogs, and the elevator jumped into motion.

"How did you know to do that?" Neros asked.

"It's not as though we are so discriminated that we are not allowed to see the bottom of the volcano," Leof explained. "But it is complicated. Aldebrande has gone, once or twice, but he needed prior approval and a selected guide." He turned to face them both fully, with an intense look in his eyes. "This cloak is not full protection. The cracks on my face give away that I am a yellow Ember. Do not reveal this information to *anyone* down there. Do you understand?"

Neros and Anthea nodded. Leof lowered his gaze, covering his face almost completely. From Neros' height, he could barely tell there were even cracks in Leof's skin—all the better, he supposed.

As the elevator descended, they passed through a thick, white fog, on the other side of which laid a stunning array of blue- and purple-hued stones fixed to the walls. The shops and stalls down here were set up the same way as the other layers, but the selection was immediately more recognizable to Neros: books, potions, small orbs with swirling flames inside of many colors, staffs, and much, much more. Hanging lanterns emitted a blue glow, and every Ember that roamed had either blue or white flaming hair. It was stunning.

There were more than simple bridges connecting the gaps across the outer rim, as well—these Embers seemed to devise small floating platforms that moved to different commands. The prince had a sudden, intense curiosity. *How much magic energy does that use up, and whose magic powers those structures? Or, perhaps the Embers devised a way to channel energy through another object, allowing these platforms to move freely with no stress to the mage who created them?*

"There you go with that love-struck look again. Yeesh, Neros, what are we going to *do* with you?" Anthea teased, ruffling his hair.

He laughed. "Sorry, sorry. I'm amazed by the technology down here! Those platforms, Anthea, how do you think they were built? Oh, perhaps we'll have time to stop and talk to a few Embers down here..."

"We're going to *have* to talk to a few of them to find out where these mysterious trials are," Leof mused.

The elevator clanked into place, and the doors opened, allowing the group to exit. Neros noted that, while it did feel warmer down here, there was still no imminent danger of burning alive. He figured it had everything to do with the lava not being active, and not much to do with his magical inclinations.

While he was tempted to wander, Leof seemed to have an idea of where to go. "I only have a vague description of their shop, but I believe I know someone we can speak with here. Follow me."

If Neros thought that he and Anthea were subject to gawking in the upper layers, down here it increased tenfold. The blue and white Embers dressed in longer, draping robes and cloaks, perfect for concealing books and staffs, but not their stares. The prince tried his best to look friendly, but he could only hold his will together through so many piercing eyes.

One figure stepped in front of them, his long flames glowing a deep indigo blue, assaulting the group with his gaze. Purple eyes brighter than the sun struck Neros' very soul. He shuddered.

"Who are you three? What are you doing down here?"

"Terribly sorry for storming in," Anthea bowed her head, extending a hand as she straightened. "My name is Princess Anthea, and these two are my traveling partners, Neros and Le—uuuh, Mako. His name is Mako. He's horribly disfigured, which is why we hide him under the cloak."

Neros saw the faint glow of Leof's hair beneath his hood, but he took a deep breath, and it dimmed.

The Ember peered at them, squinting. Carefully, he took Anthea's hand. "We have never seen an Arborian here, or...one from Vetur. You two have travelled far. And your friend, Mako? From where does he hail?"

"Him?! Oh, he's from...somewhere around here. We just met him. Found him, actually, the poor dear. He was lost. If you don't mind, we'd like to be on our way, now. I'm sure his family is just burning up waiting for him to return home."

The prince nearly slapped his forehead at Anthea's fumbling. *Is it something with Embers? Why is she so suddenly flustered?* It was much unlike the princess to act so strangely; then again, she wasn't exactly trying to *lie* to whoever this Ember was. Just stretch the truth to get by. Neros wondered if her nervousness was an act after all.

The Ember folded his arms, hands disappearing into each sleeve of his robe. "Intriguing story, travelers. Kind of you to bring this young boy home."

Neros breathed a sigh of relief as the strange figure allowed them to pass. He jogged to catch up to Anthea's long strides, leaning close to her ear. "How much of that was an act?"

Anthea's laugh came out a faint, lilting chuckle. "Not as much as I'd like. That guy really caught me off guard, coming out of nowhere like that. Sorry about faking a random backstory for you, 'Mako.' It was all I could think of."

"Anything is better than the truth," Leof said.

They continued, Leof taking the lead. Eventually, he approached a particular Ember outside of a potion shop. Neros took a good look at him; his hair was longer than most other Embers they'd seen, with blue bangs that flared around his eyes while the rest of his hair remained in an almost impressively stable bowl shape. He had one large crack running down his left arm, and it reminded Neros of lightning; it revealed an ever-shifting blue lava substance like the other Embers had. His eyes matched his hair, a bright blue emphasized by the same yellow sclera Neros had started to get used to. The clothes he wore were standard fare for the upper layer, from what Neros could recall: a plain tunic and pants with a sash around the middle. Neros felt a shudder run down his spine. He *swore* he had seen this Ember somewhere before.

His eyes widened when he got a good look at Neros. "You are the spitting image of the Dark Red Prince—except, you're blue."

"I–uh–" Neros stammered, suddenly feeling a bit dizzy. "I am?"

"Yes, you are blue. Are you unaware of this fact?"

"No, no, that's not what I meant," He ran a hand through his hair, displacing his crown. "I look…like the Dark Red Prince?"

"Yes, that is what I said."

"From the war?"

"*War?* Who told you of a *war?* Was it my brother? He spouts nothing but lies. There was a scuffle. An argument, really. Hardly anything. The Dark Red Prince was merely caught in the middle of it all."

"Then why is he called the *Dark* Red Prince?" Leof countered.

"Because his flames and cracks burned dark red. It was an unnatural color, but that is what happens when you are born a color so far away from your parents' typical range."

"Typical range…?" Neros asked.

"Gods above, you've come down all this way, and you seem to know *nothing* of us Embers. It's simple genetics, your blueness, it's not that hard to understand. If you have a red Ember and a red Ember and they bear child, the child will be red or orange. If there is an orange Ember parent, the range extends to red, orange, or yellow. Blue Embers can birth yellow, blue, or white. Do you understand the pattern?"

The prince nodded. "Right, I understand, but I don't follow you on the war—or as you say, lack thereof. I have a history text that describes—"

The blue Ember held up his hand. "No, you have an *upper layer* Ember history text. There are multiple. Hold a moment." The boy disappeared into his home, re-emerging with two texts. He handed them to Neros. "Consider these a gift, *doppelganger.* A lower level history text, and a record of Ember history as recorded by someone who left it in a chest in the desert. Curious."

Neros accepted the books, tucking them away in his satchel. "Thank you. I appreciate it, but the history lesson isn't exactly why we came here. Leof…?"

"Right. You're Ignatius, correct?"

The blue Ember raised both brows as his gaze shifted to Leof. "Oh? And however do you know my name? Surely my brother didn't tell you. He speaks in nothing but *lies.*"

Leof looked up, revealing his face to Ignatius. "I am Aldebrande's apprentice. He told me to seek you out if I ever found myself here."

Ignatius' shock faded into a smile. "Ah, of course. Come in, before anyone else sees you."

❄

"The trials you seek are the ones called the Trial by Fire."

Anthea barked a laugh. "*Trial by Fire?* No way, that sounds like something out of a fairytale."

"Believe it or not, Princess Anthea, it is the truth. The SMITH council's blue and white Embers devised it as a way of highly advanced training for mages. It takes place in the arena on the volcano's floor, and is nothing to sneeze at. Leof, has Aldebrande trained you in magic at all? I was under the impression he didn't know how."

"He...doesn't know any magic, no. I have practiced in secret, but I'm self-taught." His brows furrowed. "Why did that Oracle want me to do this...?" He murmured.

"Troubling. Well, I could teach you a bit. I am self-taught as well, but I at least have tomes and other mages to field all of my queries."

Leof hesitated. "Do you have a crash-course available? I don't think we have much time."

"Hmm," Ignatius stood, pacing to examine the bookshelf behind him. He thumbed through a few of the titles, then brought down three thin books. "These should be good beginner texts to read. They're about flow and control. Read them, then come find me in my workshop."

"Workshop?" Neros asked. "But I thought mage Embers didn't do enough hands-on crafting to warrant that."

"Ha! And who told you that? My brother? I tell you, he's a liar. He's filled your head with myths. Come, leave Leof to his reading. I'll show you."

Neros and Anthea followed Ignatius down a small hallway that opened into a circular room, one half which held three furnaces, a workbench, and a shelf full of vases and translucent orbs. Tools were strewn about in canisters, as well as blocks of vivid colors. On the other half of the room, there were smaller projects that looked like jewelry. What looked to be his current project rested in the center of the desk—a dark, black chain with various pearlescent orbs affixed to prongs throughout. A large, diamond-shaped gem rested at the bottom center, and it appeared yet to be molded in.

"Wow, what are all these furnaces for?" Anthea asked, peering into them individually.

"The vases and magic orbs you see on the shelf were all crafted using those three furnaces." Pride swelled in his voice, and it looked like he couldn't stop himself from smiling. "I'm sure it will take Leof some time to get through those books I gave him. Shall I show you how it's done?"

Neros' eyes lit up. "Of course!"

Ignatius looked pleased with himself, then rummaged through his tools before pulling out a long metal pipe. "This first furnace here contains raw materials that have been melted down into *glass*. I stick this pipe in to gather some of it on the tip of my pipe, here," He demonstrated as he spoke, spinning the stick slowly as molten-hot glass formed at the tip of the pipe, collecting like honey. "Then, we have to roll it to even out the glass and create a good basic shape to make into a bubble. I use this to do it."

Neros was mesmerized by the process. Ignatius turned and carefully rolled the glass ball over a marble table through glittering reddish dust, slowly building his desired shape. Then, he blew into the opposite end of the pipe, and Anthea gasped as the shape began to expand. Ignatius repeated this process, adding more layers to the piece before looking satisfied.

"Once the base is built and the size is right, I can create the base," He transferred the glass fixture onto a different, smaller pipe, and he took a medium-sized steel paddle and flattened the bottom. "This is the most crucial part. You can re-warm the glass from here, but I must work quickly to get all the details pulled out."

The prince admired how nimble Ignatius was in his movements. He took large pliers and pulled out a handle from the bottom, fastening it to the top. With smaller pliers, he began pulling string-like parts out, quickly fusing them to each other before bending it to wrap around the handle. To Neros, they looked like small snowflakes. Ignatius continued this process until he reached the base, where he pulled larger chunks and flattened them, shaping them to look like leaves. He folded them elegantly along the base, re-heating his glass when needed by sticking it back into the second furnace for a bit. All the while, his hands glowed faintly with warmth. When he was satisfied—

which was easy to tell, unlike other Ember they'd met—he moved it to the third furnace.

"The third furnace is called the *lehr,* and it slowly cools the glass. It needs to be in there, otherwise the glass will crack from thermal stress. This piece will take around a day or so to fully cool."

Anthea applauded him. "That. Was. *Amazing!* How are the furnaces able to stay so hot when all the lava has dried up?"

"Excellent observation. Usually, yes, the volcano's ever-flowing lava would keep the furnaces warm. However, now, I devised a way to use my own magic to heat them."

Neros' brow furrowed. "Doesn't that drain you?"

He shrugged. "Not as much as you would think. The contraptions outside were devised to hold the moving platforms up as they travel back and forth across the gap. I simply...borrowed a few of the techniques for my own purposes. I've filled discs with my own magic and placed them in slots beneath each furnace. As my magic continues to burn, rejuvenated by the alloys in the discs, the furnaces stay hot at very little cost to me. Brilliant, really; a perfect center between relying solely on the mechanics and solely relying on magic."

Just then, there was a light knock coming from the doorway.

"I think I'm ready," Leof said.

❄

"Are you certain it was a wise idea to skip all the way to the tournament, young Leof?" Pontius worried, fretting and flying around Leof like a nurse tending to his patient.

Leof tried to swat the water spirit away like an insect. "I'll be fine."

"You may think so, but you don't know what you're up against! None of us do!"

"I've got a few ideas," Leof said. "I'll be fine."

Neros worried at his bottom lip. He wanted to ease Pontius' nerves, but to be honest, they had no proof that Leof knew how to fight at all, with or without magic. Sure, he could *make* swords, but did that really matter at a time like this?

Ignatius led them down a labyrinth-like set of hallways and doors on the bottom floor of the volcano. This layer had no gaps, like the previous ones, though Neros could see the pits where the lava had dried into rock. Leof was fully cloaked again, but still they earned curious stares from outsiders. Eventually, they approached a rather tall Ember next to an intricately-carved stone doorway.

"I have an apprentice who seeks the power Hélder has." Ignatius said, ushering Leof forward.

"Name?"

"Leof," The blacksmith replied.

The guard sneered. "Show your face."

After a nod of approval from Ignatius, Leof slowly removed his hood. At once, the guard pointed his sword at Leof's neck. Leof didn't flinch.

"A *yellow* Ember?!"

"He has skill."

The guard squinted at Ignatius, who held his glare steadily. *Ignatius barely trained with Leof for an hour. Can he really tell his skill level from a few sparring matches?* Then, the guard lowered his sword, waving his hand over the door. It lit up in an array of blue and purple lights, outlining the text at the edges before glowing brightly at the center. Something clunked into place, and the door opened with a groan. Ignatius shuffled inside, grabbing Leof's wrist and taking him along. Neros and Anthea awkwardly followed behind.

Inside the doorway was a massive, empty arena, and for a moment the prince wondered how they fit something so large at the bottom of the volcano. Glancing up, he noticed trickles of daylight filtering through a white haze. *Is this the very bottom center of the volcano?* He examined the floor at his feet, noting that as they walked, some of the ground was soft. *Could it be...these were floating platforms?*

"You two should probably go up there," Ignatius pointed to a set of thin stairs leading to a set of seats that hung above the arena. "I'll join you in a moment."

"Wait, we can't fight with him?" Anthea asked.

Ignatius barked a laugh, leading Leof to the center of the arena. "No Ember who has ever fought in this trial has been allowed to do it with *friends*."

Neros should have expected as much, from something like a trial to test one's skill, but still, he worried for Leof. Their new companion had been thrust into this new role of heroism, and barely a full day had passed and he was already being put on trial to test his abilities—abilities that were previously a secret. *Will he be alright?*

As he ascended the stairs, he could only hope.

"What else do you think they use this arena for?" Anthea asked, shuffling into a seat near the edge of the overhang.

Neros sat next to her. "I can't be sure. I believe I saw a book on kinetic contraptions earlier, and didn't we see a few Embers building them as we looked around? Maybe they're displayed here."

The princess hummed. "I don't know, this place seems way too huge to become a display room."

She had a point. The arena's colossal size was emphasized by their vantage point—Leof was dwarfed by the rocky expanse around him. The door they had come in was shut and locked tight, but there were two other, smaller doors across from where Leof was now standing.

Ignatius leaned close and spoke into Leof's ear. The boy nodded, and Ignatius turned and left, ascending the stairs to join the two royals. Neros watched a figure emerge from the shadows. He was twice Leof's height, from the looks of it, with a long flowing robe and white flaming hair that wisped behind him as he walked, using his long staff for aid.

☼

"Leof, yellow Ember of the volcano," His voice boomed. "I am Hélder the White. Your trial shall consist of three battles, only one of which you may use a weapon. For the others, you are to rely only on your self-professed skills as a mage. Is this understood?"

"Yes, sir."

"And which battle would you like to have your weapon for?"

"The second." Leof was confident he'd gotten it right. After studying for hours, learning all he could about this trial and hearing of rumors murmured in the shadows in the upper levels, he knew that's when he would need the boost.

Hélder smiled, and Leof hated how it looked. "Interesting choice. You seem to know enough. I need not explain any further." He extended his staff outward and cast a spell, forming a hazy cloud of white flames. He stepped on it and lifted it until he was a safe distance from the battlefield. "Begin the Trial by Fire!"

The arena rumbled. Leof looked to its source: the door on the left. Out from it stormed a raging bull with charcoalskin and bright red horns. Its tail was made almost entirely of flames, and it looked *infuriated*. The doors, Leof had read, were mere cages that housed the creatures used in this fight. It was much larger than Leof had anticipated—he knew they were big, but this beast was nearly three times his size.

He didn't move at first, only curling and uncurling his fists. Then, at the very last second, he rolled off to one side, outstretching his arm and shouting.

"Kleine flamme!"

An orb of fire formed in Leof's palm, and he shot it outward, hitting the bull in its side. It stumbled, groaned, and prepared to charge again. *I don't think I have enough energy to simply parry like this for long. I'll have to come up with something else.*

Their back-and-forth parry continued. Leof rolled through options in his mind. He could try for a larger flame, but these battles were back to back to back. If he exhausted himself too early, he would never make it to the end.

But there was *something* he could try.

The next time the bull charged, Leof dodged out of the way, keeping one hand behind his back to ignite a spark. Then, he tried pulling it out, stretching the spark into a string, almost like a thread. Then, he'd do it again. And again. He'd only read about this theory in one of Aldebrande's books, and he was surprised that it was working. He twisted his fingers, willing the spark-strings to tie together in a braid.

As the minutes passed, Leof's rolling slowed, and his chest heaved with every breath. At last, it felt like whatever rope he had been building up was long enough—he built up three or four loops and had been twisting them around his sash.

Leof turned, casting a spell on the boar and knocking it square in the face with a fireball. Then, he looped the rope around its horns and leapt onto its back. He jumped down the other side, running around it to securely tie its legs together before dragging it to the center of the ring. He dropped it, and looked up at Hélder for an assessment.

"A most interesting approach, boy," The white Ember bellowed. "Though bait-and-catch will not always be the way to go. Fetch your weapon of choice."

From his cloak, Hélder procured a sword, three small daggers, a broadsword, a spear, an axe, and a bow and arrow, floating them down to Leof. Without hesitation, he snatched the daggers, hooking them to his belt. *Small items will increase my mobility. I cannot sacrifice that by taking something heavier. Plus, there are three of these.*

"Begin the second trial!"

This time, the rumble was so powerful that Leof wondered if today would be the day he learned what was under Endra's crust. A slow, hulking figure emerged from the second door, cracking the edges as it escaped. It had a long head and body, its tail swaying as it moved. Its beady eyes darted around, hunting for its prey. This monster had to be twice the size of the last. Leof examined the field. *I'm too small to roll away, like with the boar,* He mused. *But if I can land a hit, I can capture it.*

Instead of waiting and watching, this time, Leof ran around to the lizard beast's side. He pulled out one of his daggers, running his hand across it like he had back at his workshop before Prince Neros and Princess Anthea interrupted him. *This, at least, I know how to do.* The dagger lit up with blazing flames, and he aimed surely at the lizard beast's eye. *The one advantage to being small,* he thought, *is agility. This had better hit.*

He threw the dagger, clenching his jaw anxiously.

It hit.

"Woo-*hoo!* Go, Leof!" Anthea cheered, standing up and clapping her hands together. Leof looked the other way, his cheeks white-hot with embarrassment. *Must she be so loud?*

The lizard beast hissed and groaned, flailing its head around, and Leof took the opportunity to leap up at the monster, gripping the secured dagger for leverage. He swung himself on top of its head, engulfing another dagger in flames before stabbing it into the beast's other eye. It wailed, flailing wildly in an attempt to throw Leof off of him. He resisted, clamping his thighs around its neck and slamming his palm on the beast's forehead and shouting, again, in Embran.

"Entzünden!"

Flames whirled around him, concentrating around the arm secured to the beast's skull. The flame danced from his hand, embedding itself into the lizard's skin, the burn spreading and growing darker and darker until its entire head was black from being singed. *That was close.* It was a risk, Leof knew, and not quite what he intended, but when the lizard beast responded so violently to being stabbed, the Ember felt it left him no choice.

The beast collapsed with such force that Leof was at last tossed from its head. The Ember tumbled across the arena floor, clutching his final dagger close. His breaths came in labored puffs, the flames atop his head shrinking away a bit. *Too much.* He cursed to himself. *I've used up too much energy. The last fight is supposed to be the most difficult. I hope I at least survive.* He would hate to come all this way just to be made a fool, forced to return to Aldebrande and send the royal pair off to find someone to replace him on their journey.

Hélder descended once again on his cloud of white flames, this time lowering himself all the way to the floor. The flames dissipated around him, and he leaned down and lifted Leof's up by the collar of his shirt. He murmured into Leof's ear. "You have done well to make it this far, but I will crush you under my boot. All you've been 'til now is lucky."

He tossed Leof away, and he landed hard on his shoulder. He stood through sheer determination.

"You will now face me. You may keep the dagger. It will prove a useless crutch." The white Ember's voice was commanding, but Leof didn't falter. Hélder was one of the council of SMITHs that oversaw the volcano, and Leof knew that showing weakness would just give him a greater advantage. "Begin the final trial!"

At once, Hélder was charging at Leof, barely giving him a moment to breathe. Anthea shouted more words of encouragement from the rafters, but Leof couldn't really make out the words: every ounce of his focus was devoted to what was before him. The older Ember swung his staff in wide circles, creating large flaming rings that amalgamated into two or three large orbs, homing in on Leof's location. He tried to roll away—and managed to escape a couple—but he still had to block one with his arm. The flames stung, but he shook it off. *Not worse than what I've done on accident while smithing. I'll be fine. I'll be fine…*

"You think you can come down here, with no formal training, take this challenge, and walk away *unscathed?* You are an upper layer Ember. Your body is lean from years of smithing work, yes, but you don't know how to wield your power. You're *sloppy*, blacksmith."

"Petty words will not cause me to falter, Hélder," Leof growled, gathering his bearings. "I know the squabble that ignites the flames of unrest down here. I have come to prove myself, and that's exactly what I'll do."

With that, Leof waved his hand over the blade, and began reaching behind him again. Hélder countered quickly, summoning more flaming orbs to hurl at Leof.

This time, however, the Ember was ready. He whipped out another flame rope, using it to slice through Hélder's magic. He threw the dagger not at Hélder himself, but at his staff, cracking the surface.

Hélder wavered, needing to utilize his free hand to procure more flames, and Leof nearly cracked a smile. *Good, I've punctured his offense. If only slightly.*

"What is your goal, boy?" Hélder asked, creating a ring of fire.

"I told you. I've come to prove my worth."

"To what end?" He pressed, splitting the ring in two and approaching Leof. The younger Ember backed away, but Hélder flung the rings upward, slamming them down to wrap around Leof's torso, restricting his movement. "Why do you study magic?"

"Because…!" Leof took a deep breath. *I cannot struggle just yet. He cannot know he's bested me.* "I believe there is a better use for our powers. I have been…*called upon* by the heroes on that balcony to join them on their quest to save the cursed lands. If I go with them, I can find a way to restore the lava to the volcano. But only if I prove my mettle with magic." Leof spat out the end, as though being a prophetic hero was still a lie to him.

"Well, then," The elder Ember replied, moving in closer and tightening the flames. Leof groaned. "How will you escape this?"

Leof struggled against the magical restraint, and the elder mage spun him around and kicked him in the back, knocking him face-first on the arena floor. Leof tried to get up, but Hélder held him down by pressing his boot into his back, grinding the heel.

"You cannot win, you spineless yellow *brick*. Your miserable attempt at this trial has been an *insult* to those who spend their lives honing their craft! Tell me, did you think you could cheat your way through this trial? That you could *scrape* by without needing to use magic with the intent to kill?"

"That's…not true!" He grunted.

The elder mage lifted his staff and brought it down on Leof's tied up arms, hard, and a resounding crack echoed off the walls. Leof cried out, curling inward as pain shot up his arm and rocketed down his back. He felt part of his magma core leak onto his tunic. Instantly, he focused all the magic energy in him to the source, urging the cracked rock to close off and stop the leak. Leof had heard of Embers earning new cracks in battle, but he hadn't imagined it could be done so easily.

"What…is your staff made of?!" He grunted.

"Pure diamond at the end, there. From *years* of pressure and careful magic discipline to imbue it with power. If you are to escape now, you must turn yourself into a *real* vessel for your magic energy. I've been watching you fight. You use magic like a mere *tool*, when it is not. It is a part of you. Feel it, and escape me, and perhaps you will stand a chance."

Leof pressed his head against the ground, taking deep, concentrated breaths to focus his energy away from the crack. He cleared his mind, shoving the pain aside, and focused only on *breaking free*. He'd had enough of being belittled, tossed around by others. His quiet rage spewed forth in response, flooding as though a dam had broken, filling him with renewed vigor. The flames atop his head grew and whipped around, responding to a wind that was not present. *This power…it is unlike anything I've felt. It isn't a tool. It was locked away inside me, all this time.* Hélder stumbled backward, eyes wide with fear, and the white ring of flames exploded away from Leof's body. He stood, ignoring the crack in his arm—which had, thankfully, stopped leaking magma—and held out his hand, conjuring small balls of flames.

"Don't underestimate me!" He shouted, second hand joining the first in the conjuring of flames. They danced around him like a taunt to his opponent. "I've dealt with far worse than the treatment you've given me today. I'll show you what *my* discipline can do."

He thrust his arms forward, and the flames swirled through the air, crashing into the white Ember from all sides. Hélder grunted with effort as he tried to block a few of them, but Leof's renewed energy had him conjuring more flames by the second. His attack was relentless, and Hélder dropped his staff to the ground, throwing his hands up in surrender.

"I yield! Young man, stop!"

Leof stopped, and his hair calmed. The fierce glow that enveloped him faded, and he stumbled forward, catching himself before he fell.

"What a display of power," Hélder said, stooping to pick up his staff. "I am...sorry I underestimated you. You have succeeded in this trial. Collect your reward."

Hélder knocked the diamond end against the ground three times, and a pedestal rose from the center of the arena. On it was a set of three daggers that shimmered, iridescent black blades with handles wrapped in fine cloth. Leof recognized the metal instantly—it was infused with compressed magic essence found only in these depths of the volcano itself—something that had not been done since the time of the Dark Red Prince. *These are legendary, indeed.* "Thank you," he said.

The white mage nodded. "Take care of them. I'm sure you understand their power."

"I do," Leof said. "They should...prove useful."

"I must return to the council," Hélder turned and conjured a large cloud of white flames. He stepped onto it. "And I believe you have an adventure to get going on."

"Correct. We will take our leave from this place."

"I pray to our god Pyrrhus that you are successful in restoring the flow of lava to these lands. Good day."

Leof secured the daggers to his belt and looked up at the arena seating. Neros was on his feet almost instantly as the white Ember floated off, Anthea close on his heels. They practically tripped over each other down the flight of stairs and crashed into Leof in a giant hug. He recoiled.

"Let *go* of me."

"No way, Leof, you nearly died!" Anthea scolded.

"Is your arm alright?" Neros separated from their hug, holding the arm in question. Leof clenched his jaw. *It's not worse than what you have to contend with, Your Highness.*

"It'll be fine. The crack has closed up, so my magma core can't leak out any further."

"Will this crack ever go away?" Neros asked.

He shook his head. "No. Cracks on Embers are permanent. We all have some from birth, but others can manifest over time, as you've just seen."

"Well, as long as you don't need to be healed, we should probably make our way out of here," Anthea released her grip, then held out her hand. "Can you walk?"

"I'll be fine."

When the trio reached the lip of the volcano, the sky was streaked with blues and purples, accented by bright yellow-orange clouds catching the light from the setting sun. The fields were awash with a warm glow, and if Neros turned around, he could see a vast desert behind them, the twin moons both barely visible in the distance. Anthea had sat down on the edge of the volcano's rim, taking in the fresh, cool evening air. The prince sat beside her, and eased himself down, preparing for the climb back to the fields. Anthea followed suit, but when they both looked back up to see if Leof was following, he wasn't. He was instead captivated by the landscape.

"Leof, are you coming?" Anthea asked, quirking a brow to Neros.

"Huh? Oh, yes. Apologies." He shook himself away from his thoughts, joining the two in their descent. It occurred to Neros at that moment that Leof had more than likely never left the volcano before in his life. He had never seen Endra's moons, or the grass and trees, or snow. Neros wondered if Leof would like snow, or of it would be too cold for him.

The climb down was silent, save for a few stray warnings about falling rocks from the occasional rumble of the volcano. Neros wasn't expecting their new companion to be the most talkative, but the trip down did feel a bit awkward to him. He supposed he couldn't blame Leof for being mostly silent—his mind was likely swarmed with both the intake of the new scenery along with recovering from his marathon battles. Neros himself had questions, *so* many questions, but kept them to himself for now. The Ember had been hesitant to join them on their quest in the first place, and the last thing the prince wanted to do was to drive him back into the volcano's depths.

All Neros could do was what his parents instilled in him from birth: *be kind.* He had been kind to the Veturians, and he had been kind to Anthea, and he would be kind to Leof. At the very least, Neros hoped he could coax the other boy into trusting them both. He had his work cut out for him.

Chapter 9
Life Through Fresh Eyes

"The last time we were down here—which was a few days ago, from what I can tell—there were a lot of creatures hanging around," Anthea explained as they walked. "I think if we stick to the northern path, we should see less of them. If I remember right, more Arborians made towns close to Vetur so they could take advantage of trade."

"Trade? What of?"

"The Arborians accept wool and furs in exchange for providing Vetur with better medicines," Neros answered. "It's been going on for many generations."

"Fascinating. Do Veturians often leave the mountain, as you have, Prince Neros?"

"Please, just Neros is fine. Sometimes Veturians leave, most often to grow their businesses, but some do just want to see the world."

The three had settled into a rhythm, Leof walking between Neros and Anthea, mostly in silence, but occasionally asking a question here and there. Occasionally, Leof would stop and examine objects, taking two or three and putting them in his backpack. Neros figured it was to fuel his desire to build. Pontius had settled on Neros' shoulder, finally feeling brave enough to escape the confines of Vatnis. The prince wasn't entirely sure where they next true destination was, but their priority was getting to a town to restock on supplies that had depleted over their time in the volcano.

Pontius had a worried look in his eyes. "Not to change the subject, everyone, but don't those patches in the grass look ominous to you all?"

The trio turned their attention to where Pontius' gaze suggested, and Neros frowned. Small, purplish masses were forming in the grass, but it wasn't like the skeletal creatures before. These spots were simply spots, spewing forth blackish-purple smoke. The grass around them was less vibrant. *It looks like they're sucking the life out of the grass.*

Neros shuddered. "I fear as though wherever those spots appear, monsters will follow. We should be careful."

Keeping their eyes peeled, the group noticed the spots were infrequent across the fields. No monsters spewed forth, but the threat was imminent. Neros worried for the nearby towns, full of life and Arborians who were unaware and not prepared to deal with an invasion of mysterious origin. The three of them had their own mystery to solve, but did they have time to go from town to town and beat out the undead? Neros doubted it; to cover all the land between here and Arboria would require an army, not three kids. He sighed.

They approached a town, and the spots faded from view, replaced instead by dozens—maybe hundreds—of rose bushes. They created almost a fence of sorts, and there was a delicate metal sign with the words *Welcome to Rosefall* etched into it. There was a second phrase scrawled beneath, but it was in Arborian.

"Town of perfect fortune, huh?" Anthea murmured. "I wonder what they could mean by that."

Walking through the rose-covered entrance, they found the town to be mostly devoid of people. Logical, Neros surmised, because the sun's rapid set on Endra had left the whole place masked in darkness. A few late-night shops were open, but they were always the sorts of places Neros tried to avoid. That was how many mages in storybooks he'd read had met their end. While he couldn't say for sure that the stories were true, he felt better not taking any chances.

"We may need to wait until morning to get more supplies. Perhaps we should look for an inn?"

Anthea sighed. "I'm not sure if we have the coin to spare, Neros. We should probably just find somewhere nearby that looks safe and make camp."

"While that's typically a good idea, your highness, if we camp in town we run the risk of camping out in someone's backyard," Leof pointed out. "It's probably best if we keep moving."

"But you've been injured," Neros warned. "And we've been travelling all day. If we're caught by monsters in the middle of the night, who's to say we'll survive?"

"I hate to agree with Prince Worrywart, but he's got a point."

Leof pursed his lips, scanning the sparse houses and inns around town. He walked past the two royals, to a hut that was almost buried in overgrowth. He knocked on the door.

There was no answer. Leof tried again, then reached for the handle.

Pontius yelped at Neros' side. "Are you *mad,* sir?! That's breaking and entering! You will be severely punished by the owner of this home, surely with the blunt force of a defensive weapon. You've just barely survived your trial, sir Leof, this could be life-threatening."

Leof paused with his hand on the doorknob. "I am no 'sir,' Pontius. This house is abandoned."

He said it with such certainty that Neros was compelled to believe it. But he knew Arborians, and some of them liked their homes *incredibly* overgrown—often to the point of not knowing there was even a home there. His stomach flipped when Leof tried the handle and it opened; it could either mean he was right, or something far worse had happened.

"Don't look so mortified. Come on."

The inside was much the same as the outside; bursting at the seams with plants and vines and leaves and the like. It was a small, one-room home, with barely enough furnishings to call it livable. Neros' felt his heart sink: had this person been robbed? Perhaps no one had ever lived here, and it was simply a traveler's home, one meant to be used for their exact purpose as wanderers.

That explanation felt too convenient. Anthea examined the room carefully, coming to a stop in the center.

"He's right. No one has been inside here for a few months."

"How do we know the owner didn't simply go on vacation?" Neros worried. "What if they're coming back tonight?"

Anthea sighed and took another lap around the room, coming across piles of abandoned papers and maps and directions. She peered at them curiously for a few moments, then turned back to Neros and rolled her eyes.

"Not a chance. Looking at these papers, I know *exactly* who this place belongs to."

Leof frowned. "And how is that?"

"I recognize this inane scrawling. It's from an Arborian I grew up around who was *obsessed* with prophecy theory. He made up tons of his own, and he was constantly traveling once he got old enough. Not surprised he has abandoned homes everywhere—anyone else would have been too afraid to look in here and check if he was still alive."

Neros chuckled, though he still felt awkward being in someone else's home without their expressed permission. Leof, however, seemed to have little issue with it, as he had set his backpack down on the floor and sat in front of it, unloading some of its contents onto the space in front of him. Across from him was a single bed, and Anthea plopped in it, cross-legged with her chin in her hands. She watched the Ember carefully, and Neros looked around the rest of the room. There were maps of Endra on the walls, though in the dim light they were hard to see. The prince suppressed a yawn—all this travel had thrown his circadian rhythm awry. Pushing away his awkward nerves, he sat beside Anthea on the bed, joining her in watching Leof.

The Ember took out two books and a set of tools and a combination of small, metal pieces in all sorts of shapes. There were springs, cogs, small pointed bits that looked like the tips of pens, and a large collection of screws. He laid out his materials with meticulous care, not paying much mind to either of the other two heroes.

"Whatcha makin'?" Anthea asked, leaning forward.

"Simply continuing a project from home."

"Which is?"

"None of your business, your highness."

"Aw, come on! We're friends, aren't we? Just call me Anthy!"

He looked up at her then, narrowing his eyes. "*You two* are friends. *I* am traveling alongside you for the greater good. So you say."

"You believe it," Anthea countered. "I heard you talking to Hélder the White while fighting him."

Leof sighed but remained silent, picking up some of his tools and bending over them, lifting a structure he had partly filled with the metal bits.

After a moment, he plucked a pair of glasses from the front pocket of his backpack and slipped them onto his nose. The frames were small, and Neros assumed they magnified the project before him. A shame, really, that he was such a private person, because Neros *really* wanted to know what it was he was making. It *looked* like a pocket watch, but the prince was positive that Leof's skills were centered primarily around blacksmithing. He tried to push the curiosity from his mind.

Pontius stirred, floating into his field of view. "Prince Neros, it's not too late at night. Today has been far less taxing than those previous, so how about we have another lesson?"

The prince nodded, and they headed outside: the house was a bit too small for them to practice, especially in the event something went wrong. He didn't want to risk injuring anyone. Or soaking all the papers in the house.

"Last time, we focused on the creation of water, but I think this time, we should focus on control."

"Okay," Neros settled into a sitting position, Pontius posed in front of him like a teacher.

"Go ahead and create some water for me, *without* summoning ice first."

He tried, focusing solely on the ease and flow of water, as opposed to the brittle chill of ice he was used to. This time, the water pooled in his palm a bit easier than before.

"Good, good!" Pontius urged. "Now make more. I'll be back. Get about, oh, enough to be me-sized. See if you can move it without losing the total volume."

As Pontius floated off, Neros focused on building his orb of water. Soon enough, he had an orb around the size of a his fist; he breathed evenly, so not to disturb the delicate magic coursing through him. People often had the impression that ice was delicate and easy to break; while that may have been true for some thinner structures, on the whole ice was rather sturdy. In Vetur, it had been fashioned into thick hammers and axes—it was even the head of Vatnis, his own spear—as well as built into Castle Vetur. It was dazzling during sunrise and sunset to see the light glint and bounce off the castle walls.

Neros sighed. He missed home. The water in his palm reminded him of home, too, though in a different way. To him, *water* was delicate. Everyone around him spoke of its strength, but Neros did not find that to be so. It took years to weather rocks with water that could be snapped in seconds with other forces.

If he was to save the world, what good was water, really? Pontius showed that water had healing properties, but could Neros even pull those off? Staring at the water in his hand, it suddenly felt too small to do anything with. Those guardians in Paralia had nearly drowned him with their massive water-axes, and this was just…a ball.

As though controlled by his emotions, the water collapsed, pouring over his open hand. Neros jumped. *Oh. I suppose I must have lost focus.*

He started over, and by the time Pontius had returned—with an armful of misshapen, dead-looking flowers—he had worked up just about what Pontius had asked for.

"Good! Have you tried moving it around?"

Neros gently moved his arm from side to side, the water following slowly in his wake. It took an incredible amount of focus to accomplish, and the prince was surprised the orb didn't collapse, as it had before.

"Wonderful! You're advancing more and more each day, Prince Neros. You truly are a sight to behold! It's no wonder you're a hero of legend! Your powers are growing at an incredible rate. Now I know you're ready for the next step!"

The prince wasn't too sure about that. "Next step?"

Pontius' eyes lit up. "Spells!" He deposited the collection of near-dead flowers at Neros' feet. "I need you to hone your abilities more before we move into actual healing, but being a water mage afford you a few extra tricks!"

He quirked a brow. "I'm not sure I understand."

"Well, that's what I've got these for, your highness! Hold your horses, and I'll explain everything." Pontius settled into the grass beside the flowers, removing one and setting the others aside. "There are four important spell types that use the power, might, and grace of water to view and affect life at varying levels. They are Life View, Restoration, Ailment Erasure, and Regeneration. Tonight, I am going to teach you the first!"

"Wait," Neros interrupted. "Can *anyone* learn these spells?"

Pontius hummed. "In theory, sure, but if the mage is elementally incompatible with water—someone of Sir Leof's nature, for example—then they would, sadly, be unable to learn. It's much like any other kind of magic, Prince Neros—with enough time and energy, I'm certain even an Ember could overcome the difficulty, but no one has ever needed to in the past. So, no one has tried."

He nodded. "So, I assume this life viewing spell allows you to check on the status of another's health?"

"Exactly!" Pontius cheered, somersaulting in the air. "Like this flower, for instance. Now, unlike other magic, water spells are built on longer phrases passed down orally for hundreds of years. Spellbooks likely exist in Castle Vetur, but they read almost like poetry because of how long some of the incantations are. Checking on the status of someone else's health was very popular for Veturians back in the day, as it would be a perfect way for some of the farmers to keep track of their livestock! These days, however, someone like you or I could use it to check up on the status of our traveling comrades. Useful, right?"

The prince nodded again. "Yes, I suppose I see its benefit. But, how do I cast it? Do I need this?" He held up the slowly-spinning orb of water.

"Precisely! To use the spell, the water in your palm needs to extend to the size of the being's heart. That's too much for these flowers here, but it'd be plenty if you wanted to try it on Princess Anthea or Sir Leof!" Pontius shuffled, picking up the flower and holding it out. "Now, here's the tricky part. First, you need to press your palm toward the recipient, which is this flower. Hold out the water so it almost presses up against the heart of this flower. Right now, the water in your hand is an orb. Focus your energy and make it a disc."

"Okay." He held out his hand, turning his wrist so his palm faced the flower. The water threatened to fall away to the ground, but Neros held it steady, focusing on compressing its size. *You know, perhaps Leof would feel a bit better if he knew I was learning something new like this. I'm sure being around Anthea and I, he feels surrounded by trained skill.*

The water in his palm began to slip, and he panicked, instinctively freezing it to keep the icicles afloat. He winced from the sting that followed, and released his magic, the ice dropping in front of Pontius with a quiet thump.

"Oh, Prince Neros, you were nearly there! Try again, sure to focus your energy on nothing but the water this time! Don't switch to ice, you'll only hurt yourself from that curse."

"Right. Right, I'll try again…"

☼

Leof hunched over his project, twisting a screw into place with practiced ease, ignoring the dull ache in his arm from where his recently-cracked coalskin was healing. This stopwatch *was* going to be a gift for Aldebrande, but with this new adventure the Ember found himself on, he hadn't had the chance to finish it before leaving. To avoid the risk of him discovering it, Leof took it along. He was making it as thanks for housing him and teaching him for so long. *If I'm lucky, war will not have broken out and killed the old man before I return home.*

The princess' voice came suddenly from beside him. "Are you always this quiet when you work?"

He narrowed his eyes at his project. "Are you always this noisy when others are trying to work?"

"Alright, smart guy, do you really think that we'll let you get away with silently working on your projects all hunched over like that? At least let me make you a table."

That got him to look at her. "*Make* me a table? I don't believe we have the resources for such a project, your highness."

"Ha! You're thinking too big, Leof," She smirked, which Leof did not like, and moved to the floor, placing her palms on the ground. "Watch and learn."

She began to murmur in a language that sounded difficult to pronounce but oddly beautiful—less harsh than Emberan. Her hands glowed bright green, and the ground shook for a moment before a perfect square rose from beneath where his tools were. They quivered from the movement, and he snatched up the stopwatch and some of the smaller parts—just so they didn't get lost—and watched as she called leaves and vines to the surface, as well, wrapping around the sides of the dirt cube for no other reason than aesthetic.

When she finished, she returned to her perch on the bed, smug smirk still on her face. "See? Now you don't have to break your back to work."

138

Leof looked at the makeshift workstation. It would certainly do well, for what it was; they wouldn't be here long enough for him to dream of anything more, anyway. He placed his tools down, turning the stopwatch over in his hands to determine what part went next. "Thank you," He murmured.

"I think you can thank me by telling me about yourself!"

Instantly, Leof regretted thanking her at all. He worked in silence for a few moments, turning her demand over in his mind. Three full years of apprenticeship and ten whole years of knowing Aldebrande, and Leof ensured his mentor only knew what he needed to. These two persistent royals would have to simply deal with the same.

"You get one question," He said.

The princess swung her legs up on the bed, crossing them in front of her. She rested her chin in her hands, pursing her lips. Clearly, she wasn't fond of this agreement, but Leof had granted her enough just with one question. *She'll survive.*

While he waited, he went back to work, carefully placing the a few cogs in the back of the stopwatch. He turned them gently, admiring how smooth the movement was.

Eventually, Anthea sighed. "Since you've never left the volcano before, what do you think of Endra? Your answer *has* to be more than a sentence."

His brow lowered in concentration as he tried to place the springs in his project. "Interesting question, princess." *Pleasantly non-invasive,* he thought. *But she might just be trying to butter me up.* "I think Endra is quite beautiful, even with the apparent poison taking over. It puts imagery to the elements and landscape I had only previously read about. You two are quite curious, yourselves, and both day and night are quieter than I expected." The spring jumped away from his hands, and he sighed, leaning down to pick it up. "Does that answer your question, your highness?"

"I keep telling you, it's *Anthea.* And yes," She smiled, with some of the same smugness Leof sensed earlier—and still, he did not like it. "Yes, it does."

"Very well." Spring back in his hand, he returned to the tiny clock. He'd never *made* a clock before—much of what he was doing was simply guessing at where parts were supposed to go, and hoping that, once he closed the back, he could make it tick. Clockwork was one of the less common practices among Embers, but Leof had told Aldebrande he wanted to learn everything. He wondered absently what sort of aid flame could bring to the piece in his hand? He had seen Ignatius' workshop, with its furnaces and various vases and glasswork. Leof wondered if he could apply the same theory to this thinner metal in his hand. Surely, he had the ability to heat it—to make it soft would make it easy to carve.

"Who's the watch for?"

"I said you only had one question."

Anthea laughed, big and bold. "Ah, well. Can't blame me for tryin'!"

"That, I cannot," Leof said. He looked to her. "If you must fill the silence, why don't you tell me about your homeland? I can at least listen while I work."

"By the teeming essence of the river…by the might of the sea…"

"*Through* the might of the sea."

"Through the might of the sea…Show me the life that breathes in this vessel."

The water disc in Neros' hand began to glow a faint orange—that meant dying, nearly dead. His eyebrows drew together in sympathy for the poor flower in Pontius' hand; it looked like it had been grasping on to the dredges of its life for quite some time.

He didn't get much time to fret, however—Pontius cheered, tossing the flower off to the side and breaking the spell, faint glow fading into darkness. Tiredness pulled at the corners of Neros' eyes, and he began to wonder how long they'd been out here practicing. He suppressed a yawn; if he could stay up a bit longer and learn just a bit more, maybe Pontius would teach him how to attack with water magic. *If it's even possible,* he mused to himself. *I've never seen anyone other than those guardians in Paralia use water magic for violence.*

Pontius gathered the flowers up in his hands, planting them down behind Neros, near the wall of the building they were using for shelter. He held his hands out and sprinkled them with water, chanting something under his breath until the leaves became vibrant and the petals bloomed, full of life once again.

The water sprite wiped his brow. "Restoration magic is quite energy consuming. Let's return to her highness and Sir Leof to get some rest!"

When they returned, both Anthea and Leof were asleep. There was but one bed in the room, and Anthea had curled up in it on her side at the foot of it, leaving plenty of room for two others to do the same. However, Leof seemed to have begrudgingly taken the floor. Neros smiled to himself. *He may be a bit of a cold personality, but he is awfully respectful.* Despite everything, he wanted the Ember to get a good night's rest; but how to move him to the bed without waking him? *My hands are likely ice cold to the touch, for a being like him…This is going to be tricky.* He kneeled beside Leof's sleeping figure: his knees were pulled up to his chest, eyebrows drawn together. From where Neros was, he could see the spot on Leof's arm that had been cracked— miraculously, the rock around it had re-grown slightly to conceal the gash, leaving a thin crack that emanated a soft glow. *That healed impressively quickly,* Neros noted. He shook his head: he was here to move Leof and get some sleep. Gingerly, he slid his hands beneath Leof's knees and head, lifting him up and finding, thankfully, that the small Ember was lighter than expected. Neros was just glad there was no risk of dropping him. Lowering Leof to the head of the bed, Neros quietly dressed down, taking the space between his companions and hoping for sweet dreams.

The following morning was filled with shopping and Anthea's expertise in gleaning information from the locals. Every Arborian they passed was more than willing to share information with her, no questions asked; they were too elated to see her. There were a few Veturians in the town, as well, and Neros was sure to greet them. He wanted nothing more than to ask about his parents, about Vetur, but unfortunately, the citizens he spoke with had been living away from Vetur itself for years.

"It is a fine town, and it brightened up the moment you were born, your highness," The man said. "But ever since I left, I feel enriched! Travel has brought me new friends and a chance to see what is rarely seen, like your friend there," He gestured to Leof.

Leof averted his gaze from the conversation, and Neros looked between him and the Veturian. "Is it truly so uncommon for Embers to leave the volcano?"

"Incredibly, your highness. Folk like us typically need to trek up to the volcano ourselves just to get a glance at their supplies and precious metals.

And never have I seen one with such bright flames! That yellow is truly striking, lad."

"…Thank you," Leof murmured, but still, he kept his gaze away.

Just then, Anthea appeared behind the two boys, tossing an arm around each of them. "Hey, I'm sorry to interrupt, sir, but the three of us really need to be getting on our way."

"Oh, of course! Travel safe, Prince Neros!"

"I will!" He called, and allowed himself to be dragged away by the princess. "What's wrong, Anthy?"

"After some interesting conversations, I think I know our next best option for our adventure."

Leof shook himself from Anthea's grip. "Which is?"

"We petition the gods for help!"

Neros blinked. "…You mean, through prayer?"

She laughed, ruffling Neros' hair. "Of course not! We go to them in person, heavensward, to Andolis! Prayers alone never reach the gods. I should know; Silva has communicated with me directly before. The goddess of Arboria can only communicate one way, with those whom she chooses to. When we send prayers or perform as thanks to them, they only receive the essence or intention of the feeling."

"You realize you're suggesting we go to *Andolis* to petition the *gods*. We don't even entirely know what's wrong with Endra, your highness."

"Right, Leof, I know, but I'm saying we can find out! And the Great Ancient Tree is going to be our ticket to get there!"

The Great Ancient Tree in Arboria was the tree that, if Neros remembered correctly, trapped every Arborian in a vice grip of life-sucking roots. *If we go there, who's to say Arboria won't be in total ruins? Everyone could be dead… has Anthea forgotten?* There was no way Anthea forgot, Neros knew, but he couldn't help the nerves that tugged at his gut. But he wasn't sure what other option they had.

"Anthy, are you *sure* about this? After all that's happened…"

"Neros, I'll be okay. I just have to get to the tree and use my power to grow a vine to the heavens. It'll be a snap."

Leof sighed. "I hate to disagree, but more than that, this is a bit confusing. *How* did you come to this conclusion, your highness?"

"Anthea," She scolded. "And it's simple. The town of Rosefall, from what they told me, has been maintaining a protective barrier over their town to prevent dark creatures from sneaking in at night. It's almost *exactly* like the Arborian texts' recounting of the prophecy's first coming. The gods now are the heroes who dealt with it the first time, so surely their advice is the best advice we can get!"

Leof narrowed his eyes. "You're going to trust *one* account of the past? And what about that Oracle you saw?"

"His advice is infrequent, and I fear his power is fading," Pontius chirped, releasing himself from inside Neros' spear. "He cannot spend all of his energy contacting us and guiding us on our journey. That's why he sent me along!"

"That's right. While we freed him from deep imprisonment, I'm not entirely sure he's truly free," Neros explained, eyebrows furrowed. "But that doesn't make this a good idea."

"Unfortunately, Prince Neros, it is our only idea," Pontius said. "I think there is a chance it may work out! The gods have been said to be the grandest, benevolent beings in all of Endra. I'm sure they will be just as sage and wise as Pegaios!"

Neros worried at his lip, then sighed. "Very well. We'll press on."

Chapter 10
The One Who Ran Away

$\mathcal{T}$he road was perilous, and Neros wondered more with every step whether they'd made the right decision. They'd stopped at a few other towns, and he'd since learned two other skills from Pontius: the ability to heal small wounds, and a spell that cures minor ailments. Pontius assured him he was shaping up as a water mage, but it did little to quell the uneasiness in his heart. The Endran landscape was swiftly growing more and more lifeless. Throngs of purple spores appeared in patches, spewing dark energy that made his stomach turn. The surrounding grass and trees wilted and withered away, and towns had started barring their entrances from outsiders: one small effort to keep the smoke from spewing in and infecting the life still clinging within.

In the present moment, the trio was engaged in a fierce battle against four skeletal figures. Neros wasn't sure how, but they had started bringing weapons up from…whatever ether they rose from. The prince was inclined to believe that there was no other place these demons could spawn but the netherworld: Umbros. The same place that the darkness had come from five hundred years prior, according to what Pegaios had told them. Pontius had called them *Melanthos' monsters,* but Neros still wasn't sure what that meant for them. With all the excitement of Leof joining their team, they hadn't quite gotten the Ember up to speed.

Not that he seemed to mind. He swung his sword valiantly, often taking the brunt of the damage from the enemies' harsh swings of their own. Anthea had stuck to the rear, but Neros could tell it was frustrating her. As much as her fighting style was ranged, she still preferred to be taking bigger shots instead of simply providing support. Neros felt the same—they had fought countless skeletons of varying sizes, yet he felt like he'd hardly put in any effort to defeat them.

Leof pierced his sword through the last skeleton's ribs, yanking its bones apart and watching it crumble at his feet before sheathing his sword. Anthea approached him, gripping his shoulder and whirling him around.

"What's your deal, Leof?"

He stepped back, recoiling from her. "What are you talking about?"

"You're always fighting right at the front lines! Neros and I have barely been able to fight at all. It's like you won't *let* us, even if we try. So what's your deal?"

His expression darkened with frustration. "Is it not obvious to you that you're royalty? On a journey of this scale, with this much danger afoot, shouldn't it be clear you need a protector? If something happened to either one of you, what would become of your kingdoms?"

Neros glanced at Anthea, but she was having none of it. "Our kingdoms would be doomed if we weren't fighting for them, Leof! Curses fell over our lands, and we're supposed to work *together* to solve this prophetic mystery and save the world!"

Leof stood firm. "I didn't say to do *nothing*. But think, if either of you die along the way, what then? What of the people of Arboria, who look to their princess for aid? Or to the villagers of Vetur, who relied on the prince to help them? Your lives are not meaningless. You're reckless for behaving this way."

"Your life isn't meaningless, either! What about Aldebrande?! How do you think he'd react if he saw you throwing your life ahead of ours, practically *asking* to be killed by these things!"

He rolled his eyes. "You couldn't possibly be trying to compare my life to yours."

Neros stepped in, placing a hand on Leof's arm. "Just because you're not royalty, or even well-known, doesn't mean your life is worth *nothing*. You're not alone in this—let us fight with you."

The Ember pulled away, turning and beginning to walk. "There's no way you could understand. Let's keep going. We're beginning to lose daylight, and we should be nearing Arboria soon, shouldn't we?"

"Stop!" Anthea snagged his wrist, and he bristled. "You're not walking away from this conversation. We're a *team* now. We care about you!"

"Oh, *give it up*, princess!" Leof whirled around, flames crackling around his face. "How long to you plan to feign friendship like this? I'm just a tool, why not leave it at that?!"

"Because you care for us, don't you? Otherwise you wouldn't lay your life on the line to protect us from the skeletal beasts!"

Leof's shoulders tensed. "That's *not*—"

"You do! So why don't you expect us to care for you in the same way? Gods, you even refuse to believe your own caretaker wants the best for you. But we've put our faith in you and your abilities! Why not just *trust us?*"

"Did you have *flowers* in your ears when you were pestering master Aldebrande about my past, your highness?" Leof's eyes swam with pain. "I thought—for years—he was working with my parents, waiting to catch me infusing magic into weapons to test, and toss me to the streets for being an *abomination*. Now, just as I was getting used to being with him, he urges me to go along this adventure with you so…so *easily*. Like he *wanted* me to leave. And here I am, at your insistence, but how can I trust you? You two are… so close, I—" He averted his gaze, hands curling and uncurling into fists. "Please understand. I feel like an outsider. I have very little trust in you. Your kingdoms' histories are tied together, and my own is…removed from all that. Offering you protection with my blade is all I can do to keep from going crazy thinking about it." He tried to shake himself free from Anthea's grip, but Neros could tell it was halfhearted.

The prince felt his chest grow tight. True, Anthea and he had offered plenty of information about Vetur and Arboria to Leof, but he hadn't realized how isolating that must have felt. The stories they exchanged often related back to their childhood when they weren't talking about their peoples' interpretations of the prophecy. They had just been trying to welcome Leof into their lives, but they may have done the exact opposite.

"I–I'm so sorry we've made you feel this way," Neros said, wishing he could reach out a hand to him, but he had a feeling Leof wouldn't take it. Neros exchanged a glance with Anthea, eyebrows pulled together in concern. "What can we do to help your trust in us?"

Leof looked like he wasn't expecting Neros to express any concern at all. His cheeks glowed faintly, and he stammered through an answer. "I–I– Just *how* do you expect me to answer that?"

"Ah, I—sorry, I suppose that's not really something you can answer right away, is it…" Neros murmured to himself. "If…if you're comfortable taking the lead, we can follow suit for now. Just…don't take the burden of fighting these creatures all on your own shoulders, especially since you've recently been injured."

Anthea turned her frustrations on him. "But, Neros, how will we defeat *any* gods if we can't cooperate?"

"Cooperation takes time! Of all beings, you should know that, Anthea. *How* long did it take you and I to become as connected on the battlefield as we are? The best we can do right now is offer support until we learn enough about our abilities to work together."

The reality of his words seemed to bring Anthea back to earth. She sighed, rubbing at her temples. "Right, you're right. I-I'm sorry, Leof, for getting impatient with you. Neros is right."

"It's fine," Leof murmured, crossing his arms. "I'll monitor myself, as well."

It was an uneasy resolution, a small band-aid on a crack in the wall, but Neros felt he had to accept what he could get. Leof seemed wholly uncomfortable with royalty apologizing to him, and Anthea's patience had already run thin and fractured. Frankly, Neros' head spun just thinking about ways for all of them to use their abilities together, especially with Leof's so new to them (and perhaps himself) and Neros himself learning completely new skills.

Perhaps they had a longer road ahead of them than Neros anticipated. He sorely hoped that their idea to travel to Arboria would pan out.

Princess Anthea was, typically, an expert at dealing with other creatures. She was a natural persuader, charisma rolling off her in waves and waves; anyone she wanted information from, she could get. If there was ever someone in need, be it animal, Arborian, Veturian, or alike, she could come to their aid and they would feel compelled to tell her what was wrong. Anthea was a natural troubleshooter, and glad to do so for others—perhaps that was part of Neros' influence on her over the years.

But what perplexed Anthea was why Leof had been so gods-damned *difficult*. It annoyed her, as she had never experienced someone who had put up such resistance against her whims as he had. In Rosefall, he *insisted* against sleeping on the bed. "I'm used to arrangements like this," He'd said. "At least this ground is soft."

She'd wanted to punch him. Of course, she was glad to see him sleeping soundly in bed beside Neros the next morning (albeit curled as far away as he could get), but she couldn't help but wonder why it was that Neros had outclassed her people skills. Not that they were competing—her competitive nature against Neros had long since faded into a more playful back-and-forth—but that was just it. She wanted to know, because as frustrated as she was with *him* for being *difficult,* she was frustrated with herself for not realizing he felt like an outsider.

Maybe I came on too strong.

It was time for her to try a new tactic. They had a while before they would reach Arboria, and the skeletal beasts weren't so overwhelming in this area.

After their brief argument, Leof had taken the lead ahead of them; Anthea jogged to catch up to his side. "So, Leof, we saw you do some magic back in the volcano. How does it work?"

She saw the hesitation pass over his face—he wanted to deny her, as he had every time previous. But he sighed. "I'm not sure I know what you mean, your highness."

"*Anthea,*" She insisted, as she had been and would continue to do until he got it through his rock-hard skull that she was not like other royalty, and didn't care for titles because they were *friends*. "And I mean, how does your magic work? Are there limitations? How do you make fire, anyway, if you're a rock?"

Amusement flickered in Leof's eyes, and Anthea knew she had him hook, line, and sinker. "There are many limitations. I can make *fire* despite my form being rock because inside all Embers there is a molten, magmatic core. Fire magic, like anything else, is just energy. I pull it from within."

"But you're self-taught," She countered, interest sparking in her brain. "So how did you know to do that?"

At this, he looked away. "It was just a feeling. Once I was…alone, I used it for survival."

She could *feel* the walls being thrown up around him. *This is good; I'm starting to be able to sense when he's getting defensive.* Not that she wanted to crack him or manipulate him, of course; it was more that she wanted to know precisely where his boundaries were. To be a better friend to him, and to avoid any further frustrating outbursts.

So, she backed off. "What are your limitations, then?"

"I can't create flames for too long, or else I get exhausted," He explained. "It drains my life force, if I'm to understand the book Ignatius loaned me properly. I cannot generate lava itself, as my abilities are limited to flames. As far as I know, at least. Though I have other capabilities beyond magic," He added, fiddling with the bottom of his tunic.

"Well, yeah, there was that clock you were making. And you're a blacksmith! So what else can you do? Are you any good at it?"

He paused, and Anthea thought he may have clammed up for the remainder of their trip, when he looked back at her with a glimmer in his eye. And…was he *smirking?* "I *am* one of the best craftsmen in my layer of the volcano. Far more than clocks and blades, I can craft nearly anything, so long as I have the instructions—or, in some cases, a decent idea of how the end result should function."

Her ears perked at this new information. "Anything? Like, *anything?*" A skill set like that could be unimaginably useful. "So, say Neros' staff breaks. You could fix it?"

"Certainly."

"And if I need a bow?"

"If you've materials to spare."

"If my knapsack rips open?"

His confidence faltered. "I'm a bit more mechanical, but I could mend it with the right material."

A peal of laughter escaped her lips. "You are something else! And you really believe you aren't special?"

"I'm not," He insisted. "My skills are a result of hard work. That's all."

He's so modest. Anthea turned to look back at Neros. *Kinda like him.* He beamed at her, as if encouraging her to continue to talk casually with Leof.

"Well, believe it or not, Leof, you're special now. And *believe it or not*, that guy didn't want to answer the call to heroism at first, either." She pointed her thumb back at Neros.

Leof spared a glance at the prince. "You didn't?"

Neros' cheeks flushed purple, and he rubbed the back of his neck. "She's right. I'm *still* not sure if I have what it takes to be a hero of prophetic legend," He laughed, light and lilting. Anthea wanted to thwack his arm for being so sheepish.

Leof hummed, returning his gaze far ahead. "Interesting. I suppose you two are not exactly as you seem."

"Hey! And what do you mean by that?"

"Nothing so offensive," Leof mumbled. "Just that, with all your royal grandeur, I was prepared to presume you had no real vulnerabilities."

"Ha! Maybe Neros is, since he's nothing but fluff and snow inside—"

"Anthy!"

"Forgive me, forgive me!" She laughed. "But you'll soon learn that I am made of much tougher bark!" The princess knocked on her own arm for effect. She could feel Neros' glare on the back of her neck, but she let it roll off her shoulders. Leof only shook his head.

As Arboria grew closer—the surrounding grass more gray—Anthea felt like a rock had settled in the pit of her stomach. Fear and anxiety pulled at her limbs, rushing her closer and closer to home. What were once trees with bright leaves of all colors were now, from what she could see, nothing but barren branches that had been drained of all vibrance. Dead grass crunched beneath their feet and Anthea thought she was just about to learn *how* tough her bark really was.

Her legs couldn't seem to decide if they wanted to root in place or run for the entrance of the woods. All the trees she grew up around—the ones permanently rooted, not the Arborians—were shells of their former richness. She scrambled through brambles and stumbled into the first clearing, and she thought she may have heard Neros shouting after her, but the sound of leaves crackling beneath her was too loud. Each *snap* seemed to tear at her very heartwood, threatening to peel away its contents and leave her a husk of her former self.

No. No…!

The damage was worse than she could have ever imagined.

Arboria had once been a kingdom of Endra that could only be described as *lush*. Travelers envied the intensity of the landscape, how full and safe and soft everything had looked. How the leaves and flower petals shimmered like golden silk in the setting sun. How the trees swayed gently in the early spring wind. How every last Arborian was teeming with the ardor of *life*, clamoring over each other and laughing and singing and caring for each other, ever hungry for the morning light peeking in through their windows, a gentle wake-up call to begin their days anew.

Not now.

Now, their faces were plastered with terror. Fear. Anger. Sadness. Anthea could feel it all well up inside her, and she shoved it back down. Nearly everything was *colorless*—more than the entrance, where she had passed by empty trees and feared that the rest of Arboria would look the same. But this was worse. Branches had shriveled. Expressions were empty. The grass had disappeared, and the shrubs were hollowed out frameworks of the masterpieces they had been formerly.

She recognized so many of these faces. They were her friends—no, they were her *family*. Every one of them. There was Garrick, who had taught her to mix herbs; Pihla, who had mended her dress when she tore it; Elowen, who held her close when she cried from the pressure of being Silva's *chosen child*. Hadas and Eoghan, Iva and Ilan…even Hideki and Hiroki, a pair of maple twins who had helped her learn to shoot her bow, had gone lifeless, eyes stricken with horror. It made Anthea sick.

"Everyone is…dead…" She croaked out. She fought against the weight trying to pull her to her knees. *You're fighting for them. Be strong. They need you to be strong.*

"Oh, Anthy," Neros' voice came, soft, empathetic. "I—I'm sure they're not…not completely…" He sounded unsure, like he didn't want to jinx them by suggesting they were still alive.

Is *this* what was spreading throughout Endra? This force that turned flowers to dust, was it what everyone in every town they'd passed beyond Rosefall was protecting against? There were Arborians in all those towns, sure, but in total there were maybe a thousand at most. Spread before her, bark peeling away from some of their cheeks, hair fraying and looking nearly *singed*, were *tens of thousands of Arborians*. It was an ocean of thorns. Impossible to pass. If she looked—though it hurt to look—she could see where she had stood where it all started. She had been next to Rosea, and they were buying vials of potions for Willow, who had asked Anthea to marry him no less than twelve times that month. The girls had suspected he wanted to make a love potion, and Anthea could still hear Rosea's airy giggle.

"He wants ingredients for a love potion, right?" She had said, smiling madly. *"So, let's get the more fragrant rose vials, so he ends up making an anesthetic and passing out instead."*

Such an atypically violent thought for a typically sweet girl, Anthea remembered thinking. The princess knew her influence on Rosea had been strong, but the plan she cracked had been devilish. However, they had no time to execute it; the ground rumbled, snake-like movements shifting the ground beneath their feet. And so, the curse had begun.

"Prin…cess… An…thea…?"

Anthea whirled her head around to see Neros, crouched beside an older man—no, that was Florus, with years piled on from having the energy sucked away from him. Neros was performing some kind of water spell, maybe the life-giving or life-seeing one, and they locked eyes, his violet meeting her golden with overflowing urgency.

She rushed to his side. "What is it?"

"She…escaped…"

"Who escaped?" Her heart leapt in her chest. Did someone other than her leave Arboria?

"Para…lia…"

"Who went to Paralia? Florus, stay with me!"

"She…escaped… Princess…she…escaped…"

"Please, tell me who!"

His words slowed. "To lift…the curse…to…lift…the…"

"Lift the curse? On you? From Paralia?"

"Divine…water…to grow…"

Anthea felt her control slipping. She gripped Florus' shoulders, looking into his eyes, a rich, deep green slowly morphing into a dull gray. "Who escaped?!"

He said nothing else. Neros' hands glowed orange, and he released his grip on the spell.

"Another Arborian escaped from here. I have to find out who." She was resolute. She would get a vantage point, survey the grounds, and count them all. She would find the missing Arborian. She would know who ran away.

"Um…Anthea," Neros began, hesitant, and it annoyed her. "I-I think he may have meant *you.*"

If that were the reality, it would be simply too soul-crushing. She couldn't accept it. She *wouldn't.* She pushed past Neros, ignoring his calls after her, and scanned her surroundings. She spotted a tree with a flatter canopy—one that hadn't begun to shrivel at the top yet. The princess outstretched her hand, pulling woven roots from the ground (and wincing at their dullness) and lassoing it onto the tree, pulling herself upward in a graceful sweep.

Her eyes continued their scan, and she pushed down the discomforting churn of her stomach as she recognized more and more faces; the market was busy that morning, she recalled. Her gazed roved over again to the flower stalls, where she and Rosea were shopping for those fragrant roses. The ground had rumbled, and Anthea had been quick on her feet, jumping away immediately as panic overtook the forest. Something was off about that patch of grass, now, and Anthea stared until realization struck her.

Anthea didn't see Rosea.

There was no husk or shell, as there were with the thousands of other faces she saw. Only a large space beside the stall, with wilted rose petals on the ground. *Of course! How did I not see it earlier?* A wicked grin broke out on her face: Rosea escaped, and was looking for them!

Her stomach dropped. Rosea escaped, and *was looking for them.*

Without thinking, she swung down from the tree, soaring past Neros and Leof and hit the ground running. As the only other Arborian who knew exactly what happened that day, Rosea would be a great help to them—Anthea just had to reach her before any monsters in Paralia did.

Neros groaned, running a hand through his hair while he watched Anthea disappear into the trees. "Damn it," He muttered. He'd have to go after her. The plains were too dangerous to traverse alone.

Leof blinked at the trees, as though expecting her to re-emerge. Then he looked to Neros, brows furrowed. "Is she always this reckless?"

The prince sighed. "Since the day we met," He admitted. The feeling of Anthea's vines coiled tightly around his middle and suspending him in midair ghosted over him, and he shivered. "Best not to let her get too far ahead. We don't want to lose track of her."

The Ember looked uncomfortable.

"What's wrong?"

"I should probably stay here, shouldn't I?"

"What? Why?"

"I'm sure she wouldn't be too keen on me being involved with such a…private moment."

Neros' hands closed around Leof's, delighted when the boy didn't shy away. "Nonsense. We've been over this. We're a team, and she needs all the help she can get." He began to lead Leof back into the woods, toward the plains. "If we catch up to her, we can find out where she's going. Besides, if we separate, *you* might get lost, which isn't good either."

Leof sighed. "I suppose."

Once free from the forest's grasp, the pair broke into a run. Anthea was taller than both of them, and so her strides made her difficult to keep up with. Freed from the volcano, she had the power of the soil beneath her feet: Neros could almost see her swinging along the sparse trees until the plains flattened out, using her ability to temporarily disrupt the landscape and make slopes to slide along. In fact, he could see evidence of it around him: small lines of baby grass in the dirt to indicate where her magic had touched. And if he looked hard enough, he could see the princess, too: a slowly disappearing dot in the distance, running toward the place where their adventure began.

Neros slowed, Leof beside him, both panting from exertion. "She must be…headed for Paralia."

"How—in the gods' names—do you know that?" Leof asked between breaths.

"It was as the Arborian said. Divine water…to grow…grow *something*. I'm sure it's a clue in the greater mystery of how life can be brought back to Arboria."

"Beyond that, didn't her highness say something about using her magic to grow the Great Ancient Tree to the heavens? It…didn't quite look *alive* enough to do that. We'll likely have to find another way up."

Neros nodded. "It was unnerving to see Arboria in such a state. What a…horrific way to be introduced to the place."

"All the more reason to save it from permanent destruction," Leof agreed.

Pontius came tumbling forth from Neros' spear, eyes frantic. "We cannot be standing around! As we speak, Anthea is barreling toward Paralia at her top speed! You may not know, Sir Leof, but Paralia is riddled with mighty water beasts, but with this purple *muck* spreading around the world, who knows what sorts of evil could have been born?! She may be in danger! She is acting recklessly for a princess of her importance!"

Neros chuckled, unsteady. "Well, I doubt she'd listen if you told her. Trust me, I've tried. The best we can do is warp to her location—can you do that for us, Pontius?"

"Yes, of course!"

"Wait, *warp?*" Leof asked, a disbelieving look on his face.

"Yes. I hope you aren't susceptible to motion sickness."

Leof frowned, looking no less nervous as Pontius plucked one of his monocle chain links and expanded it to cover the two of them. There was something especially ethereal about the way Leof's hair and cracks still glowed when surrounded by water, unaffected by its properties. If he strained his ears, he could almost hear the flames crackling, muffled by the water that batted and pulled at their clothes.

Neros realized he'd been staring when Leof's discontent had morphed into curiosity. The prince waved a hand, averting his gaze to avoid the strange tug in his stomach.

It was probably just because they were about to rocket skyward.

Chapter 11
Pink Petals

*N*eros learned quickly that Leof was, unfortunately, susceptible to motion sickness. Minutes after they landed, Leof had a startlingly disoriented look on his face. Then, he stumbled to his knees and retched. The prince felt helpless, at first rummaging through his bag for an antidote before being politely reminded that motion sickness could only be cured by the passage of time and feet on the *ground*. So, he settled for kneeling beside the Ember and rubbing small circles on his back. He was…morbidly fascinated with the viscous glowing liquid in the grass but elected not to ask. It struck him as rather inappropriate.

Leof coughed harshly, startling Neros. "A-are you all right, now?" He asked, hand hovering behind Leof's back.

The Ember stood, cheeks faintly glowing. "I'm fine. Sorry about that."

"No need to apologize," Neros smiled, turning to Pontius, who was adjusting his monocle. "Any sign of Anthea?"

"Your eyes are as good as mine, your highness, so if you can't see her, neither can I!"

"Oh, I can see her," Leof said, gesturing with a nod. "See that? She's flying through the air."

Neros turned his gaze to the sky to find that Leof was right. Anthea had been grabbing hold of branches with her vines, propelling herself through massive expanses of the air at a time. She was like a graceful winged beast, and the closer she came, the clearer the fierce determination in her eyes became. She tumbled to the ground, rolling into a fighting stance with her hair poised like a whip. Her eyes darted to Leof and Neros, as if they were a threat, before realizing exactly who they were. Her jaw dropped, hand limp at her side.

"How did you—?!"

"We *warped.*" Leof said, disdainfully.

Anthea nodded. "Well, glad you caught up. We need to get looking for the lost Arborian."

She began to parade toward the falls, but Neros stumbled over to her, putting an arm out to keep her rooted. "Wait, Anthy. Wait! You just stormed off without even so much as a *hint* of who we're looking for. We can't help you unless we know!"

The princess blinked, frowned, and blinked some more, like she was trying to piece together both how she hadn't said something *or* how Neros didn't know.

"Rosea," Her voice was hoarse, he noticed. "We have to find Rosea."

"R-rosea…?" The prince's heart nearly stopped. "But how? How do you know for certain she's *here?*"

Anthea pushed past him, walking closer to the edge of Paralia. "I was walking beside her when it happened. We were laughing, planning something mischievous, you know," Her tone was light, like she wanted to revel in nostalgia, but Neros could hear the quiet quaking beneath it. "And the ground shook, and I narrowly escaped, which I told you, but I looked back there, at *every* face, and she wasn't there. There was a huge gap in the crowd where we were standing."

"Sure, you didn't see her, so you know she left," Leof supplied, following at a safe distance. "But why here?"

"Paralia was all over my notes on the prophecy," Anthea explained. "It's not surprising that Rosea would pick up on its significance. And Florus, he…something about divine water to grow something, remember? I had that in my notes. The divine water from Paralia could cure all ailments, lift curses and bring fortune to those who needed it. At least, that was what I thought initially." She stared out to the water, expression hardening. "But it turns out Paralia's waters weren't so divine."

"And now, it seems like they're hardly there!" Pontius cried, floating ahead of them.

He was right. The water level had receded greatly, revealing a treacherous-looking passage with winding twists and turns. *More labyrinth-like ruins.* Neros was sure it was a gold mine of information, but Pontius' tone had ignited panic in Neros. It had only been a few brief months since their adventure started, and already the curse over Endra had spanned so far…Arboria was nearly in ruins, as well. *What does that mean for Vetur? Or Runa, or my parents? Oh, gods, I've been gone so long…* Neros shook his head. What he had to do right now was help Anthea find Rosea.

"Well, maybe less water means less of those water beasts will attack us," Neros said.

"Yes, it would be ideal to avoid getting *soaked,*" Leof squinted disdainfully at the distant falls. "But this Rosea girl isn't going to find herself. We should get looking."

Hours passed, the group looking down muddy passages and rocky lakebeds. No monsters attacked them—it seemed that Neros' theory was right, and the lack of water meant that the beasts, if any, would need to use whatever water was left to take shape. In their own right, they must have known not to deplete Paralia of *all* of its precious resource.

The packed, damp dirt grew muddier as they approached the center of the large lake. If Neros looked overhead, he could see the vine bridge pathways Anthea had created on their first trip. As they neared the lakebed's center, the water lapped at their ankles, and Neros turned around to take in their current status.

"Is everyone alright?"

"I'm fine. No sign of any life, though," Leof said.

"I thought I sensed her this way! Look, where the water is deeper," Anthea replied, rushing past Neros to wade further. Then, she paused, looking back at Neros. "Wait, Neros, why are we getting our feet so wet like this? Couldn't you make some ice for us?"

Neros wrung his wrists in his hands. "I could…I could try. Which direction do we need to be headed in? I may only be able to do this once."

Leof looked curious, and Neros realized he'd only glossed over his predicament back in the volcano. *Perhaps it's best left alone,* Neros thought. *I wouldn't want him to worry more than he already does.* Anthea peered out into the lake, pointing near where they entered the coves.

"Maybe there," She said. "We got into the coves near that point, so maybe we can find Rosea if we start from the top."

"Got it." He stretched out his staff, casting the ice spell and watching as the water transformed in front of them. His arm arched, then burned, and before long, Neros was forced to drop the spell, inhaling sharply.

"You alright?" Anthea asked. He nodded, rubbing his arm to soothe the pain. She surveyed his progress, grinning with her hands on her hips. "Not bad, Neros, not bad!"

Something felt wrong, though. He had successfully made a bridge for them to begin crossing, but as they walked, the feeling only worsened. Before, they were trespassing on holy grounds, and it was made abundantly clear that they were not allowed to be here. Now, however, it was eerily quiet as though someone was laying in the shadows, waiting for the perfect time to strike.

The water began to ripple. They were easy to miss, like a few stray water droplets slid off the tree leaves, but they steadily grew stronger. The makeshift ice bridge rocked, and the trio gripped each other's arms to keep their balance.

"Wh-what's going on?" Anthea asked.

"I-I don't know!" Neros replied, panic rising in his throat. "Pontius?"

"I think something dormant may have awakened! It certainly isn't happy, your highness—*AAH!*"

A large tidal wave—how a wave that large could come out of so little water, Neros didn't know, but it rose higher and higher and threatened to knock them all asunder. In a last-ditch effort to block the water, Neros procured a shield made of ice, wincing at the pain shooting up his elbow.

But the water was stronger.

It tore through the ice, shattering it and scattering the trio. Neros tried to hold his breath, but water slipped up his nose and he coughed, water rushing into his lungs. He reached out, blindly, for his best friend and new companion, but the current pulled him down into a hole. His head knocked on one of the walls, and everything went black.

☼

Leof spun and swirled, down, down, until finally the vortex spat him up and he landed face-first in some dirt. He coughed, throat raw from where water had shot up his nose. He blinked, his vision hazy. His head felt cold, and he cursed; he hated when his flame went out. His whole body felt sluggish, like he was about to freeze up and die right there. He coughed again, willing the heat in his core to become more powerful to blast away some of the excess liquid. The hiss of steam reached his ears, and he relaxed. *Much better. Now, then…* With enough of the liquid gone, the flames atop his head sparked and re-ignited, and he tied it back into his low ponytail. His vision cleared up, and immediately the Ember was grateful that his two companions—he refused to say *friends*—hadn't seen his moment of weakness. *I'm sure the princess would have about twelve too many questions about that.* It wasn't worth explaining, anyway; it's not as though not knowing would deter their adventure in any capacity.

Slowly rising to his feet, Leof took in his surroundings. The air was heavy with humidity, and *he* was the only light source in the room. He could make out a short distance in front of him, enough to tell that the walls were rocky and dark. He instinctively reached for his backpack to find that it must have fallen off when the wave took him. Leof sighed, crouching and igniting a few sparks, tossing them out to light the immediate area a few times. Once he found it, he pulled out a small torch and lit it, using the glow to find any other displaced items and replacing them in his pack, then securing it to his back once more.

There were two paths in front of him, and Leof resented the choice. He would have preferred one longer, more perilous track than the chance of getting even *more* lost. If all three of them became separated like this, how could he safely say they'd all find each other again? Not to mention, neither Neros nor Anthea had bothered to describe Rosea's appearance to Leof. *I suppose she'd be the only other living creature here, but what if this is a setup? What if we're to be ambushed?* His brows settled into a deep frown as he walked; he'd chosen a path at random. It curved to the left, then the right, then left again, before dropping off into a steep slide. Leof paused, looking back and wondering if it was worth the time to search for Rosea down the other path. Normally, he wouldn't pass up an opportunity to be thorough—better to know all than to know only what was conveniently presented to you—but in the interest of his *sanity*, he thought it best to continue down unfamiliar paths. He willed his flame brighter as he slid down the slope, landing upright. He expected it to be *more* wet down here, but the air seemed lighter, and the walls drier. Small fluorescent crystals were fixed to the walls, making delicate patterns that danced under the light of Leof's torch. The Ember took a long moment to admire them; he'd seen a few crystals in his brief venture to the lower layers of the volcano, but they had been mined—these grew naturally, and they were beautiful.

He debated, if briefly, whether he should take one when something caught his eye nearby: a pink petal of…some kind. Leof kneeled, picking up the delicate object and turning it over in his hands. Was it part of a flower? *Down here? I doubt it,* he thought. *This place is beautiful, and sure, it's full of water normally, but it doesn't seem that good at sustaining life.* He moved to pocket it when light humming caught his ear. Immediately, his body tensed—the voice was unfamiliar, so it wasn't Neros, Anthea, or Pontius. He wanted to *hide,* more than anything, but he knew it would be fruitless. He was a being of rock and flame, after all.

"Is that a light…? Hello, is someone there?"

Leof's throat closed up, his body going tense. The voice that carried down the corridor was higher pitched than Anthea's, though less abrasive. *But can I trust it? Is it an illusion of the labyrinth?* Leof recalled how Neros and Anthea described the coves the last time they were here: filled with mind-bending puzzles and ridiculous riddles. Really, it sounded like paradise, but his current situation was a horse of a different color.

"Hello…? Anthy, is that you? Oh, gods and goddesses above, what have I gotten myself into…?" A girl rounded the corner, small eyebrows drawn together in concern. She had a halo of light pink petals around her head, framing her round face. Her barkskin was darker than Anthea's, but it only served to draw out the brightness of her eyes, which were a vibrant magenta—darker than her hair. Leof also noticed a small staff strapped to her back, the head shaped like a flower yet to bloom. "O-oh! I'm so sorry, I–I–um! Are you a creature of this place?"

Leof shifted his weight, feeling a bit awkward. "I'm not. Would you happen to be Rosea?"

"Oh, my! Yes! How do you know of me?"

"I know her highness." He thought it well enough to leave it at that, for now, especially after Rosea's expression brightened.

"You know darling Anthy?! Oh, delightful!" Her face fell back into concern. "Is she not with you?"

Leof shook his head. "Sorry, she isn't. We were separated."

"I don't believe I've ever met you before," Rosea said, regarding him curiously. Her stare caused an uncomfortable heat to flare across his cheeks. He didn't enjoy being scrutinized by strangers, and between Rosea, Anthea, and Neros, he'd had quite enough of it. "What is your name?"

"Leof." He had trouble meeting her eyes, still unsure if he could trust her completely.

"Well, Leof, it's a pleasure to meet you. My name is Rosea Winterflower. Shall we work together to get out of this labyrinth?"

When he looked back at her, she had her hand outstretched for him to shake. He took it, and she reinforced the handshake by clasping her other hand over his. The sheer warmth in her smile reminded him of Neros. *Maybe…maybe I can trust her.*

"Let's get moving, then."

Anthea was *lost.* Hopelessly, irrefutably lost. She had turned the same corner and rounded back to where she began no less than ten times, but every time she thought she'd taken a new path, it led her back here. She ran her hands through her hair in frustration, groaning at the ceiling.

"Is this some kind of *message?!* Or is this sheer torture? A clue of *any kind* would be great right about now!"

She knew that yelling at the walls would provide no clue, or hidden secret, or cool entrance to a second layer of labyrinth beneath the first. She slumped against the wall, sliding down until her butt made a wet *plop* against the floor. *I need to look for Rosea. I need to find her. I need to save the Arborians…all of them, they looked so…* If she wasn't fast enough, they would die. She understood the gravity of the sickly orange glow that Neros' hands emitted when checking the life force left in their bodies.

Anthea was a failure of a princess. What sort of princess couldn't protect her people from harm? She had *run away,* like nothing more than a common coward. And now, now…she couldn't even find her best friend, her one hope at finding a way forward, and she was stuck.

Her throat and chest constricted, like vines had grown and constricted the airways, and when she sucked in a breath, out wrenched a sob. Fresh tears streamed down her face in waves. The weight of thousands of Arborian lives potentially lost crushed her, consumed her, and she kept crying until she couldn't breathe. Neros was not here to ground her, and Leof couldn't offer his unusually perceptive insights. She knew she needed them both, and cursed herself for relying on them, especially since her friendship with Leof was so fresh.

The princess wanted nothing more than to be strong: for her, for her friends, and for her people. But she drowned in the helplessness of it all, and hoped that somehow, someone would be able to find her.

She wasn't sure she could stand up again on her own.

☼

There was an oppressive nature lurking behind the beauty of the labyrinth, Leof noted. While he was carefully exploring with Rosea, the shimmer of the crystals on the wall went from looking inviting to foreboding. A chill ran down his spine as they worked their way back to where Rosea was exploring: a crossroads of three pathways.

"I came from this way," She explained, pointing to her left. "And then I saw a glow coming from this hallway, and that led me to you. I'm delighted to have found someone! A place this large and winding can be awfully lonely."

"Right," He agreed, thinking of the dangerous allure of every passage. "So, is there any way we can make an educated guess for where to go next?"

Rosea pursed her lips and hummed. "Before, I tried feeling the presence of another life with the aid of the complex root system beneath Endra's surface." When Leof's eyebrows raised, she giggled. "It's an ability unique to my race of Arborians, though sadly, I'm the only one left."

"I…I see," He said. She didn't sound especially heartbroken over it, so he didn't know if she needed to be consoled. "I'm…sorry."

"It's quite alright. Arborians don't really have precise parents, as many Veturians do. And maybe Embers, considering your apology. But Arborians are born from the seeds blown from the pollen of their ancestors, so I was unable to meet any of my ancestors before I was born. A deadly wave of cherry leaf spot infected them all…it arrived very suddenly and killed many saplings before they had the chance to grow." Her expression was distant for a moment, but she smiled, and weight of her story dissipated with it. "Never mind that! I hadn't tried to locate anyone for a long while before I found you, so let me see if I can sense whether anyone is nearby."

Rosea approached the far wall, leaning her ear against it as though she were *listening* for the whisper of the root system. Maybe she was. She found a spot farther down the corridor to press her palms against, and she began speaking in the same language Anthea did whenever she'd cast a spell or summon an arrow. *Must be an older Arborian language,* Leof thought. *Since most of the townsfolk we've seen seem to speak in a different tongue to each other.* A bright, yellow-golden light enveloped Rosea and she closed her eyes, again listening carefully.

When her eyes opened, she beamed.

"I can sense Neros! He's travelling with you as well?"

Leof blinked. "You can tell who, just from listening?"

She blushed. "Well, Neros and Anthy are special cases, as luck would have it. I've spent so much time with them, I can identify their rooted rhythms—the pattern of their footsteps, the beats of their hearts, you know—I can sense that very clearly for them. I could sense you, too, of course, since you're right here. But I don't know you as well, regrettably. So, in your case, I can only tell that you're a living creature. Whether you're hostile or not…that I can't tell."

It was undoubtedly a useful skill. The thought of the prince being nearby both calmed Leof and made him restless all at once. Something dawned on him: if they could sense he was nearby, could they logically go down the hall toward the direction Rosea sensed him in? This was a *labyrinth,* after all, which were notorious for being inane twists and turns and backtracking with no hope for escape. He wished he had pen and paper to make a map of some kind. That would be far more useful than root-based echolocation.

"Neros' energy seems to be coming from this direction," Rosea said, pointing farther down the hall. "But he doesn't seem to be in good condition." Her eyebrows furrowed before she spoke Leof's own thoughts aloud. "And I'm not sure we'd reach him quickly, with how these corridors are laid out."

She shuffled around her person for a moment before pulling out precisely what Leof had been yearning for—a long piece of parchment paper, and a quill.

"Oh! I've been making a map, and I didn't even think to show you!" She shuffled back down the corridor, holding the map out for Leof to look at. "I've been keeping track of where my paths take me. Do you think it makes a pattern?'"

The Ember hummed, poring over the map in front of him. "Not all labyrinths have patterns, but this place served as holy grounds to house the Oracle for many years…perhaps he did something to shift the corridors in that time."

As Rosea explained her method of map-making, the gears in Leof's brain continued to turn. The path Rosea had walked looked like it was starting to make a shape. He could guess about where his path led from, including where the opening may have been, but *what* was it becoming…? The lines curved consistently, with stark crosses marking dead end; very few of the curves overlapped each other. Rosea had explored a *lot*, and the curves all seemed to move in the same direction when Leof traced his fingers across the page.

He had a thought, but he needed to test it.

"Let's backtrack the way I came. If we can climb up to where I fell in, I think I may be able to identify what shape this is making."

"Prince Neros, you really should not have used your ice powers back there!" Pontius scolded. His voice echoed down the wide corridor. "You may not be able to see the damage beneath the glove, but I'm sure you can feel it, can't you? You must be careful!"

"I didn't have a choice," Neros defended, though the strength in his voice didn't carry. "We needed to find Rosea, and…a bridge was the fastest way. Besides, I wasn't even entirely sure that Leof should be getting wet. As an Ember, his core is molten, and his hair is flames! Gods, I hope he's alright, what with the *tsunami* that tore us apart…Anthy, too."

Pontius hummed, vibrating from the nervous energy. "Don't even get me started. If not for your recklessness, your highness, you may not have all been separated in the first place! What if one of you dies down here? There is no food or accessible water in the labyrinthian coves of Paralia! And your supplies were scattered, so there's no doubt Sir Leof's and Princess Anthea's were, too." He miserably placed his head in his hands. "Oh, why was I not swifter to warn you?!"

"Don't blame yourself," Neros said. "It's as you said. If not for my recklessness, we wouldn't be in this situation. But Anthea and I got out once, didn't we? So surely, we can do it again…hopefully we'll be able to find Rosea along the way."

He ran his non-injured hand along the wall as they walked, willing the consistent pain in his gloved hand to fade. He did *not* want to look at it, because if the sharp sting he felt was any indication, the cracks had severely worsened. Besides, if he couldn't see the damage, it would be easier to distract himself from the pain. Or, he could just focus on the corridor, which seemed to be slowly curving to the left as they continued. *Strange,* Neros mused. *I could have sworn that Paralia was more doors-and-puzzles than paths-and-walkways like this…I wonder if Pegaios changed the layout during our absence, or if Paralia's underbelly is truly this vast.*

He was grateful to have Pontius with him, all scolding aside. He couldn't imagine being alone, like Leof or Anthea. Down here, it was dark (though perhaps Leof could light his own way) and the atmosphere felt thick with something less tangible than the humidity. Sure, it was cool and damp and it made Neros' clothes stick to his skin a bit uncomfortably, but there was something foreboding about these paths. Almost as though they were daring Neros to get lost.

Well, Neros found that quite unlikely, considering there was only *one* path for him to take. But the farther he walked, the narrower the passage became, until finally, he'd hit a dead end.

He blinked.

"Did I miss something somewhere?" He wondered. When he turned around, Pontius wasn't behind him. "Pontius? Hello?"

Neros went back; it was his only option, after all. This time, he kept his hand along the opposite wall, with the sole purpose of finding something hidden. Had Pontius gone down a secret passage without telling him? *Impossible,* Neros reasoned. *He would shout in delight, without a doubt.* "Pontius, are you out here? I swear, he was beside me just a moment ago."

Distracted by his own musings, he didn't realize his arm had given way to a hole in the wall, and he tumbled ungracefully downward. His bag tangled around his midsection, and he groaned as he landed painfully on his side.

"What was that?" Said a high-pitched voice.

"Your highness?" Another voice, and Neros recognized it instantly. *Leof.* He scrambled to his feet, brushing himself off and stumbling in the direction of the voices.

Leof and Rosea emerged from around the corner, Rosea clutching a map and Leof holding a torch. Rosea's eyes lit up at the sight of the prince, and she leapt into a hug, sending them both careening back to the ground.

"It's a joy to see you well, Rosea," He laughed.

"I'm so delighted to see you in one piece!" She said, lifting herself off and helping him up. She was taller than Leof by a hair, but still far shorter than the prince. Her smile morphed into a deep frown, and suddenly Neros felt a bit intimidated by her, just like they were children. "You are unwell. I sensed your body's energy from far away, and Leof figured out the pattern of the corridors to help guide us here. I wasn't expecting you to come tumbling out of a tunnel, but I'm glad you did. Let me examine you!"

"Wait, Rosea, why—" Neros protested, but Rosea's hands were already on his, tugging the glove off his hand. He winced. From all their battling, more vein-like cracks began to scatter up and down the length of his forearm, reaching as far as his fingers. It looked so fragile.

"Is that...?" Leof asked, hesitant. Like he didn't want to be right.

"*This* is what I've been sensing," Rosea gasped. "No wonder I thought you were so unwell. Your arm is...it's a wreck, Neros, I'll be honest with you."

"I–I know. It's a curse...my magic hurts to use." Neros admitted, voice laced with shame. "And when I do...use it, it cracks my arm...like this."

"Oh, my. Well, I'm sure that has been quite difficult for you."

Neros opened his mouth, though no words came out. From beside him, Pontius spun in front of Rosea, gesturing to Neros' opposite arm.

"We've been working on an alternative, though! Show her, your highness!"

The prince raised his opposite palm shyly, willing water magic to conjure. In his hand, a small orb of the liquid formed, and he waved it around before tossing it aside, where it bounced before collapsing with a weak *plop*.

"Oooh, water magic! I didn't know it was possible for you to do that!"

Neros rubbed the back of his neck. "Me either, until about 6 weeks ago."

"And he has been excellent at honing his skills!" Pontius quipped.

"Where *were* you, anyway?" Neros asked.

"Oh! I began to feel fatigued, so I rested on a wall when it cracked and I fell through! Then you tumbled down shortly after, landing nearly on top of me. But I stayed valiantly silent, because I didn't want you to fear for my life, your highness." He turned to Rosea. "If you are Lady Rosea, it is my honor and pleasure to meet you. I am Pontius, a water spirit born here in Paralia!"

"I see! So *you're* a creature from here! That makes much more sense. I asked Leof if he was from here earlier, because his appearance reminded me a bit of the crystals affixed to these rocky walls."

She had a point. While they were chatting, Leof had taken to sitting in the hallway with the map in his lap, slowly adding lines to it to make it more complete. A soft glow emitted from his cracks reminiscent of the rocks that occasionally glinted in the darkness.

"So, does water magic not injure you?" Rosea asked, stepping into his line of sight to continue her thorough examination of his arm. "Surely your arm didn't start with this many fractures."

"Water magic doesn't injure me, no, but…I may, um…I may have used my ice magic since."

She whacked his opposite arm, and he flinched. For being so small, she had a powerful swing.

"Prince Neros of Vetur, how *dare* you carelessly put your life in danger like this! You don't even know what this curse *does*, do you?!" When he shook his head, her anger doubled. "What if it spread to your heart and killed you? Or if you begin to lose your fingers from it cracking too much? It isn't like you to be so reckless with your life, Neros. What happened?"

When he met her eyes again, he noticed how pitying her gaze was. He shook his head; there was simply no reason for her to be burdened with his troubles. "It's nothing to worry about. I overexerted myself, and I won't be doing that from here forward," He closed his hand gently around hers, and lowered it from his arm. "I'll be okay. We need to focus on finding Anthy and getting out of here."

Rosea looked blatantly dissatisfied with the answer, but blessedly did not pursue the conversation further. "You have a point. I'd been making a map—" She patted her pockets, frowning. "Wh-where did it go?"

"I've got it over here. I apologize," Leof said, rising from the ground and holding the map out to Rosea. "Based on where Prince Neros came from, I think my theory is correct. If you could just fill in the blanks, your highness…?"

Rosea passed him the map, and he did his best to recall his previous walking path…looking down at the stark inked lines, Neros could see a shape beginning to form. If he added the approximation of where he came from, then… *It's a wave!* The shape dictated that Leof had fallen from above the path that Rosea had walked on, insinuating that he and Leof were deposited on the same strip of wave, but in different places. When Neros carefully inked in the blanks, he saw the shape more clearly.

"If this path is methodical," Leof said, taking the map back from Neros. "Then Princess Anthea should, in theory, be on a path below us. It's possible she landed above, but considering where you and I have fallen, I think we're closer to the edge of Paralia's landscape. Does that make sense?"

Neros blinked, carefully considering the map, then Leof. "Yes, I think so. Besides, before I fell, I heard rushing water, which only further pays toward your point."

Rosea beamed. "Perfect! Now all we have to do is find a way down. One should be along this wall, right?"

Leof nodded, and the group began to feel carefully along the wall. Neros was glad they didn't decide to split up—if Leof's theory was wrong, and they tumbled down *other* holes, who knew how long it would take them all to escape?

A somewhat tense quiet settled over them as their methodic search continued. Rosea broke the silence.

"I've been travelling for months, going from town to town on my way here. I…I ran after Anthea as soon as I felt the rumble and saw her spring into action, but I lost sight of her once I got out of the woods. I recalled what she said about Paralia, and its healing waters that could mend any illness or grow anything from anywhere, and I came as soon as I could."

"Were the waters this calm when you arrived?" Neros asked, stopping momentarily over a strange bump in the wall before continuing.

"They were," She said. "It was frightening, really. I'd walked into an opening left behind by one of the falls, and a door slammed shut behind me. I heard a mysterious voice…one telling me to stay because the world was too dangerous. Is…is it really unsafe out there?"

"We're not really sure *what* is happening out there," Neros admitted. "We came back this way to ask the gods for help, and when Anthea saw the state of Arboria…well…"

"She noticed you weren't there, and came running to find you herself," Leof finished.

"Oh, goodness. Leave it to Anthy to think with her heart," Rosea laughed. "But I'm happy you came. Ooh, hello, what's this?"

She stooped down to tug at some vines that were poking through a crack in the wall.

"Strange," Leof said. "I don't remember vegetation along any other path."

"I think I recognize it," Rosea said, bending closer to it before looking up at Neros. "She used to grow these when she was upset! Look, the thorns!"

The prince kneeled beside her, examining the foreign root. It was unmistakably thorny, and a rich, vibrant green. A distinct memory of these thorns being coiled around his midsection came to him, and he shuddered. "You're right. Anthea may be nearby."

"We have to break this wall!" Rosea rolled her shoulders, stepping to the far end of the corridor before rushing at it, yelling. "We're coming, Anthy!"

Her shoulder collided against the wall with a *whump*. Rosea stumbled back, rubbing at the sore spot.

Leof's hand covered his mouth, stifling a laugh. When Rosea glared at him, he shrugged. "Apologies. I'm not sure that's the best way to go about it."

"Well, do *you* have any better ideas, mister genius?" Rosea huffed. "Those thorns aren't a happy sign. Anthea could be in big trouble! We must move with urgency!"

"We can't really move with *urgency* if the wall before us isn't so easy to destroy. This labyrinth may be old, but parts of it are still plenty sturdy." Leof walked up to the vine, tugging at it briefly before feeling the wall itself. "It's soft here—maybe your shoulder loosened some of the sediment, Rosea—but we'll need something a bit more powerful to crumble it."

Neros hummed, rifling through the objects in his bag. Books, food, and other sparse materials he'd grabbed suddenly didn't seem so useful. *Maybe I could freeze the wall, and Leof could heat it,* he thought, looking it over and wondering where its weak points may lie.

"Neros, don't even *think* about it," Rosea warned. "I don't want you using any more of your ice magic to try and make this wall brittle."

He shrank back. "H-how did you–?"

"I *know* you, Neros. I may not have seen you in months, but I can still see that *scheming* look in your eye. We can figure this out without using your magic!"

"It is true," Leof added. "Don't overexert yourself. I may be able to melt it down on my own, if you'll allow me the space to try."

He and Rosea stepped back, and Leof felt up and down the wall, searching for weak points, perhaps places he could crack. Then, he reached into his pocket and took out the daggers he'd earned from his trials in the volcano. He stuck them in the wall, and together, they glowed. Neros stepped back farther, pulling Rosea with him. *I hope the wall doesn't explode...*

"Versinge...*gasmolten!*" Leof stretched out his arm placed his palm at the center of the dagger points. A bright red light burst forth from the daggers, dousing the wall in flames and swallowing Leof up with it. Neros' stomach dropped in time to Rosea's hand gripping his arm. The spectacle lasted a few moments, and the flames died down, the daggers clanging to the floor.

Leof bent over to pick them up, appearing unchanged; miraculously, his clothes were also intact. *Must be a special Embran fabric...* When the Ember caught their frightened gazes, he quirked a brow. "What? Don't look at me like that. It's open, so let's go. There are more vines littering the way down, but it's steep. We should be able to climb safely."

Rosea nodded, bolting down the passage and climbing down the vines. Neros followed, pausing at the top of the vines.

"Thank you," He said. "For doing this."

"Don't thank me. It had to be done, right? Better for you to save your strength." Leof swung past Neros and continued down. He spoke so casually of doing things that, in Neros' eyes, were really quite kind. His heart felt light as he climbed down to where, hopefully, they could find Anthea.

He *heard* Anthea before he saw her. The prince was still lowering himself to the ground when he heard Rosea's delight.

"Anthy! Princess, I'm so glad you're okay!"

"Rosea! It's true! You're–you're alive!" Anthea sounded choked up, like she'd been crying for longer than just a minute or two.

Neros turned around to see the two girls hugging like their lives depended on it. Anthea looked over Rosea's shoulder, and her whole face lit up when she saw him. She separated herself from Rosea's grip to tumble into his arms. "Neros, thank the goddess you're here too."

"Likewise. But really, you should thank—"

"Leof!" Anthea smiled, moving from Neros immediately to the Ember, who tried to back away from the princess before being *tackled.* "I felt the tips of my vines get singed, and I knew right away it was you. You're a real hero!"

"I am no such thing."

"You are! Heroes save princesses, and that's just what you've done," She laughed. "You can't deny me now!"

Leof rolled his eyes, and Neros laughed, wrapping his arms around them both.

The Ember groaned. "Must this become a group hug?"

"Yes!" Rosea called, jumping in and joining from behind. They remained that way for a few moments, and Neros felt safe then, his arms around his friends new and old. What seemed, at first, like a means to trap them here forever became instead a means to reunite. It left Neros feeling hopeful for their future.

"This is a lovely moment," Pontius piped up, perched on Neros' shoulder. "But I must remind you all we have business back in Arboria! Lady Rosea, may we take you back home?"

"Oh! I'm no lady, good sir," Rosea giggled. "But now that I've found you all, I would be happy to keep adventuring alongside you for a little while. What business did you have in Arboria?"

"We need to grow a vine from the Great Arborian Tree to the heavens of Andolis," Anthea said, separating with a serious look in her eyes. "We need to speak to the gods."

"Wow! Much has changed for you two, indeed. Well, let's not wait any longer. How do we get out of here?"

Leof sighed, appearing particularly dismayed. "We warp."

Chapter 12
Andolis Above

*O*nce everyone's stomachs settled back in Arboria, the three heroes re-counted everything they'd encountered thus far to Rosea. She was enraptured the entire time, especially when it came to their newest companion.

"So you're a blacksmith by trade?" She asked, eyes wide with wonder. "And you can make anything?"

His cheeks glowed with embarrassment. "Contraptions or weapons or tools, mostly. Many Embers are blacksmiths or something similar."

"That is incredible. And you had to fight massive beasts and a member of an elite council just to leave the volcano?"

He shook his head. "Not to leave. Just to earn something."

"Those daggers?"

"They're…of legend. I'm told."

"Well, do you believe it?"

Leof nodded. Rosea got the hint that he may not want to talk further about himself, and moved on. They were climbing over and around the husks of Arborians, toward the epicenter of life in the kingdom: The Great Arbor-ian Tree. The trek was utterly morbid, but the conversation surrounding their adventures kept it from feeling somber. As they passed through sections of Arborians, he heard Rosea chant something under her breath, and her staff would emit a soft yellow glow and puffs of what appeared to be pollen would float out of the tip, drifting gently over each group. Once the pollen hit an Arborian, it affixed itself to the barkskin, continuing to glow and turning the forest into a landscape of fireflies. *Elegaic in its own way, as it almost looks like a funeral procession,* Neros noted.

The tree itself was a wonder: long hollowed out and built into, it functioned much like a castle. The top of the tree—the roof, but really, but it was a canopy—was an intricately woven-together system of branches and leaves, and Neros was ever surprised at how structurally sound it was. Leof looked hesitant, at first, as though his hair would set fire to the treetops, but Anthea pulled him along despite his protests.

"There's got to be a good spot to grow the vine," She said, surveying the canopy. "How tall do you think it should be, Rosea?"

"Well, as long as you have the energy, as tall as you can make it. If you're trying to reach the heavens of Andolis, you may need to send someone up to tell you when to stop."

Anthea hummed. Neros looked at the sky.

"I'll go."

The group turned to Leof, who had a determined glint in his eye. "You said you could feel it earlier when I singed your vines, right? So, send me up. When we hit Andolis, I'll burn the tip of the vine. That way, you'll know right away, and you can preserve your energy."

"That…That's *brilliant!*" Anthea beamed, tackling Leof and twirling him. "Boy, I was worried when we first met you, but you are so smart and brave, Leof. You're a great fit for our team!"

His cheeks glowed again, hair flickering and crackling anxiously. "Please put me down."

She placed him in front of her, waving her hands around to spin a large leaf into existence beneath his feet. "For you to stand on," She explained, testing her abilities by spurring the growth of a vine to lift Leof on, making the leaf the platform of an elevator. "Feel steady?"

"As steady as I can be," He said.

She began to chant in the ancient Arborian Neros knew so well by now; he was sure he'd never tire of hearing it. There was something rhythmic and melodic about the words, like they were being whispered by the wind. Leof held fast to the tip of the vine as it sprung from the canopy, curling around the leaf and lifting it higher and higher, with steadily increasing speed. Neros admired his stalwart determination—being prone to motion sickness as he was, Leof held the vine steadily without a trace of discomfort or nausea on his face.

As the vine took a fatter, more robust shape, Anthea's spellcasting slowed. "Ugh," she groaned. "It's hard to pull energy from this place. I think the curse runs deeper than I first imagined…I thought the canopy of the tree would be okay, but I just don't know if there's enough energy in the available roots."

"Could you grow more?" Neros asked.

Anthea shook her head. "I'd need a lot of water to do that. In Paralia, summoning and growing vines was easy because there were small traces of water *everywhere*. But here…" She trailed off, and Neros understood her pain.

"Water, huh…" Neros looked at his hands. He outstretched the bare one, closing his eyes and calling forth the energy of running water. *Think of yourself like one of those waterfalls,* he told himself. *Conjure a river of water like how you used to build stairwells of ice.* A chill ran down his spine, and he thought he may have failed and conjured ice instead, but liquid orbs began to form and coagulate in front of his palm. He pushed it toward the vine, thus creating a personal waterfall for Anthea. He caught her eye and smiled.

"Neros, you have so many surprises up your sleeve!"

He laughed. "It really shouldn't be so much of a surprise, Anthy. I've been practicing every night!"

"Fair enough." She tested the vines, pulling out smaller strands first and weaving them together, sending them upward inch by inch. She nodded, hummed, and continued her chant. "*Crescere, crescere altius, crescere, crescere fortius…*"

The constant stream of water was visibly helpful to Anthea, but positively draining for Neros. Now that the princess had regained her focus, it was likely she wouldn't stop until Leof singed her vine. Rosea walked up next to him, putting her hand on his outstretched arm.

"Need help maintaining your energy?" When he nodded, she closed her eyes, mouthing words he couldn't make out, and sprouting more of that glowing pollen, affixing it to the prince's sleeve.

He felt lighter immediately.

Through their combined efforts, the minutes passed steadily, and Neros fell into a trance, watching the water feed the vine's growth to the sky. Before long Anthea abruptly stopped, pulling back and hissing like she'd been burned.

Because, well, she had been.

"I guess he made it," She announced, looking to Neros and holding out her hand. "Get on. It'll be faster if I climb."

Neros' eyebrows drew together, and he turned to Rosea. "What about you?"

She waved her hand. "I'll be plenty busy maintaining the life force of these Arborians while you're away. I'll keep searching for clues about this prophecy, too. Go ahead! I promise I'll be fine."

The prince's gaze moved past her, to the forest of Arborians clinging to the last threads of life. His heart swelled with a sense of purpose, but his gut sank with dread. Rosea's face was determined, and her energy seemed to double once she took her life-pollen back from Neros' arm. *I have to trust her,* he told himself. *I have to believe she'll be okay while we do what we can up above.*

He grabbed on to Anthea, who swung him onto her back—with a complete lack of grace on Neros' part—and they began their ascent.

Before, Neros had been pleasantly surprised by the stability of the Arborian Tree's canopy. Sure, the woven structure had bent under their weight, but he felt no sign of it collapsing. When he and Anthea reached the heavens, however, Neros' mind was bent even further.

They were standing on *clouds*. And clouds stretched around them as far as the eye could see. The air was crisp, but not cold, and smelled like fresh laundry. In the distance, Neros could see a large castle made of pale white stone. Its shimmer rivaled the sun itself, but he was confused by the utter *barrenness* of Andolis aside from it. He looked at Leof, who met his gaze with a shrug.

"You would think there would be guardians, but when I got up here, there was nothing." Oddly, Leof's voice didn't echo across the landscape; more that it sounded swallowed up by sound.

"Well, no guards means no fights and no roundabout explanations of our visit to people who don't care to hear it. Which makes our path forward pretty clear," Anthea said, leaning on Neros' shoulder and gesturing to the castle nestled in clouds. Neros looked at his feet. Again, he was shocked: they sank into the clouds slightly, as though he was standing in snow, but the clouds themselves were perfectly opaque, ridding him the opportunity to see Endra from so far above. *Perhaps I should have taken in the view while riding on Anthea's back to get here...*

As they began to walk, the silence felt deafening and disorienting, as not even their steps made sound. Neros checked over his shoulder now and again, just to be positive he could still see Anthea's vine poking out of the clouds in the distance. The prince tugged at his glove—his stunt in Paralia had caused his arm to *throb*, but he'd do anything to avoid the other two taking notice. *This pain will pass, just like it always does.*

"Have you thought about what you're going to *say* to the gods to explain our situation?" Leof asked.

"If the prophecy is right, the gods now were once mortals, like us. So I'm sure they remember what it was like to deal with the strange darkness and the cursing and all," Anthea waved it off. "They'll know."

Leof frowned. "If they're our gods, wouldn't they know by now what's happening to Endra? Shouldn't they have...stepped in?"

The question sat uncomfortably in the air. After a strained silence, Pontius said, "It is not typically the business of gods to interfere with mortal life. At least, that's what I believe Pegaios would say."

They continued their walk quietly after that. Neros thought carefully about Leof's question, and his mind began to swirl with all the questions he could ask. *What of my parents? Who was it that cursed them? And me? Is there a way to reverse the damage done so far?* He wondered if Leof would ask about the dried lava in the Eldur Ignis Volcano, or if Anthea would demand life be restored to the Arborians. Stress tugged at his stomach, and he tugged at his glove a bit more. Pontius seemed to sense his pain, floating down and offering some of his own healing magic to soothe it. The prince was relieved that it worked; looking down the path carved in the clouds, they still had a ways to go before reaching the castle ahead.

❄

"I didn't think there'd be a gate."

"Well, it's a castle, isn't it, Princess Anthea? Most castles have gates."

"But we couldn't see it from the distance...are you sure it hasn't just appeared now, Leof?" Neros asked, frowning at the structure. Made of clouds, the gate was golden in hue like the sun at dusk was reflecting off it.

The main part billowed into an archway, with thin, silvered spindles curling straight down into the cloudy ground at their feet. In the center was a circular insignia with a snowflake on the top, a leaf in the lower left, and a flame in the lower right. It reminded Neros of the puzzling orbs he and Anthea had dealt with their first time in Paralia.

"I can't be *certain* it didn't just appear now," Leof murmured. "Just that it's not that strange."

"Well, gates usually mean guards, right?" Anthea countered, crossing her arms. "Which means a lot of talking. So where do you think they are?"

"I BELIEVE GUARDS WOULD SPEAK LESS THAN YOU LOT."

The three of them startled at the deep voice, looking back at the gate in awe.

"Did it just *talk?*" Anthea asked, bewildered.

"THAT IS HURTFUL, YOUNG ONE. I AM NOT AN 'IT.' I AM A BEING OF WORTH, FABLED GATEKEEPER AMUND. WHO ARE YOU?"

"I'm Princess Anthea, and my travelling companions here are Prince Neros, Leof, and Pontius the water spirit. We've come to request an audience with the gods!"

"YOU DO NOT NEED TO SHOUT," Amund replied. "WHY MUST YOU SHOUT?"

"Sorry," Anthea replied, rubbing the back of her neck. "It's just… you're *huge*, Amund, and I'm just not sure where your consciousness can hear me from."

"A RIDICULOUS CONFUSION, YOUNG ONE, BUT IF IT HELPS, I CAN TAKE A MORTAL-APPEARING FORM."

"You don't have to–ah, gods damn it, he's already started changing shape." As Amund's clouds began to twirl through the air, pooling in front of them and building the shape of a man, Anthea mumbled something about this being *exactly* why she hated gates and gatekeepers and guards alike, because it required so much extra *talking* when really she just wanted to demand answers from the gods herself. Neros chuckled despite himself, raising his hands in apology when she shot him a glare.

Amund's mortal form was clumsy at best, made entirely of clouds and still twice the size of any one of the three of them. Now, he stood in front of the gate, face firm and stoic. His eyes, like the eyes of the water beasts Neros and Anthea had fought, glowed a fierce yellow, contrasting the kindness in his voice. It unsettled Neros, and he couldn't place exactly why.

"I HOPE THIS APPEASES YOU, YOUNG ONE," Amund continued; if he'd heard Anthea's grumbling, he made no comment on it. "NOW, YOU SEEK A COUNCIL WITH THE GODS SILVA, ISOLDE, AND PYRRHUS, CORRECT?"

"Correct," She replied. "Could you let us pass?"

"IF I WERE A GATEKEEPER WHO ALLOWED ANYONE WHO ASKED TO PASS THROUGH, I WOULD NOT BE A VERY GOOD GATEKEEPER," He said. "YOU MUST PROVE YOURSELF TO ME."

"Listen, if it's trial by combat, we'll have to politely decline," Anthea explained. "My companions have been injured recently, and we'd really prefer not to fight you right now."

So she knew I'd hurt myself, Neros thought, tugging nervously at his glove. He stole a glance at Leof, who had crossed his arms and remained silent.

"PROOF OF WORTH DOES NOT ALWAYS COME IN THE FORM OF BRUTE FORCE, YOUNG ONE. THAT MUCH I KNOW YOU KNOW," Amund said. His form shrank a bit. "INSTEAD, I ASK THAT YOU ANSWER MY RIDDLES THREE. ONE RIDDLE EACH, NO ASSISTANCE."

Leof frowned. "And how, exactly, are you going to prevent that?"

Amund snapped his fingers, and a bright light shimmered over Neros and Anthea, covering them each in an orb of glass. Neros' pulse raced, and he pressed his fingers to the edge of the glass, pushing against it. The glass resisted.

"THIS GLASS CONTAINMENT WILL HANDLE THAT. YOUR COMPANIONS CAN HEAR US, BUT YOU CANNOT HEAR THEM. IF YOU LOOK TO THEM FOR INTERPRETIVE HELP, YOU WILL BE PUNISHED. DO YOU UNDERSTAND?"

Neros watched Leof look between the two of them, alarmed, before taking a breath to nod at the gatekeeper in compliance.

"VERY WELL. LISTEN CAREFULLY—THIS IS YOUR RIDDLE:
THEY HAVE NOT FLESH, NOR FEATHERS,
NOR SCALES, NOR BONES,
YET THEY HAVE FINGERS AND THUMBS OF THEIR OWN.
WHAT ARE THEY?"

Leof stroked his chin in thought, and Neros slumped against the side of the glass. All he could do was watch, and it tortured him; he and Anthea used to take pride in solving all sorts of strange castle riddles when they were kids. When the prophecy came into their lives, they turned all their focus to it: it was their life's biggest riddle. But here, Neros couldn't offer as much as a wave of a hand to help Leof in his contemplation. So instead, Neros watched, almost entranced by the way his hair flickered around his cheeks as he thought. Neros could nearly see the gears in his mind spinning.

Then, he looked up. "Gloves," He said, like it was obvious.

Amund smiled. "THAT IS CORRECT." The glass dissipated from on top of Anthea, and covered Leof instead. His hair…dimmed. *Is that from the lack of air…?*

"NOW IT IS YOUR TURN, YOUNG ONE," Amund said, and he shrank in size a bit.

"LISTEN CAREFULLY—THIS IS YOUR RIDDLE:
LIGHTER THAN WHAT I AM MADE OF,
MORE OF ME IS HIDDEN THAN IS SEEN."

Anthea hummed. "Pretty short, for a riddle."

"YET YOU STALL IN YOUR ANSWER."

"I'm not *stalling*, I'm *thinking*, you impatient cloud-man," She rolled her eyes. After a few moments, she turned to Neros and asked, "More of me is hidden than seen, huh…isn't there that phrase, 'that's just the tip of the iceberg' or something?"

Neros blinked, eyebrows drawing together. *I can't open my mouth, because Amund will assume I'm helping her, but if I do nothing, Anthea will think I don't know the answer, either, but she's right…Oh, gods…*

"NO ASSISTANCE!" Amund boomed, and a wave of electricity crackled from his fingers, shooting Anthea and bouncing off her, flickering to the glass orb Neros stood in and shocking him from all angles. It was a strange buzzing sensation, and he thought he may have screamed—or maybe Anthea screamed, or maybe they both did. His eyes fluttered, and he quivered with the tingling sensation as it tickled his nerves.

When the world refocused, he could practically see the steam rising out of Anthea's ears—*was that actually steam rising out of her ears?*—and she stomped her foot, the cloud puffing up around it.

"I was *not* asking for *help!*" She hollered, trying to tame her now-frazzled vines.

Amund only shrugged. "IF YOU WISH TO AVOID PUNISHMENT, PERHAPS

The princess ran her hands through her hair, groaning in frustration. "You're the *worst.*"

Watching Anthea sit and ponder the riddle in silence gave Neros time to focus on quelling the twitching in his muscles. Leof caught his eye and sent him a questioning look. Neros smiled, and Leof sighed.

"I'm going—ugh. I'm going to stick with my initial thought," Anthea said at last, carefully unbraiding and re-braiding her hair. "An iceberg."

Amund smiled, and his form shrank further. "VERY GOOD, YOUNG ONE."

"NOW, IT IS YOUR TURN.

LISTEN CAREFULLY—THIS IS YOUR RIDDLE:

I AM NOT ALIVE, BUT I GROW;

I HAVE NOT LUNGS, BUT I NEED AIR;

I HAVE NO MOUTH, YET IF I DRINK WATER, I WILL DIE.

WHAT AM I?"

The glass around him dissipated, and he took a deep breath. He heard the magic encase over Anthea again, who had shouted "Good luck!" right before her voice was swallowed up by the glass.

Neros sat down in the clouds, rubbing his chin in thought. *Something that grows, but isn't alive…*He could think of many elemental things that fit the bill, depending on how you sliced it. *But riddles are never about contingencies… often the answer is plain and simple. I can't overthink this.* As he thought about it, he considered their adventure so far. Trekking through the volcano had been a wonder Neros wouldn't soon forget; the Embers were such incredible creatures. Neros had never realized beings made of rock with hair of flames even existed, and—and thinking about them brought the riddle's answer right to his lips.

"Fire!"

The glass orbs shattered into a bright light, and Amund shrank into nothing, his consciousness returning to the gate itself.

"YOU THREE ARE QUITE WISE," His voice seemed to carry more when his consciousness was less concentrated. "IT IS SURPRISING."

"Yeah, yeah. So, have we proven ourselves to you? May we pass?" Anthea urged. Her patience was clearly getting the best of her, and Neros understood why—there were thousands of lives at stake, including their own.

"I HAVE ONE FINAL RIDDLE FOR YOU BEFORE YOU GO. YOU THREE MUST ALL AGREE ON THE ANSWER, AND IT MUST BE CORRECT. IF YOU ARE, I WILL PRESENT A SMALL GIFT TO YOU. CONSIDER IT A GIFT REWARDING YOUR WITS. ARE YOU WILLING TO ACCEPT MY FINAL CHALLENGE?"

Anthea turned to them. "What do you think, boys? Is it worth a shot?"

"Well, his other riddles weren't exactly *difficult,*" Leof shrugged. "And it's not as though our lives are in danger if we fail. I would say it's worth the risk."

"I'm tempted to agree, but…" Neros lowered his voice, unsure if Amund could still hear them. "How will he know if we truly agree? There are some riddles with more than one answer, and even if we all *say* the same thing, but how will he know it isn't a trick?"

"We'll probably just have to trust him," Anthea peered over her shoulder to look at Amund. He didn't say anything. "I doubt he's going to trick us, anyway. This is *Andolis,* land of the gods. As a vessel chosen by Silva herself, I think that the gods have always been honest and faithful. So, we're safe to assume their subjects are too, right?"

Neros shared a look with Leof, who looked to the castle and frowned. "I can't say we're safe to assume anything. But it won't hurt to try."

The prince turned back to the gate, nodding resolutely. "We accept your final challenge, Amund!"

"A WISE DECISION, INDEED. LISTEN CAREFULLY, FOR YOUR FINAL RIDDLE IS AS FOLLOWS—

I AM SOMETHING THE GODS NEVER SEE.

I AM SOMETHING A KING SELDOM SEES.

I AM SOMETHING YOU SEE EVERY DAY.

WHAT AM I?"

Neros hummed, sinking back down to sit on the plush ground; he tried not to think too hard about how, under any normal circumstance, he would call this impossible, but the boundaries of what he knew to be possible were broken long ago. He rested his chin in his hands, thinking.

Anthea and Leof joined him. Leof spoke first. "Let's start with this: what do the gods see?"

"They see Andolis," Anthea gestured to the clouds around them. "They see each other. Probably their castle."

"They see us, too," Neros added. "Shouldn't they?"

"I think so," Anthea said. "Then, what does a king see?"

As the individual next in line for the Veturian throne, Neros had been asked this question many times. He'd puzzled over its answer, too, often reaching for the obvious instead of thinking between the lines. His tutors had scolded him for it many times, and even now their voices came to mind: *Obviously a king sees the queen and castle walls! Dig deeper! What does he see?*

When he looked up, Leof and Anthea were staring at him expectantly. He stammered. "I-um, a king sees…the troubles of his subjects. He sees solutions for those issues, and he sees that the call to action is made."

"Maybe a good answer for a future king, but for a riddle, that seems a little metaphorical," Leof murmured. "But anything else seems too obvious. Moving on, what do we see every day?"

Neros frowned. "I'm…not sure about this part. I feel like we all see different things every day."

"Me, too. I see all the Arborians, maybe some travelling merchants, and don't you see the Veturian townspeople?"

Neros nodded, thinking fondly of Veshna and the storekeepers who helped him prepare for this journey in the first place. "And Leof, you see Aldebrande and any customers who've come for wares, don't you?"

"Yes, but there must be some commonality between them all…" Leof's hair flickered around his face; Neros was beginning to suspect it *did* respond to his emotions on some level, because it amplified the thoughtful expression on his face. "I feel like there's a pattern, something to connect them."

"Maybe we're not supposed to classify them as *individual* things. Let's put them into categories."

Neros hummed. "Not a bad thought, but categories based on what? We can think broadly, like buildings or mortal beings or duty, but that doesn't feel right, either."

Leof's eyes lit up. "What if we tried a hierarchy? The gods, a king, and us seem to be arranged in that way. Neros, you said a king sees the problems of his subjects, but he also sees his *subjects*, which are beneath him, and the gods see us, but we are beneath them—literally and figuratively. But that means, what we see every day…something they don't see…"

"An equal!" They all said it at once. A grin broke out on Neros' face, and Anthea high fived Leof, and—Neros nearly fell over—was he *smiling?* Warmth spread through his chest as he stood, the other two following.

"You all seem to agree," Amund said. He didn't have a physical form, but Neros could hear him smiling. "It is fortunate. You are correct. Accept this gift, and you may proceed."

From the top of the gate floated down a thin stone tablet, with text that Neros couldn't read, and accompanying pictures. The small pictographs carved into the tablet looked like little heroes, etched in the same style as the ones Pegaios had shown him and Anthea on their first visit to Paralia.

"What is it?" Anthea asked.

"You are connected with one who knows," Amund replied. "He will tell you when the time is right."

Neros nodded, tucking it away safely into his bag. The gate opened, silent as the rest of Andolis, and the trio pressed forward on the path to the castle of gods.

✿

The second they passed through the threshold, a foreboding feeling wrapped up his insides and squeezed. He walked behind Anthea and Neros, as opposed to in front; he'd been trying to vary their placement after his argument with the princess. After seeing the prince's cracked arm in the underground labyrinth, however, Leof could only worry if they were both pushing themselves too hard. He stole a glance at the deep purple glove covering his arm, now worn and stretched out from their journey. What lie beneath the fabric was like something out of every Ember's nightmares. The cracks ran deep, and Leof was positive that if any blood *could* come out, it would have. He shuddered to think of own arm in that state—the entirety of his molten core would ooze out. He rubbed at the spot on his arm where Hélder the White stabbed him. Ember skin had a naturally quick healing ability, to prevent one well-placed crack from killing them, but Leof still understood he wasn't made of solid gold. He had to be careful.

He wondered if the prince knew that.

Shaking his head, he took in their surroundings—the palace walls were a gentle cream color, like a polished limestone. The floors were brighter, a white marble. His and Prince Neros' boots clacked as they walked, and it was the only sound in the whole place. If they were on Endra, Leof would be inclined to say the place was abandoned. He scanned the walls, looking for traps or hidden figures. None existed. No one had come to greet them; luckily, this part of the castle was a glorified hallway, so they didn't have to guess where to go.

Eventually, they heard voices trickling down the hall. They were faint, and Leof couldn't hear any complete sentences.

"You are not...that on me...you..."

"Have...rationality...look around you!"

"... hello? Amund...guests. They should...any second."

One of them groaned. "I doubt it's...we may as well..."

"They sound pleasant." Leof said, flatly.

"They are the gods!" Pontius said, his voice distant from within Vatnis, the prince's spear. "They are not pleasant nor unpleasant, here nor there, but ethereal beings! You should do well to keep snide remarks to yourself. Amund did not sense me, so I'll need to stay hidden. But best of luck! I'll be listening to everything from here!"

Leof sighed, rolling his eyes. They entered an antechamber filled with clouds acting as screens to view the world below. There was one for Arboria, where they had just come from. Leof could see Rosea, slowly pacing atop the ancient tree. Another cloud showed Paralia, and his stomach lurched. The Eldur Ignis Volcano looked drier than ever, and many of the citizens looked to be arguing. Some of the clouds were hazier, like the connection wasn't strong.

"This is incredible," Neros said, peering at all the clouds. "This must be how they keep tabs on everything going on down below. Surely they know what's been happening, then!"

"Perhaps," Anthea pointed to one of the clouds behind them. "But perhaps not. Look."

Leof turned to see a cloud that had been...torn in two. None of the clouds were labeled, so it was impossible to guess which region this one looked over, but the frayed edges from where the cloud was ripped set off a whole new set of suspicions in Leof's mind. *Did one of them rip it themselves? Did someone break in? Amund's gate surrounds the place, and I doubt his defenses are weak.*

"That is a shame," Neros said. His expression was sullen, but Leof couldn't quite place why he would feel such a deep emotion over a cloud. In all fairness, Leof had learned that the prince had quite deep emotions about many things, so he chose not to question it. He noticed the prince tug on his glove when he turned around. "I suppose there's only one way to find our answers."

There was a large door in front of them, white as the floors beneath and just as marbled. The handles were solid gold. If they were in any other situation, Leof may have admired their fine choices. As Neros knocked, however, he only felt a chill settle at the top of his spine.

The door opened, but no one was standing behind it. As they walked through, Leof had to squint—the walls in here were bright white to match the floors, and it was so bright it was *glowing*. The room was gigantic and round, with three *huge* thrones holding three *massive* gods in their seats. Leof felt his mind stretch to comprehend how beings that were this large could go unheard just down the hall. To the left sat a tall, lanky goddess with snow white hair coiffed up in a bun, longer strands falling to frame her elongated face. She had blue skin, like Neros, and a dress of deep navy blue, trimmed in furs and draped all the way to the floor. Leof assumed she must be Isolde; Neros regarded her with a sort of childish wonder. To the right sat Silva, Anthea's nature patron, and she was taller than Isolde. Her barkskin was a rich brown, and her hair—leaves, like Anthea's—cascaded down her back and coiled on the floor in heaps of reds and golds and yellows. She wore a long green dress, and Leof thought she looked a bit like Anthea, if her colors were swapped around. Her face, like Isolde's, was long and thin, and she had the strongest air of ethereal beauty. It was like she knew she was the prettiest one in the room.

In the middle was Pyrrhus, god of ash and flame. Leof knew of him well. He was stout—gargantuan compared to the trio of heroes, but stout compared to the goddesses—his shoulders were broad, and his skin had cracks like stars littered all over it. His hair flowed freely, bright red, and seemed to be seething with rage. Leof regarded him carefully. Embran folklore seemed to tip one of two ways, from what he'd read in Aldebrande's collection. They said Pyrrhus was either benevolent and kind, giving Embers all the equipment they needed to develop and foster their skills, or that he was a reckless, raging fool who only knew how to hate, and bred that hate within all

Embers so that no two Embers of a different color could get along.

Leof had not truly believed in Pyrrhus before. Neither had many Embers—they didn't feel the need to thank or worship him as past generations had, since many of the Embers had innovated beyond Pyrrhus' creations to make it their own. All Embers felt this way—they were a species of inventors and engineers, not creatures led around by a god's will.

He thought he should very much keep that to himself. Pyrrhus' flames seemed to burn brighter when he laid eyes on Leof, and the Ember shrank away.

The door closed behind them, and its slam felt too resolute. It was quiet. Leof wondered if the gods would even listen to them. Then, Prince Neros spoke.

"G-greetings, gods of Endra," He glanced at Anthea, who urged him on. "We are Prince Neros of Vetur, Princess Anthea of Arboria, and Leof of the Eldur Ignis Volcano. We've come to…to ask you some questions, if you could spare us a moment of your time. We believe Endra is in danger, and we need your aid."

Leof would *swear* Isolde sneered at him before smiling all too sweetly. "My young prince, of course we will help you. What seems to be the problem?"

"Our lands have been cursed!" Anthea said. "Have you not seen? It's displayed plainly in your antechamber! There are dying Arborians below, and Embers without any lava with which to live. In Vetur, their king and queen have been paralyzed, and their prince—Neros, right here—has been cursed. We need your help. We think things are getting worse."

"Princess, my princess, please, calm down," Silva soothed, her voice like wind caressing the leaves. "What do you mean by worse?"

"There are these…purplish spots appearing all over the fields, and skeletal beasts emerge from them and attack us at will. We've done all we can to fight them off for now, but we need to know how to stop them. I thought…well, since you are our benevolent gods, that you may have some words of wisdom to guide us."

At the mention of the skeletal beasts, all three gods stiffened. They looked to each other. Pyrrhus frowned deeply.

"Melanthos." His words scratched like gravel in Leof's ears. "That *hurensohn.*"

Leof remembered hearing about Melanthos. God of Umbros, the prince and princess had informed him, and he had gone positively *berserk* about a century ago, leaving Endra to be destroyed. His reason was unknown. Leof wasn't sure that anyone in their traveling party knew anything about that particular nuance, just that they wanted to prevent it from happening again.

"I can't *believe* he's flown into a rage again so soon," Silva sneered.

"Incorrigible. After all we went through those many years ago. We'll have to send you three down to destroy him," Isolde noted, twirling one of the curls around her finger. "For good."

Anthea balked. "Wh-what? You're *gods!* Can't you do it? Smite him with your almighty power, or something?"

Leof thought he saw Silva stifling a yawn. "It is unbecoming of a god to meddle in mortal affairs, I'm afraid. The most we can do is give you access to divine weapons."

At this, Leof became immediately suspicious. "*Access* to divine weapons? That means you won't give them to us outright."

"Correct."

"And how do you expect us to find them?"

Pyrrhus hurled another stone tablet before them. It clattered to the ground, and the young Ember blinked at it, amazed it didn't shatter. "Take it," Pyrrhus huffed. "It's a map."

Prince Neros walked forward, taking the stone gingerly in his hands and putting it in his bag, to join the other that Amund had given them. Leof noticed him wince a bit as he re-adjusted the strap. *It must be getting heavy.*

"So with these weapons, we'll be able to give Melanthos what for? And that's all the advice you've got?" Anthea implored, palms splayed at her sides.

Isolde shrugged. "You have everything else you need, child. Including a vessel from that bratty oracle. Now, take your leave of us. We must prepare in the event of your failure."

Anthea looked like she was about to protest, but a strong gust of wind came and blew the three of them out the door again, slamming it closed in their faces.

"Well, they were largely unhelpful," Leof grumbled. He turned to the prince. "May I see that map? I think I can copy it onto some parchment. It'll save you the weight on your shoulder."

The prince blushed, reaching into his bag and handing it over. "You don't have to—"

"But I should. We may need the space later," He rushed, grabbing the stone and sifting through his pack for parchment and pen before either of them could notice the faint glow on his cheeks. He set to work, tracing over the stone carvings that made a vague map of Endra. There were three x-marks on the stone, which had to be the locations of these supposed "divine" weapons. Leof could have scoffed at that—the legendary daggers in their sheaths were going to prove *far* more useful than anything Pyrrhus laid his ancient hands on.

Surprisingly, he noticed the divine weapons were close together. It had never been indicated if they were *above* or *below* the surface, but the closer he looked, the more he felt like they weren't on Endra's surface. That meant they were either up here, in Andolis, or below, in Umbros.

Leof sighed. He felt like he knew the answer to that. He stuffed the map in his bag, leaving the stone behind. "Let's get going," He said. "I can't stand to be here much longer."

Anthea, however, had an annoying amount of starlight in her eyes. "Why not? It was *unreal* to actually meet them. And they spoke in our tongues, instead of some ancient indiscernible language! Sure, they couldn't smite Melanthos for us, but their reasoning made perfect sense to me. Gods shouldn't meddle in the affairs of mortals, like Pontius said! And it's in every storybook in Endra."

"A shame we don't live in a storybook," Leof quipped, annoyed.

"Now, don't be so glum. At least we have a way forward," Neros soothed, offering a small smile. Somehow, Leof thought it was strained, despite the wonderment ebbed off him in waves. "And the map will surely lead us to those divine weapons, right? We must put our faith in the gods' ability to help us in small ways like this."

Leof sighed, feeling quite like the only one who felt as though the gods were…less altruistic than gods should be. He led the way back to the vine Anthea had sprouted, and the princess lowered them back to the surface.

Chapter 13
Fracture

$\mathcal{T}$he minute they stepped back onto Endran soil, Neros' entire body shuddered. It was impossible to tell how much time had passed while they were up in Andolis, but the air itself was thick with danger.

Rosea was where the trio had left her, pacing restlessly at the top of the canopy. She turned and ran to them as soon as they finished their descent, hugging them each individually.

"I'm so relieved you're all right," She breathed. "It's been so long, I…I feared the worst."

Neros' heart nearly stopped. "How…how long has it *been?*"

"A few weeks, maybe a month. I was quite worried! The state of Endra has been regressing faster than I could have ever anticipated…I've felt so many Arborian souls escape to the otherworlds, and I–I *hate* that I couldn't save them." She rubbed at her eyes. "Please, tell me the gods gave you assistance."

Beside him, Leof sighed. "You could say that. It's not excellent, but we have a plan. We need to go to the Umbros."

Rosea's eyes bugged out. "Wha–the *underworld!?* I…"

Anthea put her hands over her friend's. "Rosea, it'll be okay. Just stay here and protect the Arborians. We'll be back for you. And when we come back, we'll undo this whole mess. I swear it."

Unsteadily, she nodded.

Their farewells were teary, and Neros still found himself rubbing at his eyes as they crossed the threshold back into the Endran plains. To say the purple masses growing on the ground had spread would be an understatement. In the distance, Neros could see one *gigantic* mass, and figures crawling out of it—hundreds of them. He knew there were towns close by, and his adrenaline spiked with the threat to them. He swallowed, resisting the urge to shudder again.

"Oh, my gods," Anthea gasped. "It's *awful*."

"And dangerous," Leof added, unsheathing one of his daggers. "Look out!"

A large bird—if Neros could truly call it that, with its melted black wings and mangled body—soared down toward them, and Leof tossed his flaming dagger up at it. It caught, and the beast's wings set ablaze. Neros grappled for Vatnis, shaking Pontius free and giving the spiraling beast a solid *thwack*, sending the body careening into the distance. Its remains imploded, leaving behind nothing but dust.

"Th-thanks," said Anthea, voice shaking. She cleared her throat. "Thanks."

"Don't mention it," Leof replied, fetching his dagger from where it landed and returning it to its sheath at his hip. "Let's move fast. That purple mass has got to be the entrance to Umbros, right, Pontius?"

Pontius nodded. "The dark energy pouring out of that spot is massive! There's no mistaking it: that's an entry point to the underworld, ripped open fresh from beneath Endra's surface. Portals like that only stay that large for so long, so I agree, we should make haste!"

Making haste turned out to be harder than Neros thought. There were monsters *everywhere*, all emitting the same purplish smoke as those skeletons. Not all of them had the wax-like blackness like the bird, but those that did seemed to have no thread of consciousness connected to the mortal plane at all. They moved like demented puppets, and the three of them fought back, with Pontius commanding helpful orders when the numbers grew.

It was exhausting. Neros' muscles *ached*, and he sorely wished for a brief respite so they could stop and re-evaluate the situation. The closer they got to the swirling massive portal to Umbros, the more frequent the attacks became. Once, it was a swarm of rats, and Anthea unleashed her hair from its braid in order to grip them all, squeezing the life out of them until they, like the bird, imploded. Her vine-hair was caked in black dust.

Neros felt a tug on his sleeve; it was Leof. "This way," He urged. "I think there's a place we can take cover for a moment."

The three of them ducked under the overhang of a small hill, sitting and tossing their bags aside. Anthea held her vines in her hands and groaned.

"I don't think I can make my bow like this. This black mucky stuff is keeping me from using my magic on these strands."

"It is?" Neros' eyes went wide. "Is that why you haven't re-braided it?"

"Yeah, it's like I can't even move these. They're limp."

The prince hummed. "I wonder if water cleans it off," He mumbled, gingerly taking a few strands of her hair in his hands and conjuring some, sprinkling the droplets over the dust. The water gave the blackened parts of her hair a brilliant sheen, but nothing else happened. Neros sighed, and so did Anthea.

"Leof, you think you could you burn it off?"

Leof choked on air. "What? *What?* You want me to *burn your hair?* I thought it hurt you last time."

"Of course it hurts, but it's worse to be defenseless! Please?"

He regarded her warily. "Alright. I'll try to make it quick."

Neros felt especially useless as he watched Leof gather the group of vines that had been coated in dust, tightening his grip around the top like he was about to tie it off in a ponytail. He closed his eyes, and his hand began to glow. In an instant, a sharp burst of flames erupted around his fingers, a crack popping in Neros' ears. The princess hissed, but relief followed soon after. The blackened vines fell to the ground.

Growing her hair out and allowing it to braid itself again, she smiled. "Thank you, Leof. That didn't hurt much at all! You're getting really good at all different kinds of skills."

His cheeks glowed, and he turned away. "Thank you. I study frequent-ly."

The three of them took their rest gratefully. They snacked on some of their rations huddled together to avoid the gaze of most of the monsters in the distance. The crowd of them seemed to be thinning out, and as he watched, Neros noticed that many of them would simply sink back into the ground again, nothing but a plume of smoke left behind. *Why are they coming to the surface just to travel back to Umbros again?* Neros wondered. He scanned the horizon for the largest portal, and sure enough, it was still there—ominous, ever-present and spewing forth darkness like it was a machine made to do so. Examining its surroundings, Neros noticed a patch of trees, the surest sign of a town as any he knew.

"I think if we can just make it to that town," He pointed. "We should be able to stop in and rest."

"If they'll let us in," Anthea sighed. "Remember on the way to Arboria? *Tons* of towns had put up magic barriers to keep monsters away."

Neros hummed, recalling the sorry frowns and shaken heads they'd received night after night on their way to Arboria. "Maybe if we get rid of enough of the monsters, we can convince them it's safe enough to drop a doorway for us to get in. We should have at least one night's rest in a bed before going to Umbros, I wager."

"An excellent, safe plan, Prince Neros!" Pontius agreed, nodding enthusiastically. "Let's get going. The sun is beginning to set. Are you all prepared?"

"As we'll ever be," Leof said, rising to his feet. Anthea stood after, rolling her shoulders back with a determined fire in her eyes.

The longer they walked, the more Neros wished he had a glorious mount to ride upon. There were horses in Vetur, and he'd been taught to ride as a boy, but travel down the mountain with a horse was slow. Anthea had needed him…well, a bit more immediately than that. While walking everywhere had its perks, it sure had worn down his legs. His shoulders had ached, too. He was grateful for the few vials of healing potions he'd remembered to pack—he was taught they were muscle relaxants, really, but magical enough to heal the soul, too.

The town ahead must have been a few hundred feet away when his whole body suddenly seized up; a road ripped through the air and struck terror down to his very bones. He squeezed his eyes closed, waiting for the rippling sound to dissipate.

Then, slowly, he turned toward the source of the wail.

Much closer than the town, between them and the portal to Umbros, stood a hurling beast four times their size. It stood on four legs, but Neros couldn't peg what creature it must have been when it was alive—it looked like a cross between a boar and the giant Ember-lizard that Leof had fought in his volcanic mage trial. It was hard to tell; its face was blackish-purple like a bruise, though its texture seemed more like glue. Its eyes glared, a bright, piercing blue, perhaps only appearing to glow because of the contrast it struck against its skin.

The beast reared its head, and began to run straight for them. Panic shot up his spine, and Anthea spoke first.

"*Split up!* It can't get all of us if we're not together!"

"Good idea!" Leof shouted back, and they took off in either direction away from Neros. He forced his legs to move, almost tripping to follow between their paths without running directly in the creature's path. Pontius struggled to keep up.

Anthea had summoned her bow, and was taking aim while on the run. The beast had slowed its stampede, noticing the heroes running away from it. The princess took the opening, nocking an arrow and sending it flying. They connected with its back, and it roared again, and all of them froze in place. That same pulse of terror shot down Neros' spine, and he had to take a few steeling breaths to get himself to move. And again, they continued their scramble to confuse it.

Leof had been busying his hands with something, but then Neros saw the arc of one of his daggers soaring through the air, attached to some flaming rope. *Just like the trial.* He had a determined look in his eye, and when the dagger caught around one of the creature's legs, he smirked, yanking *hard.*

It stumbled, but didn't fall, instead dragging Leof's heels through the dirt. He cursed. "Anthea, fire another arrow! I'll catch it on fire as it passes!"

"You got it!" While Anthea busied herself with that, Neros kept running, trying to guide the beast's path away from the town. He heard the familiar sound of arrow striking flesh, and turned around to see how far away they'd guided it. The hillside they'd rested under was nearby, and for a moment, Neros cursed. He hadn't meant to backtrack, but perhaps it was for the best.

The beast reared its head and yowled again, and Neros endured the stricken sensation of once more, his feet rooted in place. This time, he noticed pools of purple forming in various points around the field. Orcs began to climb out, looking largely undead and snarling, their faces the same melted-black as the beast's. They seemed to know only rage, and Neros urged his body back into action with just enough time to whack one down with Vatnis.

"It can summon more monsters!" He called. "Be careful!"

"Not for lack of trying!" He heard Leof cry back, followed by a few grunts. Across the field, he and Anthea were busy battling a pack of them that had decided to horde their efforts. The beast took notice of this, and turned, preparing to charge right for his friends.

"Oh, no, you don't!" He hissed, breaking into a sprint to cut the beast off in its path. As he ran, he tried to gather a large orb of water, threading it to the top of his spear. Neros wound Vatnis in small circles, and when he'd built up enough momentum, he disconnected the liquid thread to hurl the water at the beast's face. It connected, splashing over its eyes like a water balloon. For a moment, it stopped in its tracks, looking at Neros. It shook its head, water raining down on the surrounding area.

Then it huffed, steam pluming from its nostrils, and it *roared,* continuing along its warpath. Neros' eyes widened as the beast gained speed, approaching a distracted—and *frozen*—Anthea and Leof. Adrenaline coursed through Neros' veins, and he snapped free from the vice grip strangling his limbs to raise his arm and shout: "*Vahamut!*"

Large, dagger-like ice crystals formed around him on all sides and shot forward, striking the beast and bringing it to the ground.

A lot happened in the seconds that followed.

Two cries rang clear on the field: first, that of the beast as it collapsed, crushing orcs beneath it and imploding in a cloud of black dust that caked the earth.

The second came from Prince Neros. He collapsed to his knees, heaving a breath only to let out another scream. *My arm… Oh, gods, my arm!* Underneath his glove, he felt for it, thinking it had continued to fracture to find it had disconnected completely. The ice crunched beneath his hand. In that instant, he realized the only thing keeping it connected was the fact that he was cradling it himself.

His throat closed up. *No. No…* Neros couldn't move his fingers, or his wrist. He curled his appendage tight against his chest, squeezing his eyes closed as hard as he could. His heart rammed against his ribcage, and pulse after pulse of pain seared past his elbow and seized his shoulders.

"Oh, no, your highness—shit!" Leof called, slashing through a few rogue orcs with his daggers. "Princess, I'll clean up here. Go help him! I'll catch up with you!"

"You got it!" Anthea wasted no time, firing an arrow and running as fast as she could to Neros' side. She knelt, hooking her arms under his knees and hoisting him up, bridal style. "We have to get you out of here, to cover. There's no way you can fight like this."

Prince Neros tried to speak, but only a strangled cry escaped. Anthea's brows knit together, and she continued to run, taking Neros to the hill they rested at before. Anthea lowered Neros to the ground, and immediately ran back to assist Leof. Both she and Neros knew that even if he may *say* he can handle it himself, he appreciated any help he could get. Neros didn't mind being left alone: he could barely focus on the ground in front of him. His heartbeat had finally slowed, but his vision was hazy and it hurt to *move*. Slowly, he removed his glove, and he choked back another cry. His arm—or, at least, the large chunky pieces of it—came tumbling forth, shattered ice like glass scattering across the grass.

Panic grappled and gripped his lungs. He couldn't breathe. What air he could suck in was rasped back out in short, frantic pants.

A wail escaped his lips. There was a phantom sensation that he should be able to flex his fingers, to feel where they should connect to his wrist, his forearm; and yet, there they sat on the ground, motionless. Neros collapsed back against the hill, closing his eyes tight and forcing himself to take long, deep breaths through his nose. *This pain…this is unbearable…* He cradled his jagged arm gently, as gently as he could, and he blinked back the anguished tears that flowed freely down his cheeks.

Moments—maybe hours—passed, and eventually Leof and Anthea approached him, Pontius in tow. It had grown dark, Neros noted. *Did I pass out? My arm still hurts…* Anthea sat beside him, and Leof dropped to his knees in front, immediately moving to examine the damaged pieces. Pontius floated politely at the prince's other side. Neros focused hazily on Leof; the cracks in his skin glowed with urgency, the magma core shifting and churning, his glowing yellow eyes razor-focused on the task in front of him. Anthea looked on, grabbing Neros' remaining hand with her own and giving it a supportive squeeze. Pontius, for the moment, remained silent, sensing the building distress and frustration.

A tense, melancholy mood settled over the three heroes. Neros drifted in and out of wakefulness. He wished, so sorely, that it was all a dream. *More like a nightmare.* Leof continued lifting and examining chunks of Neros' arm, and Anthea continued watching him. Pontius spoke first.

"Sir Leof, what are you doing?"

"Making sure none of the pieces are back in the field."

"Pieces? For…?"

Leof gave him a level stare. "For Neros' arm." He turned to the prince, worry slipping into his features. The Ember picked up a piece of the prince's arm, running his thumb across it. "Can you feel this?"

Neros rested his head against the grassy hillside with a thump. He sighed. "No."

"I see." Leof continued his focused work, pausing only to glance over at Anthea. "Princess, is it possible for you to elevate the ground? So we can rest the prince's arm on it."

"Oh, uh…yeah, sure." Anthea's voice sounded far away, but she released Neros' hand to carry out Leof's request. She pressed her palms against the soil, willing it to rise up to a comfortable level for Neros' amputated arm to rest on. Neros looked out at the field where they were fighting. His heart sank; they were successful in clearing the area of monsters, and they should have been on their way to that town, then to Umbros. To defeat Melanthos, and break the curse over the world. But *he* failed. *He* was gravely injured. He felt as empty as the field was.

"Leof, Anthea, I'm–I'm so sorry. I should have known…I should have been more careful," He closed his eyes and pursed his lips. "Pontius…I didn't listen. I—"

"Neros," Anthea cut him off, resting a hand on his shoulder, eyebrows drawn together. "It's okay."

"Is it?" He asked, bitterness seeping into his tone. "I lost over half of my arm because of my own *negligence*, Anthea, I've let you and Leof down. We're supposed to be well on our way to *Umbros*, following the guidance of the gods, not—not—" Neros' voice broke, free hand curling into a fist. *By the gods, it hurts so much,* he thought, squeezing his eyes shut momentarily.

"Don't cry." Leof's voice was carefully level, and partially distracted. He was dutifully arranging the pieces of Neros' arm back into their original shape below the prince's elbow, and was nearly finished. He raised his eyes to meet the prince's, and a flash of an emotion Neros couldn't place passed over Leof's face. All too soon, he ducked back to staring at the jagged pieces of ice. Neros blinked at him, eyes focused on the shards of his arm—but it wasn't *his* arm, not anymore—laying by his side, so precisely arranged he could almost pretend it was re-attached.

The silence weighed heavily on the trio, and Anthea suddenly stood, rubbing at her eyes.

"Anthy...?"

"Excuse me. I—I need to take a walk." She briskly walked away, turning the corner around the hillside. Neros watched her go, unsure of how to stop her. By his side, Pontius stirred.

"I'm going to go make sure she doesn't get lost or hurt. Stay here, you two."

They nodded, and Neros watched as Pontius, too, disappeared around the edge of the hill. Neros heard Leof shifting. He turned his gaze to find the Ember pacing, then re-settling beside the makeshift table. He locked gazes with the prince, looking inexplicably nervous. He reached for the fracture at Neros' elbow, then pulled away.

"May I...?" He ventured. "I'd...like to assess the damage completely."

Neros didn't trust his voice, so instead, he nodded.

"Good. Please tell me if it's too painful, alright? I'll stop right away."

He felt like it was going to hurt no matter what Leof tried, but he nodded again anyway. Gingerly, Leof rolled up the prince's sleeve and took Neros' broken arm in his hands, carefully tracing over where the ice had broken off. Periodically, his gaze would flicker up to Neros, gauging his reactions. The prince bit down a cry as he started to poke and prod—*I cannot believe it still hurts so much,* he thought. He screwed his eyes closed. This reminded him of when he'd fractured his leg as a child; he'd cried and cried all through the evening. His father had sat by his bed and told him: *"A king must work through his pain without worrying his people."* The moment Leof's hands stopped moving,

Neros felt like he'd failed.

"*Tell me* if it hurts too much. I told you, I'd stop." Neros opened his eyes to find Leof frowning at him, though no malice attached. "Is it painful even now?"

"Unbelievably," He rasped. While the initial shocking pain faded, the area around his elbow throbbed. His shoulders ached with stiffness. "I feel like I could sleep forever."

Leof's hair flickered viciously around his head. "We should probably keep that from happening. Bodies tend to need sleep to recover, but there's also the risk of becoming comatose from other side effects that may develop in response to this. I know it's hard, but please try to stay awake for now."

"How do you know so much about health? Weren't you raised a blacksmith?"

"I'm allowed to study other matters, you know," Leof bit back, but then shied away, as though burned by his own bitterness. He turned to the pieces of Neros' arm, slowly arranging them more precisely. "Did Princess Anthea know about your arm this whole time?"

Neros nodded, but realized Leof couldn't see him. "Y-yes."

"And Pontius?"

"He knows. He's been...teaching me water magic to avert the need to...use ice." Shame washed over him. He could sense where Leof was going with this.

"I think I can imagine why you wouldn't want to talk about it," He said, taking Neros a bit by surprise. "If it's alright, I'd like to know how it happened."

The prince shuddered a sigh. "I apologize for not saying something sooner," He started. "I...I promise, it's not that I meant to exclude you—"

Leof held up a hand, shaking his head. "Please, don't worry about it. Believe me, I can understand where you're coming from. But I think, to know how to proceed, it'd be best to talk about what happened."

Hesitantly, he nodded. "One night, I was about to go to sleep when I heard a deep rumble in the castle. It was coming from the throne room, so I went there, and I heard a voice. She yelled at my father and mother...called me a wretched mage, and laid her curse on them. When I reached out to save them, some of what cursed them infected part of me. Or maybe it was the witch herself choosing to curse me separately, I-I'm not sure."

"So when you used your magic, your arm fractured."

"Yes." His voice felt so raw and hoarse.

"And it hurt? And you continued?"

"Yes…"

Leof was silent for a long time, arranging and re-arranging the broken ice that used to be connected to his elbow. The prince wanted to badly to close his eyes and fall asleep, but he feared the consequences of doing so. *If I truly did go comatose, that would be disastrous. Moreso than this situation already is.*

When the Ember did speak again, his voice was soft. "You're very brave, your highness."

Neros' eyes welled up. "H-hardly. I was doing what I could with what I was given, and I—this wasn't brave, it was reckless, plain and simple."

Leof caught his gaze. "I don't think this is as impossible to fix as you may think."

"What makes you say that?"

"Looking at…the pieces, it gives me an idea. I don't think all hope is lost, but…I need to think about it. We'll have to stay here a while. You're in no shape to fight, and…" Leof cast a glance at the hillside. "I don't think Princess Anthea and I can do this alone. Do you…trust me?"

"With every fiber of my being, of course. You're brilliant." Neros hadn't meant to say it so quickly, so honesty, and he felt himself blush. *Of all the times…*

Leof shook his head, and if Neros thought he saw a smile, it was gone before he could register it. "Your highness, you look exhausted. Here, let me get an emergency salve from my pack, and I'll let you sleep."

Neros followed Leof's movements, watching him rummage through his belongings and pulling out a vial of dark blue liquid, thick like jelly and *cold* when he spread it on the skin above the fracture. Neros sucked in a breath through his teeth.

"Sorry, sorry," Leof soothed. "It's just in case. I don't want the area above here to get infected, for any reason. With this, at least *I'll* feel a bit better allowing you to get the rest you need. And deserve, after all this."

Neros nodded, but as he tried to ease himself into a laying position, he felt himself wanting to rely more on the arm that was gone. He lost his balance more than once. Leof had to help ease him down, and the prince was thoroughly embarrassed. *This is infuriating. I feel like a helpless child; he's certainly annoyed with having to practically babysit me, I'm sure.*

The salve eased the throb in his arm, and sleep overtook him like a tidal wave.

He dreamt of snow, slowly falling and piling up, swallowing the universe whole.

When Neros awoke, his legs felt like lead and his head felt stuffed with cotton. His body felt too light. His drooping eyelids urged him to go back to sleep, and as much as he wanted to give in, he knew oversleeping would bring nothing but good his way, like Leof had warned. He gazed across their makeshift camp in the hillside, a near constant reminder of his grueling mistake. His fracture ached and itched, and he fought back the urge to cry again when he looked down and saw nothing: just his arm resting on the dirt in the grass.

Leof and Anthea came by and spoke to him, but he could hardly process their words. The edges of the world were blurred, and it proved to be an immense effort just for Pontius or Anthea to get him to walk around—he was simply so *tired.*

"You must stay active, Prince Neros," Pontius urged. "You need your strength. We're here to help you through this."

Neros was disheartened by Leof being gone the most—his chest ached in a way he couldn't place, and he feared he'd scared Leof away from their mission for good. *I'm so incompetent, he probably couldn't stand it anymore,* Neros thought miserably.

One night, as he struggled to fall asleep, he overheard an argument.

"How could you do that?" Anthea hissed.

"Stop acting like I'm being reckless, your highness. *I* have a *plan,* unlike your reckless gallivanting." Leof bit back.

Neros strained to keep listening. "That was before, when asking for the gods' help was our only way forward! There has to be another way around this than for you to—"

"Shh!" Leof sighed harshly. "He's *finally* able to sleep without medicine. If you insist on arguing about this, we can take it somewhere else. But I know what I'm doing, Princess Anthea. I know it's not my place to ask, but please, trust me." Neros thought Anthea may have responded, or someone said something else, but he couldn't quite hear.

Instead of getting up to check, sleep overtook him.

✿

Leof's eyes nearly rolled to the back of his skull as he allowed himself to be *dragged* by Anthea away from their hillside campsite, out of Neros' earshot.

"You can't tell me it wasn't stupid and reckless of you to sell that clock! You *made* it for your mentor! And just—just—*trading it?* And some of our other supplies, as well? And for what, to get some scrap metal?"

"I've been mulling the idea over for days, Princess Anthea! I am *going* to make him a new arm, because *that* is what will be best for our *future!*"

"What do *you* know about Neros' future?!"

"You're not the only one who cares about him!" Leof yelled, hair flaring wildly around his face. "A trinket for Aldebrande is worth nothing compared to his life. We need him. So I am going to do what I can to help him heal to the best of my ability." His cheeks glowed at the admittance, but she'd drawn the words from him.

He'd had enough of arguing back and forth with the princess. She had been resistant in helping him the entire time, which made buying and selling and trading in local towns a lot more difficult. Leof was not naturally a people person, and he felt that many nearby townspeople turned him down because he simply wasn't charismatic enough. The Ember turned on his heel to walk away, feeling desperately like he needed a long session *alone* with his blueprints and the fragments of Neros' arm to calm down.

Then, Anthea snagged his wrist. He whirled around, glaring at her, only to see she had a wicked grin sprawled across her face.

"You *like* him?"

It was a harmless phrase on its own, but Leof's entire core went into overdrive from the insinuation behind it. Embers were naturally warmer than other creatures, but in that moment, Leof was positive his entire body would explode. Flames crackled in nervous spurts around his ears, and he tugged against her grip, silently begging her to let go.

"I didn't say that. I said you weren't the only one who cared about him."

"I can't believe you *like* him!"

"What is *with* you, Anthea? First you argue tooth and nail with me, and now you're teasing me?"

She barked a laugh. "You just called me Anthea! I *never* thought I'd get you to do that! You're just one surprise after another—you know, you knocked the fight clean out of me when you admitted how much you care," She singsonged, and Leof's cheeks burned. "How long have you liked him? I noticed you were always nicer to him than me."

Was it possible he could burn himself to nothing but ashes? He wasn't sure he wanted to find out. He had work to do.

"You're insufferable."

"But Neros isn't, right? He's such a sweetheart, always wanting to help everyone he sees and approaching every conversation with the *utmost* kindness and diplomacy. And he's got that precious, adorable face," She lilted, and when she clasped her hands beside her cheek to blink dreamily at the sky, Leof wrenched his arm back.

"Quit antagonizing me, princess."

"I'm not, I'm not, I swear," She raised her hands in surrender. "I just think it's so sweet how you're falling for him."

"I didn't–I never–I'm *not*. Alright? Excuse me, please. I have to go."

Pushing past her, he marched back toward camp. He couldn't face... *whatever* Anthea thought he was feeling head-on just yet. Slowing to a brisk walk, he rounded the corner to find Neros as they left him—fast asleep. Begrudgingly, the Ember had to admit that Anthea had a point: he did have a nice face. In sleep, like this, he at least looked peaceful, which Leof noted was a step up from the nights previous where his features were twisted in pain. The Ember felt a tug in his chest, and he pursed his lips, shaking his head to free his mind from the thought.

He had an arm to build.

Leof sat down, rolling out his working blueprint he'd been developing every night while Neros slept. During the day, he travelled to nearby towns to pawn his possessions, fighting and looting monsters to secure more trading tools to gather all the materials he could dream of needing. It was difficult, at first—many of the Arborians out here were just as stubborn as Princess Anthea, but the few times he could get her to agree to trade in his stead had proven fruitful (if not for the princess' constant griping). That was *before* the clock. Leof only sent Anthea to pawn off small trophies from fights, with specific instructions for what to buy with the earnings. In his bag now were scrap metal pieces of varying sizes, bolts, and blown glass orbs in various sizes.

The blueprints were vague: he'd drawn Neros' arm per the dimensions approximated from the shattered pieces that fell out of his glove. There were a lot of question marks scribbled all over his notes, like how to attack each finger together, then to a palm, and then to a wrist. The arm itself wasn't troubling—it didn't require as much range of motion. His eyes scanned the paper, then the parts. He grabbed a few pieces of metal, checking their stability. He peeked at Neros' sleeping form to make sure he wasn't making too much noise. His shoulders stiffened when the prince rolled over, but he breathed a sigh once the moment had passed. *Good. Still asleep.* The air was chilly, and Leof's brows drew together. *He* wasn't affected much by a slight chill, as his body temperature sat naturally higher. *I'm not sure if Neros is more resistant to this sort of thing, given his abilities, but…* His chest tightened at the thought of the prince getting sick, and he tugged off his cloak and tossed it over Neros' shoulders before he could think better of it. *Better safe than sorry.*

Returning to the task at hand, Leof could nearly feel the gears spinning in his mind as he began to heat up metal pieces and shape them to match the fragments. He held it up to the broken arm on Anthea's makeshift dirt table, sighing when it turned out to be too big. Reshaping and checking again, Leof fell into a steady rhythm of adjusting and comparing, comparing and adjusting; before he knew it, he'd made an entire forearm. It was a bit clunky in places where the metals didn't align perfectly, but there would be time for adjustments. *Not a ton of time, but time.*

He looked up for a moment to notice sunlight had begun to peek over the top of the hill. *Another night gone already, huh?* He sighed, and it rolled into a yawn; closing his eyes, he stretched his shoulders and neck, pushing away the stiffness that was all too familiar in his line of work.

Then he proceeded to jump out of his skin when he saw Anthea crouching right in front of him.

"Are you *trying* to scare me? You're lucky my reflexes aren't *violent*," He hissed.

"Come on, I'm not that mean-spirited. I wanted to apologize. About freaking out that you sold the clock. It's your item, right? So you should be able to do what you want with it. I just…it scares me, to see him this way," She looked over her shoulder at the prince. "I wanted to be able to help him without us having to sacrifice anything else, but it seems like that's not the case."

"It's like I said, princess. A trinket is worth nothing compared to his life."

She grinned. "Right. So, you need any help?"

He hummed, continuing to turn the forearm over in his hands. "I had a few ideas for how to make the hand and wrist, but…I need a way to test it. I don't think that's something you can help with, though."

"Oh, really? And why not?"

"I'd need something…living. To test the movement of the armature. I can't be performing such tests on Prince Neros—or anyone alive, really. It's just too dangerous."

Anthea hummed. "I could make something…sort of living. Out of vines."

"What does that mean? Do you think that would work?"

"I think it's worth a shot. I'll be right back—constructing something like that may be kinda…noisy."

As she walked away, Leof looked back at the snoozing prince. He had since pulled the cloak up around his shoulders, face partially buried in the fabric. His expression was serene, and… *Is he smiling?* Leof felt his core coil up into knots. He took a deep breath; there was no way the prince's expression had anything to do with the cloth draped over him. It was *cloth*, and a ratty one, at that. Neros was probably, blessedly, having a nice dream for once.

Then, Prince Neros nuzzled into his cloak, and Leof's intake of breath was so sharp he nearly choked on the air around him. He looked away, rubbing aggressively at his face in a vain attempt to keep himself from glowing like a star in the night sky. *No, no, no. Anthea has to be wrong. I can't be feeling these emotions…no, I can't believe I am feeling these emotions.* He pressed his palms to his forehead and curled his hands into fists. To accept friendship was one thing, but did he really have to fall in *love*?

This is bad.

Neros roused slowly, feeling warm, his nose filled with the faint scent of ash. The sun cast bright light across the plains, highlighting the dark spores churning in the distance, a bitter reminder of what lay ahead for them. His head still felt foggy, but it was…better. Better to be covered, at least; the thought of looking beneath his makeshift blanket made his stomach churn. He pulled the cloak tighter around him, suddenly wishing he could go back to sleep. He was having a pleasant dream, but now he couldn't remember what it was about; just that he felt warm and safe.

"Good afternoon." Neros turned his head to see Leof cooking. "Was your rest peaceful?"

"At the end, yes," He admitted. "Where's Anthea?"

"She may still be making a prototype for me."

"Prototype?"

He nodded, gesturing off to the side with his chin. "I need something to attach that to. To see if it'll function."

The prince rolled onto his shoulder, hissing at the stiffness in his muscles. Using his good arm, he pushed himself into a sitting position to get a better look at what Leof was talking about.

It was an arm. *For me? Of course…who else? But why? More importantly, how?* The bronze and gold metals shone in the sunlight, connected by small glass orbs. There was a spot for a wrist, and a very loose hand-like structure had been built, but it looked far less finished than the rest. *This must be what Leof said his plan was.*

"Were you working on this while I was asleep…?"

"Yes. Now, please eat. You need to recover more of your strength. Pontius will begin preliminary training with you when you're ready."

"Where is he now?"

"He spoke with Pegaios for a long time, then mentioned something about needing a cleric. I assume he may be retrieving Rosea."

Neros nodded, accepting a small plate of roasted meats and seeds from Leof. "I didn't know you could cook."

"I had to survive, didn't I?" He shook his head. "Unless you think I can't eat because of my anatomy?" When Neros flushed, he chuckled. "That's a bit silly, your highness. Embers can still *eat.*"

"O-of course! It's just, well, Anthy's diet is primarily seeds when she's not at home, and I haven't actually seen you eat at all in our travels."

"I have, here and there," He said, clearing off the makeshift dirt table to place the planks of food. "Though Embers don't need to eat as much because of our metabolisms and body structure. Mostly, I took my meals at night, while you and Princess Anthea have been asleep."

Neros blinked. "Have you slept?"

"Naturally. I would have died without it."

"No, I mean, have you slept recently? Last night?"

Leof stayed silent, choosing that moment to begin eating, gesturing for Neros to join him. Neros felt a flare of anger in his chest, but sat in silence. *Helpless. I'm totally helpless, yet Leof is having to lose sleep over this.* The question hung heavy in the air while they ate. His gaze flitted between the arm on the ground beside them and the food in front of him. The cloak he'd woken up under was wrapped around his shoulders, and he vaguely wondered if it was the one Leof had been wearing. *Just another way he's been inconvenienced.* But it was comforting, and the Ember hadn't asked for it back yet, so Neros thought it was alright to keep it for a bit longer.

Anthea rounded the corner of the hillside, dragging along a large figure made of thick vines and leaves. *That must be the prototype Leof mentioned.* The princess had even gone through the effort of giving him a little flower crown and hair, mimicking Neros' own. The prince nearly smiled at the gesture.

"Here he is!" She announced, plopping the dummy against the hillside and plopping *herself* between them, plucking a piece of meat off Leof's plate. "Took all night, but he's ready for his fitting, mister mechanic."

Leof looked between the dummy and Neros. "Looks to be the right size. It'll make do for testing. Does it…um, can it animate?"

"Sure! I made it from my own vines and magic, so I can power it up, too, if I want. So to speak. It's technically *always* powered up, strictly dependent on whether or not I want to move him."

"Fascinating. So alive, but not *alive*. Rather brilliant, princess. Does it take much effort for him to remain dormant?"

"A little. Like, I couldn't make an *army* of these things, because then I'd be too tired to draw my bow and fight for myself. Or, they'd all just be standing still."

Neros ate slowly, allowing the conversation to continue around him. He felt the warmth from earlier slowly slipping away from him, and he wasn't sure how to stop it. Eventually, Leof stood and cleared his makeshift plate away, grabbing the partly-constructed arm and moving to the dummy for testing. Neros didn't watch. He pushed around what was left on his plate and stifled a sigh. *They've both been working so hard. I wonder how long it's even been since I...* He shook his head, massaging the nub of frost. The initial searing pain had dulled, but with each day that passed he felt colder and colder. *It's like my body is giving up. But does it even matter?* He glanced at Leof and Anthea, who were both had their focus razor-sharp on the magical dummy. *They're working so hard for me. I should be happier. I should be helping. Of course, I'm grateful, but...are their efforts going to amount to anything? What if I ruin it all over again?*

The prince scooted himself away from the dirt table, back to where he'd been resting. Using his left arm, he clumsily eased himself to the ground, cursing himself for being so uncoordinated. Leof's cloak fell off his shoulder a bit from the movement, so he awkwardly shrugged it back in place before falling asleep.

A hiss followed by a *pop* woke him up. He stared blearily out into the fields. It was dark.

He willed his consciousness to fade.

Waking up again barely felt worth it. He laid still for as long as he could bear.

It would be easier for them without me.

There was the feeling of hands pulling him upright, then nothing. His eyelids felt heavy, so he let them fall closed again.

An empty conversation. Concerned voices rang dull in his ears.

I could get to Umbros faster if it all ended here.

He knew it wasn't right, to keep on like this. A tug at the back of his mind tried to get him to rise, but it felt like too much effort.

Everything was so much harder.

So much energy that he simply didn't have.

So he slept.

All her life, the princess had stayed at the prince's side. As much as they could do together, they did. She would never forget her excitement as she saw him tumble or drift down the mountain at top speed, crashing into the plains and scattering ice shards everywhere like a busted glass vase. They'd laughed together, studied together, told stories huddled around campfires in the dead of night just to see which one would spook first (it was always Neros).

But never, never in all her years of knowing him had Anthea seen Neros like this.

It *destroyed* her. She fought constantly with her emotions, her heart playing a vicious tug-of-war between wanting to smack him or drown him in affection. At this point, she felt like Neros would react the same no matter what she did, and that was probably what hurt the most.

"Your highness?"

Could she do nothing to help him? She was trying! She felt like she was even getting to know Leof a little bit better, through their struggle to cooperate in building him a new arm. At first, she thought it to be a heinous plan with no merit. Thoughtless, even. But Leof had proven her severely wrong, and his meticulous work drove her to actually *want* to give him a hand. After all, at the end of the day, Leof was right—it was to help Neros. And helping Neros meant helping the future of the world.

"Princess Anthea…?"

Doesn't he realize that? She thought bitterly, frowning at his sleeping form. *He's a part of this weird, twisted destiny! We're companions. I think it's safe to assume we're all actually getting along now, which is a massive improvement. But he's just…* She couldn't quite grasp the words she wanted. She settled for just thinking angrily at him. It was frustrating, and vastly unfair. Neros didn't deserve to go through such hurt, but he also didn't have to *wallow* in it.

"Anthy!"

She snapped out of her thoughts, turning to face Leof, who looked a bit embarrassed at having to use her nickname to get her attention.

"Are you alright? You're crying."

Was she? She put a hand to her cheek, and it came back wet. *Oh.* She supposed she was crying. But could Leof possibly understand if she tried to explain it to him?

He had been slaving over an arm for Neros for the past few weeks, and she was propping up her magic dummy while he affixed *another* test arm to it. It wasn't as though she didn't have the time to try.

"Of course I'm not alright," She sniffed. "Look at him! He may as well be comatose, he's so unresponsive. It's like I don't even know who he is anymore. How could…how could this happen so quickly? What did we do wrong to let this happen?"

"I…I don't think we could have done anything to prevent it, your highness," Leof mused, eyes trained on the work at hand. "I think…in a way, he had his own things to hide. From both of us. You know, he only ever mentioned to me he was cursed. I only saw that arm for the first time when we were trapped in that underwater labyrinth."

She sighed. "He didn't tell me at first, either. Do you think he was ashamed of it?"

"Perhaps…" Leof paused over a particular fastener, and Anthea *so* wondered what was on his mind. The way he spoke, one word led to a million silent others, and she ached to hear them. However, she had run out of time to prod more, as Leof placed his tools aside. "There. It should be solid.

Let go of the arm…?"

It looked stable. It fit around the dummy's forearm well enough, Anthea figured, since she had made this vine dummy as an approximation of Neros' measurements.

"Could you, um, try to get it to move?"

"Sure thing," She breathed long and deep, focusing her energy into the dummy itself. It rose to its feet, and she tried to lift the test arm up to wave. It followed her imagined movements, the latest model arm following along seamlessly. Leof had made what must have been *thousands* of adjustments, to the point where she had to help him get more materials, but it looked surprisingly stable now. The bulk of the arm was built from various metals, but Leof had still put significant focus on design. The twists and bends of each piece melded together, and it shone a brilliant golden-copper hue in the light. The joints were connected through an intricate series of magnetized glass—she didn't bother to ask further, as when Leof explained it, Anthea's head spun trying to keep up with magic and metrics. All the technical delicacy aside, the arm seemed sturdy. Leof gave her a set of actions to perform: wave, grab something, swing something, punch something. Testing this prototype was finicky, because it wasn't a *conscious* living being, not the same way that Leof and Neros and Anthea were. It lived on borrowed time and energy from Anthea's energy and vines, and she could often only perform testing for a few hours, max.

"That's enough," Leof said, and she released her magic on the dummy instantly, and Leof caught it before it smacked the ground. They'd lost a good test arm that way. "I think I can do some finalized fittings on this one, and we can work the logistics of…getting it to work on him."

"Do you think he'll even want it…?" She asked, her voice dying in her throat. "He's hardly said a word to us."

"I doubt he's harboring anything, Anthea. There is probably more on his mind than either of us can know. He's just…hurting."

Neros and *hurting* didn't belong in the same sentence, the princess thought bitterly to herself. She wanted to pick up his pain and hurl it across the planet, to restore the light in his eyes.

"He's always been such a pillar of strength for me," Anthea admitted. "I feel like I'm failing at being the same for him."

"Your strengths feed off each other. Forgive me if this is too forward, but I think your sadness does, too. I guess it's natural, though, considering how close you two are."

Anthea hummed. She hadn't considered it like that, but Leof made a good point. *Maybe it works both ways. Maybe if I act happier, feeding off the excitement of having an arm for him, maybe he'll start to brighten up again.* "You know, Leof, for someone who had almost no friendships or relationships, you're pretty perceptive."

He scoffed. "You two have given me a *lifetime's worth* of lessons, believe me."

If it was meant to be an insult, Anthea took it as both a compliment and an admittance that Leof was finally warming up to the two of them. She smiled, rising to her feet and crouching beside the prince. He was asleep, but not fully—she could tell his breathing was more shallow.

She placed her hand on his arm. "Hey, Neros."

He stirred, brow furrowing, though he made no move to open his eyes.

"You should sit up. You'll get stiff laying the same way all the time."

She didn't help him sit up—she noticed he preferred to do all that on his own. His hair stuck up in an odd way, so she smoothed it.

"Actually? It's been a while since we took a walk. Come on, get up!"

She hoisted him to his feet without warning, and he yelped, stumbling and having to lean on her for support. She laughed; that was the most emotion she'd gotten him to express in *days*.

"Leof, keep an eye out for Pontius and Rosea. Neros and I are gonna take a lap!"

"But his arm—"

"You can fit it to him *later*, Leof!" Anthea looped her arm through Neros' good one and led him away. "We'll be back!"

She laughed when Leof groaned. "Be *careful!*"

For a while, they walked in slow silence, arms still linked. Anthea knew Neros wouldn't speak up first; he probably had far too much clouding his mind.

Still, she had to prod.

"Talk to me."

There was a long silence, but she heard him sigh, like he was trying to find the right words, so she stayed quiet. "My heart feels like a rock," He said at last, voice rough from so much sleep. "I've thought about it a lot, and I…I don't think I deserve this. The title of hero, the arm you two have been working on. It's…it's useless, isn't it? I can't—I can't save the world."

"Neros," Anthea started, though her chest felt tight watching his eyes well up with tears. "Neros, no! Heroes make mistakes. All the greatest heroes in the world make mistakes. Some make life-ending mistakes, and they become regarded as legend! Your journey isn't over yet. Leof and I—uh, mostly Leof, actually, but he made an *arm!* For you! I never thought he'd even want to consider us friends, but he's even—well, he's gone through a lot to get this arm together. And we'll attach the arm to you, and we can continue to Umbros, like we planned!"

"What if…I just mess up again?" Gods, his voice sounded so small. And *wounded.* "I'm holding the both of you back. It–it would be better if you left me behind, for the monsters—"

"No no no no *no,"* She stopped walking, releasing his arm in favor of facing him and gripping his shoulders. "We are *not* going down that road. Look at me, Neros. *No, look at me.* There is not a snowball's chance in the volcano that we would leave you behind. You are my *best friend.* And I need you. We *both* need you, and for so much more than the prophecy states. When we were all lost, looking for Rosea, I was freaking out. I cried more than I thought I could. I thought I'd die alone down there, on a foolish mission to save my friend, and I regretted dragging you both along. I was too proud to admit I made a mistake, so I sat on the floor and I wept. But you know what got me to get up again?"

He shook his head, bewildered.

"You. I thought of what you'd tell me if you were there. The Neros-in-my-head told me it would be okay, and that nothing would be solved by sitting around. If there was a path to take, we'd take it. If there wasn't one, we'd *make* it. We were unstoppable, do you realize that? I almost killed you when we first met. I was totally ready to. But you told me I wouldn't, because I was a good person." She laughed, feeling herself getting choked up. "I don't know if you were on the mark, really, but that bravery struck me."

Neros managed a chuckle, himself. "I was actually terrified, you know."

"I *know!* That's what made it even braver to me. You have such a strong heart, Neros, and we need that. Me, and Leof, and Pontius, and everyone on Endra needs your unique strength. Please, don't give up on us. You mean so much to me."

She was crying again. She felt the dampness on her cheeks, heard the quiver in her voice, but he had to understand, so she just let her emotions ravage her while she maintained eye contact.

Neros' expression crumbled, and it was like watching him wake up from a bad dream. Immediately, his hand was wiping the tears off her cheek. "Anthea…" He said. "I didn't realize…I–you're my best friend, and I…I'm sorry. I've been so selfish. I didn't think…I wasn't thinking of how all this must have been affecting you."

She sniffed. "That's not the *point,* you idiot. Don't try to hide things from me anymore. If you're in pain, tell me. If you're worried, tell me. If you're sad, please, *talk to me.* I know it's hard, but you should *never* feel like you have to put on a brave face for me. For anyone. You're stronger when you know when to ask for help. You taught me that, right?"

He looked taken back by that. He moved to hug her, stopping short and looking horrified with himself. "I-I'm sorry! Sorry, I shouldn't, it's probably weird, with–with my arm, as it is…"

Anthea wrapped her arms around him anyway, lowering her head to rest on his shoulder. "I don't care, Neros. You could lose both of your arms and your legs and just be a body with a head and I'd still love you for you, okay?"

She smiled when she felt his arms around her in return. "Right. I… thank you, Anthea. Thank you."

"Good, you're back. Could you sit? I need to fit this to you."

Neros blinked at the intense look in Leof's eyes. He nodded, sitting where Leof gestured him to and propping up his arm. Immediately, Leof's nimble hands set to work, taking the prototype arm Neros had seen earlier and matching it up to the nub of ice. He held up various clamps, measuring their size against the arm and his flesh, until deciding on a few. *That prototype looks a bit different than I remember,* Neros thought to himself. *Though, I suppose I didn't get a good look at it in the first place.* While Leof worked, Neros wondered how much time had passed. The plains were looking darker with each passing minute. He noticed Pontius wasn't around, either, and he began to worry when a warm hand began to poke and squeeze around his upper arm.

"Does this hurt?"

"Not especially," He commented. "I-I can still feel it, though."

Leof hummed. "Good. This will have to be my entry point."

"Entry point…?"

"This arm is made of metal and glass, fused together with various bolts and magic streams. But once it's on you, it's as good as a paperweight unless I can connect it to your own energy system. For Veturians, that means…your complex systems of veins, correct?"

Neros could see where this was going, and he wasn't sure how he felt about it. "You're going to attach it…to my veins?"

"You'll need to operate it with your life energy. You were technically doing the same with your previous arm, but it was innate, so you didn't notice any difference. These clamps will secure it to your arm initially, but…we'll have to…uh, perform a bit of surgery to keep it there permanently."

The prince swallowed thickly around a lump in his throat. "Surgery…?"

Leof looked to Anthea, who continued to explain. "I'll have to essentially sew it to you. Leof and I talked for hours about the best ways to do it, but the prototype testing was most successful when the prosthetic was connected directly to the nervous system of the dummies. It's not an exact science, but…it's the only thing we've got."

"We sent Pontius to get a healer," Leof sounded oddly calm, though Neros could see the slightest quiver in his hands. "Once he returns, I'd like to make an attempt to attach this to you. I've got the clamps on, so would it be alright to…fit it one more time?"

Neros nodded, suddenly feeling numb and too nervous to trust his voice. Leof's hands returned to his arm, this time anchoring each clasp in place. They pinched at the skin above the ice, but there wasn't much pain beyond that.

"Try to move your arm a bit and tell me if that feels too heavy."

Nodding again, he did as he was told. The appendage was beautifully crafted, and honestly, Neros didn't expect anything less from someone like

Leof, who had been creating things from metal his entire life. His arm broke below his elbow, so he could at least still bend it to lift the prosthetic and test the weight—it was surprisingly light. He ached to try and curl the fingers and see if he could pass magic through it, but the wrist hung limp.

"I-it isn't too heavy."

The Ember looked visibly relieved. "Good. Are you able to feel some of the magical fusion emanating from it?"

If Neros focused, he could feel it: a small pulsing from his elbow and coursing through his veins, seeping into his heart with every breath. It wasn't unpleasant, but it did feel a bit foreign. Warmer than he was used to. *Is it because it's Leof's magic? Will Anthea's feel…grassy?* He smiled at the thought. "I have to focus my efforts, but I can feel something faint. It's warm."

"Incredible…" Leof's relief quickly melted into deep fascination. "Veturians really are something. Most of my construction was based on educated guesses, but to see it in action…" He cleared his throat, cheeks glowing faintly. "Anyway, Pontius should return soon. Then, the hardest part begins. I won't try and dress it up, your highness: this may be the most painful thing you've endured in your life. And I don't know what'll happen if we fail."

Neros shook his head. "You won't fail. I trust you." He turned to face Anthea. "I trust you both."

As if on cue, a large orb of water came hurtling from the sky, halting just short of the ground and collapsing into a puddle to reveal Pontius, accompanied by Rosea.

"You rescue me from an underwater cave labyrinth, leave me to watch Arboria, and you get yourself into such trouble that you need me again? Honestly, Prince Neros, what has gotten into yo—" Rosea stopped short when she saw him, almost dropping her staff. "No, *no*, not your arm…oh, gods, Pontius told me it was an emergency, but I thought…"

"I-I'm sorry," Neros said, like a reflex. "I don't mean to trouble you. I'm sure it took much preparation to come all the way out here."

"It did, but it was worth it. Arboria will be fine for now, and I can focus my efforts on helping you with this." Rosea's eyes were glued to the prosthetic. "Where did you find something like that?"

"Leof made it!" Anthea tossed her arm around his shoulders, and he just as quickly shrugged her off.

Rosea opened her mouth to compliment him, but Leof stopped her. "I understand you're impressed, but we need to get this attached to Neros as soon as we can. We've lost quite a few weeks, and I'm sure you saw the state of the plains on the way out here. It's dormant, but dangerous, and leaving Neros in a state unable to fight puts us all at a higher risk."

She nodded. "Right. What do you need me to do?"

The prince had been stripped of his tailcoat and undershirt, leaving him shirtless and propped up with his shoulder forward. Leof sat behind him, holding his arm steady. Anthea was beside him, prepared to stitch the prosthetic on. Rosea, at his other side, gripped his good hand with a wide array of salves and potions rolled out on a cloth beside her. Neros focused his energy on taking long, even breaths; he didn't know what to expect, and he was honestly terrified of the procedure. *But this is our only option, with the way things are. I'm lucky to be able to get a prosthetic in the first place,* he reminded himself. He thought about what Pontius had told him about learning water magic; to keep his mind open and receptive to new feelings and ideas. Water magic was a fundamentally different set of skills, and Neros wondered if attaching an arm and re-learning how to use it (and cast magic with it) would be similar.

He could only hope.

"You're–you're sure there's no way I could, um, be asleep for this?" He asked, voice shaking.

Leof looked to Rosea, who shook her head. "I'm sorry, Neros. We need to be sure your body will accept this foreign object before administering anything of the sort. Besides, if I put you to sleep with my strongest spell, it creates two problems. First, that your body is being influenced by my magic energy, which may in turn influence your acceptance or rejection of this prosthetic. Second, it'll only put you to *sleep*, not numb you. So you'd still jolt awake when we started, which complicates the process even further."

"I'll try to go as fast as I can," Anthea added. "Without making any mistakes. Rosea has a salve that'll make your veins visible to me, so I can stitch this bad boy right in!"

"And I'll follow behind Anthea's movements to twist some of the final gears into place and cauterize the wounds that open, to prevent excess blood loss. Though, ideally, she won't be slicing anything open any wider than a pinprick."

Rosea rummaged through her apothecary collection, procuring the salve Anthea spoke of and applying it to Neros' skin. He shivered at the first, but he watched her spread the jelly around, forming a cuff above the ice. Once it had taken shape, it began to glow, lighting up the dozens and dozens of veins traveling beneath Neros' skin like string lights on a winter festival tree.

"Fascinating," Leof breathed. "Absolutely fascinating."

"Well, Neros, I think it's time. Are you ready?"

The prince closed his eyes, taking a deep breath through his nose, letting it out through his mouth. *Mother...Father...I must be strong for you.*

"I'm ready."

No sooner than the words came out of his mouth did thousands of tiny vines erupt from Anthea's fingers, pricking his skin and sinking deep beneath his skin. It *stung,* and he could hardly watch as they wove under his skin and looped back out, tying intricate knots around the metal clamps before diving back in. Neros' eyes watered from the sensation. The more she sewed, the more the joint began to *pulse,* thrumming all the way to his skull. *This must be the magic energy Leof infused into the arm.* He had to...accept it as part of his own body, right? He tried to focus his mind, but it was difficult to get past the pricking *sear* ripping its way around his arm, over and over. His muscles spasmed, and he struggled against Leof and Rosea's grip. The pain from the vines shifted into a pressing, as though they struggled to break free. Rosea's mouth moved—was she casting a spell?—and light traveled across him, though he couldn't tell precisely where.

His shoulders jerked again as a particularly strong pulse shocked him to his bones. The prosthetic twitched erratically, and he was beginning to feel its movements—he could almost control them, but it was like the metal kept locking up on him. *Is it...rejecting me?* He swallowed, breathing roughly through his nose. He would *force* his magical wavelength to merge with the prosthetic's. They couldn't afford a complication.

Rosea grabbed his cheeks and turned his face to hers. Was she saying something? His ears were ringing, so he couldn't tell; she began to wipe at his face with a cloth. *Oh. I must be sweating.* He thought he'd felt damp, but it may have been his tears. Or had he started to bleed? He didn't want to look.

He feared he had to.

Tearing himself away from Rosea's grip, he stole a glance—instantly, his gut lurched. Anthea's process had slowed, but Leof was diligently closing any open wounds, accepting salves from Rosea to urge the areas to heal. The woven structure Anthea left behind was a beautiful, intricate braid. The veins were thin and frail-looking, but the woven knot surely boasted strength.

Another jolt from the arm's magic slammed him back into the hillside, and he could begin to hear a voice or two beneath the ringing.

"Prince Neros, you're doing fantastic!" Pontius, that had to be Pontius.

"We're nearly there, nearly there…" That was Rosea.

Neros felt a warmth keeping him steady, followed by a series of rhythmic, metallic clanks. He hissed from the sudden burning sensation but knew his arm wasn't actually on fire—it was more of the magic energy fighting to fuse with his own. He breathed roughly through his nose, crying out again as the energy buzzed in his veins. That warmth—was it Leof's hands?—rubbed slow circles in his arm, and the feeling ebbed away.

"It's over, your highness. It's over." Leof's voice was low and clear in his ears. Neros wondered if anyone else could hear him. "Breathe, nice and slow. There you go. You can rest, now. You made it. You're okay."

Thank the gods, but it still…hurts so much. The corners of his vision began to blur. His head spun. He blinked, slowly, trying to see past it, but then, everything went white.

Chapter 14
Recovery

"*A*re you sure you don't need a break to rest? He's pretty heavy!"

"Calm down, Pontius, I've got it. The town is close and those monsters have finally stopped being so active. We need to take this precious window of time to make progress."

"You may not need to handle him for much longer, princess. I think he's waking up."

Neros peeled his eyes open, blinking blearily at his surroundings. They were mostly being blocked by Anthea's hair. *Anthea's hair?* He was moving... but he wasn't using his legs. *Oh. She must be carrying me.* The crook of his elbow still pulsed as though the strings of vines Anthea used to sew his prosthetic were threatening to burst open and come undone. He had to tell himself that wasn't likely.

He flexed the fingers on his prosthetic hand. Slowly, they responded, and though they were stiff, the prince was shocked at how *real* they felt.

"You can move your hand?" Anthea said, giddiness evident in her tone. "That's fantastic! Good morning, by the way."

"Morning," He replied. "I–Anthea, you can let me down."

She laughed. "Right, right." He rocked uneasily on his feet when she set him down, but Rosea held the small of his back while he righted himself.

As they continued walking, Leof fell into step beside him. His expression was uncharacteristically bursting with inquisitive wonder and awe, and Neros felt a tug in his chest. *Why does his face make me nervous?*

"How does it feel? The arm, of course. Now that your magic energy seems to have synced with it, does it feel…proper?"

He flexed the fingers again, watching the way the metal curved around each glass orb in sync. He rolled his wrist around, testing the limitations of the movements and shocking himself to find that they were the same as his regular arm. *Is it because I can't imagine spinning my wrist around any further? Or is the structure really that accurate?* When he curled his hand into a fist, tightening his grip like he was holding his spear, sparks of pain fired at his elbow. He sucked in a breath.

"It feels proper enough…I think? It's a bit soon to tell." He stifled a yawn.

Leof's cheeks lit up and he rubbed the back of his neck. "Sorry, you've only just woken up and I'm barraging you with queries. Take your time to adjust to it, and if you find something is out of place, let me know immediately. I can make adjustments."

"Aw, it's so cute that you're worried about him!" Anthea chimed.

Leof's hair flared out like a minor explosion had gone off, and he quickly fell out of step with Neros to walk behind them. "I'm only ensuring the product functions at full capacity for the client. It's *business*."

"You're really quite attentive," Rosea commented. "It's a charming quality."

Leof stayed silent, and Neros didn't look back to see his brightly glowing face, instead focused on the parameters of his new arm. He wondered… could he cast magic? Would it be dangerous to try doing so, this soon after his surgery? Looking ahead, the town they tried to get to earlier was close. *I should probably wait until it's safe, just in case something goes wrong. I wouldn't want to hold us up yet again…*

The town was enclosed by a magical barrier, and Anthea pressed her palms up against it once they approached. She groaned. "I get why they did this, but did it have to be impenetrable to *all* creatures?"

"It wouldn't be safe otherwise," Rosea placed a calming hand on Anthea's forearm. "The people who live in this town probably can't trust any creature out here. Who knows what sort of possessed or ill will they may bring to this place?"

The princess huffed. "Fair enough."

"It's all we can do to hope they trust us," Neros said. "Just use your winning smile, Anthea. I'm sure that'll do it."

They shared a laugh as the princess knocked on the barrier. To everyone's surprise, a Veturian approached. His hair was long and pale, wrapped in an intricate fishtail braid. He was decorated with jewelry beyond the prince's comprehension; he shimmered in the bright afternoon sun. His eyes widened when he saw Neros, rushing to the edge of the barrier and opening a small hole to speak through.

"Your highness? Why, I never thought I'd see you out here. Is this your travelling party?"

"Y-you could say that, yes. I, um…" Neros scrambled for the stranger's name. *Of course he knows me, and I could swear I've seen him—no, I know I've met him…but his name escapes me!*

"Dorian, your highness. No offense taken, I assure you. Are you passing through?" When Neros nodded, Dorian looked relieved. "Well, then, come in! It's a mite dangerous out there, too much for someone of such high accord like yourself. Come, all of you!"

He expanded the hole so it became a doorway of sorts, and the four of them shuffled inside. He closed it tight behind them.

"Pardon my curiosity, but are you the mage operating this portal?" Neros asked.

"Yes, I am, your highness! I moved away from Vetur some time ago, but I used to be an attendant at the castle just before you were born. You were waddling around at the time I moved away—to study magic, that was my reason, right, so I travelled Endra in search of a master to teach me! I ended up learning quite a bit from all sorts of folk, and who knew I could really become what I'd dreamed of, huh?" Dorian laughed as though he couldn't believe it himself. "Living in Vetur, I thought that magic was limited to the royal family line. Imagine my surprise!"

Neros would have been surprised as well, if not for Pontius' history lesson. He did his best to feign shock. "Truly? I had no idea myself."

"I'd hate to change the subject, Dorian," Anthea slid between the two, wrapping an arm around Dorian's shoulders. "But do you know somewhere we can sleep tonight? We'd love a cozy couple of beds to rest our weary heads!"

"Of course, who am I to deny you? I'll show you to the inn."

The inn was a collection of rooms on top of a library. They were given two rooms, each with one double bed. Neros wanted so badly to pour through the books and lose himself like he used to as a child, but he had other matters to handle before he slept. Anthea immediately pulled Rosea off to one of the rooms, claiming they had a lot of catching up to do (and only so much time to do it), leaving Leof with him and Dorian.

"Make yourself at home, your highness. I'm sure it's not as plush as you're used to, but we do our best."

"It's more than I could ever ask, and believe me, this is leagues more comfortable than our previous situation. Thank you for your hospitality."

He picked the room opposite Rosea and Anthea's, perching on the edge of the bed. Leof sat in a chair opposite him, regarding him curiously.

"Are you all right? You look…pensive."

The prince wrung his wrists. "It's Dorian. Well, not him, so much as his magic. It's so *powerful*. I never thought water magic could hold such effects, and I…I'm curious as to how he did it. I…know that I should rest, of course, but…" He swallowed around a lump in his throat. "I've done enough sitting around. I want to find out what more I can learn."

Leof blinked at him. "You're not sore? Or in horrible amounts of residual pain?"

Neros blinked back, glancing at his new arm. He flexed the fingers again, still a bit amazed at how fluid it felt, and how frankly gorgeous and intricate the mechanism looked as it moved. Sure, it ached when he'd first awakened, but after walking through town he'd grown used to it. Honestly, it was no different than the ache he felt *before* his arm broke. "I feel…fine, as surprising as that may sound."

"Well, then I can't stop you from going to talk to him. Just take Pontius with you."

"Yes, a fine idea!" Pontius said, floating up from his home in the tip of Neros' spear. "I can provide bountiful informational commentary from the sidelines, your highness!"

Neros chuckled. "Very well. I'll be back before it's too late, alright? But don't wait up for me. If you're tired, please, go to sleep."

Leof nodded, and the prince took his leave. Frantically, he retraced his steps to seek out Dorian. He left the inn, and found the man walking down the street toward some shops.

"Dorian, wait!"

He turned around, eyebrows shooting to his hairline. "Prince Neros? Is everything alright?"

"Yes, I just…" He stopped short in front of him, catching his breath. "I wanted to speak with you. About your magic. I–I have a few questions. May I…?"

An earnest grin broke out on his face. "By all means, your highness. Let's take a walk."

✿

Leof waited for Neros to leave before unpacking his bag. He needed to be sure they had enough provisions to survive down in Umbros, whenever they managed to get there, and he'd done *excessive* trading to get the parts for Neros' prosthetic. *It's a miracle that he healed so quickly. I'm hesitant to believe him, but he's behaving normally.* He stopped himself. *Well, as normally as I've never known.*

He sighed, pushing the thought (and the strange yearning that came with it) aside in favor of counting and recounting his supplies. He gently dumped the contents of his pack on the small table in front of the chair he'd sat in. There were instructional books he'd nabbed from Aldebrande—too precious to trade. He stacked them and set them aside. He had spare nuts, bolts, screws, and glass orbs. He compared his tools on hand to what he'd used according to his blueprint. *I have enough bolts and screws to replace any should they come loose or get lost. I shouldn't need any of the nuts. I could trade those for a fair price around here, I hope.* He put the bolts and screws in a small pouch, moving the nuts to the other side of the table and placing the pouch near the books. With them, he'd placed his daggers, blueprints, and the glass orbs. *I have enough orbs for that arm to fall apart completely once.* He sighed, sincerely hoping it wouldn't. There was a meager amount of food—bread and cheese rolled up into packages, and he set those aside with the books, too. *We'll need a fair bit more than that to survive down in Umbros.* He knew Anthea could survive on seeds alone, but he and the prince needed more substance than that. *Though I need less than him. If need be, I could always survive on some of my emergency potions.*

He continued to sort through his various strings of twine, salves, potions, and knickknacks, when there came a knock at the doorway. Leof stifled a groan.

"Hey, Leof, what are you up to?"

He answered her without looking up. "I'm a bit busy, Princess Anthea, what do you need?"

The sound of wood scraping against the floor told Leof that Anthea had *not* taken the hint to leave him alone, instead sitting across from him. "I never said you weren't busy, I asked what you were doing. Rationing out your belongings?"

"Figuring out what to buy, sell, and trade in the wake of Prince Neros' surgery, yes."

"Don't worry about it too much," Rosea's voice floated in from the doorway. "There are a lot of Veturians living in this town. If it's for the prince, I'm sure they'll understand, and put together a care package for him!"

"Oooh, what a great idea, Rosea!" The princess added, leaping to her feet. "Come on, Leof, grab what you don't need and let's see if we can't get a care package together."

They'll do it that easily? I suppose being royalty affords that sort of privilege. Leof shook his head. "I had wanted to spend some time in the library—"

"You can do that later! Come on," Anthea urged, tugging at his arm. He sighed, scooping up everything he'd put in the trading pile and allowing himself to be dragged out the door.

❄

"Incredible, Neros! Your power is growing even more!"

Neros laughed, feeling it brighten his entire mood as he swung around a small water-axe in front of him. Dorian had taught him nearly everything he knew about water magic, and because he was Veturian, he could explain how to conjure and twist and reform the magic in a way Neros could digest. Of course, the prince's lessons with Pontius provided the foundation all the new knowledge could be built upon, but both of them knew that as a water spirit, there was only so much he could do.

Beside him, Dorian clapped his shoulder. "It's true, your highness! I'm surprised that new arm isn't giving you much trouble; though it should be no wonder that your skill is so impressive—the royal family has always been special."

Neros dissolved the axe into a mist, turning to Dorian and shaking his head. "No, I–I really don't think we are."

"Nonsense, Prince Neros!" He protested. "Don't sell yourself short."

"No, no, I'm serious," He looked to Pontius, who urged him with a nod. "*All* Veturians used to be able to use water magic, hundreds of years ago. At some point, the goddess—the goddess Isolde, who watches over Ve-tur—I think she just *picked* someone to be royalty, and gave them special extra ice abilities to be passed down from then on. I don't know much else, but I think she may have wanted the royal family to serve some sort of purpose."

Dorian frowned. "Then, if I may, your highness…why would she have allowed a curse to befall you? And the king and queen…?"

The gears began to spin in Neros' mind. *Veturians in this town have redis-covered their abilities away from home, and they're all…rejuvenated. Isolde couldn't have been suppressing them; Veturains back home simply feel they don't need their magic. But if she wanted the royal family to serve a purpose, what purpose was that…?*

Neros shook his head. "We must not have…fulfilled her desires, what-ever they were." But they had *met* Isolde, and she was the picture of grace and power—wouldn't she have made it clear to them long ago what she had wanted? "I can't be sure."

"Don't worry about it, then. So, you say all Veturians used to be able to do magic like me and the others in this town? Where did you learn that…?"

"From me, sir Dorian!" Pontius chimed, puffing out his chest. "Veturi-ans have a fascinating history, and I was surprised to hear that Prince Neros didn't know the whole thing! For some reason, the magical abilities of Veturi-ans must have been removed from recorded text. Fickle things, sometimes, those history texts can be."

"Amazing…! To think we've simply reclaimed what was thought to be lost…well, I'm happy to keep tutoring you, Neros, if you have the energy. I'm sure you're exhausted."

The prince looked out toward the horizon, beyond the boundary of the town. The sun was beginning to set, and the twin moons were glimmering brightly. He still had time before he'd told Leof he'd be back.

"Let's keep going."

✿

Anthea and Rosea had insisted that they gather a large care package, much to Leof's chagrin. *How will we transport this?* He wondered, as the other two had to carry the basket stuffed with goodies back to the inn together.

They'd plopped it unceremoniously onto the table, looking too pleased with themselves.

"It was so nice of them to give us Veturian-crafted clothes!" Rosea smiled, feeling the fabric between her fingers. "In case Umbros is as cold as they say, I'm sure these will keep you warm."

Leof frowned. "You speak as though you're staying here."

"Well, yes, I am. I'm not suited for battle, and I would hate to slow the three of you down. Rather, I'd prefer to stay here and gather information on the state of Endra while you're away. There are a couple other nearby towns, and if I'm careful to time my passage properly, I can speak to lots of folks while you're gone."

He hummed. It would've been rather useful to have someone with clerical abilities on their trip to the underworld, but Leof supposed it *would* be infinitely more dangerous down there. And if Umbros was anything like Andolis, time would pass differently. It would be helpful to have someone on Endra to keep tabs while they were away.

"Very well," He reasoned. "All that being said, are you two turning in for the evening? The sun is about to set."

"Sadly, yes," Anthea sighed, looking truly remorseful. "As much as I'd *love* to stay and pick your brain about a few things, we Arborians have a pretty strict sleep schedule."

"I've noticed." He was going to pointedly ignore whatever *picking his brain* might have meant.

"Rest well, Leof! We seek passage to Umbros tomorrow."

He nodded, and saw them off, sighing in relief when their door closed across the hall. He turned back to the care package. Truthfully, he had to call it what it was: a glorified gift basket. *We'll be lucky if Neros finds anything of use in there,* Leof mused, turning over some of the fabrics in his hands. There was some food, which would be useful, but mostly the Veturians tossed in trinkets: bracelets and earrings and other such toys and clothes that Leof felt had no place being packed in the prince's bag.

Instead of fretting over it, he decided to spend some time in that library, like he'd wanted to *all day.* Like any good library, the books went from the floor to the ceiling, and Leof felt momentarily overwhelmed deciding what to study first. There were a few tomes for water magic, which he quickly dismissed, but noted to tell Neros about later; his eyes glazed over the history books—not his preferred subject of discussion. *History texts are always written by the winners,* he grumbled. *What can I learn down here?*

Plucking a book on Veturian anatomy, a book on flowers and gardening, and a curious book titled *Shadowes and Monstyrs: Veturian Myth,* he settled into a remote corner of the room to read.

❋

The sun had *long* since set, and at last Neros allowed himself to be guided back to the inn.

"I cannot thank you enough for your insight, Dorian. I've learned so much today."

"Please, your highness. Don't forget, I used to be a castle attendant. Assisting royalty like yourself has become second nature to me. It's an honor to teach you." He held the door open for Neros at the inn. "Now, rest well. I'm sure you have a long journey ahead of you."

"We truly do. Thank you again."

"And…Neros?"

"Yes?"

"Good luck with saving your parents."

The prince smiled, his heart twisting up in longing to see them again. He choked out a quick "Thank you" before ducking into the library.

As he passed through the stacks of books, a flicker of light caught the corner of his eye. He turned to see Leof, his nose buried in a book. Neros smiled. *I wonder if he even knows how late it is. If he's anything like me and Anthy, I doubt it.*

"Go on ahead, Pontius," Neros said. "I'll catch up with you in a bit."

"Are you going to speak to Sir Leof about something?"

A flush crept up the back of Neros' neck. "Something like that."

Once Pontius had taken his leave, he approached hesitantly, unsure if Leof would be frustrated at being disturbed. Unsurprisingly, the Ember didn't even look up as Neros approached: he was totally engrossed.

"You've had enough late nights, haven't you?"

"Hm? Oh, I'm sorry, your highness, I didn't hear you come back." Leof placed a makeshift paper bookmark into the book and closed it, giving him his undivided attention. "Have you thoroughly picked Dorian's brain?"

Neros collapsed into the chair across him, practically glowing with elation. "Oh! It was wonderful, Leof, he tutored me all afternoon and well into the evening. Veturian water magic is truly a thing of beauty, and I'm... amazed at the breadth of its power. I'm ashamed, partly, for not knowing our history with it, but now, when I return home, I can teach it to everyone! It'll be a new wave of magical prowess, and we can discover all sorts of new things all over again, I'm sure of it. It'll be like a rebirth, or renaissance! I've read about so many of those in history texts growing up, and they always sound so romantic...ah! Sorry, sorry, I don't mean to ramble," He rubbed the back of his neck. "What are you reading?"

"It's *Shadowes and Monstyrs: Veturian Myth*, actually," He turned the title so Neros could see. "Funny you should talk about Veturian water magic, since I've spent the better part of the evening reading about it. There are dozens of legends of Veturians who walked into the ocean and were consumed by a creature they called the *Steinhvalur*, never to be seen again. The legend describes them as creatures of the sea, and speaks...at some incredible length of this city, *Kivinki*, that's supposed to be hidden far in some corner of the vast Endran sea. Deep underwater, of course. No real evidence of the place exists, but I think it's interesting that your people have so many myths related to water when none of you actually practice water magic in the town."

Neros had heard of Steinhvalur before, a long time ago when he was studying mythology under Runa. He hadn't paid much mind to it at the time, thinking it was myth and therefore fictional. *I suppose it had some grounding in reality, though, considering the truth.*

"I'm familiar with the tale," Neros nodded. "I was enthralled with it as a child, and I wanted to ask everyone in town to tell me more, but Mother and Father forbade it. I wonder why..."

"Perhaps it has something to do with why nobody living in Vetur realizes they have the capacity for magical prowess."

The prince stifled a yawn. "Perhaps so. I discussed the same anomaly with Dorian, while we were training. It all seems so *odd*. We *met* the gods, and Isolde didn't..." He paused. *Did* she seem all-knowing and kind? Generous, even forgiving? He thought back to their time in the heavens, and how *small* he felt standing before them in their throne room. "She didn't seem like the type to take magic away from her people."

"Maybe she didn't," Leof reasoned. "Maybe that Melanthos guy in Umbros has something to do with it. And that, we can find out tomorrow. It's late—you seem tired, your highness. Go on ahead; I have to put these away, but I'll join you in a bit."

Neros nodded, feeling a wave of exhaustion pass over him. He trekked back to their room to find a large gift basket on the table, stuffed full of various goods. *Where in the world...?* There was a small note attached to the handle, and the prince picked it up to read.

Dear Neros,

I hope you enjoy your care package! Sift through it and pack up the rations you want. Rosea, Leof, and I just took anything the townspeople offered. (I think Leof even had a good time!)

Love, Anthy

The prince smiled, sifting through the contents of the basket. There were three corduroy cloaks in a rich deep purple; he unfolded one to find they were lined with plush fur. It was an *incredibly* valuable Veturian product. In the basket were dried fruits (which may have come from the Arborians he saw wandering around), bread and cheese wrapped delicately in cheesecloth, soaps, and *dozens* of pieces of jewelry. Sapphire and amethyst earrings, pearl necklaces and bracelets—all things Neros knew would fetch a fine price at the right shop. He began to sort through them, picking through what was best to take along, and what would simply be too cumbersome.

He heard Leof come back before he saw him sit gingerly at the table.

"Sifting through what to keep?"

"Yes. If we're leaving for Umbros tomorrow, I'm afraid I won't be able to take all of this. My bag simply won't carry the food and clothing *and* all the jewelry."

Leof hummed, then stood suddenly to grab something out of his bag. He returned with a cloth, unrolling it to reveal a wide array of fine metals and picks organized into pockets.

"I may be able to take a few."

"Brilliant. So, are these your tools?"

"More or less. A couple of them broke while constructing your arm, so I had to melt them down and turn them into other things, but these are most of the important ones."

Guilt pressed at his chest. "O-oh, I'm sorry…gods, I meant to thank you again for…all of this. All you've done to help me after we dragged you along with us on this adventure."

Leof waved his hand, covering a faint glow on his cheeks. "Don't concern yourself with it. I came along willingly, and we all need to be in peak condition before venturing to the underworld. Now, which one is your toss pile?"

Neros flushed, gesturing to the largest pile of jewelry. Veturian accessories were delicate and gorgeous, but truly, the prince's priorities lay elsewhere.

"Even those?" Leof pointed to a pair of diamond-shaped amethyst earrings with silver metal curling up the sides, pointing to delicately placed snowflakes embedded in the center of the gems. Neros thought they, like everything else, were beautiful, but he had no real use for them.

"Yes, even those. Why?"

"I—" He stammered, looking intently at the table. "Wouldn't it be polite to keep just one?"

"Oh, you think I should…wear them?" His parents were never the type to be decorated in fanciful jewelry, so he'd never taken up the habit himself. The only exception, of course, being the crown on his head. His ears had been pierced long ago, by a vendor in town who was kind enough to offer him a sample pair even though the prince was later discouraged from wearing them. *I wonder why Leof suggested these…maybe I'll give them a try.* He picked up the pair in his hands, clasping them into his ears and fastening them closed. They dangled, tapping at the edge of his jaw, but they were light.

There was no mirror, so he had to ask Leof. "Do they look alright?"

Leof's hair crackled and popped. He cleared his throat. "They suit you."

Neros smiled at the sentiment when another yawn passed through his lips. The moonlight was bright in the window, casting a long pale glow across the bed. He rose to draw it closed, and looked to Leof.

"Will you be sleeping tonight?"

Part of his earlier frustration had edged into his voice, and he wanted to bite his tongue. *If he doesn't need as much sleep, that's fine. It shouldn't bother me.*

He hadn't meant for the sentence to come out rude, but Leof, to his surprise, chuckled.

"You sound like my mentor. Yes, I will sleep, your highness."

Neros thought about Leof's answer as he closed the curtains. Darkness fell over the room, save for Leof's candle-like glow. "You won't try to sleep on the floor again, will you?"

Leof blinked at him. "…That was *you?*"

"Of course! I hated seeing you curled up on the floor. Anthea had left room for both of us in that bed, and you deserved somewhere comfortable to rest."

Leof just stared at him for a few moments, and Neros felt a flush creep up the back of his neck. "If it'll make you more comfortable, I'll sleep beside you. I just—well, I thought you'd want the space."

Neros shook his head. "I'm…after the last few days, I think the last thing I need is more distance. Thank you for the sentiment, though."

Leof simply nodded in response. They remained quiet for some time, silently preparing for bed together. It gave Neros some time to think about what lay ahead. The underworld was the sort of place he'd only read about in stories, its danger being vastly exaggerated in some ancient history texts he'd nosed through when he was little. He was wondering just how exaggerated the texts made Umbros out to be when his sleeve snagged on his arm. He hissed—the area surrounding Anthy's needlelike stitching was still tender, the muscle aching underneath. Though he'd brushed it off before, he cursed under his breath. *Of course the additional training from Dorian would result in more strain. I should be careful not to break anything, either.*

Leof was at his side in an instant. "What's wrong?"

"N-nothing, I just…it caught on my sleeve and I tugged a bit hard, is all. The ache will fade."

Shaking his head, Leof ducked into his pack, sifting through until he pulled out a pink-hued salve, approaching the prince and popping its cap. "Let me. You'll end up re-injuring yourself if you don't allow it to heal properly."

Neros opened his mouth to protest, but the look in Leof's eyes told him he wouldn't take any argument. He allowed the Ember to rub the liquid into his upper arm, careful in spreading a thin layer. When Leof was done, the liquid shimmered bright pink, dissolving into his skin and leaving a faint glittery appearance behind.

"That's…interesting," Neros said. "What sort of salve is that?"

"One Rosea concocted," Leof explained. "She took a few different ones from town and blended them with some ingredients to make this. It's supposed to encourage muscle strength and pain relief. She studied medicinal magic quite intensely, so she told me. But she wouldn't tell me why it…shimmers."

The prince hummed. "That makes sense. Leave it to Rosea to give a salve extra flair." He laughed, finishing dressing down for bed and resting his clothes on the table. *I'm glad we were gifted new cloaks,* he thought. *Our clothes have really seen better days.*

Leof allowed Neros to settle in bed first before climbing in beside him, gingerly, turning to face away from him. "Good night, your highness."

"Goodnight, Leof."

❄

Neros awoke feeling warm, the faint smell of ash tickling his nostrils. He blinked, eyelids settling back down in a desperate plea for five more minutes. The prince was curled up against his pillow; he nuzzled his forehead into it, only to find that it was a bit rougher than he remembered. Something was *actually* tickling his nostrils, too—he felt the urge to sneeze. Blinking his eyes open, his breath caught in his throat.

He wasn't nuzzling his pillow. It was *Leof.* The flames of his hair had been flickering and weaving around the prince's nose, and his own arm had curled around the Ember's front. *Is Leof still asleep?* Neros slipped his arm out from over him, curling it back to his own chest.

"Did you sleep well, your highness?"

Neros' heart thudded in his chest. *He was awake?!* "I–um! Yes, I did. Thank you for asking." He swallowed. "Did you?"

Leof sat up, stretching. "It was fine. We should dress soon, though. Arborians seem to be notoriously early risers, and if I know Princess Anthea by now, she'll want to get going to Umbros as soon as we can."

Neros followed suit, sitting up and stretching down to touch his toes. His back ached, but he felt warmer than he had in days. *It's incredible what the support of my friends has done for me.* The prince smiled. *I think I could even say*

Leof is a close friend, now. His heart fluttered at the thought, and he stood to gather the rest of his things.

"Do you think we're ready?" He asked. Leof paused, looking up from his backpack.

"Maybe. I don't know what to expect…I've read many things about Umbros. Some have said its darkness is all-consuming, leaving no sound or presence in its wake, but others have said it's a flaming hellscape that's so noisy you can hardly think. I don't know which to believe, and I don't know if we'll make it out of there alive." He shook his head. "But we have to do it, don't we? So…I'm not worried."

"Your lack of fear for the underworld is concerning, Sir Leof, but your determination is something else! It's no wonder you're the third hero of legend," Pontius piped up, floating into the room.

"Gods, Pontius, where have you been?" Neros started. "I thought you'd been asleep in my staff."

"He was meditating with us," Anthea chimed in, entering their room with Rosea in tow. "You sleepy cuddlebugs were too boring for the valiant and heroic water spirit!"

Pontius laughed jovially. "That's right, Princess Anthea! And I have news for you all. Pegaios requested I contact him when you were all gathered up and ready to go." He gestured for all of them to stand around him, and he raised his arms, spinning three times in each direction. Then, droplets of water began to form around his head, more and more until they completely covered him. When Pontius re-emerged, he wasn't Pontius at all, but a water projection of Pegaios.

"Ah, heroes. You are alive, I see. But I must speak quickly…my power is…fading."

"Fading? What do you mean?"

"It costs a great deal of energy to communicate long distances…and the dark power grows stronger with each passing minute. You must hurry to Umbros, but you need to know how.

There is a sacred ritual that requires the power of all three of you to complete. It is known as the Trinity Seal, and it was performed by the previous heroes before you. Your weapons are not the same, but your power rings true. You must…strike the ground…fill the air…flames…pass vines through…the portal, and you will be done. Do you under-

stand?"

The three looked at each other helplessly. The small projection of Pegaios was glitching in and out of existence, Pontius' features returning to view.

"We understand, Pegaios. We'll figure out what to do!" Neros declared.

"Good. Now, there is one other thing you must know. It is about Melanthos—"

Suddenly, the water projection popped apart and Pontius returned in its place. "I'm so sorry, your highness! I couldn't maintain our connection any longer...Pegaios' power has faded drastically!"

"It must be a side effect of the rest of this," Leof said. "We should get going."

Rosea stayed behind; Neros debated pushing to bring her along, but the dangers that lay ahead in Umbros outweighed his desire to take a friend along. *If possible, I'd prefer my arm to be the only casualty that results from this adventure.* So he, Leof, and Anthea stood at the portal to the underworld.

"So it sounded like the rite had me striking the ground, then Leof fills the air with flames, and Anthea, you...channel vines through the center? Toward the portal?"

Anthea hummed. "It should be more connected than that." She snapped her fingers. "Oh! Neros, what if you line the outer edge of the circle with water, and I grow my vines through that, shoot them up, catch them with Leof's flames, and throw them to the center of the portal?"

The boys blinked at her for a moment, then Leof said, "It's worth a shot."

Neros got himself set at the edge of the portal and imbued a channel of water around its edges. The water mingled oddly with the plumes of purple smoke pouring out from the space, but he tried his best to ignore it. Anthea shouted something from the other side, and suddenly vines were growing—at breakneck speed—circling around and around. Leof followed suit with his own magic, casting a large circle of flames that spun overhead. It was a spectacle to behold, especially once Anthea commanded her vines to rocket skyward and catch fire. In a moment, they came hurtling back down to the portal of Umbros, and the ground quaked angrily at the intrusion. Then, Neros noticed the purple smoke swirling at his feet: the portal was growing wider and wider, the darkness scooping him up by the back of the knees and dragging him far below.

The portal closed overhead once all three of the heroes were inside, and the thing that stuck out most to Neros was the sensation of dread that followed behind his plummeting stomach as they fell.

Chapter 15
Umbros and the Wisps

*T*hey landed with varying levels of grace. Anthea caught herself with a frantic spell, pulling decayed vines from the ground to cushion her. Neros was not as resourceful; he landed on his shoulder (of his good arm, thank the gods) and tumbled onto his back, at the very same moment Leof crashed down on his side and tumbled into him. The Ember groaned.

"Is there no *normal* method of transportation to any part of this gods-forsaken planet?"

"Well, I don't think this is the *normal* way that people come here," Anthea pointed out. Neros shivered.

"That in mind, I'm glad we're all still in one piece."

Standing to brush themselves off, Neros took in their new surroundings. It was dark, first of all, but he could have expected as such. They landed in an open courtyard, lit by occasional orbs of floating, blue-purple flames. Neros saw a river in the distance with a ferry boat gliding along it as though the river was made of air. And there were tons of small, pale blue orbs floating about. When they drifted by, their hushed whispers passed through Neros' ears. He couldn't make out any words. One of them landed on his shoulder, and a sharp tingle prodded at the nape of his neck, crawling down his spine until he gave in to the urge to shudder. The orb floated off, like a speck of dust.

"Leof, do you still have that map?"

The Ember dug through his bag, pulling out a few pieces of parchment before swearing under his breath. "The map must've snagged on something else in my bag when we fell." He stood up, and they gathered around to examine them. "Weirdly enough, there are only three pieces. Like how there are three of us."

"And one mark on each piece," Anthea hummed. "Those are supposed to be places in here where special legendary bad guy-killing weapons are, right? You think that if we find those first, we'll find the way to Melanthos?"

"It's possible. The more we explore, the more clear the layout of this place will become." Leof looked around. "Prince Neros, where's Pontius?"

Neros panicked. He checked his spear—still in one piece, but with one less glowing orb inside. "Oh, no. I think—he may still be on the surface."

"So we don't have our oracle-sanctioned guide."

Guilt settled into his stomach like a rock. "We do not."

Leof sighed. The eerie quiet settled over the three of them, and more of those dust orbs came floating by. Neros shooed away a few of them, but they seemed to resurface in hordes.

"Perhaps we can think and walk," The prince said. "These creatures are starting to give me the creeps."

Deciding Leof should lead the way (*"Really? Just because I'm my own light source?"*), the three of them headed toward the river. Leof tried piecing the map back together, frowning at it as they walked along.

"The landscape down here seems to mirror that of the surface, but only to a certain degree. This place is clearly not as big, at least, not from what I can tell." He groaned. "It would be useful if we knew *whose* weapons were *where*. It would save us a lot of guesswork."

"These paths are *really* far away from each other, too," Anthea commented, peering over Leof's shoulder. "So if we split up and got lost, or we were wrong, then it would take an awfully long time to correct."

"And since this is an otherworld, like Andolis, we don't know how fast time is passing while we're here." Neros worried.

"Or slow," Leof pointed out.

"Exactly. Maybe we should worry about the weapons later. We're here primarily to find Melanthos, right? Perhaps the creature running the ferry up ahead will have an idea."

As they approached the riverbank, the dusty orbs began to cling to the heroes' arms and legs. They weren't slowed by them, exactly, but their whispers grew harsh in Neros' ears. When he brushed them off, they faded, and the silence stuck to him like humidity. He wasn't sure which he preferred.

Standing at the riverbank, Neros peered into the water—or what he thought was water until he looked in. *This must be where those creatures are coming from,* he noted, watching the cyan orbs flickering beneath the surface. There was no water, but instead a long stream of wispy purple smoke. The ferry was on the other side, dropping off a pair of ghosts. ...*Ghosts?!*

"Leof, Anthea, do you see that...?"

"The ghosts over there? Yes." Anthea said with the same tone she'd use to talk about the weather.

"I think I know what this river is, then."

"The fabled River Myst...?" Neros guessed.

"It has to be, right? There aren't that many legends of rivers that cross over the dead to the other side."

Before Neros could say anything else, the ferryboat arrived back on their side of the river: there wasn't a dock so much as the boat approached whoever was standing along the bank. The boat was small and wooden, and its ferryman was gaunt, with a pale gray face and thick purple robes. His hair was smoky like the river, wisping slowly atop his skull.

When he spoke, it was hoarse and raspy, like the smoke in the river. "Do you wish to cross?"

"Are you...Melanthos?" Neros asked, hesitant.

The ferryman laughed, but it sounded more like a cough. "This job is not suited for the god of Death, young one. Do you wish to cross?"

"Y-yes."

"Then get in."

"Wait," Leof said. "We're not dead."

"I noticed," rasped the ferryman.

"Will we still be alive on the other side?"

Another raspy cough-laugh. "If you want to be, you will be. The living may find it taxing to be here. The Wisps tend to be attracted to the living. They feed on your energy."

"Wisps...?" Anthea asked. She brushed a few stray glowing dust-orbs from her arm. "Is that what these things are called?"

The ferryman nodded. "They are creatures born of lost souls, wandering here, seeking purpose. Their souls disconnected from their bodies when they died, but they were dissatisfied with their time on Endra, and so they did not accept Melanthos' judgement."

"His judgement?"

"He decides what section of Umbros to send them to." The ferryman waved his hand, and distant lamps glowed brighter in the distance, revealing more of Umbros. There were hundreds upon hundreds of pagoda, stacked 5 stories tall and laid out in what looked like small neighborhoods. *How did we not notice these before?* Neros wondered, but the ferryman kept talking. "There are many creatures and beings on Endra, and Melanthos individually determines their lives post-mortem."

The neighborhoods were busy, but Neros couldn't always make out the ghosts' structures. They seemed translucent, yet not, flitting in and out of existence as they walked and went about their routines.

"The Wisps disagreed with Melanthos, and so he settled them all here, just beyond the reach of town, to wander until they understood their lives were over. So they cling to the living, sometimes wishing to be transported back to Endra. But they cannot follow you there."

"Can they follow us once we cross the river?" Anthea asked.

"No," The ferryman replied. "They will be pulled back here."

The prince thought that sounded like an awfully sad way to exist after death. "So, since we'll be alive once we cross, and the Wisps will remain here, could you tell us one other thing?"

"What is it?"

"Are we headed the right way to get to Melanthos…?"

The ferryman smiled wryly. "Umbros is a mysterious place, young ones. There are many illusions here. When you think you may be on the right path to Melanthos, something may come in your way. Here, you must find your own truth. Many ghosts are checking in. If you can find and follow them, you may find your way to the god of Death.

I will ask you one last time: do you want to cross?"

Neros looked back between his companions, and they nodded at him. "Yes."

❋

Crossing the river had been loud. The trio hadn't been able to speak to each other since disembarking, silently agreeing to let the hiss and whir of the whispers vacate their skulls before trying to communicate again. The other side of the river was brighter, for what it was worth, but Neros couldn't quite shake the tight, uneasy feeling pushing at the walls of his stomach. They opted against entering any of the neighborhoods, instead following a small congregation of ghosts. This was much harder than Neros thought it had any right to be—with the ghosts flickering in and out of view, they appeared to jump farther away from the group no matter how swiftly they walked.

"Gods, this is tiring," Anthea mumbled. "Are you *sure* that map isn't useful, Leof?"

"Not since the ferryman lit up the rest of the world down here," Leof sighed. "It doesn't match at all. I thought it might be flipped, but all the pagodas throw off my sense of space. Are there *more* than when we crossed over?"

"No, I think there are less," Anthea reasoned. She frowned. "Right?"

"I didn't think it changed," said Neros. He fiddled nervously with the edge of his sleeve. "Um, guys? Where did the ghosts go?"

The princess gasped. "Oh, *damn it!* I...they were this way, weren't they?" She began to walk toward a neighborhood with three pagodas, but Leof shook his head.

"No, last I saw, they were away from the neighborhoods."

"Wait, you two, I don't really think we should split up—"

"Come on, Neros, it's right over here! I promise I'll be right back."

"I know the ghosts are this way, we should continue forward."

"But this is so much closer!"

"Guys, *seriously*, we need to stick together—"

As Neros was trying to corral his friends, he was overtaken by a twitching, itchy feeling, and a screeching noise stabbed at his eardrums. He closed his eyes, plugging his ears from the noise, and when he opened them, he was in a room.

And Leof and Anthea were nowhere to be found.

✧

When Leof turned around and Prince Neros wasn't there, that should've been his first sign that something was wrong. When he watched

Anthea disappear in a mass of sketch-like, shimmering blue lines, that should have been his second sign.

When those same lines wrapped their tendrils around him, it was already too late. He felt the same sensation as when Pontius warped them places—like his entire body was balled up and shrunken down to be flung across the universe at unimaginable speeds. This time, he felt *itchy,* and he felt no relief from it until he was deposited...somewhere. There was a ringing in his ears, and the lines—they looked more like threads, now that he could see a bit better—scrambled across the room, disappearing beneath the cracks in the walls.

The Ember frowned at them. Then, he took in his surroundings: the walls were the same as everywhere else in Umbros: a deep purple, with darker and lighter hues of blacks and blues making ever-shifting shapes that...circulated, somehow. The floor was the same dirt as he had been standing on. *Was there a box of a room put around me, or was I really taken somewhere else?* There were no windows, nor doors; only lamps with the same wisping blue flames as the ones on their path. Leof turned behind him, beginning to feel along the wall for a door, or a clue of some kind.

"You won't find a way out that easily."

Leof froze. He hadn't spoken, but he swore that was *his* voice he'd just heard. He turned around, and his breath hitched. Standing in front of him was...himself. Almost a carbon copy, save for one thing: his flames were blue. It carried through the rest of his body, too: the blue core, the pale blue irises, all of it. Leof opened his mouth to speak, then closed it again. He swallowed thickly.

"What's wrong? Are you scared? Or, perhaps more accurately, are you *jealous?*"

"Who *are* you?" So his own voice worked. That was a start.

The stranger—the copycat?—smirked at him in a way that made Leof's stomach turn. "Isn't it obvious? I'm you. But...I guess that's not really true. I'm *better*. I'm what you've always wanted to be, aren't I?"

It was true. All his life, Leof wished he had been born to a different flame color—he wanted to be able to freely learn and experiment with magic. *But...why is this stranger appearing before me now?* He flexed his hands into fists, uncurling them again only to curl them back. He wanted to reach for his daggers—

—but his own wrist, glimmering blue under his coalskin, stopped him. "Don't try to fight me. I know you don't really want to."

As if this...blue-Leof had control over Leof's mind, the urge to fight completely left his body. "Where did you come from?" Leof said.

"You," blue-Leof replied, circling back around to stand in the center of the room. "I have a family, too, you know." He snapped his fingers, and from the ceiling descended those shimmering navy threads, spinning them-selves into Embers that looked like Aldebrande and another older woman—like his own mom, if she had a kinder face. Her white flame hair was braided elegantly, draped over her shoulder. Aldebrande's flames burned blue. "You would do anything for a life like this. To have parents who coddle and care for you, instead of leaving you to your own devices."

"No," His voice cracked. He cleared his throat and tried again. "No, that's not—"

"But it *is,*" blue-Leof urged. "You're not happy with yourself as you are now. You want this. And I can take you there."

"Wh-what?"

"I can let you trade with me," blue-Leof said. His parents each rested a hand on his shoulder, smiling down at him *so damn warmly.* "I can take you to a universe where this is possible. You will have a family, magic training at your fingertips, and you'll become everything the Dark Red Prince wished he could become."

Leof swallowed, backing up and shaking his head. He jumped as he hit the wall behind him. "What's going to happen to this world if I let you do that...?"

"Does it *matter?* You want this, don't you? It's only logical to follow along with it."

Leof frowned. "I can't trust you."

Blue-Leof rolled his eyes. "I was afraid you'd say that. Fine, look." He dismissed his parents, the threads transforming into a mirror-shape, opening a portal to the bottom layer of the Eldur Ignis volcano, looking the same, yet different, than the one he knew now. He—or rather, the copycat—was speaking with Ignatius, and they had blueprints drawn for an elaborate-look-ing kinetic machine that looked to be fueled by magic. Watching his own eyes light up with excitement and fervor made him ache for it, but he didn't step toward the portal.

"That's me—what you *could* be," blue Leof said. "I'll take you here. You can have this life instead."

Leof bit his lip. His chest felt tight with emotion—through the portal, blue Leof's parents had come to check on his progress, giving him some snacks for fuel. His mother gave him a hug and kiss on the head, and his father *(Aldebrande, did it really have to be Aldebrande?)* pointed at the blueprint, no doubt giving some manner of sage advice.

"They love you," blue Leof said. "Like you always wanted someone to."

Leof wiped at his eyes. *Stop. Stop.* He didn't need his parents—he didn't need *parents*—that was what he'd told himself when he was seven. Aldebrande was a fine caretaker, but he didn't need him to be his father. He had turned out just fine. Besides, he couldn't just abandon this world (and thus the prince and princess) just because he wanted to start over with a new life.

Right?

Anthea slid open the door to the pagoda, stepping inside only to have the door slam shut behind her, a high-pitched sound like nails on a chalkboard stinging her ears. She groaned, screwing her eyes closed tight. When she opened them, she noted that the pagoda was empty. There were no stairs, but the ceiling was high enough for the building to support five stories.

"Hello?" She called, stepping further into the room. "Is anyone here?"

No voice replied. She supposed she wasn't surprised—if she were an army of ghosts, she might not respond to the voice of a random stranger, either. As she approached the center of the room, the sharp snap of a whip cracked in her ears.

Anthea whirled around, seeking its source. "Who's there?"

A girl descended from the ceiling, her hair long and navy and braided just like her own. Her eyes were yellow, like Anthea's, but they had an eerie glow to them. Her skin was navy like her hair, braided and stitched together. A wave of unease crawled up Anthea's arms. It was like looking in a mirror, but distorted. The edges of her didn't seem *fully there*, like she was a moving sketch, ready to flicker to the other side of the room in an instant.

She ended her descent, hanging and staring at Anthea with unblinking eyes.

"Hey, princess. What do you think you're doing down here?"

Anthea laughed. "*I'm* trying to find a way to save Endra. What are *you* doing with *my* voice?"

The mystery girl laughed, and Anthea was annoyed that it rang exactly the same as her own. "I have your voice because we're the same. I know everything about you, Anthea."

The princess had to resist the urge to shiver. Suddenly, this girl wasn't quite *interesting* so much as she crossed the line to being *creepy*. "That's impossible."

"Is it? I know about your whole life," The girl said, slinking her feet to the floor and bending around to face Anthea. "See? Check this out." She commanded her hair—something Anthea *knew* was an ability unique to *herself and herself only*—and the strange, blue, sketchy lines made a small projection in front of them. It was a flashback to her childhood: specifically, the moment she met Neros. He was tied up in her vines, and she was threatening him, and the projection was, somehow, from Anthea's point of view.

"That's you," the girl said. "You're terrorizing that poor boy."

Anthea scoffed. "I was *not*. I was trying to protect myself."

"Against a *Veturian?* Princess Anthea, *please*, you knew for a fact that Veturians had a trade relationship with Arboria in the past. This kid posed no threat to you. You just wanted to have fun with him, toy around a little. And look, look where that led you!" The image on the hair changed, to her dragging Neros down the mountain. "You never even noticed how much pain he was in."

"But when he told me, I was careful with him!"

"Were you?" The fake Anthea tilted her head, maybe a little too far, and her neck creaked, its groan reverberating all around them. Anthea flinched. "From what I remember, you just used him. And when Pegaios told you what to do, you ran ahead of him."

The projection changed again, and again, and again, flickering through different moments where Neros looked uncomfortable or uneasy.

"You practically left him and Leof in the dust—right after meeting Leof, no less—because you wanted to find Rosea."

The image changed again, and Anthea stumbled back at being shown her companions' dismay.

"But you kept going. Talking your way through everything." Her fake turned her head all the way around to glare at her. "You manipulated them into doing whatever you wanted. You took charge, because you can't take the back seat."

Anthea felt a strange tightness in her chest at the words being said using her own voice. "No, that's...you're wrong. They don't feel that way!"

Fake Anthea collapsed the projection, re-braiding her hair as she adjusted her body to match her head. "How do you know? Did you ever ask?" At her silence, the girl continued, stepping closer and closer to the princess with each word. "You argued with Leof to assert you were the only one concerned for Neros' health, not even bothering to consider Leof's own feelings. Then, you antagonized him. You've done nothing but make him uncomfortable since you met him. You called him *useless* behind his back."

"That was before—"

"*Before you realized he could be useful to you!*" Fake Anthea shouted, face contorting into a scowl. "You're a *monster*, Princess Anthea."

When the princess tried to step away from her fake, she found herself backed into the corner of the room. Her breath hitched, eyes darting frantically for an escape. The fake's words couldn't be true—Neros was her best friend. He'd stuck with her through thick and thin, and this adventure had handed them both their fair share of adversities so far. He couldn't think she was a monster...Leof, either. They had a rough start, sure, but he was opening up to her—and to Neros, too. She didn't think Leof was the type to think someone a monster so soon after meeting them. *Right?* But her fake had a point, and doubt filled her heart where her frustration fled. Anthea buried her face in her hands. *Maybe I am a monster.*

"I know a way to fix you right up, Princess."

She looked up, frowning. "Yeah, I doubt it."

"No, you have to believe me! I know everything about you, after all, so what reason would you have not to trust me...?" The fake Anthea blinked, and Anthea had never seen herself look so innocent.

A horrible pain tugged at her chest. *Maybe this is what I look like to people when I'm trying to get information from them.*

"You want to be on top, right? You want to be in control," When the other Anthea said it so soothingly, the princess thought that didn't sound so bad. She nodded, hesitant. "I can get you to a place where you're on top. You're the queen! You don't have to listen to anyone, not even Silva."

Anthea blinked at her counterpart. "But...what will happen to Endra?"

"It doesn't *matter* what happens here," The other Anthea said. "That'll be for me to handle. I can take care of everything, don't worry."

Something sour settled into the pit of Anthea's stomach. This felt *wrong*. Leaving to some different future where she was a queen meant leaving Neros and Leof behind. It meant leaving Rosea behind, and all the Arborians who needed her help.

In that moment, Anthea remembered what the ferryman said. *There are many illusions in Umbros...that's it!*

She shoved the fake princess away from her, hard. "You're just an *illusion!*"

The fake scoffed. "What?!"

"You're a total fraud, *and* you're lying. You only know everything about me, *not* about my friends. We trust each other, and we're doing what we can to work together to save the world. No friendship is going to be perfect, but I love all of mine. I need to stay here, to *save* this world, and *you* have got to *go!*" The princess pulled her hair into her bow, whipping one of the vines taut to be the bowstring. She was *livid*. This creature had wormed its way into her subconscious, and she allowed it to happen, and she almost let it convince her to *leave*.

The illusory Anthea seemed prepared for this fight, however, and pulled out her own bow and a pair of golden arrows. "Hah! Fine, if you can't come so easily, I'll just have to take you down myself!"

Arrows flew. Anthea had to make her own, as she always did, but the illusion's two golden arrows simply kept flickering out of existence from where they landed and re-appearing at her fingertips. It ran the princess ragged, fast: Umbros didn't have *excellent* landscaping opportunities, so her own arrows were wilted. The golden arrows the illusory Anthea were using called out to the princess, and the princess wanted them in her own hands so *badly*.

Anthea rolled out of the way of one of the illusory princess' shots, and she stomped down, sending a thick vine careening through the floor and whacking the fake down. Anthea then sent her own hair out, wrapping up the illusions' wrists and tying them together.

"Give up," Anthea spat. "Or maybe I'll show you what a monster *actually* looks like."

Illusory Anthea coughed, then sighed. "You're stronger than you look, Princess. Fine. You win." The threads at her sides started to unwind, and she began peeling apart, slipping through Anthea's constraints and returning back to her true form: snaking, hapless threads that wiggled toward the corners of the room. She left the arrows behind, and Anthea scooped them up, spinning them in her fingers before putting them into the quiver at her back.

"Wait!" The princess called. The threads stopped squirming. "One last thing. Are we headed the right way to Melanthos?"

The threads hesitated, then swirled back together to make a circular portal shape. "Come. I'll deposit you somewhere that your paths will all cross. Where the way to Melanthos is clear."

The voice that spoke was no longer Anthea's own, and while she was hesitant to trust it, she figured it was better than staying in an empty pagoda (with a gaping hole in the floor, now). She allowed the mini-portal to take her away.

☼

"You...never answered me," Leof said, carefully. "What would happen to this world if I were to go...?"

"I told you, it doesn't matter," blue Leof said, clearly exasperated.

"Yes, actually, it does," Leof bit back.

"Oh, *why?*" blue Leof squinted, and Leof thought he saw threads dancing around his shoulders. "Don't tell me you're happy *here*. You were *thrown away*. You're alone. You have to do everything for yourself. Don't you wish you had someone to support you? Someone to *love* you?"

This blue Leof sounded *hurt*. *Is he hurting on my behalf...?* He looked down, wringing his wrists. *If he won't tell me the consequences of leaving, that just means I have to think of what may happen myself.* It was hard to think about—he knew nothing about interdimensional travel, for one, and he wasn't sure if the blue Leof would then take his place in this world.

Leaving this Endra...it meant leaving Prince Neros and Princess Anthea. *Would they notice my absence?* Princess Anthea was a very keen girl, and

Leof figured she would undoubtedly notice if his personality shifted away from what it was now. The prince may not notice right away, but Leof felt his stomach tying itself in knots just thinking about him. A heat wave crashed across his cheeks. Leaving *this* Endra meant leaving behind everything he'd done for Prince Neros, too. That arm was one of his finest inventions. *Aldebrande would be awfully proud of it*. Hell, *he* was proud of his own handiwork—and it had lifted Neros up from that dark, dangerous place Leof knew all too well.

"Won't you just go?" Blue Leof pleaded.

Leof had worked hard for his whole life to try and improve his situation. And now, finally, things were starting to look up. He wasn't about to turn his back on it.

"No," Leof said. "No, that's—that isn't what I want." He looked at the impostor before him, and now the threads poking out at the edges of the figure were clear. *He* is *an illusion. This was a trick*. But his determination and resolution felt the same. "I have people to support me. And I may not have someone to love me, but…" He took a deep breath. "I have someone I love. I can't abandon this world."

Blue-black threads unwound themselves from the Illusory Leof's face, and Leof recoiled at how unnatural it looked. "Fine," He rasped. "I suppose you've earned your place." The threads continued to unwind, and they slithered away, glimmering like stars in the sky.

The room he was in collapsed around him, and he tumbled forward, catching himself on a stone. He looked up—there was a golden sword resting on it, with an orange and red glass-blown guard and a hilt wrapped in strong black leather. When he took it in his hand, it ignited. Magic energy coursed through him. He scrambled for a sheath, but one appeared at his hip, spooking the living daylights out of him—*did I summon that here?*—he wondered. He carefully sheathed his sword to rip the map out of his pack.

Two of the dots had disappeared. *Does that mean someone else found their divine weapon, too?*

Before he had a moment more to think about it, a familiar voice roused him from his thoughts. "Hey, Leof! Wow, that illusory princess was right. Are you okay? You look like you saw a ghost."

❅

The room Neros was in was large. It felt small, but that was simply because it posed a stark contrast to the wide expanse of Umbros before he was...*How did I get here?* He walked toward one of the walls, running his hand along the grooved texture in search of a way forward.

He heard the click of a lock, and turned around to see a blue door. *Interesting,* he mused, walking over to it and carefully pushing the door open. It led to another room: this one, he recognized. *This is my room, at the castle.* The floors had the same fractal blue pattern laid across it, and the pale columns rose up to arch at the ceiling, where Neros had painted constellations when he was a child. His bed was made, and his vanity was clean. *I think this is a bit different than when I left it.* His eyebrows drew together at the memory: the distinct rumble of the castle that led him down to the throne room. For him, that moment started it all.

"Reminiscing?"

Neros gasped, whirling around to see a figure in his chair. It was... himself. Looking at the figure was like looking into a mirror: he had the same color hair, the same eyes, the same crown, and even the same clothes. The only difference was that Neros was wearing a cloak, but the double...was not.

"Who are you?" The prince asked, hand hovering as though about to reach for his spear.

"Calm down, I'm not *dangerous,*" The alternate prince said, standing up and laying his palms open. "I'm you. And you're not dangerous, right?"

Neros shook his head.

The alternate smiled. "That's what I thought, too." A beat. "Do you miss this room?"

Neros nodded, a wary feeling creeping toward his heart. "Of course. Doesn't everyone get a little homesick when they're far away...?"

"I guess so." The alternate Neros sounded *so similar* that Neros himself was beginning to feel lost. "But I wouldn't know anything like that. I've always been here. Mother and Father aren't too keen on letting me leave."

"They...they aren't?"

The alternate prince shook his head, sitting down in front of the vanity mirror. "Unfortunately, no. I had a sour run-in with an Arborian girl many years ago, and they've never let me out of the castle since."

Neros paused. *Wait. A sour run-in...?* "You mean with Princess Anthea?"

"Oh, I never asked her name," Alternate Neros looked at the prince, doe-eyed and innocent, and Neros felt a pang in his heart. "She wrapped her vines so tightly around me that it gave me strange lacerations that got infected, and…well. I've been here ever since." He tilted his head, and Neros swore he saw the alternate's eyes flicker to black and back. "Can you tell me about your life? You're a far ways from home, you said. Why?"

The prince stammered a little. "I-it's a bit of a long story," he started. The alternate urged him on. "My parents…o-our parents? Were afflicted with a horrible curse, turning them to ice statues. As for me, well…" He gestured to his prosthetic arm. "My arm was cursed; if I ever used my ice powers, it hurt, and…I-I broke it. I made a friend, though, and h-he fixed it for me.

The girl you had a sour run-in with…I met her when I was small, too, but my time with her was much less…detrimental. Her name is Princess Anthea, and she's one of my best friends. When I found out about my curse, she told me of one affecting her people, and…well, we started a journey together. As it turns out, Endra is under terrible duress. It's the second coming of an old prophetic tale, where three heroes join together to take down a terrible darkness inflicting the land."

The alternate's eyes sparkled. "That sounds so exciting! Much more than my own life."

Neros frowned. "Really…? Don't you…love your mother and father?"

Alternate Neros fiddled with the ends of his tailcoat. "I do, but…I rarely see them. Mother travels abroad to do trading with other territories, and Father is cooped up always with political agreements with other nations. In a year, he'll begin grooming me to be king, and I'll need to take a wife."

The prince's breath hitched. "A wife…?"

"Your life is so thrilling. The true life of a hero." He looked down, then back up, and an odd pang hit Neros' heart. "Won't you trade places with me?"

"*What?*"

"Trade places with me," The alternate stood suddenly, and Neros stumbled back when he gripped his arm. "Please. I would do anything to be in your shoes. You know, I'm you, right? So I can trade plenty of things with you."

Neros looked down at his arm where the alternate was grabbing it. He was scared to say anything, but his grip felt a bit too tight.

"Are you worried about your arm? I can give you mine," The alternate said, and with a wave of his hand, their arms had traded places. Neros' arm was restored to its original, soft blue skin, and the double had the hand that Leof made. It was beautiful, and whole, and real, but...

It felt *wrong*.

"I—could you give that back, please? I-it's quite dear to me."

"But why? It's broken, and now you're fixed." He pouted, and Neros thought it looked quite...unbecoming on him. "You've never wanted to be broken."

When Neros didn't say anything, the alternate continued. "I can see it in your eyes. You were sad when it broke, right? But it's because you think this new arm makes you less beautiful."

"That's not—! This arm—the one on you, rather—*is* beautiful, I..."

"You don't have to hide anything from me. I know all of your secrets," The alternate smiled, but it was too wide, and Neros tried to take another step back, but the alternate's grip just got tighter. "You've been hiding many things from Anthea and Leof, Neros."

"What...? What are you talking about?"

"You want to be everything your parents dreamed for you. A poised, natural, easygoing prince with no worries in the world. Someone who could connect with others. But you're afraid you can't be that anymore. You're sad. You're worried about your parents, the world, your friends, and it plagues you. You don't want anyone to see the pain you're enduring." The alternate's thumbs pressed down, and Neros felt tension building in his wrist. "You need to be happy, or else they won't look to you for help you so desperately need to provide. You need to keep your suffering to yourself so no one else is inconvenienced by your pain. You need to be beautiful. And this," He squeezed tighter, and Neros cried out when his wrist orb cracked, pieces of glass falling to the floor. "This is not beautiful."

"Pl-please let go of me," Neros choked. *How did he crack it? He was squeezing my arm—his arm on me, rather, not his own.* "I-I have to go back."

The alternate Neros' eyes grew angry and black, but only for a moment. If the prince looked closely, he could see its crown beginning to crumble. "Please don't leave," he begged. "I need to switch places with you. Please!"

Neros pulled his wrist from the alternate's grip, and their arms switched back to their original bodies. He rubbed some of the soreness out of his wrist, lamenting that Leof may need to fix it for him. *If only I could do it myself…*

"I can fix it for you, remember? All you have to do is trade places with me."

Neros frowned. "But what about Endra?"

"What do you mean, Neros? This *is* Endra."

The prince shook his head. "No, I mean *my* Endra. With Leof and Anthea, and *my* parents."

The alternate laughed, and Neros flinched at the sound. *"Your* parents? The ones frozen solid in the throne room, slowly rotting to death under the ice? Hah! Hahaha! Why would you want to go back to a world of such suffering when I can offer you salvation?"

Neros backed up to the door, moving to discreetly try the handle. "Because I'm dedicated to my friends and my family. I've built my own life, and there…I want to fix the fate that has befallen us."

The alternate prince's eyes clouded, becoming pools of sheer black, and threads of glimmering starlight exploded from his shoulders. He charged at Neros, and the prince was barely able to scramble out of the way.

"No!" It screeched, and Neros felt the same fear as he did fighting those large black birds in the field. The way this figure was coming undone, however, set the gears in Neros' head spinning. *It was odd to meet a double of myself, but is it unstable because it's trying to communicate with me…?* His double's head turned, and the prince recoiled because *his neck should not be able to turn that far.* "You can't leave me! I don't want to be left alone. You have friends, and—and don't you have feelings for someone special? I have no one. My parents barely talk to me. The people in this town don't know who I am. It's just me. I'm all alone."

Neros stumbled away. The alternate began muttering to himself, a pitiful expression on his face. The prince had to digest what he asserted: *feelings for someone? But, wait. Is there truly no one to support this version of me?*

The prince shook his head. "Neros," he started, stuttering around the odd feeling of addressing himself. "You're not alone here. You'll never be alone. The castle attendants are so much more than just servants to keep you prisoner. They're every bit as good of a family as Mother and Father are."

Alternate Neros' eyes brimmed with tears, seeming to melt his face as they spilled onto his cheeks. "That's not true," he hiccuped.

Swallowing thickly, Neros slowly approached the double. He gingerly placed his hands on the double's shoulders, rubbing slowly up and down, like his parents used to do for him when he was young. "Of course it is. All you need to do is reach out to them. Talk, and have a conversation. You'll connect in no time, and you'll feel less alone."

The alternate continued to unravel, his crown crumbling into dust as he twisted into thousands of threads, glimmering and floating like they had minds of their own. "Perhaps you're right," came the airy whisper. "I should accept love and care from those close to me when I need it. Don't forget that."

Neros wasn't sure if the whispers were telling *him* not to forget or if it was the alternate telling itself not to forget, but suddenly the room around him was fading, wall by wall, and Neros realized it had been an elaborate illusion. The threads lifted the prince and carried him down toward where he had originally split from Leof and Anthea, but deposited him a bit further up the path, dropping him on a fork in the road with a sign directly in front of him.

Before he could read it, he was barreled into from behind.

"Neros! Oh, thank gods, you're okay! You're okay, right?"

The prince laughed, turning in Anthea's grip to embrace her. "I'm fine...I think. What happened to you two?"

"We found our divine weapons!" Anthea cheered, reaching into her quiver and pulling out two glimmering golden arrows. She urged Leof to show off his, and he meekly pulled out the sword with the glass-flame hilt. Neros' eyes widened.

"Wow! These are beautiful..." He gasped, whirling around to see if the threads from his own illusory self left behind anything special, deflating a little when there was nothing but the dim glow of lavender-hued flames around them. "I–I never found my own. Only an...odd, distorted version of myself."

"We encountered the same," Leof sheathed his sword. "Ours tried to trick us. To get us to go somewhere other than here. We had to fight them off or subdue them in order to get these."

Neros hummed. "I...my illusion tried to get me to stay, but it...was crying, so I comforted it, and that's when it dissipated." He rubbed at his wrist, fingers grazing over the small fracture in the orb there, the only proof he had that it even happened.

Leof consulted their map. "It looks like there's still a dot here." He showed it to Neros, who took it to look more closely. "What happened to your wrist?"

"O-oh, the illusion gripped it a bit hard. I-I'm fine," He reassured, offering a smile. "It doesn't hurt."

Looking back down at the map, Neros noticed the small dot was moving. If he traced his finger from where they started back at the river to where he thought their current position might be, it looked like it was straight ahead.

The prince glanced at the sign. There was only one direction on it, and it read: *To Pazemes Pass and the Sanctum of Postmortem Affairs.*

"Whatever my divine weapon may be, I think Melanthos has it. It looks like this path may lead us right to him."

"Well, there's only one way to find out," Anthea said, looping her arm through Neros', then Leof's. "Let's go!"

Chapter 16
The Sanctum of Post-Mortem Affairs

$\mathcal{T}$he longer the trio traveled through Umbros, the heavier their bodies began to feel. Neros' head was clouded by a weight and sadness he just couldn't put a name to. Along the path to the sanctum (and, he hoped, his divine weapon), the landscape diminished. Surrounding them now was an expanse of the same, ever-shifting purple ground they'd been walking on, and very little else. Ghosts flickered in and out of existence ahead of them, a congregation of souls headed toward their final judgement.

For the umpteenth time, Neros shivered. He couldn't shake that horrible, creeping feeling that lingered around the base of his neck. Alongside it was a weariness that wore away at his bones, tugging and tugging and tugging, a feeling he could only describe as heavy.

"It's much easier to follow all these ghosts now, at least," Anthea said. "And two-thirds of us have new weapons!"

"Right, but don't you get an odd feeling that this may not go as we thought it might?" Leof countered. "We don't know what kind of person Melanthos is. He could be more evil than those sludge creatures we fought in the plains."

Neros nodded. "Pegaios had wanted to tell us something about him, didn't he? I wonder what that could've been."

"I hope he's okay," Anthea lamented. "He seemed to be fading out pretty fast during that last remote communication."

Leof nodded. "I hope Pontius is alright, too."

Soon, they approached a tall, thin door leading into a castle built as tall as they could see, stark black spires stretching up toward whatever passed for the threshold between Umbros and Endra. A significant contrast to the pagoda neighborhoods that served as purgatory, this castle had delicate wrought-iron detailing snaking and clawing around its walls and windows. It emanated power, but also something darker. Neros rubbed his arms and tugged his cloak tighter around his body.

They walked inside, not knowing what to expect. There were no receptionists (and Neros wasn't sure why he felt he should expect one), though the ghosts would stop in place and close their eyes, eventually floating toward the ceiling and dissipating. *Is Melanthos capturing them as they walk?* The heroes remained untouched, though Neros caught snippets of distant conversation.

"I deserve better!"

"You must go where you are told."

"But...how...why am I here...?"

"My babies! I must go back for my children, please!"

"I supposed it would eventually come to this..."

They climbed a winding stairwell that creaked under their weight, and down a long, carpeted hallway. In a twisted sense, this place reminded him of his own castle. And as they walked, Neros felt that truly, it was *dark*: shadows closed in on them from all sides, their weight settling heavy in Neros' chest.

"Do you guys feel that..." The prince asked.

"It's like a pressing on my chest. Like—like loneliness, but..."

"But it changes?" Anthea guessed. "It feels lonely, but then it feels angry. I wonder if we're being affected by the emotions of the deceased while we're here."

"How troublesome. I hope this doesn't mean that Melanthos will be distracted when we try to talk to him."

Neros nodded. "I guess we'll find out soon."

At the end of the hallway, they arrived before a door that stretched toward the ceiling, carved with intricate patterns and boasting two golden handles; a stark contrast to the rest of the darkness surrounding them. For a moment, Neros wondered if it was going to speak to them, the way the gate did back in Andolis. He thought it would be fitting, since the rest of the walls seemed to ooze with the whispers of the dead.

His hand hovered over the handle for a moment, listening. No voice came to assert that he stop before disturbing Melanthos and offering riddles in exchange for passage.

Yet he hesitated, still.

"Are you afraid?" Leof's voice came low from his side.

To be honest, Neros didn't know how to answer. The same pressure had been pushing and pulling at his insides for the last *gods-knew* how long, leaving him unsure what was nerves, what was fear, and what was fabricated. Anthea appeared at his other side, wrapping her arm around his and grabbing the door handle.

"It's okay, Neros. We're right here with you. Let's open this door together!" She smiled encouragingly, and the prince's heart felt lighter.

Leof gently added his hand to the pile, and Neros swore his entire body warmed from the sensation. "Right," He squeaked, clearing his throat. "Right. Let's go. Together!"

And together, they pushed open the door. The room beyond was large and empty save for one obsidian desk straight ahead. The body in the chair behind it, Neros assumed, was none other than the god of death: Melanthos. *He's massive,* Neros thought. *Though I shouldn't be surprised: so were the other gods.* However, the prince wondered if *massive* was the right word: more than that, he was *tall.* His face was long, and gaunt like a skeleton's with pale grey skin stretched over it. A long black robe draped over his shoulders, with marks that seemed to be moving across his back and up and down his body. He had long, silvery hair that was, at present, tied back into a low ponytail. A small pair of glasses rested on the tip of his nose.

As soon as the door closed behind them, Melanthos looked up. His eyes were small dots of light inside of larger black sclera. Neros felt compelled to stop moving under his gaze.

"Excuse me," the prince started. "Are you Melanthos?"

Melanthos' gaze narrowed, and he removed his glasses, placing them on the desk. He stood—he was tall, taller than any of the gods. When he walked in front of the desk, his cloak billowed behind him, revealing his (surprisingly plain) black clothes underneath. He stopped and stared, but his cape continued to billow. His hair fell out of its wrapping, and now floated like a halo of webs around his head. He looked...*angry.*

"*You,*" He growled, reaching an arm out to summon a stone scythe taller than he was. *"You three…you degenerates ruined me…but I will not let that happen again! Now, you shall* perish.*"*

"Uhh, I think you might have the wrong trio—*whoa!"* Anthea scrambled out of the way, taking the two boys with her just as Melanthos' scythe swung down, sticking into the ground and shaking the floor. Immediately, he lifted it, winding up for another swing. The three split up, scrambling out of the way as more debris flew.

"Did he say *again?* We've never met before, have we?" Neros called, unhooking his spear and searching for an opening.

"No way! I'd remember a face that tired!" Anthea called back, spinning her hair into a bow. She summoned two glowing golden arrows from her quiver. Melanthos caught sight of them, and his aim was locked onto her.

"Princess Anthea, watch out!" Leof shouted, dashing to her side and summoning—Neros gasped. *Is that the same blade he showed earlier?* It was gorgeous when ignited, and apparently strong enough to parry Melanthos' scythe. The god brought his weapon back again, scowling. Neros stuck to the shadows, hanging by the wall out of the god's view.

"Pyrrus…Silva…you ruined my life! You will pay!"

Neros paused. *Those are…the names of the gods?* Suddenly, it clicked. "He's gone berserk because he thinks we're the gods!"

"We'll keep him busy, Neros!" Anthea yelled, shooting him a thumbs-up before squealing and rolling out of the way of another vicious attack. "Try to climb up on his back and knock some sense back into him!"

"Right!" *How am I supposed to do that?* Melanthos was *constantly* moving and about twenty times their size. *Find a way. Find a way, Neros. Your friends are in danger.* He crept as fast as he could along the wall, keeping a close eye on Melanthos to ensure he wasn't seen. He seemed fully preoccupied with Leof and Anthea, and Neros wondered if it was their divine weapons that drew the god's attention and ire. Suddenly, the prince felt lucky that he was unable to acquire the divine weapon he could call his own.

Sticking close to the wall, Neros noted that the room they were in wasn't actually as large as it appeared, and he wondered if that was an illusion brought about my Melanthos to seem more imposing. He approached the corner and rounded it, sprinting now toward the god's desk. *It's tall enough…if I can get onto it, maybe I can attack him from behind…*the gears in the prince's head were spinning trying to think of ways to get up, and fast. *I could build stairs out of ice, but...there's too much risk. This curse hasn't been lifted, and I can't risk infecting another part of my body. If only I could use a rope, I could transport myself easily...or if Pontius were here, he could...Wait!* Neros' eyes lit up with delight, and he immediately set to work by channeling a small platform of water. *This works just like other magic, right? Those water barriers were solid, and so this should be, too, if I just...* When he stepped on it and didn't sink—his theory proven correct—all that remained was for him to lift himself. Albeit awkwardly, he willed his water platform up to the desk's edge.

The desk had a much better view than the floor, Neros had to give it that. He could clearly see the flames of Leof's hair and the trail of Anthea's vines as they scurried across the floor, dodging or parrying Melanthos' mighty swings. His heart swelled with pride—the two of them were cleverly dodging so the god wouldn't have to turn around. Neros shook his head. *Focus! What can I do from up here...?*

Melanthos seemed to be falling into a pattern: he would swing, his scythe crashing down, then he would wind up and swing again. Every other time he struck the floor of his office, the Scythe would catch, and he'd struggle for a moment to release it. *Maybe I can attack him while he's struggling... but with what?* Neros looked around—the desk was sparse, save for a stack of papers and a cup of pens that were as tall as the prince himself. They looked too heavy to lift without aid. *I'll probably have to conjure something myself...I wonder if I can cool off some of my water magic if I channel it through Vatnis. It is made of ice, after all.* He nodded to himself—it was worth a shot. Focusing his energy, he felt the flow of a river through his veins, and from his hand sprouted thin trails of water. Neros channeled them through the base of his spear, and as they emerged out of the tip, they swirled together with ice crystals, forming a disc of water and ice that was spun around and around like a small hurricane.

Neros grinned. *Perfect.* He willed it to grow larger and larger, and then he waited. Sure enough, the moment Melanthos' scythe was stuck, Neros guided the disc to float above the god's head, and dropped it.

It exploded into a wave of water and snowflakes, and Melanthos stumbled forward, his scythe dissipating to dust the moment he dropped it. He sucked in a harsh breath before going completely silent. Neros felt the blood rushing through his heart and thrumming in his ears as he waited for what would happen next.

"This water…but also, snow…?"

Melanthos turned around. He bent over and squinted at Neros. Realization flashed across his face, followed by momentary guilt before settling back into a faint frown.

"You aren't Isolde, are you." It wasn't a question.

"N-no, sir." Neros answered, trying his best not to feel crushed under the intense weight of Melanthos' blank stare.

The god turned to Leof and Anthea, and he sighed. "And you two aren't Silva and Pyrrhus. Right. How foolish of me, to be deluded. It's been a long day." The tiredness that ebbed into his tone made his voice akin to crumbling ashes. He moved back around to his desk, sitting unceremoniously. With a snap of his fingers, he summoned a few shimmering threads—like the ones Neros had seen earlier, with the illusions—to pluck Leof and Anthea from the ground and place them on his desk as well.

"Apologies. I'm not usually so violent."

"Kind of a weird thing for the god of the underworld to say," Anthea quipped.

Melanthos only sighed, a fog floating down from his lips and casting a brief haze over the trio. "Perhaps we should start over. You seem to know who I am, but I will reiterate. Melanthos, ruler of Umbros, keeper of the dead. Who are you, and what brings you here? Seeing as the three of you are clearly too *perky* to be dead yourselves."

"We're on a vitally important quest," Neros explained. "I am Prince Neros of Vetur, and this is Princess Anthea, and this is Leof. Endra is in grave danger, and we were told you were its root cause."

Melanthos lifted a brow, less amused by the assertion. "Am I, now?"

"We've gone to Andolis," said Anthea, and Melanthos narrowed his eyes. "The gods were up there, and they told us you were up to no good down here, and that's why big portals have opened all over Endra to spew out black sludge-covered *monsters* that attack everyone!"

"They gave us a map," Leof added. "And instructed us to come down here and find you, and defeat you using divine weapons we'd find on our way. Princess Anthea and I have found ours, but Prince Neros is missing his, and…no offense, um, your holy–uh, undead-ness…but you don't seem quite as bent on destroying the world as the gods told us you might be. Seeing as the three of us are…prophesized to save the world, perhaps you can explain that?"

"Astute observation," The god deadpanned. "You may just address me as Melanthos. I am the ruler of the underworld, Umbros, but my circumstance allots that I am not yet quite its god."

"Not yet its god…? What does *that* mean?"

"Allow me to paint you a picture, Princess Anthea," Melanthos summoned more of the shimmering threads, and they spun themselves into a yarn replica of a piece of the Endran plains, with yarn-spun clouds floating overhead. "You are aware of the prophecy you three have been…written into. But I fear you three do not know the whole story, for no history has been kept since the first coming of this prophecy."

"Why is that?" Leof asked.

Melanthos sighed, folding his hands. "Because it was destroyed. By me, mostly, and the army of dark figures I created. You see, around eight hundred years ago, I arrived to Endra…a different god." The yarn diorama moved along with his explanation, even creating a mini Melanthos. "I used to live in Andolis. With Pegaios the sage Oracle, and the two of us were meant to keep the peace. By manner of many conflict and discrepancies, he…struck me down here. Banished, you could say, but I was displeased with the arrangement and fought back. I sought power from the magic of Endra's soil…and it corrupted me greatly."

On the yarn diorama, small purple portals began to scatter across the world, growing larger and larger. *Just like what's happening on Endra right now,* Neros thought.

"Pegaios called to the land, to see if he could find heroes that would hear and answer his call. And three did."

Threads spun into the shapes of three heroes who Neros admitted looked *startlingly* like Leof and Anthea, though the third was a girl with long flowing blue hair like waves of the ocean. They appeared determined, with special weapons in their hands: Neros immediately recognized the arrows and the sword as the ones Leof and Anthea carried with them now.

"Isolde, Pyrrhus, and Silva fought their way to my domain and knocked the sense back into me. I retreated further into Umbros, where I re-side now, and took to processing the spirits of those whose lives I had taken. A bit of divine punishment, as you may consider it. I had plenty of time to reflect on my actions. For their troubles, they were rewarded with godhood by the Oracle."

The mini gods ascended to the mini yarn clouds, settling into the thrones Neros recognized from their trip to the heavens earlier. "They were given the task of repopulating and restoring Endra to its former glory, as I had nearly brought its ruin with my rage."

Anthea frowned. "Huh. *Rewarded* godhood? So they were mortals, like us?"

"That is correct."

"But you're not raging."

"That is *also* correct."

"Then who's creating the darkness!? We were mauled by dozens of creatures that imploded into black dust when we defeated them, and there are weird portals like the ones in your story everywhere. People are sheltering themselves in their towns, desperately trying to keep the encroaching darkness out. My people in Arboria were attacked by our Great Ancient Tree, and Leof's civilization is on the verge of *civil war* because of the dried-up lava in the Eldur Ignis Volcano. And Neros' parents are frozen ice statues, and he was cursed by a witch to never be able to use his ice magic without pain!"

Melanthos raised his eyebrows. "Perhaps you should have led with that, young ones. Curses have befallen your kingdoms?"

"*Yes!* And the gods didn't seem to understand it at all, waving us off to Umbros in search of you and divine weapons to kill you with."

"I thought it was odd," Leof added. "They seemed surprised that we were there, but hardly willing to listen to our story. Pyrrhus doesn't have the best reputation in Embran legend, but I still imagined him being a bit more… benevolent."

Melanthos hummed. "The creatures I bore from the darkness down here were most powerful when I had sucked away Endra's magic and made it my own. Perhaps…that is why you saw some of them on the surface. Endra is a world used to being imbued with magic, and without it, it cannot survive. It will revolt. Do you understand?"

Neros remained quiet. *Endra's magic being…taken?* The prince thought that made sense—his magic was technically taken from him, and Leof and Anthea's entire kingdoms had had the magic that made them unique sucked right out of them. *But if not Melanthos, then who...?* He thought back to the witch who cursed him, and the words she spoke. *She said we defiled her legacy, but who was she...?*

Neros gasped. Realization hit him like a freight train.

"The goddess Isolde!"

"What? What about her?" Leof asked.

"It was Isolde who cursed me and froze my parents," Neros breathed. "I thought she sounded familiar when we were in Andolis, but...I never put it together until now. It was her voice that shook the castle, and her words... she said we defiled her legacy. I didn't know what it meant at the time, but she *must* have been talking about the statues I created. In years' past, we had always created a statue of Isolde in honor of her gift to the royal family, the gift of ice magic. But this year, I...I crafted one of my parents instead." He turned to Melanthos. "Is it possible...that the gods are the ones who could have done this?"

Melanthos shrugged. "If they let their powers of godhood get to their heads, I wouldn't be surprised if it was them. All I can tell you is that it isn't me. Those monsters you're seeing on the surface are a response to the diminishing magic in the world—even when I first summoned them, I didn't have control over them."

Neros nodded, deep in thought. *Had I only realized it was Isolde's voice earlier...maybe I could have avoided...* He looked down to his arm, with his wrist still fractured. He sighed. *There's no point thinking about that now.*

"But if you angered the goddess Isolde, that only means that we—or our people—must have angered Pyrrhus and Silva in some way," Leof reasoned. He turned to Anthea. "Does that make sense to you?"

Anthea hummed, frowning. "I don't know, the gods didn't seem that... awful, to me."

Leof quirked a brow. "Really? They barely wanted us there, immediately shifted the blame elsewhere, and literally *threw* a stone tablet at us for us to use as a map to find divine weapons with no description or aid, and we've only happened across them all by chance." He glanced at Neros, who fiddled with his cloak. "Almost. They called Pegaios *bratty,* and used powerful god wind to blow us out of the room when they were done with us. I don't think they were *nice*."

"You just don't trust Pyrrhus because he was a little brash! I've been spiritually connected with Silva my whole life, I think I would know what kind of goddess she is!"

"Oh, you have? Then why hasn't she told you anything about how to save the thousands of dying Arborians in your kingdom? That's right, because 'gods don't meddle in mortal affairs.' But what happens when all the Arborians die and she has no kingdom to oversee? Don't you think she would care even a *little?*"

"Shut up! Just because you don't trust anyone you first meet doesn't mean you have to force that belief on everyone around you, Leof."

"Hey, *hey!*" Neros interrupted, physically stepping between his friends. Leof's hair flared and *popped* around his cheeks, while Anthea's eyes were narrowed into slits, thorns beginning to spawn at her feet. "Stop it. This is no place to argue."

"The prince is right," Melanthos said. "I've told you all you can, and the dark aura of this world is clearly beginning to get to you all. I'll send you back."

"But, Melanthos…we don't even know if the gods are truly the ones behind all this." Neros said, a bit helplessly. "I…how will we know if we're right?"

"I'm sure the signs are there, Prince Neros. Perhaps you should consult again with that bratty oracle they mentioned."

"Pegaios?"

An odd emotion that Neros couldn't place settled on Melanthos' face, pulling down his brows and dulling his eyes. "Yes, him."

"But, his power…it faded. I don't think we can speak to him anymore."

"Then that gives you your answer, doesn't it?" Melanthos squinted. "Now, please go. I have a lot of freshly deceased souls to process."

The god waved his hand, summoning dark tangles of that starlit thread and wrapping it around each of the heroes, making wings for each of them. Neros watched him tuck something into his own pair of wings, but he couldn't make out what it was. With another wave of his hand, the three of them began to float upward, into the darkness. The higher they rose, the quicker Neros realized that the darkness was becoming *lighter*, like sunlight trickling between clouds, and the heaviness pressing on his bones ebbed away. Neros looked back down to Melanthos one last time, and his eye caught on a pair of ghosts. His breath hitched.

The weight that had just lifted from his heart crashed back down, knocking around his insides and settling into the pit of his gut. They flashed out of existence before Neros could be sure, but he would swear upon all gods in the universe of what he had seen. It was unmistakable.

He had just seen his parents.

Chapter 17
Howling Winds of Winter

The trio settled peacefully back on the surface, their glittering wings sliding off their bodies and back into the darkness. Behind them, the portal they entered in zipped closed, leaving nothing but dead grass behind. Immediately, they heard a cry of joy, but it didn't come from any of them.

"Your highness! Princess! Sir Leof! Oh, I thought I had lost you forever!" Pontius came flying faster than Neros had ever seen him, crashing into the side of the prince's face to give him a tiny hug. "I was out of my wits waiting for you."

Neros feared to ask. "How long has it been?"

"Three days, your highness," Pontius said, tone grave. "And so much has happened since then. Some of the portals have sealed, but the monsters you've all been fighting are still here. And what's worse, many of the Veturians and Arborians in the nearby town have started to panic because their magic isn't working anymore!"

"*What?!* In just three days? Wait, we've only been gone three days? Oh, my gods, I don't know whether to be relieved or terrified," Anthea ran her hands through her hair.

Neros nodded, a lump stuck in his throat.

"So, your highness?! What did you learn? Must you train more and face Melanthos again?" Pontius urged. Neros blinked.

"Oh, no, Melanthos…was nice, actually."

The water spirit's eyes nearly bugged out of his head. "What? *Nice?* He's a god of death, your highness, how can that be so?"

"He gave us a lot more information about the prophecy than the gods ever did," Leof seethed. "It turns out *they're* the ones responsible for this whole mess."

"But we can't know for sure unless we confront them again," Anthea argued. "So we need to return to Arboria."

"Sure thing! I can warp us right there, no prob—"

Neros held up his hands. "W-wait. I...I need to go to Vetur first."

Pontius deflated. "Prince Neros, I can't quite warp us *there*. I could get you close to the base of the mountain, but...what business do you have there?"

"I...it's hard to explain, but, well, I left home without any warning at all. Not to say that I need to explain everything to everyone before going, but...it's been months. I need to know if they're safe."

"The Veturians?" Anthea quirked a brow. "Shouldn't you check on them after we confront the gods?"

Neros shook his head, guilt mixing with hastened anxiety in his stomach. *My parents.* "Please, Pontius, will you take us there? Leof, Anthy, if you both want to begin travel into Arboria, I can meet up with you—"

"Not a chance. We need to do this together, right?" Leof said, sparing a glance to Anthea. "So let's go together. Besides, you still don't have your divine weapon yet. Maybe your hometown will have some clues for how to obtain it."

Anthea and Pontius nodded, and once they were surrounded by his orbs of water, they warped back to the base of the mountain. For the first time, Neros felt queasy for the entire trip.

As the water cleared from Neros' vision, he examined the mountain that led to his home. There was a large, circling cloud of winds that blocked the view to the peak, the landscape shrouded in fog. More than anything, it was *cold.* The prince pulled his cloak tighter around his shoulders. *It shouldn't be this cold at the mountain's base. Something is wrong.*

His legs started moving before he could think better of it, and he barely heard the cries of his friends behind him. He began climbing, his muscle memory taking over and leading him up the swiftest path. Every so often, the mountain would plateau and he would run forward to the next wall, vaulting himself upward higher and higher. Now, he could see that the cloud of winds was a blizzard, caught in a whirlwind pattern circling the mountain's peak. *Where Vetur is. Where the castle is. Of course. It must be Isolde!*

A hand caught his wrist before he could continue.

"Neros, *stop!*" Anthea's desperate plea came. He startled—he hadn't even realized she'd been following. Leof, too, with Pontius beside him. The water spirit fled immediately to Neros' spear, where it was safe from the winds picking up around them.

"Wha–? No, you can't follow me, I–I need to meet up with you later!"

"Leof said we're in this together, and I agree!" She shouted. The snow was falling faster here, flakes sticking in Anthea's hair and dulling the flames atop Leof's head. *They must be so cold.* "Don't run ahead, we can do this as a team!"

Neros stumbled back, away from her. Urgency tugged at his stomach. "N-no!"

"What do you mean, *no?*"

"I have to do this alone!" Neros yelled as the wind picked up. He clutched his cloak to keep it from blowing off his shoulders. He gripped his spear in his other hand, the metal groaning against the temperature. "It's too dangerous for you to follow me!"

"Are you out of your *gods-damned mind?!*" Leof and Anthea shouted at once, both throwing their arms out to their sides.

Anthea continued. "After *everything* we've been through, you're going to leave us here?"

"No, it's not like that, Anthy—you, both of you, it's too cold, your lives are in danger! Think of yourselves!"

"And when have you thought of *your* life, Neros?!" Leof yelled, his hair blowing wildly in the winds, but strangely brighter and fiercer than Neros had ever seen. "You have sacrificed so much for us—you *blasted your arm to smithereens* to prevent our deaths from coming too soon. You left this place ages ago to help Anthea when she needed you. The least we could do is come to your aid!"

"There is a very real chance you will die, Leof!" Neros shouted, swinging his spear and causing his companions to take a step back. "It is freezing here. If we continue climbing, your magma core may not survive. Too much ice will get in your cracks. And Anthy, you'll…your barkskin will stiffen. I can't risk your lives like this! You have to understand!"

Anthea stomped her foot into the snow, hands curled into fists, thorns sprouting around her feet. "*Stop underestimating us!*" Her breath came in labored huffs. "Who do you think we are?! We won't roll over dead so easily! Neros, why don't you want us going with you?"

"There's strength in numbers, Your Highness," Pontius chimed from inside his spear.

Neros backed up, shaking his head. He was running out of time. He had to go, *now.* "This weather is too dangerous! You *cannot* come with me! I won't let you!" He pointed his spear toward the ground, eyes watering and panic hot in his chest. "Vatnis, *build!*"

The prince erected an ice wall between them, tossing his spear to the ground. He turned sharply on his heel, running up the mountain despite the piercing winds stinging his cheeks. He could hear Anthea and Leof swearing, but before long, their shouts were drowned out by the howling wind. It bit at his skin with every step. Surely, it was beyond freezing, colder than Neros had ever remembered Vetur being before. And these winds—Neros wondered if this was what Melanthos meant when he said Endra was rebelling; that magic had been sucked away, and this was the world's counter-measure. He feared for the fate of his people—and his parents. His legs ached, and his prosthetic arm stiffened and screamed as he moved it to climb, but Neros knew he couldn't stop. Stopping meant quitting, and he refused to give up now. If what he'd seen in Umbros was true, he needed to confirm it for himself.

Vetur was a ghost town. Neros' heart sank with every step he took. Compared to the climb, the town was completely silent. Every crunch of the snow beneath his boots seemed to echo across the expanse. The prince wasn't sure if the town was empty because citizens had evacuated, if people had died, or if they had fled to the castle. *The castle…mother and father…gods, I should go to them. I need to.* He picked up his pace, nearly stumbling on a few patches of ice on the way there. As he passed through the courtyard, he saw the statue he left all those months ago, now torn and broken into multiple pieces.

He sincerely hoped it wasn't a sign.

There were no guards at the castle gates, and the doors were locked. *Maybe that's a good thing. Maybe that means there are people inside...either that, or it's one of Isolde's tricks.* Neros shook his head. He couldn't assume the worst—he had to figure out the truth, quickly, and return to Anthea and Leof's side so they could find a way back to Andolis. Luckily, Neros knew of a back passage he could use to get into the castle courtyard. He scurried past the left side of the castle, keeping an eye out for rogue beasts. Neros hoped Melanthos had *some* control to pull most of them back to Umbros, but he didn't remember seeing many on the path up here to begin with. *I bet it's that raging snowstorm that's keeping them away.* Neros went about halfway around the curve of the castle, and he immediately began shifting bricks. *Top to the right, bottom to the top, right to the left, and...* The stones shifted inward, rumbling with a small bit of magic that Neros thought may have been entirely gone. The wall gave way to a passageway, which Neros crawled through to end up in the castle courtyard. Like the rest of town, it was barren. His stomach twisted, and the prince immediately tore off in the direction of the throne room. *They have to be there...they have to.*

He threw open the castle doors and ran down each hallway, slipping on yet more patches of ice. *Indoors, too? This isn't good.* Reaching the tall doors to the throne room, he heaved them open to see what lay beyond.

At the throne were both of his parents, exactly as he had left them—frozen and lifeless. But Runa and some of the councilmen were there, and they turned to look when he entered. A mixture of emotion crossed all their faces: some relief, some surprise, some anger. Neros worried at his lip.

"Neros," Runa spoke first, turning fully to him with her hands resting delicately on her hips. "And here I thought you had left Vetur for good."

The prince swallowed. "I–I could never abandon—"

"But that's what you *did*, is it not?" Runa's eyes narrowed as she began to cross the throne room. Neros tried to look past her, at the statues of his parents—the real ones—but Runa's fury blocked his view. "You stormed away from the castle like a *petulant child*, and you come crawling back now, after *months* have passed, and for what? For aid? To check on the sculptures you left behind? Did you notice the state of the town, Neros? The people have fled. Every day, it grew colder. They could not handle its frigidity any longer. Without a King and Queen to look after them, and without a *prince* to throne, the council and I could only hold the fort for so long. What, pray tell, were you doing on your 'adventure?' Did you find a way to 'save' your parents?"

As she spoke, Neros shrank into himself. "I–Runa, I'm so sorry—"

"Sorry does not fix your egregious blunder. You left your people to die, and we are tasked to fix this mess." Runa turned to the councilmen and gestured for them to come to her. After casting the prince various angry, disappointed glances, they collected their belongings and began to follow her out of the room. "I am going to discuss our current situation with the council. In the meantime, perhaps you ought to try some of those life-saving techniques you learned in your near-year absence on your parents." When Runa looked Neros in the eye again, her tone softening to a pity he didn't expect. "It doesn't look terribly positive, little prince. I–You have my condolences."

Neros swallowed as Runa and the council left the room. He was taken, for a moment, back to when Isolde first cast the curse; before Neros even knew who it was. The prince walked to the thrones, heart hammering in his chest. He wished he had a lucky charm, or someone at his side to help ease the swelling nerves and ache in his heart. *Why did I throw Pontius aside? Leof and Anthea may have survived past the climb with some extra help, but Pontius didn't deserve this...* He shook his head. *No. I needed to do this alone. Not only were their lives in danger, but I couldn't—they can't see Vetur like this.* Neros swallowed, approaching his parents. His fists curled and uncurled, anxious sweat coating his palm.

"Hello, mother. Father. I...it's been so long," He breathed, reaching out his hand and focusing the flowing energy of water through it. "With this...teeming essence of the river, the might of the sea...please, show me the life that breathes in these vessels." He waited for a light to appear, glowing around their hearts as it had worked for him and Pontius before. When nothing showed up, he repeated the chant, shifting to touch the ice that encased their bodies.

It was so cold. Neros shivered as he waited. "Show me...please! Show me the life...that breathes..." His breath came in short pants, panic rising in his chest and seizing his heart. His cheeks felt wet, but he kept trying. "By the teeming essence of the river, through the might of the sea, *please!*"

It was so, so cold.

☼

"Neros, *no!*" Leof ran to the wall, slamming it with his fists. "*No!*

Gods…*damn it!*" He turned to see Anthea doing the same thing he was—trying to break through the *ice wall* the prince erected to keep them out. It was wide, too; Leof wondered where Neros got all that power from, all of a sudden. His gut twisted at the thought of the damage he may have done to his arm beyond the fracture, or worse, beyond the joint where the prosthetic was fixed to.

"We have to go after him," Anthea's voice was hard. "*We have to go after him.*"

"I agree, but how? I can't see the edges of either side of this wall."

"There are trees, aren't there?" Already, the princess was growing vines from the ground. With her other hand, she reached into a pouch to pop a glowing yellow seed into her mouth. "I'll get us to the top of one, and we can swing ourselves to each tree until we reach the top. It's how I used to get up all the time. We'll have to run at the end of it, but so will Neros. We'll catch up. We have to."

A woven strip of vines carried the two of them up to the treetops. Leof cried out, scrambling for purchase as she deposited him on a thicker branch.

"Couldn't you warn me next time?"

"No time. Get on my back."

"*What?* Anthea, slow down. What are you planning?"

"You're not as nimble in this environment, and I'm on a serious time limit with the sun seed I just ate. Neros was right, my limbs will stiffen in weather this windy and cold. Just trust me so we can help him!"

Leof groaned. Trusting people was hard enough when it didn't involve high-speed movement through the skies. "Fine. *Fine.* I am only agreeing to this because it will get us to him faster than on foot. Let's go."

Before they could make the first leap, they heard the faintest shout from below.

"Hey, wait, Princess Anthea! Sir Leof! Neros left his spear here, with me in it! Take me with you!"

Anthea snatched up the spear with her hair, and Leof had to marvel at her quick thinking. *Even if she's reckless, she's clearly skilled with her magic. It's like second nature to her.*

"I'd tell you to hold this, but it's literally as tall as you are," Anthea said.

"So it's staying strapped to my back for now. You've got more pouches and straps, so you can take it off my hands when we're on flat ground again."

"Fine by me," Leof agreed. "Let's go."

The trees were coated in a thin layer of ice. Anthea leaped between them with intense precision. Her face was hardened with a focus he had yet to see on her before. Leof remained silent, both out of respect for her attention to what they were doing and out of a slight fear at how *fast* they were flying through the trees.

"He's *never* done anything like this before," She said. Leof frowned. "He's never run away from me. Something is seriously wrong."

"But you've been friends since you were kids, right...? Haven't you ever fought before?"

"Of course. All friends fight. We even fought a few times on the way to find you. But we always made up. He always came to me to talk it out, but...why? Why would he run from us?"

Leof's chest tightened. "I can imagine a few reasons, I think."

"It just hurts, you know? Thinking that he was keeping all this inside him, like he had to keep it from us instead of just letting us know what's wrong. We...gods, Leof, you just met him a few months ago and you already fashioned him an arm. You'd think...I-I don't know."

"Sometimes it's difficult, even with those you care for." Leof said, thinking to all the times he'd closed himself off from Aldebrande to deal with his problems on his own. "We need to be there for him when we can. Especially now."

"*Especially* now," She agreed. "We don't have a minute to waste."

❄

Neros was gutted. He gripped the knees of his parents and sobbed. Though he refused to believe it, what he had seen in Umbros was true—the ghosts of his parents, walking to Melanthos to be processed and placed into one of the underworldly neighborhoods. The prince hiccupped, tears streaming freely down his cheeks. His legs gave out, all hope falling away as he collapsed to the floor. Melanthos had sealed the portal to Umbros behind them. There was no telling whether they would go back in their entire lives, and what had he done when he saw them in the distance? Nothing.

"Gods, I'm such a fool. Mother, father, I'm so–I'm so sorry I couldn't save you," He choked, coughing and sniffing before wiping at his nose. "I'm sorry…I never–! I–I never got to say goodbye…!"

He wept and wept, until his throat was raw and his eyes stung. This was *everything* he had been fighting for. This was what he hoped to fix. This was the only thing keeping him moving forward when he snapped his arm off—the promise that in the end, they would be okay. That he could return home, un-freeze his parents, and continue his life as he left it. *I was so naïve to think that it could end that way. Runa was right. I abandoned Vetur for nothing.* Now, he felt lost, his heart cast adrift in a freezing, lonely sea.

Neros lost track of how long he had been sitting in the throne room, crying. His body was heavy. The will to stand was lost. What was the point? Vetur was a ghost town, anyway: the Veturians who weren't Runa or the councilmen seemed to have fled to the plains, or elsewhere. If his hometown had become like this, was there even a chance they could fix Arboria? Could they get the lava to flow in the volcano? Neros knew, deep down, that Leof and Anthea needed him to thwart the gods' petty will. But he felt rooted in place, as though thick chains had wrapped around his limbs. It reminded him of how he felt trapped against the hillside, arm propped up by Anthea's dirt block. The spot where it was sewn to his skin now burned from his efforts to climb here as fast as he could.

It was all for nothing.

His tears didn't stop.

What do I do now?

He heard the door open, but didn't move.

"Neros!"

"Prince Neros!"

The voices sounded familiar. The *footsteps* running across the frozen tile sounded familiar, but Neros couldn't let himself believe it. Suddenly, his shoulders were being gripped, and his body turned, and he was face-to-face with Leof and Anthea, his spear—and presumably Pontius—resting on Anthea's back.

Neros looked between them, guilt swimming in his gut. He opened his mouth to speak, but fresh tears welled in his eyes, and he tore his gaze away. His shoulders shook as he sobbed. "I'm sorry. I'm so sorry. You shouldn't have–shouldn't have followed me here."

He tried to curl inward, but warm hands pulled him forward, resting his forehead between Leof and Anthea's shoulders. Leof's entire body radiated warmth, and Anthea wrapped her arm around Neros' back to complete their collective hug.

After some time, Leof spoke. "…They're gone, aren't they?"

Neros nodded. He wasn't sure if Leof felt the gesture, but he spoke again. "I…I know nothing I say can quell what raging sadness is tearing you apart. You don't deserve this."

"How did you know?" Anthea asked. "We had been adventuring for so long without returning here, but after Umbros, we came with…such urgency…wait. Did you…did you *see* them down there?"

Neros nodded again, and the room fell quiet aside from his intermittent sniffling.

"That ice wall you threw up was a pain," Leof said. "Anthea had to hop treetops the rest of the way up the mountain. She had me on her *back,*" He scoffed. "It was humiliating."

"And then the *castle* was locked. I was gonna scale it, but Leof figured we should put ourselves in your shoes. I could never forget that weird side-castle brick-shifting entrance you showed me when we were kids. I'm glad you used it—it made you easier to track."

"Then there were the councilmen, and that bookish one. Luna…?"

"Runa," Neros supplied weakly.

"Sorry. Runa," Leof continued. "We had to explain a few things to her to justify our sudden appearance. She was decidedly less surprised by the princess as she was by me, which was logical, considering my circumstances."

"You should've *seen* the look on her face when we told her what's been going on. She looked *so guilty.* What did she say to you? Probably some real nasty stuff. But don't worry, we set her straight."

Neros nodded. He felt numb to their hands rubbing small circles on his back. He wanted to laugh at their quips, but the shock and sadness overpowered him still.

His friends shifted, and Neros felt Leof's hands lifting his head. Then, he pressed their foreheads together. Neros saw the myriad of emotion that swam in his eyes—the lava beneath his skin churned and glowed, and the prince found it to be intense, especially for Leof. *I don't think he's ever been this close to either of us before.* Neros felt heat creep up his neck at the sheer intensity of the Ember's expression.

"Why did you conceal so much of your heart from us?"

Neros blinked. "I–I don't know what you mean." He tried to shift away, but Leof held him in place, hands held firmly on the back of his head.

"You do," He said, his voice low, but not threatening. "It's as though the longer we adventure together, the more closed-off you become. You pushed us away."

"I thought…the weather…"

"Too cold? I am a being of pure molten rock, Prince Neros, and you know the Princess has devised every sort of seed imaginable to survive. We are not the Veturians, who are more affected by this damn frigid cold than you are. We are stronger than that. You *know* we are stronger than that." Neros felt warmth pulse through Leof's hands as the area beneath his cheeks glowed, his eyes searching the prince's face. He looked so *hurt*, and it was what Neros had wanted to so desperately avoid. "So, tell me, why…? When you urged me over and over to open up to you, to Princess Anthea, yet you… you drifted further away from us. Why…?"

Neros' eyes welled with fresh tears. "I—my problems are greater than myself, but this—my parents—it was my own cross to bear. I was…I was spoiled to have them, and–and it would be selfish of me to bring it up. I didn't realize–I didn't know that Vetur had become so unstable in my absence."

Anthea peered at him, eyebrows drawn together. "Neros, did I put that thought in your head that it's selfish of you to talk about your parents' curse? From…from that argument in Barmwich? I—" She wrung her wrists. "I'm so sorry. That was so long ago, and I was in such a hurry to find answers and move forward, I wasn't thinking of you, too. I didn't mean to diminish your problems just because I thought mine were greater. This…the consequences of your curse were just as devastating," She paused, looking to the frozen statues of Neros' parents and looking away, blinking furiously to keep the tears at bay. "If not more. I'm so sorry."

"None of us saw the signs of what you were hiding from us," Leof said, idly wiping Neros' tears away with his thumbs. "You know you don't always have to put on a brave, cheerful face for us all the time. We've been through so much together…Princess Anthea and I understand. This is hard—your parents meant the world to you, and so do the Veturians. You are allowed to lean on us in your sadness. There's no chance we'll think any less of you."

Neros opened his mouth to speak, but only a broken sob escaped. "Leof…"

The Ember scooted closer to Neros, pulling him into a hug. Neros buried his face in the crook of Leof's neck. Anthea kneeled, wrapping her arms around them both and resting her head atop Neros'. If he was quiet enough, he could hear Anthea's shaky breathing: a sure sign of her trying to conceal her own tears. It only made his fall harder. Leof's hand rubbed slow circles on the small of the prince's back, and he allowed his breathing to even out amidst its warmth.

After some time, his cries quieted to soft sniffles. Despite everything, Neros chuckled a bit. "Gods, Leof, you truly are quite kind, aren't you?"

Leof huffed. "D-don't get used to it."

"It's a far cry from how you used to be," Anthea added. Neros could hear the smirk in her voice. "But I don't think there's any going back for you now, Leof. You're nice forever."

The Ember sputtered, his body going tense. "I-I don't—What is that even supposed to *mean?* You know what, no. Don't answer that."

Anthea threw back her head and laughed in response, and Neros joined her, his head still resting on Leof's shoulder. His heart was warm and full, then. Leof had been right, and Neros felt ashamed and ridiculous for not relying on them sooner. It brought to mind what his double had said in Umbros: *I should accept love and care from those close to me when I need it.*

He wrapped his arms around Leof, and gave him a tight hug. "Thank you," He whispered. "Truly. I don't know where I would be without you."

Neros thought he felt Leof emanate a flash of heat—*embarrassment, maybe?*—but it was gone before he could really tell. "I—Listen, just. D-don't mention it. I-it's just the natural thing to do. We need you to beat up these gods, you know."

"Ohh, that reminds me!" Anthea stood suddenly, detangling something from her hair. "I believe this belongs to you."

Neros turned to her and accepted his spear. "I'm sorry for tossing you aside, too, Pontius. You deserved better."

"Oh, your highness, don't worry about me!" He chirped, coming out of the spearhead. "I'm just relieved you're safe. Oh, and, by the way, look closely! I think Melanthos affixed something to Vatnis."

Pontius was right—below the icy spearhead was a bright green gem, glowing faintly. "Was it always glowing?" Neros asked.

"I don't know! I was hiding inside it. But I would venture that it's been glowing since you left Umbros."

The glow felt insistent, like it was asking him to do something. He pressed into it, and it locked into place, glowing brighter, asking him to continue. His mind spun, landing on something his father had taught him years ago, during his training when he passed Vatnis down to him. *If you focus the energy into your hands, it will pass into the spear.* Neros had done this countless times with ice, but never with water alone. When he tried it in his fight with Melanthos, the intention still resulted in an icy typhoon. *What will happen if I try to ignore ice completely?*

So he tried. The same method he'd used with his father, but with the water magic he'd learned from Pontius. He was careful not to pull from the powers of ice. *Imagine a riverbank, or the ocean, or a creek, or a puddle,* he told himself. *It's flowing and freeing, like Dorian said.*

As the water passed into the spear's shaft, it sank into the wood, and the gem responded in kind, pulsing with light before becoming enveloped with it. It was blinding, and Neros closed his eyes.

"Oh, my gods. Neros, what is that?"

"Your highness! *Your highness,* this is incredible!"

Neros opened his eyes to find is father's royal spear had changed form. His eyebrows shot up in shock. It was still a spear, sort of. The shaft split at the top and curled into two parts, one that held a floating diamond that Neros recognized instantly as Vatnis' previous head. From the other half dangled a box holding a teardrop that was the same green as the gem—now gone—that Melanthos had affixed to it.

Leof pulled out their map he'd copied from the gods' stone. "There are no more roaming dots. I think that's your divine weapon, Neros."

My divine weapon…? Was it always destined to be part of Vatnis? Was it, like the royal ability to wield ice magic, a gift from Isolde? Neros shook his head, blinking in disbelief.

"There are *two* places for me to tuck myself away! Oh, joyous day!" Pontius cheered, circling between the teardrop and the ice diamond. "Neros, you've outdone yourself. I always thought you were a special prince, but this takes my theory over the moon!"

He blushed bright violet. "I–no, this isn't even my own spear, originally. It was passed down to me from my father, so…"

"Don't be so modest!" Anthea said. "If I can have glowing arrows that always return to my hand and Leof can have a blade with a glass-blown hilt that does whatever he commands, you can have a fancy half-water, half-ice spear. It's one benefit of this whole prophecy business!"

"And now that you have that, we can be sure we have the upper edge against the gods," Leof said. "We should make sure we're in peak condition before confronting them, but we shouldn't wait too long."

"I agree. Perhaps I could even build a bridge of ice from here to the heavens to hasten…our…what? Why are you both looking at me like that?"

"Neros, do *not* use your ice again," Anthea scolded. "Just because we fixed your arm doesn't mean you're not still cursed! We don't know what'll happen to the rest of your body, and—and we really need you, okay?"

"Speaking of using ice, did building that ice wall inflict any further damage to you?" Leof asked.

Neros blushed again. When he meant business, Leof's gaze was certainly intense. "I–well, no, but there is…"

"The crack, in your wrist?" Leof guessed, looking between his wrist and his face. "You said it wasn't bothering you in Umbros, but we should probably take a look at it and make sure it isn't affecting your movement."

"There's an old doctor's quarters down the hall from here, isn't there?" Anthea asked. Neros nodded. "Leof, take him there! It'll give you some privacy and I bet you the doctor's tools are still there."

"Princess Anthea, not to disrespect you, but I don't think I'll be using the same tools."

At this, she laughed, hoisting the pair off the floor and pushing them toward the door. "Sure, sure. Just go! I'll go catch up with Runa some more." Neros thought he saw her give Leof a look, but she turned toward the library before he could ask.

Neros led Leof to the infirmary, long out of use since the royal family's in-house doctor left when Neros was younger. Now, he preferred to be on call, choosing to visit nearby villages to provide his practice to others. As such, his quarters were left mostly untouched, though in extreme emergencies the beds had been used to sleep extra guards. Like the rest of Vetur, though, now it was empty.

The prince perched himself on one of the beds, and Leof sighed. "The princess is a little ridiculous, sending us here. I don't need an entire room just to look at your wrist."

Leof removed his cloak, draping it on the bed behind Neros. He placed his backpack on the desk, unrolling a separate pack with his own tools inside. He rolled up his sleeves, and Neros noticed that the crack he'd earned back during his test in the volcano had nearly entirely closed off, save for a few thin slivers. *What incredible recovery power. And it's quite striking, too…*

The Ember raised an eyebrow at him. "What are you staring at? Come on, let's see it."

Neros' heart skipped a beat, and he awkwardly thrust his wrist forward. "Right! Here—here it is."

Leof gingerly took Neros' hand in his, scrutinizing the delicate glass orb that was now his wrist. He squinted at it before prodding at it with his thumbs. "Does this hurt?"

"A little."

He hummed. "That's dangerous. A book Ignatius gave me about these glass-blown orbs warned me about this sort of thing. We're lucky this crack looks small—any larger and we'd likely have to conduct surgery and replace it."

Neros shuddered at the thought. "So, what can we do?"

He was already digging through his backpack. "The book mentioned ingredients for a special salve…ah. Here it is." He popped off the top, taking Neros' hand back and pouring a few drops of the liquid over Neros' wrist. He massaged it, liquid filling up the cracks, and the prince sucked in a breath. It stung, but it eased away some of the pins-and-needles feeling he'd been getting.

Neros took a moment to marvel at how gentle Leof was. It was the last thing he'd expected—he noticed Leof had a bitterness in his eyes whenever they first met, and as they were adjusting to each other, Neros didn't know that he'd ever see another side to him. But they did; Leof was kind, and caring, and sweet for someone whose past gave him no reason to be any of those things.

"Y-your highness, you're staring again."

Neros' face heated up. "S-sorry! It's just…you're practically glowing. Were there others you took care of back home?"

"Not in particular," He said, turning and exchanging the salve for a soft-looking, tiny cloth. "You could argue I took care of Aldebrande sometimes, but he mostly took care of me. I'm going to buff out your wrist to prevent the crack from growing, and then we'll test the movement. Okay?"

"Okay." As Leof thumbed the cloth over his wrist (in the most gentle motion), Neros continued to admire his focus. "I'm glad you seem to enjoy it."

"Taking care of you? Of course." A glow passed across Leof's cheeks, and he cleared his throat. "Y-your arm, I mean. It's my most complex project, so I–naturally, I'm dedicated to the upkeep."

Neros' heart felt warm, but he couldn't place exactly why. He supposed he was happy his companionship with Leof worked out so well—after all, their third prophetic hero could have been someone catty or indignant or passive, but Leof fit with he and Anthy better than he could have ever hoped.

He was snapped back to the moment when Leof spoke. "Can you roll your wrist for me?"

Carefully, the prince rolled his wrist in each direction, smiling when he found his pain severely lessened. "What wonders that did. It feels much better."

"Good. Can you try to conjure some magic with it?"

Neros extended his palm, conjuring an orb of water and shaping it into various things—a flattening it into a disk, shaping it like a diamond, and then like a flame.

Leof smiled. "Very funny. Does it hurt?"

Neros grinned back, dissipating the water into a fine mist. "Thankfully, no. I believe such pain is still reserved only for ice."

"Good." His face grew serious. "Promise me you won't use that ability so recklessly again—there's a lot at stake in our very near future."

Neros promised, just as there was a knock on the door. Anthea poked her head in, before allowing herself to fully enter.

"Well? How ya feeling?"

"Just fine, thanks to Leof." Neros grinned at him, and Anthea had that glint in her eye again. "So…what are our next steps?"

It was a difficult question to ask, and one that the prince had been avoiding until now. They had fought one god—Melanthos' abilities were nothing to sneeze at, and they were lucky to be distract him enough to cool his head—but Neros knew they would have to be far more punishing with the gods. Anger seized him, knowing the battle that lay ahead. It would not be easy. First of all, the gods were *gigantic,* and they'd had enough trouble with gargantuan monsters on their journey; tackling three at once would be no simple feat. They would need to be cunning—luckily, Anthea was the most cunning person he knew, and Leof seemed prepared for any situation.

Leof spoke first. "We'll need to train. A lot. Together. In a very short amount of time, we'll have to come up with some very powerful moves to use."

"Something they won't expect," Anthea said. "They were the heroes who smote Melanthos hundreds of years ago, but when we met them, they didn't seem terribly coordinated. But us? We have something they could only dream of."

"The element of surprise…?" Neros guessed dumbly.

"No! We're *friends,* you *walnut.*"

Leof laughed, and Neros' heart stuttered in his chest. "Ridiculous insult aside, Princess Anthea has a point. We have a lot of potential for combining our abilities to make greater power from them."

"Oooh! I have a few ideas, brave heroes! Prince Neros, do you have a training hall we can use?"

Neros smiled. "Of course!"

There wasn't much time to train; that much, Neros knew. With each passing day, darkness spread across Endra and the blustering snowstorm across Vetur only worsened. For as many hours as they could stand, the three of them wracked their minds and bodies in the training hall, testing powerful combinations on the dummies while getting acclimated to their new weapons.

Leof discovered a way to utilize his daggers in tandem with his sword, and Anthea was empowered more and more by her magic arrows the more she used them. Neros...was clumsy, with his dual-lantern-spear, but it was far more potent at casting magic than anything he'd ever used before. Training helped ease the pain he felt, and working with Leof and Anthea to develop powerful magic moves together fueled his own fire to beat the gods senseless.

Three days passed. Runa and her council accommodated the heroes well while still remaining distant. Neros felt Runa's sympathy, but her disappointment in him overlaid it all like a thick blanket of ice before snowfall. However, the time had come for them to leave yet again. The trio donned their woolen cloaks, packed their bags, and headed for the castle doors.

Yet again, Neros hesitated.

"What's wrong?" Anthea asked. "You look like you forgot something."

"I need to speak to Runa. A-alone, if you please. I left once without notifying her at all; the least I can do now is talk to her before our departure."

Leof and Anthea looked at each other, then nodded. "Do what you need to do," he said.

❀

Anthea hated waiting. She and Leof sat together on the front steps leading down to the main doors of the castle. Neros had left his divine lantern behind, instructing Pontius stay behind alongside it, and all that did was make Anthea anxious. She'd argued for him to take *someone* along, even if it wasn't her, but Neros insisted. Pontius was too nervous to argue, and instead chose to pace the halls while they waited. "I promise, I'll be back," the prince had said.

Neros always kept his promises. And he was feeling better, Anthea could tell—over the course of their training, the obvious tiredness tugging down his shoulders or bogging his movement began to lift. The pain of losing his parents had struck him hard, but that just meant she and Leof had to work even harder to get him back on his feet. It seemed to work, for the most part. Leof performed regular maintenance on Neros' arm, and Anthea redoubled every supportive effort in the book. Now, the princess had started to see some of the familiar light return to his eyes for the first time in months, so she trusted Neros would come back to them.

It was Runa she didn't trust.

"Princess, you alright? You look ready to stab someone." Leof's voice made her jump out of her thoughts, and she shrugged at him.

"I just hope she doesn't ban him from saving the world."

"Runa?"

"Yeah. She's always been a stickler for the rules, but she's *also* one of Neros' favorite mentors he's ever had," She scoffed, idly kicking the ground. "It kind of annoys me."

"Did you have a mentor you liked?"

"I never really had a mentor, so much as a rotating cast of old Arborians who told me I wasn't suited to be princess," She explained, threading her fingers together and holding the back of her head. "Too brash. Too outspoken. Too clever. All that nonsense." She slumped. *Maybe I'm just jealous.*

"Nonsense is right. Those who rule should be those unafraid to speak their mind, and certainly they should be clever. But Runa…" Leof shook his head. Anthea could read him a lot better now, and by the way he was wringing his wrists and his hair crackled and curled around his ears, she could tell he was conflicted. "There's something about her. She influences him heavily, and if she says the wrong thing…"

"She'll reset all of our progress."

Leof nodded, sagging. "Exactly. Grief is a delicate thing to balance."

"Especially when it comes to someone you love."

At this, Leof's cheeks lit up, his hair an explosion of wisps and pops. "Wh-what are you…? Don't insinuate something like that, it's not…I'm not—!"

Anthea giggled, shoving his shoulder. "*Relax,* Leof, that's not what I meant. It's too easy to get a rise out of you, really. Especially when it comes to Neros."

He sighed, rubbing at his face and holding it until he calmed down. "I don't understand why my emotions amuse you so much," he mumbled.

"Because you're my friend, and I want it to work out for you."

Leof rolled his eyes. "Right. Well, there's a *lot else* to work out, first. Like saving the world."

Before Anthea could give him a reassuring speech about how everything would work out in the end, the doors behind them opened, and Neros walked out. Pontius immediately zoomed down the hall to be at his side.

Anthea leapt to her feet, grinning wide.

"You're back! So, you all squared up? Ready to save the world?"

"Yes, of course." Neros smiled back, but his eyes looked puffy. Like he'd been crying. *Gods, Runa. What did you say to him?* Anthea knew the look Neros was giving her, though—he didn't want to talk about it. It would distract from their mission. "So, shall we set out for Andolis?"

Anthea's shoulders sagged a bit. "Well, Arboria is a long way from here, Neros. And the storm outside is awful…we made it up, but I'm not sure we'll make it *back.*"

"Luckily for you three, there's an *alternate* way to travel the world!" Pontius chirped.

Leof groaned, and Anthea gasped. "Warping! Perfect! We've been there before, so it really is that easy! Alright, let's go!"

Water covered their bodies, locking them into position, and with a flash, Pontius lifted them to the heavens.

It was time to kick some sense back into those gods.

Chapter 18
The Last Stand

*T*hey stumbled, more or less, to the surface of Andolis. Neros had begun to sense that Pontius' water-transporters had started to loosen toward the end of their trip; it felt like only a few minutes in total, but Neros knew that if the warp power faltered for even a moment, their containments would collapse and they would be in a life-ending freefall back to Endra's surface. Luckily, they breached the cloudy ground-level of the heavens before Pontius warned them their descent would be…less than ideal.

"Watchoutwatchoutwatchout!" He clamored, trying (and failing) to create landing pads for them. "If we can't land properly, I can't say that we won't just fall through the floor! Y-y-y-your highness, you have to do something!"

Neros couldn't imagine the cloud ground being painful to land on, but he didn't want to find out if what Pontius said was true or not. Scrambling for his weapon, he cast out a large disc of water, shaping it quickly to make a slide. His heart leapt into his throat as they landed on it, sliding down and coming to a stop at the base.

Anthea breathed out a laugh. "Wow, quick thinking!"

Leof pat the disc around him before standing. He frowned. "How is it not wet?"

The prince stammered. "W-well, I think it has something to do with Vatnis, actually. When I build structures, I send the magic through the staff first, and whether I like it or not, it tends to freeze it a little. It must be extra power from this crystal," He pointed to the diamond-shaped one locked in his new staff. "It doesn't hurt like using my ice magic has been."

From beside them, Pontius wailed. "No! It cannot be! *My monocle!*"

The three heroes looked to him, and Neros gasped. "Your monocle… it's gone!"

Pontius fished out a small pair of glasses from his waistcoat and put them on his face. He sighed, the picture of dejection. "Without my monocle, I cannot warp us to safety if it becomes too dangerous for us." He bowed, sniffling. "I'm sorry, your highnesses, Sir Leof! I have failed as your protector."

"You weren't really a protector," Leof pointed out. "More of a guide. And you got us here, so you've done your job as planned."

"Besides, not being able to leave just means we can't go back until we finish this, right? So let's finish this."

Pontius grew weepy, rubbing frantically at his eyes. "You three truly are legendary souls…! Prince Neros, I will sequester myself into your new divine weapon, per standard. I will provide advice as needed."

Neros laughed. "Thank you, Pontius. I'll be counting on you." He turned to the path ahead of them. Andolis was vast, but there was only one place for them to go—toward the guardian gatekeeper, Amund, and the heavenly castle beyond.

❄

As they approached, Amund looked…decrepit. As much as it was possible for a cloudy gate to look deflated, Amund was very much so. What was once bright gold and silver had become faded and rusty. The feathery appearance of the gate had wilted, and the insignia at the top had been broken into three separate parts. Neros' gut twisted. *Don't tell me the gods' absorption of Endra's magic is even affecting their divine guard. How foolish.*

"Amund?" Neros called. "What's wrong?"

The gate stirred, grumbling incoherently. "Hm? Who is it that desires passage into—oh, it's you three again. Did you not find satisfaction in your journey before?"

"Hardly," Anthea said. "Could you let us by again?"

He had no face, but Neros could hear his frown. "I would certainly oblige, but heroes, my hinges are stuck."

Leof was already walking toward it, rolling up his sleeves and muttering, "You've got to be kidding me."

The Ember set to work, digging through his pack and procuring long, black sticks that he placed into an empty vial and heated using flames from the palm of his hand. He gripped the gate's framework, tugging at various locations to, Neros could only assume, test exactly how stuck it was. Then, he began to pour the liquid onto the hinges, and over the locks at the center.

"That is quite painful, young Ember."

"You'll get over it. Brace yourself," Leof mused. He snapped his fingers, shooting out five small fireballs that ignited at each hinge and the gate's center. He murmured, and five tiny explosions went off.

The gate's doors squeaked as they fell backwards, cloud puffing up around them as they landed soundlessly on the surface behind.

"You have destroyed me."

"You don't sound *that* mad about it."

"Then I shall only say I am surprised you were able to unstick the hinges so quickly."

"I'm a blacksmith with training in other mechanical areas," Leof explained, already packed up and beginning to walk through the archway toward the castle. "It's my job."

Neros smiled at the pride he could hear in Leof's voice. "Don't worry, Amund, we'll ask the gods to rebuild you once we're done."

"And if they don't, we'll breathe new life into you ourselves!" Anthea shouted, following behind Leof. Neros jogged to catch up with them.

From behind them, Neros thought he heard the gate chuckle. "I look forward to your success."

❄

The stone-walled, marble-floored palace was just as big and just as empty as it was when they last visited. With every step, he felt a surge of magic in his feet. The walls practically glowed with it, and to the prince, it was sheerly blinding.

"Was it this *bright* when we were last here?" Anthea asked. "And powerful? Do either of you feel all this power?"

"I feel lighter on my feet than on Endra," Leof said. "It's concerning. Is this where all the magic energy is going?"

"If it makes us more powerful, it'll make them more powerful, too," Neros added, his heart unable to decide if it wanted to pound in his chest or leap to his throat. "We have to be careful."

"We will."

If Neros thought about it, the gods' palace felt almost lonely. It was only the three of them, with no one else here—though Melanthos had mentioned he used to live up here with Pegaios. Neros wondered if it meant Pegaios had stayed with the gods, when they were newly made immortal. He recalled the guardians around Paralia, who asserted that the Oracle had been locked away. Neros thought initially that it had been for his own good, that he knew some knowledge the gods wanted to keep away from too-curious mortals. Now, he thought just the opposite: Pegaios had been cast away there to be imprisoned. If not for he and Anthea being a pair of far-too-curious mortals with a mettle for problem solving, Pegaios might have still been locked away.

He shuddered to think of what the gods might do to them if they couldn't succeed.

They re-entered the vestibule of clouds, and looking at each image, his heart sank. He could see the decaying Arborians, and Rosea running between them all, struggling to keep their life forces afloat. The Eldur Ignis Volcano was in worse shape: the upper layers showed Embers working hard to mass-produce weapons for throngs of younger, sprightly Ember soldiers. Below, there were rigorous mage trainings using those gigantic enemies Leof had fought as fodder. Now that he had seen so much of the world, he knew what the broken cloud was: Vetur. There was no other visual for the region. Neros could only assume it had been destroyed during Isolde's rage.

He clenched and unclenched his fist. There was boisterous arguing coming from the throne room again, but unlike last time, it sounded playful, like the gods were having *fun* while the very face of the land they came from was being destroyed below.

A white-hot rage flooded through Neros, and he burst through the door to the inner sanctum, ignoring Pontius' insistent protest in his ear. The gods were sitting, infuriatingly, as they had been before. Isolde, then Pyrrhus, then Silva. Their laughing ceased when the heroes entered.

Isolde frowned, but spoke first. "You three? What brings you back here, children?"

Silva leaned forward in her seat, eyes glowing. "Ooh! Don't tell me you've defeated Melanthos and have come to collect your reward?"

"Though we have no reward to give you," Pyrrhus drawled. "Isn't saving the world enough?"

Neros opened his mouth to speak—to *yell*, to give them a true piece of his mind—but Leof stepped in front of him.

"You misunderstand, your graces," Leof called. "We're actually hear to have council with you. We have a problem."

Silva quirked a brow. "Problem?"

"Endra's still shrouded in darkness! And what's worse, I think the magic energy is being sucked away," Anthea explained. The quirk in her lip showed Neros that she'd much rather be fighting them than talking, but she kept herself calm and patient. "We traveled to Umbros, and met with Melanthos."

"You met? That sounds fairly *cordial*, little girl," Isolde sneered. "What of your meeting?"

"You see, he explained a few things," Anthea said, as though Isolde hadn't addressed her at all. "And these things shed some light for us. You know he's just down there, minding his own business? He's managing the dead, and doing quite a fine job. It's pretty peaceful down there.

You know what else is kind of odd, Silva? Melanthos told us a little story. Well, first he tried to attack us, thinking we were you, but my best pal Prince Neros over there subdued him, and he was kind enough to take some time out of his day to chat. But his story was pretty insightful, and we learned a few important things. First, that he actually used to live up here, hundreds of years ago. Second, that *Pegaios the Oracle* lived with him here, and that the oracle was the one who called out to Endra to find heroes. And those heroes were you three! How interesting that was to learn that you earned immortality as a reward for your hard work."

The entire time she had been speaking, she'd been building a vine staircase. She was now eye to eye with Silva, who looked all-too-pleased at Anthea's compliment. But Neros knew Anthea wasn't truly complimenting her, but instead buttering her up—even from the ground, the prince recognized the spark in Anthea's eye. She was *furious*.

"My friends and I have a *lot* of questions to ask you, but I'll start with the most simple: why is it, then, that we found Pegaios—your mentor, if I'm understanding Melanthos' story—all the way in Paralia, hidden behind layers of dense puzzles and dangerous water guardians?"

"You *believe* the story Melanthos told you?" Isolde asked. "Why not believe us?"

"I'll get to that in just a second, if you could answer my question."

"We wanted to keep him safe there," Silva explained, voice carefully even. "So he wouldn't get hurt."

"Hmm, you see, I *met* Pegaios a long time ago, and he definitely didn't seem safe. More like trapped." Her stairwell was now becoming a bridge, a means for her to pace in front of the gods. "Which brings me to another point. Isolde, you asked me why I believed Melanthos. I must be honest, I was hesitant to. But he said a few things that tipped me toward his favor.

Endra survives on magic energy. It pulses through the ground beneath us, exists in the airwaves around us, and flows through the veins of every creature on the planet, whether they utilize it or not. Without that energy, dark, chaotic forces become restless and begin to take over. I said Umbros was peaceful. Melanthos was able to be subdued by us. Yet, when we returned, the air was heavy. The skies were gray. The world was rebelling from this lack of energy flowing through it, like a sapling crying for more water."

Anthea turned sharply on her heel to face Silva. "It made me think of how my journey started. Our great ancient Arborian tree rebelled against us, its roots shooting underground and wrapping itself up and around every Arborian in the forest—except two who escaped. Myself being one of them. When I returned later, hoping to discover a solution, we learned instead that the life force of the Arborians was being *sucked away by the tree.* It was more than just an attempt to keep itself alive, wasn't it? Silva, Melanthos had no idea what was going on up on the surface, just that he had an extra influx of *dead souls* to attend to."

With each of her next words, her voice dropped lower, her hidden anger finally peeking through. "You are the governing goddess of our land. What. Did you. Do."

Silva recoiled, frowning at Anthea before a shrill laugh left her lips. "What? *What?* What did *I* do? If you need a reason for your kingdom's misfortune, girl, look no further than yourself! You're the one who flippantly ignores advice from her elders for the sake of her own adventures with *that* boy." She gestured rudely to Neros. "When you were born princess, I knew it'd be over for Arboria. What good comes from a kingdom with such a headstrong princess?"

"So you thought it would be alright to *kill everyone?!*" Anthea cried, her voice cracking in rage.

Neros tugged on Leof's sleeve, gesturing for the them to head up Anthea's stairwell to give her some backup. He nodded, and they moved swiftly.

"Oh, please," Isolde corrected. "No one's killed anyone, darling. Don't overreact. If you're this distraught, why not just ask Melanthos to give them all back?"

"Life doesn't work that way," Anthea seethed. "Wouldn't you know? You're the one who killed Neros' parents!"

Isolde's gaze dropped to the prince, and he froze in his steps. Leof ran into him, but Neros couldn't bring his limbs to move. *Is this…her power?* He gritted his teeth, forcing his legs to move against her piercing stare. He glared as he watched a wave of understanding come over her.

"Ah, so it *is* you. I thought you looked familiar…little princeling," She cooed, and Neros hated how the nickname sounded on her lips. "You're that little vermin that thought it would be cute to break tradition. Do you know where your delicate, revered ice powers come from? *Me.* And yet you saw fit to honor someone else…pathetic."

Her words stabbed him like icicles, but he continued to climb the stairwell. "You brought incredible misfortune into my life, Goddess Isolde. You were once mortal, were you not? So why…why would you destroy the lives of others?"

"She doesn't need to answer," Pyrrhus said. "This world belongs to us. So if the mortals are doing what we say is unfit, they get punished. Easy as that."

Isolde dropped her icy glare, and Neros bolted up the rest of Anthea's stairwell two at a time, Leof close behind. The prince stopped in front of Pyrrhus. "So you all admit it, then? You're really the ones destroying Endra right now!"

"We're not doing anything wrong!" Silva complained. "We're just ruling over the land, like Pegaios told us to."

"Then wouldn't you want his guidance?!" Neros snapped. "Instead you locked him away, and what did he do? He named Anthea and I as new heroes of the prophecy. He feared a second coming of destruction, and had you not thrown him away, perhaps you could have prevented it!"

"Is he with you?" Isolde sneered. "How do we even know you're telling the truth, and that you haven't been brainwashed by the dark cretin Melanthos?"

"His power faded, your grace," Leof said, plucking the three daggers from his waist. "We came to stop the destruction you've so clearly started. Your ignorance is proof enough that you are acting recklessly. The time for talk is *over.*"

He moved quickly, igniting the daggers and sending them careening through the air to catch the two goddess' heads on fire. Silva's leafy locks cooperated instantly, sending the goddess into a shrieking rage. Isolde dampened the flame with a flick of her wrist, but the dagger itself caught her ear, and she hissed.

"Anthea, get me a bridge to Silva!"

"You got it!"

Anthea built as Leof ran, which left Neros glancing between the remaining two gods. *It'd be smarter of me to go after Pyrrhus while Isolde is distracted... but how should I get there?* He thought of the ice bridges he'd built in the past, and an idea struck him. He grinned. *If Anthea can build bridges, so can I.*

"Vatnis, build." He whispered, and as he channeled magic energy into the spear, semisolid water was cast forth, making him a clear-cut path to the fire god. He ran across, curving his path to keep away from Pyrrhus' direct view—the god was busy laughing at Silva's struggles, but when he noticed Leof, his demeanor changed. He realized they were under attack.

Neros had to act fast.

He forced the bridge to split, following a lower path that would loop Pyrrhus' feet and sending the other cascading toward his chest. He slowed the path in front of him to focus his energy on dousing Pyrrhus. He slowed, looking back at his friends.

Leof was just about to pull out his sword from its sheath, and Anthea nocked a golden arrow, but in an instant, both weapons disappeared.

What? Where did they...?

A large, sturdy blade crashed through Neros' waterfall and cut the bridge in front of him. The prince fell to the ground, rolling himself out of the way to avoid the next strike. As Neros scrambled to his feet, he noticed the glass-blown hilt. His heart stopped. *Their weapons...!*

Pyrrhus bellowed a laugh. "Thanks for returning these for us, mortals!"

Silva had managed to put out her hair and aimed a golden arrow at Leof. "Really, you're too kind. Now get out of our home so we can rule in *peace!*"

Before she could shoot off the arrow, vines whipped up from the stairwell and wrapped around Silva's neck, tightening until the goddess dropped her bow. Leof took the opening and ran, but Pyrrhus' blade slashed the bridge and sent both he and Anthea into a freefall.

No...!

He pointed his staff before he could think, building a slide out of semisolid water and catching his friends before they could fall any further. He guided the body of the slide toward him, and Leof and Anthea barreled toward him at a frightening speed. Neros tried to hold his arms out, but the two tumbled on top of him anyway.

"Oof...thanks, Neros," Anthea said, picking herself up quickly. "We've gotta get a plan together, fast."

"I'll need to get my daggers back," Leof grunted. "I threw them so easily...ugh, what a pain. I really wasn't expecting them to steal our weapons, but it makes sense."

Neros gripped Vatnis, and glanced over his shoulder to Isolde. "I wonder if she couldn't take mine because Vatnis was my father's..."

"We can use that to our advantage," Anthea said. "And we'll probably have to take them down one at a time, unless we can get them distracted enough."

"We're not trying to kill them, though, and I think that's what we need to make clear," Leof added.

Vatnis glowed, and Pontius poked his head out from his hiding spot. "If you need a good distraction, I might have a plan that can work, heroes!"

Hesitantly, Neros nodded, and the more Pontius explained, the more he felt like it might actually work.

❄

The gods, in the meantime, had begun to quarrel, as was their nature.

"I cannot believe you'd let them catch your hair on fire," Isolde hissed. "What do you want them to take you for, an amateur?!"

"Oh, that's rich, coming from you! Had you not meddled so closely, we might have been able to keep all this power we've gotten!"

"Instead, some nasty little mortals have come knocking down our door. As if Endra isn't fine as it is," Pyrrhus growled. "They'll live. We did."

"It's what they get for being so ungrateful," Isolde sneered. "We gave them this renewed Endra. The least they could do is respect us."

"I don't really think you command that much respect, Isolde," Silva said. "What do you even do for the Veturians, anyway?"

"How dare you! At least I'm not sitting around like a lump of coal the way Pyrrhus is! He's just letting the Embers do whatever they want, with no regard for anything!"

Pyrrhus exploded, heaving his sword toward Isolde. "Shut up, witch. They used to respect me and my desires, but now they've become so damn advanced that I had to punish them. At least I punished all of them, instead of one or two like you."

"It was a *calculated punishment!* I *knew* it would create a *slow-acting* ripple! I had a reason! Your and Silva's recklessness is the real reason we're in this mess. It escalated everything!"

"Heroes of the heavens, have you truly forgotten who you are? Cease this bickering at once!" A wise, old voice boomed. Before them rose Pegaios—though he looked a bit smaller than he once was. He took his typical form of an older man with a long beard.

The three gods stood silent. Neros cheered silently, from the ground below. *Perfect! Now's our chance.* He gestured to Leof and Anthea, and the three of them nodded. Neros began to circle Isolde, using Vatnis to paint a moat of water around the goddess' legs. It was something he learned from speaking to Dorian, the elegant Veturian they met who maintained a force field around his town. An important part of Pontius' plan was to recreate this type of shield, but around the goddess Isolde. *"She may not seem like it, but her powers are the most deadly!"*

"P-Pegaios?! What are you doing here?" Silva screeched. "We locked you away a hundred years ago!"

"But I am here now, am I not? Do tell me, heroes, that you have been keeping Endra's lands at peace?"

"You've got some nerve, askin' that," Pyrrhus growled. "We've been watching over it, just like you asked."

"It was not a request for you to acquiesce, but rather a command, Pyrrhus. You tell me if I look upon the world, I shall see no harm? You have been kind to Endra, your home?"

Silva shied away a little at that, but still barked, "Of course we have!"

Beneath them, Leof and Anthea were building ropes of flame and vine. They gave Neros a thumbs up, and the prince broke into a run, circling around Isolde's front. Her gaze caught his, and he smiled up at her.

"Wait, that's not Pegaios! The mortals—!" She yelled, but Neros had erected the force field. Borrowing from the style of the one Amund locked them in during their riddle puzzles and adding the protective energy Dorian taught him, he encased the goddess. She screamed silently, clawing at its edges and trying to break through.

"Isolde!" Silva cried, frowning deeply at the heroes. "You'll pay for that! And for distracting us!" She tried to summon her arrows, but they were chained to the feet of her throne with the flaming-vine ropes that Anthea and Leof created. Throwing her bow aside, she reached her arms down to tackle Leof and Anthea herself, but Anthea caught her wrists with more vines. They began to grapple, Anthea pushing back against the goddess and giving Leof ample time to run.

Neros knew what he had to do next, and it involved Pyrrhus directly. The god was slower than the two goddesses due to his sheer mass, and Neros was grateful for it. His lungs were staring to burn from all the running he'd been doing (really, if they were once mortals, did the gods *have* to choose to be colossally-sized?!) and his legs were beginning to feel like jelly. But he steeled himself: his people were depending on him. Thousands and thousands of lives were at stake.

He stopped, glaring at Pyrrhus. He looked like the other strong red Embers Neros had seen in the volcano, but there was a twisted rage in his eyes that the prince knew he needed to quell. He twirled his staff, amassing water into a gargantuan axe. Neros stumbled—the axe was surprisingly heavy, and wielding it through the power of his staff wasn't exactly precise—and he stood, swinging it toward Pyrrhus. It crashed into his blade with great force, and both the prince and the god stumbled. Neros bolted while Pyrrhus re-centered himself, and Neros re-formed the axe and swung wide at the god's legs.

It brought Neros a wave of pride and satisfaction to see the liquid soak the god's boots, causing him to groan as he struggled to move his legs. The prince grinned, wondering how far he could take this water-weapon magic. He began to conjure up a long javelin, aiming it carefully and releasing a burst of magic energy to toss it. As it collided with Pyrrhus' shoulder, he screamed in dismay, his sword dropping to the ground soundlessly.

Chaos ensued in the moments following. Leof leapt from the throne he'd been climbing to secure Pyrrhus' wrists into flaming handcuffs, Anthea wrestled Silva's arms behind her and tied them there, then tied her *again* to her chair, chest heaving from the effort. Isolde put a crack in Neros' entrapment chamber, but he closed it, returning all his magic efforts to keeping her contained. Pontius wheeled over a large array of cloud that mirrored what was contained in the antechamber, except the view to Vetur wasn't broken. On each cloud, blown up to the gods' size, was a view of Endra and the turmoil it was enduring.

"Look!" Anthea yelled, forcing Silva's eyes toward a decaying, decrepit Arboria. "Look at what your actions have caused! You three saved the world a hundred years ago, and restored it! For what!? For it to return to this? You were *heroes!* I read thousands of stories about you, encrypted and hidden away in tomes my elders didn't want me to find. I *admired* you! I *trusted* you! Those books said you would watch over Endra and allow peace to prevail and prevent darkness from returning!"

"The Embers are going to war," Leof said, struggling to hold Pyrrhus back in his confinement. "There are many legends about you, Pyrrhus, but they all said you had a deep respect for the Volcano, right down to your core. This war will tear the volcano apart, and you're going to allow it to happen!? *So what* if we've innovated. I read a legend, once, that said you always sought out bigger and better challenges. Is that not what we're doing, but with our own minds? And now all of that will be set back by thousands of years, because you saw it fit to dry out our resources!"

"Hasn't this gone on long enough?" Neros pleaded. "You fought and subdued Melanthos because he was acting unjustly to you and wreaking havoc in the world. It was merciful of you to keep him alive, and yet you continue to act like this? When to us, you have always been legends?"

"You *whelps* never showed us even an ounce of gratitude," Isolde seethed, cracking through Neros' protective barrier. "After all we did for you!"

"But we never knew what the world was like before you—*aaah!*" Anthea was thrown from her position as Silva broke free of the vines, using them to whip Anthea around the air and slam her into Neros, sending the two of them tumbling toward the screens. With Neros' concentration interrupted, Isolde broke free; Pyrrhus found new strength in the freedom of his companions, and twisted his body to launch Leof over the top of his back and barreling into the other two.

"Insolent children! Now you will get what you deserve."

Leof and Anthea rolled off Neros, heaving pants of exhaustion. Pontius swore under his breath, flitting between the three of them. "I shouldn't have used so much magic on those cloud views," He cried. "Come on, your highness, you must put up a barrier between you and the gods before they attack!"

Neros nodded, focusing himself and his magic energy into his arm— he wished he could channel it through his staff, but it was blasted away from him when Anthea crashed into him. He conjured the barrier, encasing himself and his friends safely inside.

The gods had each extended their hands, and bright blue, red, and green light began to emit from their palms. *Some kind of powerful combo magic attack…?* Whatever it was, the prince felt it borrowing from all the excess power that was coursing through the clouds. Neros had to put more and more focus into the barrier to keep it up, and it was exhausting. The gods' aim was directly at the three of them.

They fired off a blast, and Neros braced himself for the worst.

As the gods' magic struck the barrier, he felt a jolt in his veins. He groaned as it continued to push against it, fracturing the edges and looking horrifically familiar to the prince.

Had the gods been toying with them this whole time? Was this their full, renewed power?

Neros closed his eyes, fighting to swallow past the lump in his throat. *This is the end. There's nothing else we can do.*

We're going to die here.

Suddenly, a hand wrapped around his wrist. There was a distinct warmth, and suddenly heat flowing through his veins—*this magic energy isn't my own, but...*

Neros opened his eyes. "Leof?" He croaked, awestruck.

Leof said nothing, gritting his teeth against the strength of the magic they were defending against. Weakly, Neros saw Anthea reach her hand over as well, gripping Neros' arm and doing the same, transferring her magic energy to him. He felt it course through his veins, dancing and swirling and combining with his own, and with their support, his strength was renewed—and growing. As he continued to borrow energy, he noticed he was beginning to borrow from the same power the gods had been. Specks of bright light drifted up from the ground, latching on to the edge of Neros' barrier and glowing, brighter and brighter until the prince could barely keep his eyes open.

Then, the barrier cracked, and everything went white.

Neros had not expected to wake up, but he did, bleary-eyed and drained. Slowly, his surroundings came into focus: he was collapsed on a cloudy ground, so that meant... *I'm still in Andolis. But...what about Leof and Anthea?* He sat up, arms shaking with the effort. Leof was to his left, Anthea to his right, both still out cold and farther away than before, as though they'd been blasted apart. Pontius was behind him, next to stir, and instantly flew inches from the prince's face.

"Your highness, are...are you alright?" Surprisingly, the water spirit was whispering. He caught Neros' gaze and looked to Leof and Anthea. "Oh! Of course, you're worried. Well, let's check on them with the spe—" he cut himself off, deflating. Neros' eyebrows drew together. They both knew that neither one of them had the energy to manage magic right now. The prince sighed; the old-fashioned way would have to suffice.

First, he scooted himself closer to Leof, too tired to stand and walk. Unconscious, his mouth was parted slightly, and the prince felt his heart stutter at how...serene it was. Neros gingerly reached a hand out to feel for a pulse when he paused, flushing with embarrassment. *How do I even check for his pulse…? Perhaps I should just see if he's still breathing…* He moved his wrist under Leof's nose, waiting to feel the breath on his skin and watching the flames of his hair wisp slowly in the air.

When he felt the warm puff of air against his wrist, he smiled and sighed in relief. He moved over to Anthea, testing the same. He pushed some of the vines away from her face to find she, too, was still alive. *Thank goodness.*

He heard footsteps, and out of the corner of his eye Neros noticed three figures—much, much smaller than before—that perfectly resembled the gods. Neros looked between his unconscious friends, then struggled to his feet and into a protective stance, searching for where his staff had dropped. *If they want to attack us again, I have to protect Leof and Anthea. No matter what.*

"Calm yourself, Prince Neros," Isolde said, her voice still cold, but less harsh than before. "We…we surrender to you."

The prince blinked. Moments ago, they were going to kill him and his friends. Now, they were conceding? "What?" He asked dumbly.

Silva twisted the ends of her hair. She looked vulnerable…almost mortal. "While you were knocked out, we had…some time to think. Your powers reflected our magic back at us, and beyond being super painful, it…you guys got knocked back, and your friends are still out cold, and…you're right in front of those screens, and…Endra looks horrible." She hung her head.

Pyrrhus huffed. "More than that, unfortunately, you gave us a logical argument. Brought about a few words from the *real* Pegaios that we forgot about."

"He told us…to restore Endra. Then, to rule it justly and fairly, should the darkness not return and the prophecy not repeat."

"We thought he was insane," Pyrrhus said. "So we locked him away, and took to our own bidding."

"Clearly, we…lost ourselves." Isolde sounded pained to admit it.

Neros didn't know what to make of this. Or if he could trust them.

"So what do you plan to do?" He asked, tentative.

"First, your friends have to wake up. But then, we have a deal for you." Silva said, and she extended her arms to release a throng of petals. Neros flinched back, at first, but he watched them drift carefully over his two best friends, swirling around them and dusting pollen over their bodies.

Anthea stirred first, sitting up slowly, then standing quicker once she realized who was standing in front of her.

"Anthy! I'm so glad you're okay."

"Neros, the gods! They're behind you!"

"No, no, they…" He glanced over his shoulder, noticing Leof beginning to stir as well. "They have a deal for us."

"A deal…?" Leof asked, sleepily standing. "Why the change of heart?"

Neros started to answer, but Pyrrhus stopped him. "Have you ever convinced yourself that you were living your life the only way you could, only to one day be shown that you were wrong? That there was more to life, to the way you could live, than you first thought?"

Leof looked down, nodding. Pyrrhus seemed satisfied with the response, and continued. "When we were mortals, we defeated Melanthos and sent him to the underworld Umbros to become the keeper of his own darkness. Pegaios offered us godhood as a reward for our valiant efforts. We only see it right to offer the same to you."

Neros was struck. To become immortal…? That would mean they would have access to all the power, the magic that the gods held at their fingertips. They would oversee Endra, just the three of them. But as he looked around, doubt tugged at his mind. He had duties back home, and he wasn't sure if he was ready to accept the responsibility of being a governing god to the people of Vetur. His heart sank to join the guilt in his gut. *I can hardly commit to being their prince, in Runa's eyes.* He shook his head—there was more to it than that. To be a god, he would be revered—or maybe worshipped—by the citizens, but all his life Prince Neros had never wanted to be treated that way. He preferred to live amongst them, as an equal. And he knew Anthea felt that way, too.

He caught Leof's gaze, and the Ember read his expression immediately.

"We're declining the offer."

"What!?"

"We don't want to risk becoming like you. You're still young, immortally speaking, aren't you?" Leof challenged, and the gods looked sheepish. "So like anyone, you still have learning to do. Just…learn from this."

The gods mulled it over, sharing glances and stares between them that

Neros couldn't even begin to guess at the meaning of.

"Fine," Isolde agreed. "But at least let us loan you the power to fix what we've done."

She summoned, from thin air, a large bag full of what appeared to be finely ground diamonds—pixie dust? No, more like stars—and handed it to Neros. "This should be enough. Scatter this across Endra, and the magic energy will infuse in the terrain and the seas, and the darkness will be driven back to the shadows of Umbros where it belongs. Endra will be healed, and you three can return home."

"What about Prince Neros' parents?" Leof asked. "Or his arm?"

Isolde's eyebrows drew together, and she shook her head. "Some things cannot be reversed. Death is one of them. As for your arm, your highness, I'm sorry, but I cannot fix that either. The most I can do is reverse the curse I placed on you."

Leof's hair whipped around his head in frustration, but Neros stepped in before he could voice it. "I'll take it."

"While you do that, I'll summon these three heroes a ride for their magic-spreading!" Silva cheered, walking off and dragging Pyrrhus with her.

Isolde held Neros' prosthetic arm in her hands, and slowly waved her fingers over it, drawing out long shards of ice from invisible crevices all up and down the prince's arm. He was in awe of the spectacle, as every time he thought it was over, more shards would lift from his skin and arm and drift back to rejoin Isolde. It was strangely painless, and once it was done, he felt...

Well, he felt the same.

Isolde stepped back, gesturing to Neros. "Go on. Try."

It had been a conscious effort to avoid using his ice magic before, but when he extended his hand to summon small crystals with next to no effort, a grin broke out on his face. "Oh, thank you, goddess Isolde. Thank you." He felt quite like himself again, sending the crystals skyward and watching them explode into snow flurries with a giggle.

Pyrrhus and Silva rode down from between the flurries on a large cloud, stepping off and gesturing grandly to it. "Ta-da! Your magical carriage awaits! It should be sturdy enough for one trip around Endra. Just spread the magic from the bag and watch the world come back to life at your fingertips."

"Can't you do this yourselves?" Leof asked.

"Listen, you didn't want godhood, but you still deserve a reward for showing us what for," Silva countered, ushering them onto the cloud and pushing it toward the entrance of the castle at a worryingly quick speed. "Learn to accept a gift from the gods and *go!*"

With one final shove, the cloud rocketed forward, and Leof immediately clung to the prince and princess for purchase. They soared past Amund, who was upright, locked and shimmering, before plummeting to the world below. The wind rushed against their cheeks, and Neros grabbed a handful of the magic stardust and tossed it into the breeze, watching in awe as the decaying, purpled grass was restored to its former lush glory. Anthea whooped at his side, grabbing a fistful of her own and tossing it another way.

They continued this for what felt like hours, soaring over the plains, through the woods, across the ashen terrain. They crossed rivers and dusted treetops, and summoned waterfalls grander than any had seen before—an invitation of new life into the world. Leof sprinkled stardust into the volcano and heaved his own sigh of relief as the lava spurred back into motion, the surprised cheer that erupted from the volcano loud enough to hear from miles away. The more of the gods' power they used, the lighter Neros' heart felt. Life was being restored, and the darkness receded into the shadows like Endra was waking up from a horrible nightmare.

❄

As the cloud drifted back to the surface, it dissolved, and the trio settled into the grass, staring at the renewed world around them. It was as though nothing had happened at all—the air was warm on their weary bodies, and Neros enjoyed the breeze on his face. It looked like any other spring day, though somehow the prince could sense the peace and serenity in the air around them.

It was over. He breathed a sigh of relief, but the feeling twisted into guilt and sadness and settled back into his chest.

"Neros? What's wrong?" Anthea asked. "We did it! Endra is saved, and you look so down. Why?"

"I…Of course, I'm happy we succeeded, but…" His gaze turned toward the mountain. "When I return home…I won't be able to see either of you for quite some time. Runa is placing me under castle arrest, effective immediately, until I am fit to become king."

His companions' faces dropped. "What? For how long?" Leof asked.

"It's undecided. I assume however long it takes for her to see me as a suitable inheritor to the throne."

"That's…that could be *years.*" Anthea's voice sounded small, suddenly, and Neros could tell her heart was a storm of emotions. He understood. They had barely been apart for more than a month since they were *seven,* and he'd sprung this on her without warning. Leof looked conflicted, himself, hair crackling and whipping as it tended to when he was deep in thought.

"I'm sorry," was all Neros could say.

Silence settled over them, the peaceful serenity of the world a secondary thought. Neros' gaze dropped to his feet. The grass was so green around his boots, once pearly white but now well-worn and dirty.

"This–this isn't going to be goodbye forever," Leof broke the silence, and the prince's head snapped up to look at him. "It's only goodbye for a while. Right? Runa can't keep you locked away for life, but if we hesitate to part ways, she may be inclined to be harsher on her judgement of you."

"Good point! So…I guess…I guess this is goodbye for now," Anthea added. "Like a see you later!"

Neros couldn't bring himself to say the same. When she wanted, Runa could be *ruthless,* and he had no doubt she would be upon his return. Vetur was devastated, and the gods-given magic only erased the physical evidence of all the torment. Everyone's memories would remain. Could the people even trust him anymore? How long would it take to rebuild that trust? Neros could easily see himself under Runa's lock and key for five years, maybe more. He rubbed his arm, pushing down the urge to despair about it.

He shoved the thoughts aside, looking to his friends with a smile.

"It's been a wonderful adventure. I promise…I'll work hard so we can see each other again soon." Neros took a step back to start walking home.

But he was stopped by Leof's voice.

"Wait!"

The prince and princess looked at him, puzzled. Neither of them said anything, so he continued.

"This…this feels wrong. We've been adventuring together for…a *year,* at least, and I won't—I *can't* let either of you walk away without saying something more than just 'see you later.' So…hear me out for a minute." He took a breath. "The two of you can be…an insufferable duo. You're reckless, assertive, and maybe a bit spoiled by your upbringing, but you're both so gods-damned *smart,* and kind, and caring, and earnest, that it's almost painful. I–you know my background. I'd never left my home before, *ever,* and the two of you just scooped me up into your traveling party without even so much as a blink. And just like that, you…accepted me. There was nothing, *nothing* I had done in my life to deserve such care and generosity to be given to me, and yet it was all you two had to offer.

This journey was, without question, the most reckless, stupid thing I've ever done in my life. But I wouldn't trade it for the world," Leof admitted, his voice wobbly. "You two have become so dear to me, and I—this feels like it's too soon, a-and—*gods,* I'm going to miss you both…!"

Neros' chest constricted when he saw tears, *actual tears* begin to fall from Leof's eyes, bright yellow like his magmatic core. He sniffled, aggressively wiping at them and turning away.

Anthea let out a loud sniffle beside him. "Oh, damn it, Leof! I thought–I thought I was going to get away from this without the *waterworks* coming, but…I'll miss you, too!" She wailed, collapsing into Leof and hugging him.

The prince's vision clouded, and he wrapped his arms around his two best friends, and he cried with them. He pulled them close, as close as they could get, and wept with them until their sobs quieted back down to sniffles and uneven breaths. Suddenly, bright balls of light burst forth from their chests, coalescing into one larger orb in between them. The trio stepped back, looking between each other in confusion, until the orb split back into three parts, dimming and dropping to the ground.

Neros moved toward them first, kneeling in the grass to examine them. They were necklaces. The chain was woven intricately with deep green vines, with strong-looking bronze clasps to keep them closed. The charm at the end of each one was different, sculpted immaculately from ice: one snowflake, one flame, and one leaf. They were gorgeous.

"Did we…make these?" Anthea asked. She picked one up, tugging on the vine. "I can't break this."

Leof crouched and plucked the flame amulet necklace from the grass, trying to set sparks upon it. Nothing happened. He tried to melt the clasp between his fingers to the same result. "The metal is unbending."

The snowflake looked delicate, Neros thought. He lifted it, his curiosity leading him to try to snap it in half. He couldn't.

"Was it a gift from the gods, perhaps…?" He thought aloud.

"No, that light…came from *us*. Did it…manifest?" Leof guessed.

"That would be my best guess, sir Leof!" Pontius chirped, emerging from Neros' staff and surprising the three of them. He was wiping away a set of his own tears. "The power of your friendship was strong enough to forge unbreakable charms! It's something I've only heard of as legend passed through oracles in training. A true honor to see it in person!"

"Wow, so the last of our god-given powers became these! There's an Arborian legend about how good luck charms made with the powers of gods can never be broken, but items like that are so rare I thought it was a complete myth. I guess not."

Neros smiled, unclasping his and putting it around his neck. "I think they're perfect for us. This way, we'll always be close to each other's hearts."

Leof looked like he was about to cry again as he followed suit, along with Anthea. He looked at Neros like he wanted to say something else, but he shook his head. "Good luck with the restoration and care of your kingdoms, both of you."

"Tell Aldebrande we said hello," Anthea replied. "And thank him for allowing you to come along with us."

"And truly, Leof," Neros said, clasping Leof's hands in his own and offering a warm smile. "*Thank you* for all you've done for us. For coming with us. Of all the creatures and beings in Endra that could have been our third companion, I'm glad it was you."

Leof's cheeks glowed, and he rubbed his arm awkwardly. "Right. Just…write me when you're allowed."

Neros laughed. "Of course! When my coronation date is set, you'll get the first invitation." Anthea cleared her throat, and he laughed harder. "Fine, fine! The second."

Leof smiled. "I look forward to it."

The prince couldn't take it: he pulled them both together in one last hug. Then, hearts heavy, they parted ways. It shouldn't have felt so bittersweet. Leof was right, after all—it wasn't goodbye forever.

But as Neros climbed the mountain to Vetur, his anxiety and dread building like steadily falling snow, he suddenly wasn't so sure.

Chapter 19
The Years Between

$\mathcal{L}$eof was home.

In the past—before all this traipsing around the world to find a cure for the curses infecting Endra business—he resisted calling this place his home. When he was young, this volcano was a prison, and he was locked away in solitary confinement with no hope for exoneration. Many days, he struggled to survive. He pickpocketed once or twice, but the feeling of doing so made him so sick he'd swear off sustenance for the next few days. When Aldebrande found him, the magma in his core had nearly slowed to a stop. It would have been easier to let him die, Leof knew—he was a child, and children were a pain to care for—but Aldebrande didn't give up. He nursed Leof back to health, gave him a place to sleep, and taught him the tools of the trade. Leof thought he was cursed; he should have died. He was an *abomination*, after all, knowing how to use magic and using it. That stuff…it was dangerous, everyone thought so. Leof knew it wasn't. But that's what everyone said, so he tried to hide his affinity for it.

Aldebrande would never have that, of course.

Leof could say he was lucky to have a mentor who was willing to let him practice magic. Little did either of them know that his affinity for the practice would lead to him saving the world, alongside an equally magical prince and princess.

He'd put his life on the line for either of them. They saved the world together, and with the help of the petty gods themselves, they restored the magic energy and brought new life back to Endra.

The lava flowed freely in the volcano once again, and as such, Leof knew he had to return.

He shook his head, smiling faintly and the absurdity of it all. Now, he was at the workshop with Aldebrande, sequestered away from the rest of the bustle that came with the approaching kinetic contraption competition, an annual tradition among Embers challenging them to build the most intricate system to perform a mundane task. Embers of all hues would stop in, requesting this piece or that, this size bolt, nuts and screws, copper tubes and steel plates; just about anything Leof could think of, some Ember would need.

He hated this time of year. The shop was so noisy, and Aldebrande usually asked Leof to take extra shifts at the storefront, due to his mentor's "advanced age" (which Leof rolled his eyes at—Aldebrande was barely over 200, and Embers could live to be centuries older if they took good care of their health). Thankfully, today Aldebrande allowed Leof to take the day off to use the workshop instead of face customer after exhausting customer.

With his newfound freedom, Leof took to his latest project with a laser-focused fervor. Small glasses perched on the edge of his nose, his hair wrapped high in a bun on his head so its flickers wouldn't distract him from the minuscule cogs and gears in front of him. This wasn't a project that would become a kinetic contraption—not like Aldebrande always hoped. Instead, Leof put his efforts into a more intricate, delicate piece.

"You'll be more satisfied with this product than if I worked on some large, whimsical contraption," he'd told Aldebrande.

"Perhaps. Yet, you and I both know that with your mental prowess, you could take the volcano by storm, young boy," the elder Ember had replied with that all-too-familiar competitive glint in his eyes. It had made Leof's entire core churn in discomfort.

He had spent nearly every moment since his arrival home dedicated to blueprinting and gathering materials. He wouldn't dare show it, but it excited him. His travels around the world opened his eyes to new magic and environments, and he'd be hard-pressed to say he wasn't inspired by it. What he had in the works had certainly never been crafted before (at least, to his knowledge) and Leof craved the challenge.

In front of him now was a small prototype, a platform with a lever sticking out that spun against a sideways cylinder with raised dots affixed to it. Currently, he was in the process of placing the second mechanism—a thin set of metal prongs that would be struck by the dots on the cylinder. He struggled with the placement of it, the screws he was using being impossibly small. *Maybe I should have started with a larger prototype…but I don't want to waste materials.* He held his breath while he turned the screw in place, afraid that even the slightest movement would send everything rolling off the side of his desk. *This doesn't need to be perfect, but I need to figure this out before too long. I have no idea when he'll write me…* He felt heat at the back of his neck, and he closed his eyes, placing his screwdriver on his desk after securing the piece in place. He rubbed at his face. *It's been months, but he's fine, right? Surely, he's fine. It's pointless to worry. Anthea said he'll send a letter when he's good and ready, so I had just better work hard until then.*

"Leof? You still up in here, my boy?"

The Ember nearly jumped out of his coalskin, whipping around in his seat to face his mentor. "Aldebrande, I—is it that late already?"

At this, he chortled. "No, no, just teasing you. You've got a letter."

His heart leapt into his throat, but he swallowed hard to shove the feeling back where it belonged. *It could just be the princess.* It probably was Princess Anthea, now that he put a bit more thought into it. They'd been corresponding over the last several months, after her initial contact to him with her…oddly desperate cries of boredom. Leof had to laugh, reading her first letter—it wasn't as though he could go visit so easily. She was nearly halfway across the *world,* as he knew it.

But when he took the parcel from Aldebrande, he couldn't help the stutter in his chest. It wasn't the princess' handwriting—it was far more delicate, and his name was in such a beautiful script that he must have stared at it for a few minutes too long.

"Who is it from? That princess in Arboria?"

Leof snapped out of his reverie. "No I think…I think it's from the prince."

"Oh, that one with her…Neros was his name, wasn't it? He had an odd glove on one hand. I quite liked him. He was very polite. Could this be a request to visit him? It looked like a letter to me."

"Y-you opened it!?" Leof sputtered, turning the envelope over to see the seal had, in fact, been broken. His cheeks glowed. "Why did you…?"

"I had to make sure you weren't in trouble with a far-off royal court!" He laughed again, and Leof rolled his eyes. "You've become pretty famous since your adventure, lad. I never know what to expect in our mailbox."

Leof scoffed. "Famous? Hardly. You were just prying."

Aldebrande's eyes glinted in the same way Princess Anthea's did when she knew something Leof didn't. "Perhaps I was. I'll be in the study, if you need to find me later."

"Sure," He answered distractedly, pulling out the parchment from the envelope. It was embossed with a delicate pattern of waves and snowflakes printed in gold and blue—an obscene detail and totally unnecessary to put on a letterhead, but sure enough, elegantly-scrawled lettering lay in the space below. Leof should have expected it, but still he marveled at how proper and neat the prince's handwriting was. He read it in a daze.

Dear Leof,

I sincerely hope this letter finds you well. I had hoped to write you sooner, but unfortunately Runa's had me under strict watch these last several months—I've hardly had a moment alone until now. Technically, I am still writing to you in secret; Pontius has graciously agreed to sneak the letter into the outgoing mail on my behalf, but you must (please) resist any urge you may have to write back, if such an urge exists at all.

An ink blot covered up a small sentence, as though Neros had written something mistakenly. The letter continued:

My studies have been rigorous. Being a king is not something I expected to do at my age, but Vetur needs a ruler, and I think Runa is finally finding me fit to be so. The Veturians have been receptive to my return, though many questioned why I left and what I had done when I'd gone—it was all so sudden, after all. We've held counsel after counsel with the townspeople, and we've build up emergency committees spearheaded by Runa herself to help keep Vetur at peace.

I hope we pick the date for my coronation soon—I want to see you again, and ask all about how you've been. Have you been able to visit the lower levels of the volcano? Was the civil war suppressed? Do you have any new projects you're working on? I want to know everything you've been up to.

    They have a castle jeweler who has been able to do tune-ups on my arm, but he doesn't understand the intricate structures of it. Some of it is connected by magic, after all, and that perplexes him as it's not Veturian magic. I'm not in pain, or anything, but it would be nice to have you work on it again.

There was another ink blot, a space, and another, and then there was a set of words that made a shock so hot jolt through Leof's body that he nearly lit the paper on fire.

    I miss you.

Leof stared at that sentence, reading it, then re-reading it. Reading it again. His chest felt tight, so he put the letter down and distracted himself with his project for a few hours. Once the cylinder's ridges were properly set in place, plucking against the thin metal prongs to ring out a song into the quiet of the workshop, he deemed himself calm enough to keep reading.

    I think of you every time I catch sight of the pendant on my neck, knowing—and hoping—that you still wear yours. I think you do. I feel a connection to you both through it; maybe it's some kind of effect of the gods' magic. Or perhaps I'm just imagining it. Pontius didn't have an answer for me.

    Regardless, I look forward to seeing you at my coronation. I hope you anticipate receiving the invitation as much as I anticipate sending it. In the meantime, please take care of yourself, and give Aldebrande my warmest regards.

    Yours,
    Neros

He felt like he'd been doused in water and set ablaze all at once. He instinctively reached for the necklace tucked into his tunic. It *did* have a peculiar magic energy emanating off of it, but Leof had never really investigated. *I wonder if it's possible to turn them into communication devices...* He shook his head. Neros was hard at work, so there was no room for him to be distracted by this. He placed the letter in a drawer by his bed, and then turned back to his workshop bench, rolling his neck to release some of the stiffness.

"Let's do this."

Anthea knew it was going to be difficult to be separated from Neros: her best friend, partner in crime, fellow lover of research, and excellent listener. She had been forcibly separated from him before—an accident in her youth had led to the elders locking her in her room with strict supervision for a few months. But as she lay upside-down on her bed, staring up at the light filtering through the leaves, she thought that it was much harder when *he* was the one under house arrest.

Arboria had needed *much* grooming when she returned, and nearly everyone had to be nursed back to health. She and Rosea had taken excruciating care to wide throngs of Arborians, and within a few months, the forest was lively with fresh energy that she hadn't felt in years. She was grateful the casualties suffered were few.

But it had only taken a few months, and yet more months had passed since then—she passed some time writing to Leof, but letters took *eons* to get between Arboria and the Eldur Ignis Volcano. And sure, Leof's blueprints were interesting. He was making a globe with a miniature Vetur inside, that was meant to play a song when you wound it up. It looked hard, and Anthea commended his immense effort, and wasted absolutely no time teasing him for it. He insisted it was just a gift, demanding that she stop insinuating that something more would come from it. She laughed. She knew better than to try and convince him otherwise.

And yet, even that entertainment was fleeting.

She found it within herself to groan, flopping onto her stomach and nesting her head in her arms.

"Rosea, I am *so bored,*" She whined. "Are you sure there's *nobody* in town that needs help?"

"The world isn't ending twenty-four seven," Rosea laughed. "But we can go to the market if you'd like."

Anthea was glad she didn't have to lose *both* of her best friends to house arrest. She supposed that was the singular perk to Neros being the victim this time. Sliding forward off the bed and tumbling into a standing position, she scooped Rosea off the ground and looped their arms together.

"Sounds great! Let's see what herbs and flora inspire us while we're down there. We may be able to hatch Endra's next hottest potion."

The princess was admittedly a little nervous as they approached the marketplace—the last time she had gone perusing was when disaster struck her kingdom, and though the merchants were resilient in returning to their stalls to sell, Anthea had pointedly avoided them until now. With Rosea's arm looped through hers, it surfaced a memory she thought she'd squashed.

"You alright, Anthy?" Rosea asked, gently pulling them toward a stall overflowing with different breeds of flowers.

She smiled in a way she hoped was reassuring. "Yeah, I'll be fine."

Rosea took to examining the flowers, bending and crouching and lifting them to look at them from all angles. The merchant kept trying (and failing) to get her attention, and Anthea couldn't help but chuckle. Rosea's laser-focus when it came to plants was unmatched, and it was too amusing to watch poor shopkeepers try to grapple for her attention.

Suddenly, she stood up straight, a bushel of assorted roses in her arms. "I'll take these, please!"

"Eh!? Ah, right, yes, of course, that's…that'll be a pynt and two quart, young lady."

"What a steal! Anthy, hold these," Before she could protest, Rosea had shoved the flowers into her arms, and Anthea was immediately struck by the smell. It was overpowering and warm and it made the princess's head all foggy…but at the same time, she wanted to bask in it for hours.

Rosea took the flowers back, sticking them into a bag at her hip. She caught Anthea's expression and giggled. "Wow, I wasn't expecting them to be so strong to you! Must be because you're an oak, huh?"

Anthea blinked away the fogginess, frowning slightly. "H-huh? What do you mean?"

"Those roses have a rare, high pollen count. It makes them incredibly effective for medicinal and potion mixing of all kinds, though they can be dangerous if you've got a sensitive nose."

"And what kind of pollen do they give off, exactly?"

"That bundle was a mix of pollen that makes you happy and wistful. Mixed with other ingredients, it strengthens healing remedies and elongates the effects of stuff like your frost seeds."

"Impressive!" Anthea cheered. "So, what are your plans for these?"

Rosea smirked at her. "Come on, Anthy. You *know* you're going to want to stay in Vetur longer than you strictly need to once Neros is free. I'm making both of us some extra frost seeds!"

"Come on, that's never all you're doing." Anthea smirked.

Rosea looked away, blinking coyly. "I may have a side project…"

"Share!"

"Maybe later," She said, bounding off to the next stall. Rosea always knew how to play Anthea for the long game. But the princess made note to pick every corner of Rosea's brain later.

❀

They were crushing rose petals using a mortar and pestles when they heard a distant, excitable voice.

"Your highneeeeess…!"

The girls looked at each other, baffled, until the owner of the voice made himself abundantly clear by barreling through Anthea's open window, splatting into her bedside table and immediately swirling back into the air, practically buzzing with excitement.

"Pontius!" Anthea cheered, her heart filled with warmth at the sight of him. "I didn't think you were still hanging around. What brings you all the way out here?"

"Funny you should ask, Princess," He beamed, straightening himself up and adjusting his tie and monocle. "I've come with fantastic news from the castle. Let me just…find it…" He dug around his pockets, procuring a (miraculously dry) envelope. "Ta-da!"

The princess snatched it, ripping it open and tearing the contents out. She yelped in delight.

"*Finally!*"

"Finally what, Anthy? Is his coronation date set?"

"*Yes! Yes!!* We'd better finish those frost seeds fast, Rosea. We haven't got a minute to waste. We'll have to get just the best outfits commissioned, and—oh, oh! We'll have to get him a gift." She whipped her attention back to Pontius. "Does Leof know?"

Pontius looked startled. "Oh! I! Well, Princess, Neros requested that you be the first to know."

"Do you have his letter? Can you warp like you used to?"

"Yes and yes! I will deliver it posthaste, princess!" Pontius adjusted his monocle, preparing to warp himself to the Eldur Ignis Volcano.

"Wait, mister Pontius! Bring him here when he's ready. We can house him and all go up the mountain together!" Rosea added. Pontius nodded, promising them both he'd soon return with Leof safely.

✿

"You just wanted me here for the warmth, didn't you."

"What? No! Neros invited all of us together. Why would I dare dream of attending his coronation without you, his *favorite person?*" Anthea smiled at him in that knowing way she always did that made Leof want to light her hair on fire.

"Wouldn't that technically be *you?* You're his best friend, aren't you?"

"Yes, but *you're* his beloved mechanic and long-time travel companion! You saved his life!"

"Don't forget that you also traveled with him for a long time, *and* helped in saving his life."

"So you admit to being his beloved mechanic?"

Heat flared up around his cheeks. "What!? No! That's not what I said!"

Rosea laughed. "I think it's nice that you love Prince Neros so much, Leof. I didn't expect that from you when we first met!"

Leof groaned. Were these Arborians ever going to give him a break? He thought Neros and Anthea were a troublesome duo when they stormed into his life at the volcano, but *Rosea* and Anthea was almost too much to handle.

"You don't need to feel bashful about it. Anthea and I will keep it a secret, right?" Anthea nodded in agreement, though it did little to quell his anxiety. "I really do think it's wonderful, and I think you're such a good match for him."

He *desperately* wanted to change the topic of conversation, but he didn't know what to say. He fiddled with his sleeves—billowing dark red bishop sleeves with embroidered gold trim on the cuffs that matched the decorations on his collar and waist sash. It was too fancy for him, but Aldebrande had insisted. "I—thank you, I think."

Rosea rested her hand on top of his, catching his eye with a gentle smile. "I can tell you don't believe me. You don't have to right now. Let's just enjoy his ceremony together, okay?"

For what it was worth, Rosea was too nice for her own good. He nodded, and they continued their hike up the mountain. Pontius had left soon after dropping Leof off—the Ember had grown used to the nausea that came with warping from place to place, but it didn't mean that it was *enjoyable* for him. Anthea and Rosea had fawned over his clothes, and he sorely hoped it wasn't a sign for how others at the ceremony would be treating him. He'd wanted to make a decent impression, sure, but he didn't want to *stand out*. Suffice to say, Leof was not the biggest fan of parties. Especially with throngs of nobles flitting about, where every word seemed to have a hidden political meaning.

He sighed. It was going to prove to be an interesting night.

Chapter 20
Ceremony for the King

"*Y*ou look dashing, your highness!"

Neros smiled at Pontius in the mirror, awkwardly adjusting his ceremonial garb. It was a bit stiff, if he was being honest with himself. He wore a cape that draped to his ankles, wrapping and clasping in the center with a brooch adorned with dozens of small snowflakes. Underneath the cape was a pressed shirt, vest, and pants with whimsical embroidery stitched down each pant leg. It was an entirely new outfit—Runa had it commissioned especially for the occasion. They were beautiful clothes, but still the prince felt an ache in his chest as he wished his parents were there to see. He shook the thought from his mind; tonight was not the night to be thinking of that.

Tonight, Neros was to be crowned King of Vetur. After a couple of vigorous years of study under Runa's close, careful watch, she (at last) deemed him ready to take the throne.

It was a gruesome adjustment. He'd spent long nights pouring over books on behavior and etiquette and politics and governing, all of which had such dry writing that he swore his eyes would shrivel up and roll out of his skull. Longer still were the days of practicing all which he'd been reading, and meeting with the counsel Runa had set up upon his absence. Weeks and months were spent apologizing and reconciling the town's issues that had developed while he was away. Yes, the world was no longer ending, but the Veturians had fled in the brutal snowstorm, and needed aid to restart their lives. Neros took blame and fault as graciously as he could manage.

He was lucky that Pontius had snuck back up the mountain with him, tucked away in the head of his staff. Runa had him strictly cut from any communication with anyone outside the castle (which seemed largely unfair, as he was sure Veshna would appreciate a chat and help tending to her sheep). It promised to be painfully lonely, but the water spirit made even his most dismal days a little brighter.

A knock at the door snapped Neros out of his thoughts. "Yes?"

"Your highness, you have a few early guests arriving," It was one of the guards—based on the all-too-proper tone, it was Brynjar. "It would be most wise to come down and greet them."

His heart skipped a beat or two, anxious nerves performing acrobatics in his gut. He only knew one person who would show up so early to his ceremony, and it took every ounce of energy he had not to bolt down the stairs at full speed. (He may have failed at this, and Brynjar may have scolded him for allowing such fine garments as his cape to flap gracelessly behind him, and that it was no way at all for a king to behave. Neros didn't care.)

Anthea's delighted shriek was music to his ears; never had he so quickly tumbled into someone's arms as he did hers. He pressed his face into her shoulder to hide his teary eyes from her view—he knew she'd poke fun at him for it.

"I missed you," She whispered, and Neros was relieved to hear her voice was a bit wobbly, too. "Gods, am I glad we caught you before you got swept up in coronation duties."

Neros agreed, releasing her only to have Rosea attach herself to him. "Arboria simply isn't the same without your cheery face around every now and again!"

He laughed, and she released her iron grip from him. Neros turned to greet Leof, and his heart stuttered. *Gods, he looks lovely.* Before he could say so, a voice called from down the hall, interrupting him.

"Your majesty, please allow Brynjar and Agnar to handle the guests. We must review your speech for this evening."

His hope snapped in half; he looked apologetically at his friends, only to get smiles in return.

"Go ahead. We'll all catch up later."

✿

"*We'll catch up later?* Leof, are you *nuts?!* You know how busy he's gonna be, right?" Anthea scolded as the three of them were escorted to the main ballroom, where the majority of the evening would be spent. "At this rate, you'll never get the chance to tell him how you feel."

Leof shrank back a bit, and the three were ushered into a set of seats near the back of the room.

"I shall return posthaste. More guests should be arriving soon," Brynjar informed them. Anthea waved him off, and he seemed to take offense to her, stalking off in a huff.

Once he left, Leof spoke. "He doesn't need to know how I feel."

Rosea's eyebrows knit together. "But Leof, didn't you work very hard on a coronation gift for him?"

He did. It was sitting heavy in a pouch tied around his waist, hidden mostly by his decorative sash. He breathed a sigh through his nose. "It's just a gift. Everyone will have one for him."

"Yes, but you worked hard to make yours. Because you have feelings for him, right?"

"*Must* you two *really* keep talking about this with me?"

"Listen, Leof, we're not trying to antagonize you," Anthea chimed in, face suddenly serious. "We *support* you. I think Neros really needs to hear your feelings. You never know, he could feel the same way."

Leof shook his head. "N-no, I...no, Anthea. I couldn't burden him with that. He's a prince, about to become a king. I'm sure there's...there's someone more suitable for him than someone like me."

Rosea frowned. "Why do you say that?"

The Ember focused his attention on his sleeves. "It's...difficult to explain." He could feel the girls' eyes on him, and it was beginning to make him uncomfortable. "Listen, I'll–I'll think about it."

The answer seemed to sate them, and they continued to sit in silence long enough that other guests began to filter into the ballroom. Some were Embers, which surprised Leof; what surprised him more was when a few approached him. He recognized one immediately as Hélder the White. He could only assume, then, that the two beside him the blue and orange Embers from the council Hélder belonged to, based on the colors of their flames.

"Word of your adventure has reached our ears, young boy," Hélder said, nodding in this sage way that made Leof shift in his seat. "We are proud of your journey."

When Leof didn't say anything—frankly, he was confused—the blue Ember chimed in. "An Ember who travels between levels with a prince and princess of foreign lands doesn't just go unnoticed," She laughed. "Most Embers who leave the volcano end up in the deserts, living their lives as thieves or scrubs or other degenerate occupations."

Leof shifted uncomfortably in his seat. *The world may be saved, but tensions are clearly still high at the volcano.*

"Either way, we thank you for your great service to your people. Enjoy the ceremony," Hélder said, and they took their leave.

"Boy, that was a little tense, huh?" Anthea said. "You alright?"

"Hm? Oh, I'm fine. I'm just not used to the attention, I guess."

"Well, you shouldn't have to worry about it too much," Rosea commented. "Most of the guests here will be focused on the king-to-be."

As if her words summoned him, Leof caught sight of Neros as he entered the ballroom. Guests piled in by the minute, their murmurs and chattering like a dull roar in his ears. Leof tried to ignore the anxious pull in his stomach.

❄

"Relay the itinerary for the evening to me, Neros."

"First, there is the ceremony, where I'll give a speech and be crowned. I'll be appointing Brynjar and Agnar to be royal knights of the…first court, after which we'll separate to the banquet hall for dinner and mingling. Then, I will perform the annual dance typically accompanied with the winter festival, done tonight as a good show of new beginnings. Right…?"

"Good," Runa smiled, and Neros' shoulders sagged in relief. "I expect you'll be nothing less than perfectly gracious this evening."

"Of course," Neros reassured. She pat his shoulder and led him down the hall to the ballroom.

"By the by, Neros…thank you. For all the dedication you've given Vetur upon your return. I have been ruthlessly vicious to you these last two years, and you have accepted it and grown beyond my imagination."

"I–I appreciated your guidance, as ever, Runa. And besides, I didn't have much of a choice. I had to give back to Vetur…to all the people who helped raise me."

She smiled again. "And that is why you'll make an excellent king."

Confidence surged through him as they opened the doors to the main ballroom—and as he was instantly swept up by guests, he allowed himself to be carried from group to group, making polite small talk and establishing diplomatic relations with counsel leaders from other kingdoms. He was surprised to see a few Embers—the volcano was a long distance away, and he was unsure what, precisely, made them think that a relationship with Vetur would prove useful. *I suppose they just want to see how I carry this kingdom forward,* he thought to himself. Other kingdoms could be that way, as he read in the dozens of history books Runa pushed him through. Thankfully, many of the Arborians simply wanted to hear the regaling of his adventures abroad—and he was happy to tell the story *many* times, his gaze often flicking to his dear friends in the back corner of the room.

Eventually, he made his way to a stage with a small podium, and the room's attention was drawn to him and Runa. Runa raised her arms, in greeting and a plea for silence.

"We thank you all for gathering here today. Our small kingdom has endured much over the last two years, as many of you know, including the loss of our beloved king and queen. I would like to begin today's ceremony with a moment of silence in honor of the fallen King Vasilias and Queen Heilsa, please."

It was a somber beginning. Neros steeled himself with careful breaths through his nose. Two years was not enough time to heal the loss of his parents—and he knew he was not the only one who missed them. A few Veturians in the crowd wiped tears away with kerchiefs, and Neros could even see that Anthea had closed her eyes and bowed her head.

"Thank you. We deeply respect the lives they led, and their guidance throughout their time ruling us. Now, we are here to celebrate and honor a new beginning. Tonight, Prince Neros will ascend the throne and become King of Vetur. The council has prepared the crown," Runa gestured to her left, where the royal king's crown rested on a pillow, made of delicate-looking (but sturdy) ice crystals, made to wrap around the back of the wearer's head and adorned with shimmering snowflakes. It was not his father's; that had been frozen to his skull when Isolde cursed them. Instead, Runa and the other councilmen drafted a new design that Neros made himself, with the help of a few jewelers from town. "And the prince has prepared a few words for you all. Prince Neros, if you will."

He stepped forward, nerves flitting around his stomach in a wave like butterflies seeking a migratory pattern. He sought Anthea, Rosea, and Leof's faces in the crowd, and took a few breaths to steady himself on the podium.

"I would like to begin by thanking all of you for coming," He smiled. "Normally, an event like this would not be so grand as to attract Embers from the volcano in the west nor so many Arborians and Veturians who have long since left their homes here to start new lives, but I am touched to see all of you. It is with a heavy heart that I stand here today. I–I never imagined I would ascend the throne so young."

He paused. *Deep breaths.* He had no intention of weeping in front of this entire ballroom.

"None of us in this room are strangers to loss. Loss affects us all, no matter its greatness. Endra has just returned from the brink of succumbing to a great, unspeakable darkness—and I'm sure the loss of my mother and father are not the only losses we suffered through. Arboria was in a state of decay, and the Eldur Ignis' great lava had stopped flowing entirely. Endra may have recovered, thanks in no small part to the power bestowed upon me and my travel companions by the gods, but those memories are pressed into our hearts and minds forever.

There is no simple way to heal the deep wounds left by loss. Time simply makes it easier to cope with. We need support to handle such trage-dy—and that is where all of you here come in. My family was never just my mother and father. It extended far beyond the castle walls as well as within it. Runa has supported me and stepped in as the strongest mentor-mother figure I could have asked for. Princess Anthea was, and always will be, like a sister to me. And the Veturians—all of you—are irreplaceable in my heart. From a young age, you've all cared for me as your own son, and I–I'm lucky to feel like I have such a large, supportive family." Again, he had to pause, wiping a stray tear from his eye.

"Two years ago, I returned from nearly abandoning Vetur in a reckless, yet necessary journey to try and save the lives of my parents that ended all too soon. In the years that followed, none of you had any reason to trust me. To trust that I wouldn't do it again. But many of you did—and I worked with many of you who did not to rebuild that trust. I wasn't sure if I could regain it. But you've surprised me, perhaps as I may have surprised you. You accepted my apologies. You were patient with my mistakes as I learned what it truly means to be devoted to your people. You were understanding and kind, and firm when the situation called for it. I am grateful to you all beyond my own expression.

There are two people in the crowd in particular, that, without their help, I would not be standing here today." Neros' voice wobbled, but he knew it would only get worse if he stopped again. "I would instead be roaming the afterlife alongside my parents' souls. They lifted me, carried me, and supported me when I had no right to ask for such aid. I would not have been ready to make the journey to kinghood without them. You have both provided me a shoulder to cry on, warm meals when the days were bleak, and…so, *so* much more. Thank you, from the bottom of my heart."

He paused again, rubbing his eyes to stop the tears that had built up there. When he addressed the room again, it was with a broad smile on his face.

"I stand before you, king-to-be, with a promise in my heart to continue to do the very best I can to help our people rebuild. To make our family stronger than ever. Thank you."

The crowd erupted in roaring applause, and he spotted Anthea and Rosea as they leapt from their seats, whooping and hollering in a way that, to anyone else, would be wholly embarrassing, but for Neros, it warmed his heart. He chuckled.

Brynjar announced that the crowning was to commence, and Runa took the crown from its place on the pillow and held it to Neros, who bowed forward to allow her to place it on his head. In turn, he knighted both of his guards. The cheers grew louder, and Runa spent a few minutes trying to wave everyone back to silence before sighing and raising her voice.

"I now present to you, King Neros of Vetur! We shall be moving into the banquet hall for food and drink. Please follow the guards to keep in an orderly fashion, and enjoy the celebration."

❄

The remainder of the evening was chaotic, but not unwelcome. Neros was passed around from guest to guest, making conversation and connections. Many of the older ambassadors from Arboria seemed eager to work with him, and Runa was ever present, occasionally resting her hand on the small of his back in a quiet display of support. He flitted around the banquet hall, shaking hands and exchanging greetings until his cheeks hurt. This wasn't *unusual* for him, necessarily, as he had grown quite used to having meetings with council members and villagers from all over Endra. With the threat of the end of the world out of the way, Neros could take his time getting to know the people of Vetur much better, along with their neighbors in the many scattered towns his traveling crew had passed through on their journey. However, the chaos of his coronation had left him teetering on breathlessness the entire evening. It was moments like this where he missed his companions.

The king (and it was so odd to be addressed as such, really, he had been a prince for his whole life, and *king* had such an unfamiliar weight to it) felt a tap on his shoulder. He whirled around, putting on his best diplomatic smile.

"Yes?"

Anthea beamed back at him, holding out her hand. "May a princess from a foreign land ask *His Majesty the King* for a dance?"

Neros blinked, feeling his new title sink into his shoulders yet further. That, and Anthea was positively *stunning*, and he hadn't had the chance to admire her before now. Her hair was coiled up in a bun, a few stray vines curling down to frame her face. Her dress billowed out, the fabric light and airy—much like Anthea herself—in a pale green, a color Neros thought much too soft for her bold personality.

His expression softened. "Of course."

Allowing himself to be led to the dance floor reminded Neros of when his adventure began: yet again, Anthea was leading him around, but this time (thankfully) the king knew what he was doing. The orchestra began to play a lilting waltz, upbeat and friendly. Around him, folks began pairing off and swaying to the music. He placed his hand on Anthea's waist, and she took his hand, resting the other on his bicep, and they danced along with the crowd.

"I always forget how light on your feet you are," Anthea laughed. "But you *do* perform for the Veturians annually, don't you?"

"I do," Neros said. "And tonight will be no different."

She laughed. They danced and twirled to the music, and then Anthea met his eyes with a curious gaze. "Do you ever regret it?"

"What, exactly?"

"Not choosing to become gods," She explained. "We *were* all resolute in our decision, and it was fun to turn Endra back to normal. We got this fantastic jewelry out of it, but...do you ever think we made the wrong choice? What if the gods make a mistake again?"

"Then we will be certain to smite them from the heavens again," Neros said. "Or someone else will, if Pegaios thinks we're too old, or for some reason we're no longer tied to this prophecy. But I like to think we broke it for good."

"Oh, yeah?"

"Yes. I am confident in that." He was. For once, he didn't feel any lingering pressure or anxiety surrounding the future, or the gods, or the end of the world. He'd spoken with Pontius and Pegaios at extreme length regarding the future, and they agreed that this seemed like the absolute end. The gods had been shown their place, and with the throne no longer thirsted after by those destined to take it, the formula simply didn't add up anymore.

They turned, and Neros' eye caught a flicker of light. He turned his head to look, but it disappeared.

"Looking for Leof?" Anthea asked, a mischievous glint in her eye. "Are you finally thinking of telling him how you feel?"

A flush ran up Neros' neck, covering his cheeks. "Wh-whatever do you *mean?*"

Anthea leaned down as they danced, trying to catch Neros' averting eyes. "Come *on,* don't play dumb with me. I know you're in love with him."

"D-don't say that so loud!" He cried, then hushed his voice to a whisper. "Gods, Anthy, how–how long have you *known* about this?"

"Ah-ha! So you admit it! You do love him!"

"St-stop!" He stumbled over his feet, squeezing Anthea's hand to regain his balance. They turned again, and she swiftly swapped their positioning, taking the lead away from him. "Just answer the question."

"You've had a childish look of wonder in your eyes ever since you two met. You used to stay up late with him as he tweaked your arm. Don't think I didn't see those sidelong, *pining* glances you'd give him at night when we stopped at an inn for the evening. You even snuggled up to him without thinking about it! You care about people in a special way, Neros, but I know love when I see it. And you have got it *bad.*" She giggled, twirling Neros and pulling him back into her embrace. "I think it's cute. I've never seen you so wrapped up in someone before."

Neros felt the tickle of anxious ice forming at the base of his neck—a habit he thought he'd kicked *long* ago, when his ice magic was cursed and unusable. A stress he wasn't accustomed to tugged and pulled at his insides. "Truthfully, I don't even know where he's gone. He mentioned we'd get the chance to catch up later, but…I've been so busy. He could have gone back home…"

"Neros. You know him. We traveled across the world and smote *gods* alongside him. He wouldn't skip out on seeing you tonight."

The king worried at his lip. "I thought I saw him right after the crowning ceremony, but I–I got swept up among the crowd. Gods, I hope he's not lost."

"I doubt it, he's a pretty smart guy. Stop worrying so much! You know he's here."

Neros sighed. "You're right, I know he is. I've met with many Embers, and they've sung all his praises—"

"Which I'm sure you were *eager* to return."

"Hush, Anthy! I–so what if I did!" Anthea laughed at him, and he shook his head. "That's not the point. They all mentioned him, but when I asked, none of them said they saw him around here."

"Well, he's not exactly the most *social* creature we know."

"Yes, but—"

"And just because five or ten Embers didn't see him doesn't mean he's *not* here."

"I know, but—"

"And if you don't go find him when this song is over and confess your feelings, you *will* regret it for the rest of your life."

"Anthy," Neros whined. "I get the idea. I'll go find him, okay? Gods, you're persistent."

She beamed at him, and Neros knew it was one she reserved for when she was feeling especially satisfied with herself. The song ended, and they bowed to each other, as the couples around them followed suit before dispersing. For a moment, he was tempted to blend in and escape Anthea's view, perhaps sit with some guests over the refreshments. He knew that if he tried to, the princess would find him in an instant and toss him from the ballroom. His gut twisted; that would cause a scene, and Runa wouldn't be very happy about it.

Carefully, he escaped from the banquet hall. Brushing himself off, he thought about where Leof might be. Not in the ballroom, of course, but probably not in any of the main halls. Not in Neros' private quarters, as that entire floor of the castle had been shut off to guests for the evening's festivities. The library was a bit far of a walk from this part of the castle, but Leof could have been there. Neros closed his eyes, mind reeling back through the evening's events. *I know I saw him at some point…* He thought of the flicker of light he'd noticed while dancing with Anthea. *But which way did it go? The song wasn't too long, so he couldn't have gotten too far away from the banquet hall…ah!* There was a balcony that wrapped around the castle outside the doors. He had access to it from the hallway, and thus that was where Neros went to investigate.

The chill of the wind hit his face as he opened the door, cooling the flush on his cheeks and introducing a wave of calm over him. The evening sky was clear, thousands of stars visible with the naked eye, and Neros drank in the sight. It was beautiful, as ever, and it took him back to the many nights he'd spend out on the balcony when he as young and unable to sleep, thoughts of the world's history and the prophecy swirling through his mind. *Odd to think that I would be so wrapped up in it,* he mused to himself, starting to walk down the balcony in search of Leof. *It started as a simple fascination, but now…I wonder if mother and father would have been proud.* His chest tightened, and he swallowed thickly, shaking his head. He'd had enough of those thoughts for today. It was like Pontius had told him: *"Focus on what's ahead, Neros."*

What was ahead frightened him almost more than what he left behind. As he rounded the corner, he saw exactly who he was looking for. Leof's hair flickered and swayed with the wind; he was turning an object over in his hands. Now that Neros had a moment to look, he noted Leof looked ethereal; he wore a dark red shirt with puffed sleeves and ornate gold embroidery on the front, complimented by a gold sash around his waist, dark pants, and dark boots. At the volcano, Neros was sure an outfit like this would blend in, but in snowy Vetur, Leof struck a powerful contrast against everything around him. It was no question why he'd come out here to hide out.

As Neros approached, Leof looked up at him, hiding the object in his hands, tucking it away before he could make out what it was.

Neros smiled. "So this is where you've been hiding, huh?"

Leof's cheeks glowed, and he turned to rest his forearms back on the railing overlooking Vetur. "I'm not trying to hide."

"You know I'm only teasing," Neros walked up, leaning on the railing next to him. "Have you been enjoying your evening?"

"It's crowded, but not terrible. The food is good. Some curious Veturians and Arborians have tried to make conversation with me—maybe thinking I'm important—but it's been easy to steer the conversation away."

He chuckled. "Is that so?"

"Yes, by speaking of you. Everyone seems to have faith in your abilities as king."

Neros let his gaze fall on a distant mountaintop. "Do they, now...?"

"I do, too, you know. Congratulations, by the way."

"Thank you. I'm glad you could make it."

Leof turned to face him fully, quirking a brow. "Did you really think I wouldn't be able to come?"

The icy sensation from earlier returned to tickle the back of his neck. "W-well, you see, I–I know you have the kinetic contraption competition coming up, and Aldebrande really wanted you to compete, didn't he?"

The Ember ran a hand through his hair, huffing out a laugh. "You're insane, Neros. You should know better than to think I'd make some contraption for that contest. Aldebrande's been bugging me about it for a long time, but your coronation is more important to me." His cheeks glowed again, and Neros loved how faint it looked in the moonlight. Leof turned back to the railing, but Neros kept his eyes on him.

Gods, Anthea was right. I've got it bad. He rubbed the back of his neck. "I–I'm still glad you could come. Doubly glad I found you—I've met so many Embers this evening, and I...well, I was really hoping I would find you. It's been so long, and I wanted to catch up with you."

Leof smiled—a gentle upturn of the lips, and it was one of the ones Neros loved the most, he thought, the kind where you could barely tell that it was there. "Funny," He said. "I was out here working up the nerve to find you, as well."

Neros felt hot and cold all at once, the stressful threads from earlier yanking hard. *Deep breaths.* "Truly? Was there something in particular you wanted to talk about?"

Conflict crossed Leof's face—though Neros couldn't begin to imagine why. He opened his mouth, closed it, then reached for the satchel at his waist.

"It's not so much of something to talk about more as it's...um, a gift. For you."

Neros smiled. "Is that so?"

"Yes. I...well, it's what I've been working on in the time we've been apart." He shuffled around a bit more, turning his head to give Neros a very serious stare. "Close your eyes, your majesty. Please."

The king obliged, and he felt the warmth of Leof's hands raising his own before a weight was dropped into them. His heart stuttered in his chest at the touch.

"Alright, you can look."

Resting in his palms was an ornate replica of Castle Vetur encased in glass and affixed to a sturdy base with snowflakes carved all around it. The glass orb was filled with liquid, and a substance that, when Neros gently shook it, swirled to the top and floated down gently, like snow. It was breathtaking, and Neros found himself at a sheer loss for words.

"There's, um, there's a bit more to it. It actually plays music—h-here, let me."

Gently, Neros handed the snow globe back to Leof, who flipped it over and wound it, flipping it back for Neros to take. From somewhere in the base, a gentle, lilting melody floated into the air, singing in Neros' ears. It was beautiful, and nostalgic, and spurred a rush of emotion to well in his chest, tears pricking at his eyes.

He wiped at them, smiling broadly. "It's astonishing, Leof. Thank you. Did you compose the song yourself?"

Leof's cheeks lit up in the night, and he ducked his head, hiding his face with flowing flames. "Somewhat. I'm not much of a musician, but the clockmaker near Aldebrande's workshop plays music as a hobby. So she helped. I told her that I—" He stopped suddenly, clearing his throat. "I told her what sort of song I wanted, and she gave some guidelines. After some refining, I made the structure that plays it."

"You're incredible," Neros breathed, though the impact of his compliment smacked him as a rush of heat flooded his cheeks. "I-it's such a thoughtful gift. Gosh, I almost wish I could go to my quarters and display it right now."

Leof chuckled. "I can hang on to it for the evening, if that makes you more comfortable."

Neros hummed, staring back at the castle. From the view of the balcony, he could see into the ballroom—packed with people dancing the night away. Nobody *seemed* to be looking for him yet. *Perhaps now is my chance...*

"What are you thinking."

"D-don't say it like that, it's nothing so mischievous!" Neros laughed, holding his free hand up in surrender. "I just—well, why don't we pop upstairs for a bit? I can take this gift to my study, and we can have a few more moments away from all the excitement?"

That same conflicted look flashed over Leof's face, but something else seemed to win out because he sighed and said, "Alright. I suppose it would be unwise to deny the king."

Grabbing hold of Leof's hand, he tore off at a brisk pace circumventing the castle. *I assigned all the guards to their posts, so I should know better than anyone how to sneak past them.* It felt impulsive, reckless, and absolutely nothing at all like what a king should do at his own coronation. *It'll only be for a few minutes. Then we'll return and round out the evening with my performance for everyone.* He tossed a smile he hoped was reassuring over his shoulder, giving Leof's hand a squeeze. He only offered Neros an exasperated grin in return, yet Neros still found his heart trying to beat its way out of his chest.

✿

Leof's very core churned and spun and twisted and knotted with anxiety at every turn. The castle halls were dimly lit by lines of low-burning candles behind wall sconces, all the proper lighting being fed to the ballroom where the main party was being held. They were on the second floor, sticking close to the edge of the wall without windows, Neros' hand still firmly clasped to his. If they separated, the Ember knew he had no hope of find-ing his way back, because his entire focus was drawn to Neros. He cursed himself every minute of it, as it had only been two years, and the king had no right being that breathtaking.

Especially not with the childish, wonderesque grin he was sporting.

Footsteps sounded farther down the hall, and Neros tugged hard on his hand, pulling them both into an alcove and pressing their bodies flush together. His cloak wrapped around Leof to drown out the light, and it was *everything* to keep his emotions under control. The flames whipping around his skull threatened to pop and crack, which would give away their location.

"S-sorry," Neros whispered. "It'll only be a minute."

"S'fine," Leof rushed, continuing to urge himself to calm down. He had been *close* to Neros before, but never quite like this. The king's arm was wrapped protectively around his waist, and the lack of space left his limbs squished awkwardly between them. How, in all their travels, they had never ended up in a situation like this absolutely baffled him, but the longer they remained, the more Leof was grateful he didn't have to deal with it. *This is it. This is when I learn whether Embers can spontaneously combust.* He could feel Neros' nervous heartbeat thumping strong in his ears, and Leof was sure it was be-cause he was afraid of being caught. *He probably thinks I'm worried, too, but to be honest I couldn't care less about someone stumbling across us. Neros could make an excuse, couldn't he?* Neros was so close, *so* close, and after being away for so long, Leof felt absolutely suffocated by his emotions.

Then, all at once, Neros slipped away, grabbing his hand and continu-ing to lead him down the hall and up a set of stairs. Leof knew his cheeks were glowing red-hot, and he could only pray that Neros wasn't paying atten-tion. What was once too much now felt entirely too little, and Leof ached to close the distance between them again.

Neros let go only to open the door to a semicircular study, lined with bookcases that stretched to the ceiling and a modest desk near the window.

"This is it," he announced, a bit out of breath from the trek. "It's technically my father's study, but since...well. I inherited it from him, and I've taken most of my lessons here with Runa."

"There is certainly a wealth of knowledge at your fingertips," Leof noted, thankful for the conversation to distract him. "How often is this

library updated?"

"Twice annually," Neros explained, walking over to his desk and setting the snow globe gently on top of it. "The older texts are moved to the main library on the first floor, and updated versions are bought and traded and placed here. It's quite the process, but I enjoy it."

Leof hummed, walking to the shelves to examine some of the titles. The fattest were the history books, and there was a generous amount of instructional magic tomes. A pang of jealousy struck him before realizing that it was likely Neros didn't have enough time to absorb everything on every page.

He started when he felt a hand rest on the small of his back. "It's quite formidable, isn't it? These rows and rows of books. Exciting, like a challenge, but demotivating because...well, we can't even see the top."

Why must he stand so close? Leof looked up to find Neros was right: he couldn't make out where the books ended. He hummed in agreement. "You should have a bit more time now, shouldn't you? Now that you no longer need to jump through Runa's hoops of kingliness?"

Neros chuckled. "Yes and no." His hand squeezed at Leof's waist, and he glowed. "Tonight might be the most real free time I have. I wish this could last a bit longer."

Distant, faint music drifted in the space between them. Leof allowed it to hang comfortably for a few moments. *I wonder how long it'll be before we meet again, after tonight.* He suppressed a sigh; they'd been away for long enough. Neros only wanted to drop off the snow globe before heading back to the party.

"I think I understand what you mean," Leof said, turning to face Neros. "We should probably head back—"

"Dance with me."

"What?"

"I, well, um," Only a moment ago, so bold and now, so bashful, Neros rubbed the back of his neck. "If you please. I know I won't see much of you once we go back, and it has been *years*, and, well…"

Leof fiddled with his sleeves. "The music is a bit faint, isn't it? Besides, I don't really dance."

Humming, Neros smiled, as though he'd discovered the world's greatest invention. "But we *do* have a song, don't we?" He walked over to the desk, picking up the snow globe again. "You wrote it yourself."

"That…doesn't change that I'm not much of a dancer."

"It's only you and me," Neros pointed out, a hopeful grin on his face. "And I could take the lead."

Leof sighed, though a smile crept over his face in its wake. "I did say it would be unwise to deny his majesty, right? Very well."

It was selfish of him to say yes, he knew. He knew that it was a temporary fill for his yearning to be closer to Neros, but he decided to throw away such anxieties for now. There would be time after the ceremony to ponder the weight of his actions: sneaking off with the *king* to dance in his private quarters.

But now, Neros' arm was wrapped around him and their hands were clasped and he was leading Leof around the little study in gentle steps and small circles, and Leof was trying desperately not to be so enchanted. He was clumsy, but if Neros noticed, he didn't say a word, only looking at him like he was the only person who mattered in the world. *How can he just look at someone like me like this?* It was becoming overwhelming. Was he supposed to smile back? Did Neros expect him to? He found he spent a bit too much time staring at their feet and the shared space between them.

"Leof," Neros' voice snapped his attention to his face. "Try not to look down. It'll be easier if you just go with the flow. Follow my lead."

He nodded, unsteadily, and their slow dance continued. For what it was worth, Neros was right—it proved far easier to follow along with Neros' gentle pushes and pulls than to try and calculate where his foot should go next by staring at them. However, he knew the music box wasn't built for *long* songs, and as the music slowed, so did they. A hopeful, anxious pull tugged at his chest, because he didn't want it to end but he wasn't sure how to keep Neros close to him for much longer.

The last note echoed in the study, and they held each other's gaze. The dim light blended with what emitted from his own hair and danced across Neros' face, his cheeks flushed violet.

He was breathtaking.

"Neros…"

"Y-yes?"

Leof swallowed. *If there has ever been a moment, it's now. I either do this here, or I don't and regret it for life.*

With shaking hands, he reached up, slid his hands over the back of Neros' neck, and pulled him down into a kiss.

❄

Oh. *Oh.* Leof's lips were pressed to his, intently and lovingly and *warm*, and Neros found it difficult to breathe. He'd sucked in sharply through his nose, but it had gotten caught, and now he was a bit distracted—where should he put his hands? They were clinging quite desperately to Leof's waist, but he wasn't sure if that was comfortable. Was there a normal place to put your hands when someone suddenly kisses you? He couldn't think straight. The lack of air in his lungs was an unfortunate problem.

Leof must have been able to tell, because he pulled away, leaving Neros gasping and chasing after his lips again. He was breathless and speechless and he had to *say* something, but all that came out was a stutter.

"I...L-Leof, I..."

"I-I'm sorry," He rushed, struggling to put a bit more distance between them. "That...that was uncalled for."

"No! No, gods, no, that's not–that's not what I was going for," Neros urged, moving his hands to cup Leof's cheeks. "You've surprised me, that's all."

"Well, I surprised myself, if I'm going to be honest. Neros, I..." Leof's eyes flitted about the room before settling back into Neros' own. "I love you. I've been in love with you for...months. I didn't expect to. I...tried to stop myself from it. But I...you were beautiful, and I knew if I didn't do something now, I would kick myself for the rest of my life."

"Beautiful?" Neros smiled, feeling a vulnerability bloom in his chest. He brought Leof closer, pressing their foreheads together. His thumb traced the lines of the crack striking a bolt down Leof's cheek. "I'm relieved you did. Because...I feel the same."

Leof's face told Neros he couldn't believe it, which almost made him laugh. Instead, he pulled Leof closer, brushing their lips together again. "Why do you look so surprised?"

"I—you're—you're *royalty*, and I'm...just a blacksmith's apprentice. Isn't there someone else who...who could be a better suitor for you?"

"Someone better than the one who put his life on the line for me, who traded scraps for parts to make me an arm from nothing? Better than the one who consumed my every free thought over these last two years? You've lifted me from my deepest, darkest moments, and we've shared ups and downs of all sorts in between. Even if there is a so-called better suitor, I don't care. I love *you*."

Leof's cheeks glowed from the sentiment, and Neros loved the pleasant warm buzz it sparked beneath his fingertips. "H-how can you say that so sincerely?" He huffed, tearing his eyes away.

"Because it's true."

At that, Leof smiled. "Ever the earnest one, of course. How romantic."

Neros could only return it with a laugh, still running slow strokes over Leof's cheeks, lost in the moment and wishing now more than ever that he could remain in this shared space in time forever.

A knock at the door followed by its opening interrupted his thoughts. His heart leapt in his throat. *I was sure no one was following us. Unless…has it really been too long? Has Runa sent as castle search party?* He moved to pull Leof as close as possible, frantically seeking a place to hide when an all-too-familiar squeal and cheer hit his ears first.

"Oooh, I had a feeling you'd be tucked away here! I so hoped to find you together!" Anthea bounded into the study with Rosea in tow. The grin on her face was maddening. She gasped dramatically. "You're both here…and Leof, that embarrassed look on your face…did you actually confess!?"

Neros' face bloomed violet, and Leof nearly choked. "I–th-that's—!" He started, burying his face into Neros' chest.

Anthea giggled. "Gosh, you are so cute. I bet Neros said something really dorky and heartwarming to you, too, didn't he?"

"Of course he did," Leof grumbled, voice muffled by fabric. Small embers were separating and flickering around his head as he spoke, and Neros' heart swelled at the sight.

"Leof made the most astonishing coronation present, Anthea. Come, look." He slowly peeled himself away from Leof's grip and moved to the desk, lifting the snow globe and presenting it to her.

"Ooooh!" Anthea cooed, turning it over in her hands and winding up the bottom. Once the song began to play, her jaw dropped. "Wow! You've really outdone yourself, Leof!" She grinned. "I can really feel all the love you put into this."

He narrowed his eyes at her. Neros laughed. "I could, too. It's certainly something special."

Anthea hummed. "Agreed. Now, I wish I could have left you alone all night, but Runa is looking for you, Neros. I think it's about time for your performance."

"Ah, yes, of course!" He turned to Leof. "You've never seen one before, have you? Come, we should hurry back. It's quite the spectacle."

"His majesty is quite skilled on his feet," Rosea added, her smile slipping toward sly.

"S-so I found."

"You *danced* together too? Oh, you'll have to tell me *everything* on the way back down."

Anthea and Rosea's excitable chatter filled the air as they walked back to the ballroom. A few of the guards looked surprised to see them, but made no move to stop when they noticed the king was in their midst. To Neros' surprise, Leof was entertaining every minute question the girls had to throw at him, which surely kept his face stark violet for their entire walk. He only hoped this didn't mean he would flub part of his performance for the Veturians tonight.

He chuckled to himself. *Even so, I would say it was worth the trouble.*

CPSIA information can be obtained
at www.ICGtesting.com
Printed in the USA
LVHW010057230620
658655LV00006B/929